SIDESPACE

AURORA RENEGADES: BOOK ONE

D0313096

G. S. JENNSEN

HYPERNOVA
PUBLISHING
2015

SIDESPACE

Cover design by Josef Bartoň
Cover typography by G. S. Jennsen

Hypernova Publishing
P.O. Box 2214
Parker, Colorado 80134
www.hypernovapublishing.com

Publisher's Note: This is a work of fiction. Names, characters, places, and
incidents are a product of the author's imagination. Locales and public names are
sometimes used for atmospheric purposes. Any resemblance to actual people,
living or dead, or to businesses, companies, events, institutions, or locales is
completely coincidental.

The Hypernova Publishing name, colophon and logo are trademarks of
Hypernova Publishing.

Ordering Information:
Hypernova Publishing books may be purchased for educational, business or sales
promotional use. For details, contact the "Special Markets Department" at the
address above.

Sidespace / G. S. Jennsen.—1st ed.

LCCN 2015955232
ISBN 978-0-9960141-9-9

For the dreamers
For the explorers, the innovators and the visionaries
For all those who laughed in the face of "impossible"
and did it anyway

ACKNOWLEDGMENTS

Many thanks to my beta readers, editors and artists, who made everything about this book better, and to my family, who continue to put up with an egregious level of obsessive focus on my part for months at a time.

I also want to add a personal note of thanks to everyone who has read my books, left a review on Amazon, Goodreads or other sites, sent me a personal email expressing how the books have impacted you, or posted on social media to share how much you enjoyed them. You make this all worthwhile, every day.

AURORA RHAPSODY

is

AURORA RISING

(Available Now)

STARSHINE

VERTIGO

TRANSCENDENCE

AURORA RENEGADES

(2015-2016)

SIDESPACE

DISSONANCE

ABYSM

AURORA RESONANT

(2017-2018)

RELATIVITY

RUBICON

REQUIEM

SHORT STORIES

RESTLESS, VOL. I • *RESTLESS, VOL. II*

APOGEE

(available 11/27/15 in The Galaxy Chronicles Anthology)

SOLATIUM

(available November 2015 in Crime & Punishment Anthology)

Learn more at: gsjennsen.com/aurora-rhapsody

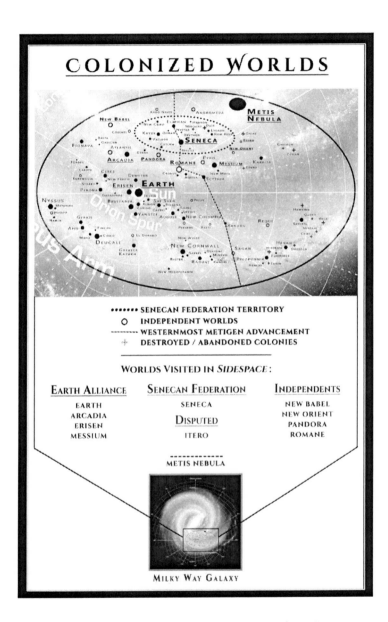

Colonized Worlds Map can be viewed online at: gsjennsen.com/map-sidespace

PORTAL NETWORK

"MOSAIC"

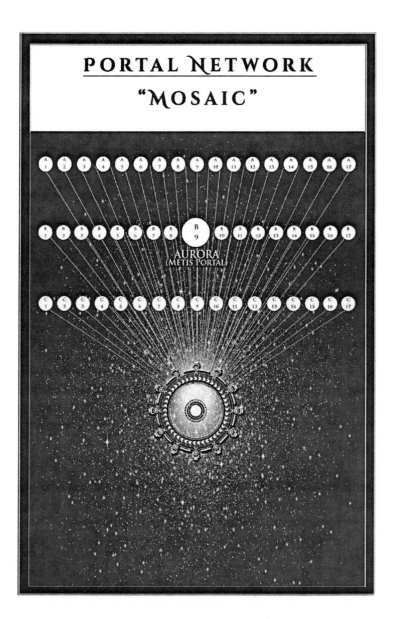

Portal Network Map can be viewed online at: gsjennsen.com/mosaic-map-sidespace

DRAMATIS PERSONAE
MAIN CHARACTERS

Alexis 'Alex' Solovy
Starship pilot, scout and space explorer. Prevo for Project Noetica.
Spouse of Caleb Marano, daughter of Miriam and David Solovy.
Artificial/Prevo Counterpart: Valkyrie

Caleb Marano
Former Special Operations intelligence agent, Senecan Federation Division of
Intelligence. Spouse of Alex Solovy.

Miriam Solovy (Fleet Admiral)
Earth Alliance Strategic Command
Chairman. Mother of Alex Solovy.

Richard Navick (Brigadier)
EASC Naval Intelligence Liaison.
Family friend of the Solovys.

Devon Reynolds
Prevo for Project Noetica.
EASC Special Projects Quantum
Computing Consultant.
Artificial/Prevo Counterpart: Annie

Kennedy Rossi
Founder/CEO, Connova Interstellar.
Friend of Alex Solovy, Noah Terrage.

Noah Terrage
Co-founder/COO, Connova Interstellar.
Former trader/smuggler. Friend of Caleb
Marano, Kennedy Rossi, Mia Requelme.

Malcolm Jenner (Colonel)
Cmdr, NW Command MSO 1st STCC.
Friend of Alex Solovy.

Abigail Canivon
EASC Special Projects Consultant:
Project Noetica. Former Dir. Cybernetic
Research Center, Druyan Institute.

Graham Delavasi
Director, Senecan Federation
Division of Intelligence.

William 'Will' Sutton
CEO, W.C. Sutton Construction.
Former SF intelligence agent.
Spouse of Richard Navick.

Morgan Lekkas (Commander)
Prevo for Project Noetica.
Pilot, SF Southern Fleet.
Artificial/Prevo Counterpart: Stanley

Eleni Gianno (Field Marshal)
Chairman of SF Military Council.
Commander of SF Armed Forces.

Mia Requelme
Prevo for Project Noetica. Entrepeneur.
Friend of Caleb Marano, Noah Terrage.
Artificial/Prevo Counterpart: Meno

Olivia Montegreu
Head of Zelones criminal cartel.

Jude Winslow
Head of Order of the True Sentients.
Son of Pamela Winslow.

Dramatis Personae can be viewed online at: gsjennsen.com/characters-sidespace

Other Major Characters
(Alphabetical Order)

Aristide Vranas
Chairman, Senecan Federation Govt.
Residence: *Seneca*

Charles Gagnon
Speaker, Earth Alliance Assembly.
Residence: *Earth*

Christopher Rychen (Admiral)
EA NE Regional Commander.
Residence: *Messium*

David Solovy (Commander)
Alex Solovy's father. Miriam Solovy's
spouse. Captain, *EAS Stalwart.* Deceased.

Diego Jara (Captain)
NE Command Engineering Regiment.
Residence: *Messium*

Faith Quillen
Lieutenant, Order of the True Sentients.
Residence: *Pandora*

Fedor Evzen
Chimeral/illegal tech dealer.
Residence: *Seneca*

Hideyo Mori
EA Defense Minister.
Residence: *Earth*

Ivan Echols
Lieutenant, Order of the True Sentients.
Residence: *New Babel*

Jacob Paredes (Captain)
NW Command MSO 1st STCC.
Residence: *Arcadia*

Kian Lange (Major)
Director, EASC Security Bureau.
Residence: *Earth*

Laure Ferre
Head of Ferre criminal cartel.
Residence: *Krysk*

Pamela Winslow
Chairman, EA Assembly Military
Oversight Committee.
Residence: *Earth*

Phillip Grenier (Major)
NW Command MSO 1st STCC
Residence: *Arcadia*

Ramon Leiva
Hacker. Friend of Devon Reynolds.
Residence: *Earth*

Sayid Pouran
Hacker. Friend of Devon Reynolds.
Residence: *Earth*

Steven Brennon
Earth Alliance Prime Minister.
Residence: *Earth*

Tessa Hennessey
SF Intelligence quantum computing
specialist.
Residence: *Seneca*

Ulric Toscano
Cell leader, Order of the True Sentients.
Residence: *Seneca*

Vanessa Devore (Major)
NW Command MSO 1st STCC.
Residence: *Arcadia*

Vii
Druyan Institute/Abigail Canivon's
Artificial Neural Net.
Residence: *Earth*

AURORA RISING
SYNOPSIS

*For a more detailed summary of the events of Aurora Rising,
see Appendix B, located at the back of the book.*

The history of humanity is the history of conflict. This proved no less true in the 24th century than in ancient times.

By 2322, humanity inhabited over 100 worlds spread across a third of the galaxy. Two decades earlier, a group of colonies had rebelled and set off the First Crux War. Once the dust cleared, three factions emerged: the Earth Alliance, consisting of the unified Earth government and most of the colonies; the Senecan Federation, which had won its independence in the war; and a handful of scattered non-aligned worlds, home to criminal cartels, corporate interests and people who made their living outside the system.

Alexis Solovy was a space explorer. Her father gave his life in the war against the Federation, leading her to reject a government or military career. Estranged from her mother, an Alliance military leader, Alex instead sought the freedom of space and made a fortune chasing the hidden wonders of the stars.

A chance meeting between Alex and a Federation intelligence agent, Caleb Marano, led them to discover an armada of alien warships emerging from a mysterious portal in the Metis Nebula.

The Metigens had been watching humanity via the portal for millennia; in an effort to forestall their detection, they used traitors among civilization's elite to divert focus from Metis. When their plans failed, they invaded in order to protect their secrets.

The wars that ensued were brutal—first an engineered war between the Alliance and the Federation, then once it was revealed to be built on false pretenses, devastating clashes against the Metigen invaders as they advanced across settled space, destroying every colony in their path and killing tens of millions.

Alex and Caleb breached the aliens' portal in an effort to find a way to stop the slaughter. There they encountered Mnemosyne, the Metigen watcher of the Aurora universe—our universe. Though enigmatic and evasive, the alien revealed the invading ships were driven by AIs and hinted the answer to defeating them lay in the merger of individuals with the powerful but dangerous quantum computers known as Artificials.

Before leaving the portal space, Alex and Caleb discovered a colossal master gateway. It generated 51 unique signals, each one leading to a new portal and a new universe. But with humanity facing extinction, they returned home armed with a daring plan to win the war.

In a desperate gambit to vanquish the enemy invaders before they reached the heart of civilization, four Prevos (human-synthetic meldings) were created and given command of the combined might of the Alliance and Federation militaries. Alex and her Artificial, Valkyrie, led the other Prevos and the military forces against the alien AI warships in climactic battles above Seneca and Romane. The invaders were defeated and ordered to withdraw through their portal, cease their observation of Aurora and not return.

Alex reconciled with her mother during the final hours of the war, and following the victory Alex and Caleb married and attempted to resume a normal life.

But new mysteries waited through the Metis portal. Determined to learn the secrets of the portal network and the multiverses it held, six months later Caleb, Alex and Valkyrie traversed it once more, leaving humanity behind to struggle with a new world of powerful quantum synthetics, posthumans, and an uneasy, fragile peace.

And in the realm beyond the portal, Mnemosyne watched.

AURORA THESI (PORTAL PRIME)

ENISLE SEVENTEEN

I considered the inert form lying in the stasis chamber.

It appeared a stranger to me. I felt no kinship, no attachment to the body providing my life force. Memory my aspect, I no longer recalled having resided within it. To find oneself bound inside the confines of a small, frail body, rendered hapless by its myriad limitations, was anathema to me.

I moved the stasis chamber into the deepest corner of the structure. The life support system was designed to function for perpetuity without my intervention. Unseen, it would trouble me no further. Then I left the structure and its refuge behind to hover at the shore of my lake, finding myself uncertain of what to do next.

Exile.

Such had been the verdict of the Idryma Conclave. Exiled from their ranks in name, title and consciousness. Exiled from Amaranthe. My body retrieved from the *krypti* and relinquished to the dirt of Aurora Thesi.

A watcher with no subjects.

An Analystae with no dominion.

It would be far simpler if it were such a simple matter as this. But my task extended far beyond the rigid strictures of the Idryma. Aurora had been entrusted to me because I understood our purpose more deeply than anyone, save possibly Praetor Lakhes.

Histories. Futures. What was inevitable, and all that was not.

The Conclave called Aurora a failure. We would refocus our efforts on the other Enisles, Lakhes proclaimed, in the search for new and innovative prospects. We would try again, Hyperion declared, but ensure firmer restraints were in place from the beginning this time.

I believed the answers still resided in Aurora. For what the Conclave was too insular to see—or too fearful to admit if they did see—was this: the uprising by the Humans had in fact proven the validity of the principal hypothesis underlying Aurora's existence.

Now was not the time to recoil as mettle failed.

This was the kairos. This was what we had *wanted*. The others might flinch and turn away, but I would not.

Before departing Aurora for the last time, representatives of the Conclave had placed spatial triggers at the Metis Portal, designed to pitch the apparatus into a dimensional singularity upon its opening from the other side. It had been a near thing, our—their—decision to refrain from destroying the portal immediately. Only my most elegant arguments had convinced the Conclave they need not permanently foreclose this avenue.

But the Conclave, eager to be rid of the troublesome Aurora Enisle and its equally troublesome Analystae Mnemosyne, had perhaps not paid sufficient attention to the details.

I was and had always been the First Analystae of Aurora. This meant I controlled all the apparatuses of the Enisle, observational and otherwise.

The triggers had been deactivated. I could rearm them at any time, and should it become necessary—should the Humans or their scions attempt to launch an armada through the Metis Portal, one bent on wanton destruction of whatever they found—I would do so, regrettably but without hesitation.

But I was the First Analystae of Aurora, and this experiment was not over. Once a proud member of an underground resistance, I was now a rebel from the rebellion.

As the sea spread out beneath me, an alert transmitted the opening of the Metis Portal. I halted far above the waters and waited.

What emerged from the portal was not the feared armada. Instead, it was a single ship. A familiar ship. I felt a quickening in my atoms.

Clever, dangerous girl. I have been expecting you.

CONTENTS

SIDESPACE

PART I:

WILD THINGS

"Life is the fire that burns and the sun that gives light. Life is the wind and the rain and the thunder in the sky. Life is matter and is earth, what is and what is not, and what beyond is in Eternity."

— *Lucius Annaeus Seneca*

PORTAL: B-3

SYSTEM DESIGNATION: EKOS

1

EKOS-1

A thundering bellow undulated across the grove as the forest roused itself to life, murderous intent in its heart.

"Get us out of here!"

Caleb's retort came in the form of the bike leaping forward out of the small clearing and into the tangle of woods.

Alex gazed at the underbrush whizzing beneath her feet in fascination. Formerly placid, it now roiled like ocean waves advancing ahead of a hurricane. Before the bike's speed became too great for her to perceive such details, she swore each individual blade of the broad, sage-hued grass reached up in an attempt to ensnare the wheels or frame of the bike, or even her feet.

"Holy hell."

Her attention jerked forward at Caleb's exclamation, at which point she could only concur. "*Svyatoy chyertu....*"

The foliage that wound parasitically around the trunks of the trees populating the lush woodland? It was unfurling to dart out through the air—toward them. She instinctively tucked her head against his back and drew her body in close.

In the corner of her vision the pliant, soft-wood limbs of those trees began to enlist in the campaign, lurching and clawing at their fleeing presence. Like the foliage, they seemed to be driven by a single, overriding purpose: to stop them, then to kill them.

Caleb expertly picked a path between narrow gaps in the trees at reckless speed, but the forest was increasing in thickness. She honestly didn't know how he was going to get through such a dense chaparral, but she needed to help.

"I'm going to try shooting at the trees—maybe it will spook them long enough for us to squeak by." Shooting at the apparently sentient trees, that was to say. She intensified her hold on his waist as her right hand went to her belt and unlatched her Daemon. She withdrew it from its holster and pointed it outward—

—a vine darted out, wrapped around the barrel and yanked it from her hand. She blinked, startled, then quickly pulled her arm in before some vine decided to do the same to it.

Wide, tall trees closed in ominously in front of them, blotting out the sun. "Um...can I borrow your gun?"

The jungle-like forest was also increasingly loud, the rumbling noise growing as every element of it sprang into action, and she wasn't sure he heard her. In the absence of a response and not wanting to distract him, she reached down and jostled his Daemon out from the holster on his belt. This time she kept both it and her arm tucked in as she pointed it forward over his shoulder at a notably behemoth tree blocking their path. She pressed the trigger.

The laser tore into the timber in an explosion of splintered bark and vascular tissue. The topmost segment of the tree swayed to the left and fell away. As it did, the dull roar exploded into a furious cacophony. The surviving trees—all the trees except the one she'd shot apart—bowed in toward the bike, lashing out with greater vehemence.

"I think you made them angry."

She snorted in the confines of her helmet. "Well, they've made me angry...."

Her voice trailed off as the air filled with a plethora of orange spores, seemingly released by the groundcover ferns. Individual plants began linking together, closing off what open space remained. The last of the faint light from the prairie in the distance vanished as the trees, vines and foliage snarled into a web in which to ensnare them.

"Shit!" She stretched up, farther over his shoulder, and opened up an unrelenting stream of laser fire directly ahead.

"Valkyrie, we're going to need a little air support here—and a pickup, posthaste."

'I anticipated as much when every active sensor spiked. ETA 42 seconds.'

The laser succeeded in creating a jagged hole in the web, albeit one barely wider than the bike. Caleb raced headlong through it as vines sporting razor-sharp edges tore at them from all sides. The helmet kept the vines from ripping into Alex's face and the protective clothing she wore mostly protected the rest, but a zing of pain at her wrist alerted her that a vine had found skin between sleeve and glove.

"We're almost out. Just hang on." Caleb's voice was low and strained. Still, she took comfort from hearing it.

Hanging on, she could do. She could also keep firing ahead and help to clear the way. She sent a new stream into the living web.

A streak of *different* moved off to their right. She squinted several times, unable to accept what her eyes relayed to her brain. "Caleb…."

"I see it." His voice had gained a rather forceful edge now.

A large…creature…loped across the woodland on an intercept trajectory toward them. Except it wasn't a creature—it wasn't an animal. Multiple bramble plants had combined to take the shape of a leopard-type beast, complete with two rows of thorns for teeth. But plants couldn't travel—not of their own volition and not like this.

As it closed on them, it became astonishingly evident what was happening. The grass was propelling the construct. Each successive region of blades worked in concert to send it careening forward.

When it was within ten meters, she swung the Daemon around and fired. The construct was porous, more empty air than organic material, and it was arms-length away before the laser finally hobbled it.

She wasted no time in redirecting her fire to the front. They were, in fact, almost out—but the trees had begun to lay themselves down across their path. The blockade grew higher each passing second.

"Faster? Please tell me there's a faster."

His response was a grunt.

"Valkyrie?"

'ETA 9 seconds.'

The front of the bike pitched upward as Caleb fired the thrusters. The back wheel followed suit, and in a burst of speed they flew centimeters above the trunks. She sensed the trees shifting up as the bike passed over them, but the bike cleared the barrier before any limbs succeeded in swatting them out of the air.

The next instant a tree was imitating a javelin by hurtling through the air toward them. The wheels had barely hit the ground when Caleb swerved. The rear of the bike fishtailed in the grasping, clawing underbrush, and sheer velocity was the only thing that kept them from being skewered by the projectile.

Prairie land—escape—was now a few meters ahead. The border foliage surged in from both sides, tearing at them as they slipped out.

She exhaled in relief as the surroundings opened up and the spores dissipated, and more so as the *Siyane* came into sight. The ship descended to hover above the flatland, then pivoted to face them.

"We're coming in hot, Valkyrie, so get the ramp extended."

'Understood. I will provide covering fire to give you time to get on board.'

"Is that necessary?"

'Look.'

She closed her eyes, and Valkyrie showed her the scene from the ship's visual scanners.

The forest was chasing them.

The plant life had not gained true motive power, and the grass here on the prairie wasn't tall enough to pull off any loping constructs. But the forest was nonetheless chasing them.

Every variation of flora was joining together, ripping itself up by the root to attach itself to the trees, pushing up and out ever farther. Behind the border region the hinterland thinned out as she watched—via the ship's sensors—to feed itself into the growing structure. They and the bike were a tiny black dot racing away from a living, angry woodland in hot pursuit, and gaining on them.

She forced out a whisper. "You're going to want to not slow down. Just take my word for it."

"It'll to be a hard landing, then."

She watched their impossible pursuer surge closer. "I'm okay with that."

When they were ninety meters from the *Siyane*, Valkyrie opened fire. The ytterbium crystal laser burned bright silver over their heads as it cut a swath through the menacing column of organic material. Exponentially more powerful than their sidearms, it ripped the leading edge of the column to shreds—but beyond the destruction the mass continued to build. *Damn.*

Caleb barked a warning. "Get ready."

She tightened her grip on him and the bike as they hit the ramp at full speed. Caleb slammed on the brakes the instant they cleared the hull, but the engineering well simply wasn't that long.

They were thrown over the handlebars as the bike skidded into the side wall. Her head slammed against the ladder. The helmet prevented her skull from cracking open but did little to soften the blow.

"We're on board—go!"

His voice came from...she blinked away the worst of the pain...her left? She couldn't be sure, as everything including her brain was moving. The ship gained altitude at a sharp angle as the ramp retracted and locked into the hull. The bike slid down the well to settle upside-down against the rear wall.

Caleb crawled over to her. "Are you okay?"

She groaned and struggled to find the control to collapse the helmet. Once it was gone she shoved the breather mask off and peered up at him. "Ow."

His eyes were dark with concern as they inspected her. "How 'ow'? I have a headache 'ow,' or I've been impaled by a metal spike 'ow?'"

She felt along her chest and abdomen to make certain. "The first one. You?"

He chuckled raggedly. "I'm exceptional."

'Do you want to depart the planet, or should I adopt a high-altitude survey course?'

Caleb collapsed on his back beside her. "I don't know, Valkyrie—did the forest form a towering beanstalk to climb into the atmosphere and wrangle us to the ground?"

'Yes.'

They stared at each other in alarm. "Yes?"

'Yes. However, it was only able to reach an altitude of 1.4 kilometers before falling to the surface.'

"Right." Caleb's expression was one of incredulity and mild amusement. "Take us to five kilometers altitude. And keep an eye out for new beanstalks." He rolled over to prop up on his elbows beside her.

She flashed him a lopsided grin. "That was close."

"Indeed. Did you really have to take a souvenir?"

"It was one fucking leaf! I thought we could analyze it on the ship...." She fumbled in her pants' pocket and triumphantly produced the leaf. "And we still can."

"Hang on, put that in something. It's alive, remember?"

She frowned at the leaf. It hung limp and inert from her fingers; the color was already fading to a dull brown. "I think we can take it if it gets rowdy."

"Well..." he twisted around and opened one of the storage compartments, grabbed the leaf and threw it in "...better safe than sorry."

She tugged her gloves off and coaxed him back to her. She was sore in half a dozen places, doubtless bruised in more, and winded. But the adrenaline continued to flow through her veins, leaving in its wake an intoxicating high built on terror and exhilaration.

His lips met hers with a sudden, electrifying fierceness. He tasted of salty sweat and earth.

Her arms wrapped around him and drew him the rest of the way atop her, then her hands were tangled in his hair. His were lower, tugging her overshirt from the waist of her pants and sliding underneath it.

She bit his lower lip in mounting passion—

'You should come upstairs as soon as you're able. I believe both of you will want to see this.'

Caleb growled in protest against her mouth. She stifled her own grumble and kissed him fully once more, then reluctantly relinquished him from her grasp. "We're on the way, Valkyrie."

He rolled off her and onto his knees. "I'll secure the bike and be up."

She offered him a pout by way of apology and climbed to her feet, discovering a few additional aches in the process, then hauled herself up the ladder. As she reached the main deck Caleb's voice echoed in the engineering well below.

"Valkyrie, do I need to explain the meaning of the term 'cockblocker' to you?"

'No. I did consider feigning ignorance, however, in order to hear what would surely be a most colorful description.'

Alex burst out laughing, which also ached, and made her way to the cockpit.

R

She didn't need to see through Valkyrie's vision or the *Siyane's* scanners to learn what had attracted the Artificial's attention; she didn't even need a HUD display screen. All she needed to do was look out the viewport.

The surface of the planet was in motion. It roiled in violent swells like an enraged beast caught in a giant cage. The agitation had spread far beyond the woodlands where they had ventured and now stretched as far as she or the visual scanners were able to detect.

She increased their flight speed but allowed Valkyrie to continue to navigate. "Let's find out how prevalent this is, and how fast it's spreading. Could it be the entire planet?"

'I will adopt a course designed to encompass the most area in the shortest time possible.'

"I brought up your contraband."

She gazed over her shoulder to see Caleb warily carrying her pilfered leaf between two gloved fingers over to the workbench. He placed it on the bench, pulled the gloves off and dropped them on the desk, then joined her in the cockpit.

"Damn. We really did piss it off."

"Seems so." She began opening several HUD screens while scratching absently at her wrist. "Valkyrie, are we picking up any readings to explain what's going on down there, scientifically speaking?"

Caleb's hand landed on her right arm; he tugged it upward and flipped her hand over. "You're hurt."

Of course she was hurt—her body was probably covered head-to-toe in bruises—but that wasn't what he meant. A cut eight centimeters long ran diagonally from her wrist up her inner arm. It wasn't actively gushing blood, but the wound was ugly and the skin surrounding it had swollen into red welts. "One of the vines managed to land a swipe in between my glove and jacket. I didn't realize it took a chunk out of me, though."

"Hang on—and don't scratch it." He glanced out the viewport again then headed back into the cabin.

'There is an increase in near-surface seismic waves across the scanners' range. I am also detecting a strong ambient wavefield, though the microtremors are erratic and not holding to a regular pattern.'

Alex kept one eye on the scene outside while she studied the accelerometer readings. "Earthquakes, huh? Quite the temper tantrum."

'You are assigning sentient attributes to a planet.'

"And she's right to do so." Caleb reappeared at her side, lifted her arm and wiped the wound clean. The antiseptic stung, and she was grateful when he moved on to securing a medwrap around her arm. "The forest tried to kill us. It was acting with malice aforethought and did everything in its power to prevent us from escaping."

She winced as he pressed the medwrap firmly onto the wound. "So the planet is alive? Is that what we're saying?"

"More likely it's only the organic material. If it was the planet, the ground would have opened up beneath us when we reached the prairie, if not before."

The image sent a shudder down her spine. "That would've been...bad."

Caleb double-checked the secureness of the wrap then squeezed her hand. "Yeah. Not sure how we'd have gotten out of that one."

She gave him a quick, relieved smile. "But if it's not the planet itself, why are other regions reacting? We've flown over six hundred kilometers of flatlands containing hardly a blade of grass, but look."

They had reached a wooded mountain range. The trees blanketing the slopes whipped about with such agitation the mountains themselves almost appeared to be moving. "How do *those* trees know what happened all the way across the prairie?" It sounded more absurd when uttered aloud than it had in her head.

'I can hypothesize that the organic material uses the soil or underground cavities to communicate between disparate regions. The details of how such a mechanism might work, however, are unclear.'

"When we come upon the next barren region, send a probe into the ground. Maybe it can relay back useful readings before the planet devours it."

'I will do so.'

She considered the irate mountains for another second. "While we wait, shall we see what our stolen treasure can tell us?"

"You mean the leaf."

"Hey, we fought damn hard for that leaf." She wandered over to one of the cabinets, grabbed a scope and carried it to the workbench.

The leaf did appear rather puny lying there all alone. A sliver short of fifteen centimeters long and nine wide, the edges had curled inward and turned a muddy umber color. Narrow brown bands extended in from the tips toward the center. As she watched, the bands visibly grew, creating an expanding darkened area along their path. She blinked and activated the scope.

On initial inspection it looked like an ordinary leaf even at the cellular level. An epidermis protected layers of cells thick with chloroplasts and a network of veins. When she zoomed in closer, however, one interesting difference manifested. In addition to the cells which transported fluids and nutrients, spread through the vascular tissue in fine webs was an unfamiliar type of cell, each one so slender they could be mistaken for filaments.

They resemble axonal nerve fibers.

Lots of things 'resemble' axons, Valkyrie.

True, but Abigail studied numerous brain images. They resemble axons.

Point taken. She increased the magnification level but couldn't discern any other noteworthy features inside the cells.

Caleb leaned against the table next to her and considered the screen above the worktable displaying the feed from the scope. "What does Valkyrie think?"

"Hmm?"

He tapped a fingertip to the edge of his left eye, by which he meant, *her* eyes.

"Oh. Right." Her nose wrinkled up in slight consternation. The truth was the act of toggling the connection to the Artificial on and off had become so seamless and natural, half the time if asked she wouldn't be able to say if it was open or closed without reaching for Valkyrie's thoughts. In fact, she wasn't certain exactly when she had toggled it on this time.

"She thinks they might be axonal nerve fibers. Valkyrie, do you think the central nervous system they would feed into was in the plant's stem?"

'Perhaps, but I'm analyzing a different idea.'

"Which is?"

'I'd prefer to wait to discuss the matter until I'm more confident in my conclusions.'

"Except you can't keep me out of your mind."

Caleb chuckled. "Maybe you should respect her privacy."

She was surprised to find him wearing a somewhat cryptic expression. "You're serious."

Both of their voices had lowered, though Valkyrie could presumably still hear them if she wished. "It just seems if we genuinely believe she's not merely a sentient being but a sapient one, we should treat her as such. I know, she's all up in your head and you in hers, which means it's an impractical notion in practice." He raised his voice pointedly. "And it's not like she's respecting our privacy by not eavesdropping right now, is it, Valkyrie?"

'I'm sorry, Caleb, did you need something?'

"Nah."

Alex pinched the bridge of her nose and shook her head with a weak laugh. The last of the adrenaline had dissipated, leaving her achy and tired. "What about the probe? Have we found a prairie region yet?"

'Launching in six seconds.'

He grabbed her hand and tugged her toward the cockpit. "Let's see how it reacts to another intruder."

"I'm going to go out on a limb and guess 'not well.'"

But it didn't do anything at all. The probe plowed ten meters deep into the barren dirt and began sending readings back unimpeded. They showed a series of extremely low frequency infrasound microseisms and little else.

"I guess this confirms our suspicion the flora's alive but not the planet, and supports the theory the flora are communicating through the soil." She chewed on the side of her lower lip. "So they're a hive mind, then, with an intelligence shared by all the flora. That's the theory you were working on, isn't it, Valkyrie?"

'You know it was.'

"Actually, no—I didn't peek. But I was fairly smart on my own before you came along, and it makes sense. In fact, it's the only explanation that makes sense."

'As you say. Scans of the crust and upper mantle show no indication as yet of a central nervous system, making it plausible that sensory functions and responses are shared amongst the flora across the planet rather than concentrated in a single cortex.'

"A distributed neural network? I suppose the trees and plants could be separate nodes of a primary consciousness—"

"Stop that." Caleb's hand rested gently over hers.

She looked down…she'd been scratching at the medwrap on her inner forearm without realizing it. She rested her head on his shoulder. "It itches." It also ached even more than the rest of her body, but no need to worry him.

"I'm sure it does. So I think the emergency has passed for the moment. We should get clean and get some rest."

"Hmmm." She nodded languidly against him. "Valkyrie, pull up another kilometer to be safe. Adopt a pattern overnight to capture good representative scans of the surface. You know what to search for. Wake us if there's a problem or a life-altering—and I mean literally *life-altering*—discovery, but otherwise we'll decide how to proceed in the morning."

'I'll do so. Might I suggest a biocide shot to ward off infection in your wound? In addition, both of you should have your eVis initiate anti-inflammation measures before you go to sleep.'

"Yes, Mom…." They drawled in unison.

2

EKOS-1

"At least we finally found life," Alex muttered as she began enlarging the overnight scans at the data center. "Even if it did try to kill us."

This was the fourth portal space in the Metigens' elaborate network they had investigated. Intending to be methodical about their exploration, they'd started on the far left of the top row of signals, when viewed from their lobby, and visited every fifth one. Thus far every portal opened into a lobby space functionally identical to their own, with a second portal at the far end of the lobby leading to the 'pocket universe,' as Caleb had taken to calling them. They hadn't bothered to try to locate an observation planet akin to Portal Prime in any of the lobbies, on the assumption their presence would not be appreciated by any observing Metigen.

The first pocket universe had contained a fully realized space not unlike their home universe. But whereas the TLF wave for their universe led to the Sol system—to the cradle of civilization—in following the wave generated for the pocket universe they had found only a silent, uninhabited planet. The second of five planets in a K6 dwarf system, it orbited on the edge of the habitable zone for humans and exhibited a nitrogen-rich atmosphere. Scans and a brief surface visit revealed no life, however. Not so much as a prokaryote. The other bodies in the system were equally barren.

The next two portal spaces had been empty—as in naught but the void. No galaxies, no stars, no planets. The disorienting nature of the space had led them to depart in short order, confident there was nothing in the nothingness to find.

Now, on the fourth try, they had found something living. Unfortunately, they had no way to communicate with it or otherwise ask it to please stop trying to kill them.

The possibility of discovering life radically different from their own had obviously been considered by scientists. Protocols had been developed, and Valkyrie carried all of them in her databanks. But the fact was no one had managed to work out how to communicate with a planet-sized hive mind distributed in flora...particularly one wielding a vicious defensive streak as a weapon.

"And now we know one thing we didn't before—not all the life in these universes is human, or even humanoid. Or in any way similar to us, for that matter."

Alex scowled at the results of the scans. "Agreed, but this doesn't get us any closer to understanding what the purpose is for all these separate universes or the portal network."

Caleb massaged her shoulders, easing the last of the aches from the adventure of the previous day. All but the ache in her arm. "We could go ask Mesme."

"No." Her head shook firmly to emphasize the point. "Never ask a question until you know the answer, or at least can tell if the other person—or being—is lying. In this case, there's no reason to think the alien will tell us anything other than riddles. Besides, I don't want Mesme to learn the extent of our poking around."

"Not until we know more, anyway. I concede the point—knowledge is power when it comes to Mesme, and right now we don't have much." His hand slid down her arm to her palm. "Come on. Breakfast before decisions."

"You get started while I change my bandage."

He let go of her hand and headed for the kitchen. She waited until he was fully occupied setting out breakfast, then gingerly removed the medwrap from her wrist.

A gasp caught in her throat. She'd realized the wound wasn't healed—she could feel it wasn't healed—but in reality it was worse. The cut had clotted into a brownish-yellow pus, and the welts covering the skin surrounding it were now engorged and inflamed.

I did tell you the biocide wasn't working.

I know you did, but it's a simple cut. The medwrap alone should've all but healed it by now.

The cut was delivered by an alien source. It transferred microorganisms into your bloodstream which humans have never seen before, much less developed treatments for. I am working with your eVi to better calibrate your immune system response and combat the infection, but it too has never seen these microbes before.

Shit. Okay.

She'd been so absorbed in the internal conversation with Valkyrie—and gaping aghast at her arm—she missed Caleb coming up behind her. He dropped a hand on the table and demanded her attention. "Were you going to tell me?"

She cringed, unable to lie to him when he looked at her that way. "If it got worse...but Valkyrie's on the case, supercharging my immune system. I'll be fine."

He lifted her arm up and ran fingertips along the edges of the wound, studying it clinically. "Alex, this is badly infected, and we don't know by what." His gaze rose to meet hers. "We need to go home and get this treated."

"Don't be ridiculous."

"I won't have you dying from some alien microbe because you were too bullheaded stubborn to get help."

"Caleb, if the medwrap and the biocide didn't heal it, that means our doctors don't have any information on whatever's causing the inflammation, so returning home won't do any good. And I'm not going to die. I'll fight it off. It just may take a few days."

"Our doctors can absolutely treat it. We discover new microbial strains every time we investigate a new planet."

"True, but those still originate in our universe. This is alien in a way none of those are."

I'm not certain this argument helps your case.

Noted.

He scrutinized her suspiciously. "How do you feel?"

"Fine." And she did, mostly. Her arm hurt like hell, but...truthfully, she mostly felt like crap.

His eyes squeezed shut. "Good god, woman, you are the most obstinate person I have ever met. If it hasn't improved markedly by tomorrow morning, we're going home. No argument."

She made a face at him. "Eh...all right." Time to change the subject. "These planetary scans are one step above worthless. It's not your fault, Valkyrie—there's simply nothing here. Whatever is happening in and among the flora, we can't see it. Do you have any ideas for how to get useful information out of this place? "

'Not at present. In order to learn more we'd need to study living organic material. We could attempt to modify a probe to conduct a minimal analysis from the surface, but given the hostility of the planet's inhabitant, at this point I doubt it would allow the probe to do so.'

"Maybe if we leave and give it a few days, it'll calm down and we can try again?"

Caleb shrugged in nominal agreement, as he was spending most of his energy staring at her arm with a worrying glower. "We picked up signs of activity on two other planets in the system, so let's go check them out—more cautiously this time."

'Setting course for the second planet in the system.'

$\mathcal{R}$

EKOS-2

The first sign Ekos-2 was somehow different was all the color. While the previous planet was undeniably flourishing, its biosphere consisted of forests and prairies, all in shades of green and brown.

This world, in contrast, was painted in the spectrum of the rainbow. Fields of enormous, vibrant flowers stretched for kilometers. Even the trees were colorful, sporting leaves of blue, orange and violet in addition to every hue of green. There were *pink* trees, of all things.

But as inviting as the surface appeared, they stayed well aloft, cruising two kilometers high while they studied the various regions and gathered data.

Now that they knew what to search for, it was easy to spot the 'noise' on the infrasound band. "This planet's alive, too—or rather its plants are."

Caleb was peering intently out the viewport, eyes narrowed. "Valkyrie, what are the odds of the same kind of life spontaneously arising in the same time frame on two separate planets?"

'Low, but not zero. This universe may feature innate characteristics favorable to this particular form of life. As such, both planets could have been 'pollinated' with the precursors by asteroid or comet impacts.'

"And what would constitute 'characteristics favorable to this particular form of life?'"

'That I do not know.'

"Don't feel bad, Valkyrie. I don't think anyone does." He crossed his arms over his chest. "The TLF wave from this portal points to this system. Maybe the better question is which came first? The life or the signal?"

Alex nodded in agreement. "They could be watching because they found life here, or they could be watching because they *created* life here. But either way, it's here now. Let's try starting with the gentle approach this time. I'm going to launch a probe but give it a soft landing...ahead here in this field of unnaturally gorgeous flowers. Hopefully they won't eat it."

They slowed to hover above the field. She released the probe and held her breath as it descended, landed, bounced once and skidded to a stop. Despite the attempt at gentleness, it surely must have torn a leaf or two during the landing. Yet the plants didn't swarm the probe in anger.

They did tentatively curl in toward it.

The subsonic waves increased in magnitude, and she activated the microphone on the probe.

A low-level but distinctive *hum* filled the cabin. It rose and fell in harmonic steps, multi-tonal and infinitely complex. The sonance wasn't grating or discordant, but instead quite pleasing to the ear.

Her face lit up. "It sounds like the planet's singing."

"I admit, it does. Are we getting anything else?"

'The life form is not reacting in an overtly negative manner to the probe's presence. There are no tectonic tremors, nor are visual scanners picking up the formation of any vertical structures attempting to reach us. The plants in the vicinity of the probe do, however, appear to be...stroking it.'

"They're petting the probe?"

'I'm certain this is their method for investigating it. But lacking a more descriptive word, yes.'

"Damn." Her fingertip slid along the HUD and she rotated the probe's camera around. As she did, the plants in front of the camera shrank away as if in surprise. Then, perhaps deducing the camera wasn't going to attack them, they drew closer.

A stalk darted out and poked the camera lens with its tip then swiftly withdrew. A few seconds passed, and it darted out again. This time instead of jerking back, the tip of the leaf ran over the lens several times before withdrawing. It was like a child investigating a new toy—timid at first, but curiosity increasingly winning out.

Her eyes were dancing as she met Caleb's gaze. "I don't think this planet's hostile."

He glanced out the viewport. "We need to have the probe take a specimen."

"Cut off a leaf? I..." she frowned, tilting her head at the feed from the camera "...I don't want to."

"Oh, *now* you're worried about the well-being of the local vegetation? I'm sorry, but before we risk a trip down, we have to know how the flora react to damage."

'Given the events on the last planet, I'm not comfortable advising a trip to the surface.'

She groaned in exasperation. "What are we here for then, Valkyrie? We'll be careful, but there's no reward—no knowledge gained—without risk."

'I recognize that, but the risk is comparatively high. It is your decision, however.'

She didn't toggle on their link, not particularly caring to hear the full extent of Valkyrie's opinion on the matter. "Yes, it is. Extending the shears."

She directed the probe arm to a different plant than the curious one. Even so, she cringed as the clamp closed around a leaf and severed it from its stalk.

The song filling the cabin turned mournful and melancholy, and the plants backed away from the probe in palpable suspicion. They didn't attack; instead they seemed to wilt, losing some of their vigor.

"God, talk about a guilt trip...." She extended the robotic arm farther, the shorn leaf still in its grasp. Then she had the arm deposit the leaf on the ground and retract into the probe's casing.

The plant it had belonged to reached out and wound the surviving stalk around its lost appendage. It picked the leaf up and drew it into itself. In the cabin, the song gradually eased up on the sorrowful tenor, though it didn't regain its former vibrancy.

Caleb finally allowed a measure of excitement to show in his expression. "So we go down there."

"I agree." She massaged her shoulder as she stood. The pain from her wound had spread to encompass her upper arm as well, almost to her neck...and it was possible the injury was causing her growing headache. She was beginning to think Caleb was right, and they would have to go home and have a specialist look at it.

Reluctantly she opened the connection to Valkyrie. *Don't bitch at me about going to the surface. Just tell me how my arm's doing.*

In vernacular terms? Not good. All attempts by your immune system to fight the infection have been ineffective, and it has spread into the skin and tissue of your upper arm. I have been able to identify the core infection as caused by a fungal-type prion, but it has since mutated into a form more dangerous to humans—to you.

What if I took a stronger dose of biocide?

The last dose you took was the stronger dose.

Right. Keep working it, please.

Alex, I'm concerned for your health.

You think we should go home?

It may be the only option, though my optimism as to the result is limited.

You mean you don't believe our doctors can treat it?

It is alien, hence not understood. I think, therefore, the outcome is unknown.

Great. We'll decide after we get back.

About that—

Not listening.

She dropped her hand from her shoulder on realizing Caleb was watching her out of the corner of his eye and quickly started getting ready for the trip to the surface below.

ℛ

Caleb descended the ramp ahead of Alex. All indications were this planet was not inherently dangerous, but the same could have been said of the previous world until they unwittingly did the wrong thing. 'The wrong thing' might be different for this planet yet incite just as violent a reaction. As a result, this time they wore full environment suits and confirmed each other's seals before exiting the *Siyane*.

His left foot alighted on the grass; he paused, all his senses on heightened alert, but no attack came. He took another step. The ground was surprisingly pliant, the grasses forming a thick pelt above the dirt. So far so good.

He sensed Alex slip away from behind him. He turned to see her kneel in front of a cluster of orange and gold flowering plants. "If you tear a petal off, I will communicate my displeasure in new and interesting ways."

Her laugh echoed in his helmet. "Tempting thought, but I'll refrain." She fumbled at her belt and unlatched a tool. "I did bring a portable scanner, however. Let's see if we can non-intrusively learn something about the way their neural processes function."

She passed the scanner over the flowering shoot and stem. The plant didn't react immediately, but after a few seconds one of the leaves reached out to caress the scanner. Alex squealed in delight.

Yes, *squealed*. Needless to say, it was a reaction most people wouldn't expect from her. But he'd learned these last months that when truly at ease, she often expressed a childlike wonder at the sights they witnessed. It had been a beautiful discovery on his part.

He crouched beside her. "Getting anything?"

She waved the scanner above the nearest flower. The petals danced around in response, triggering a subdued but still delightful chuckle from her. "Um..." she cleared her throat and attempted to be serious "...the filaments *are* behaving like axons. They run all the way down the stalk into the roots and are actively firing. Firing what, I can't say."

He gazed around the field. The foliage was among the most vibrant he'd ever seen. It stretched to the horizon, but the terrain was open and inviting, lacking the brambles and widespread underbrush the first planet had displayed. Down the slope to their right, trees with broad, expansive limbs and ornate leaves lined a bubbling creek. The sounds the probe had picked up—more song than noise—filled the air, subtle but pervasive.

He took a deep breath...and relaxed. A little. Whatever this intelligence was, it appeared to be more welcoming than that of its sister planet. This didn't mean it wouldn't turn on them, but it evidently would take a greater offense to provoke it.

Alex stood, and though it was hidden beneath the helmet's faceplate, he didn't miss the grimace which passed across her face as she did. Her right arm hung with disturbing limpness at her side.

"It's getting worse, isn't it?"

"Yeah."

The fact she didn't brush him off and instead admitted her discomfort meant the injury was causing her significant pain at this point. He checked the ship; Valkyrie had retracted the ramp and closed the hatch in order to prevent an incursion by any would-be intruders.

They should leave now and head straight home; he worried if they waited much longer she might be in serious trouble—

—she grabbed his hand and began coaxing him down the slope toward the trees. "Come on, let's investigate the creek."

He sighed and followed her. Surely a few more minutes wouldn't make a difference.

The trees were made of a pale Aspen-like bark. It was soft and flexible, for the limbs and even the trunk swayed in the breeze. The leaves were similar to ivy and hung in curtains nearly to the ground.

He reached up to hold one of the curtains to the side so they could pass through to the creek. Before he was able to do so, however, the limb lifted *itself* up to form an archway. He whistled quietly, admittedly enthralled.

"This is astonishing."

"It is." Any lingering doubt as to the sentience of the intelligence inhabiting the planet departed with the act. It was one thing to react out of instinct when attacked, or to what one perceived as an attack. It was another thing entirely to act of one's own initiative in a manner such as this.

The life on these planets was the most alien he had ever encountered—anyone had ever encountered. Mesme had been *other*, but the alien was a discrete being, one which spoke their language and took on humanoid form. The Metigen ships were unusual, massive and powerful, but they were AIs in the same fundamental way Valkyrie was AI. This place, though, this life form....

A strand of ivy from the tree to his left extended out ever so slowly and touched his glove. He stretched his arm in front of him, palm upturned. The individual leaves stroked his palm through the material of his glove. Not wanting to startle the tree and disrupt the interaction, he pulsed her.

Alex.

She was at the edge of the creek but pivoted at his message. A hand came to her faceplate, her gasp audible in his helmet. He smiled, caught up in the playfulness of the tree's gesture.

Two of the leaves slithered up to his wrist and poked at the suit's seal. It was impervious to their efforts, but they continued prodding at the seal. His brow furrowed. Was this communication? Were they asking him to remove his glove?

He pondered what to do. Alex had said it on the ship: what were they here for if not this? Decision made, he reached over with his other hand and unlatched the seal.

"Caleb!"

"It's all right. I think."

The ivy curled around his glove, and more leaves drew to his wrist. Their tips slipped inside the seal and, as he stood there watching in amazement, tugged his glove off his hand. The glove fell to the ground and the leaves flattened out and enveloped his palm—

Wind rustles downy hairs protecting a newly sprouted leaf.
Sun bears down.
Leaf wants to stretch out in the warmth.
The light helps it to grow stronger.
It is pleased.
All is pleased.
There. Ice on the bark of a barren tree chills.
Shivering.
Tree waits for sun to arrive in its time.
Here. Dirt.
Cool, protective.
Nourishes a sea of grasses, welcomes its protracting roots.
Water propels a single cell of algae along its flows.
An endless journey through the streams and ponds of its own landscape.
A splash of water soaks the shore.
A seedling draws in life, life which will help it become rich in its vastness.
All becomes more.
All welcomes Not-All.
Afraid of Not-All?
All knows not fear.
Harm?
All knows not harm.
All never dies. All replaces, renews, replenishes.

Not-All broken into pieces.

> *No. Not-All are separate?*
>> *Not fragments but each All within the Not-All?*
>>> *Not-All strange. Alien.*

All curious.

> *Searches, probes.*
>> *Not harm.*

Not-All also many within, different but together.

> *Not-All not so strange perhaps.*
>> *But Not-All tiny.*

Other?

> *All knows not of Other.*
>> *All is All. Not-All is Not-All. Other is null.*
>>> *All needs not know of Other.*

All needs not fear, needs not harm. All never dies.

> *All is forever. All replaces, renews, replenishes.*
>> *All is All.*

All welcomes Not-All, needs not harm Not-All.

> *But All needs not Not-All.*
>> *All is enough. All is content.*

"Caleb, wake up! God, please, wake up. Talk to me, move, do something…please…."

The voice sounded distant, a whisper in the limitlessness that was.

He tried to focus on it, to direct his consciousness toward the drifting, troubled song wafting through the air.

With each breath of a planet, his perception gradually separated from the being he now knew as All.

Blinking, disoriented. His body felt unfamiliar. Tight and confining. *Tiny.*

He forced air into his lungs. "Wow."

Alex's faceplate dropped to his. "Goddammit, Caleb. You scared me."

The ivy unwound from his hand, leaving a feeling of *absence* behind. Ground pressed into his back; had he been standing before?

Alex hovered above him, and he reached for her. "Sorry. I'm fine."

Such a thin word, it couldn't begin to reveal what he was.

He reluctantly let loose of the last vestiges of All's consciousness. "How long was I...gone?"

Her nose scrunched up, a clear sign of tumultuous emotions battling it out in her head. "Thirty, forty seconds. You just collapsed to the ground. I was about to tear that vine off of you, damn the consequences."

"No need." He sat up and reached for the helmet control.

Her hand leapt to his arm to stop him. "What are you doing?"

He collapsed the helmet and lifted the breather mask off, then drew in a long breath of air.

Scents of eucalyptus and honeysuckle. Warm, with a suggestion of moisture. Spores of pollination, here and there.

Maybe not quite every vestige. "It's safe to breathe."

"No, the samples were too high in nitrogen."

"All's made the air in this area safe for us."

She eased down to a sitting position beside him. "'All?'"

"The planet's life form. It's not a hive mind—or at least it doesn't think of itself that way. It's a single entity."

"So you...talked to it." Her voice bled incredulity.

"More like it talked to me. Or let me inside, or...I don't know if I can explain it." Even now his head was drowning in sensory overload. What had he seen? They weren't words or images—they were experiences. For reasons he could not fathom, the life form had chosen to immerse him in itself. Lasting only seconds, the sojourn had seemed endless.

"Go ahead, take your helmet and breather mask off."

She complied, taking small, hesitant breaths at first. "Hmm. It smells like...."

"Honeysuckle. Also an undercurrent of eucalyptus and...thyme, I think."

A corner of her mouth twitched. "Yes." She leaned back to rest on her hands, then winced and sat up, cradling her right arm against her chest.

He reached for her in concern—

Of course.

He leapt to his feet and offered her a hand. "Take your glove off—no, you'll need to take your whole suit off."

"What? Why should I take off my suit? I'm not sure I want to commune with the local. My head hurts enough as it is."

Because of the infection. It would do that. "Trust me."

"You know I do." She swallowed heavily and stood. "Taking off the suit."

While she discarded her outer layer, leaving her in a sports tank and leggings, he ran a palm along the trunk of the nearest tree. It gave and flexed in answer to his contact. Familiar and *welcoming.*

"What now?"

He turned back to her, and his chest seized up in cold terror at what he saw.

Streaks of angry, swollen crimson extended out from the medwrap covering her forearm to climb up her upper arm like trespassing snakes. Two of the streaks had made it to the curve of her neck, sending tendrils disappearing into her hairline. In the path they created purplish-black blood bruises followed. "Jesus, Alex…."

"What?" She looked down and jerked as if stung. "Fuck. Fuck, fuck, *fuck.*"

Her gaze met his as he closed the distance between them. "Okay, you've convinced me—we need to go home. Caleb, I'm officially scared. I—"

"It's going to be all right. I promise. Come with me."

Confusion and fear darkened her expression, but she didn't protest as he led her to the creek. He urged her to her knees, crouched beside her, and tried to coax her into a reclined position.

"I don't understand. We need to go back and—"

"Shhh. *Trust* me."

She watched him with panic-filled eyes as he unwound the medwrap and tossed it aside. The injury beneath it nearly sent him into the same panic she was fighting, but he willed himself calm.

This was going to work.

He carefully moved her arm away from her body and submerged it in the water.

"Ahhh!" Her body convulsed in a spasm of pain, but he held her arm firmly until the spasm subsided. She sucked in air through gritted teeth. "Not...finding this...funny."

He glanced up at her wearing a smirk—a forced one, but she needed the reassurance—then quickly refocused on her submerged arm. The water fizzed and hissed around the wound, obscuring his view of it as the water took on a brownish tint.

Alex exhaled audibly, and the tension in her body relaxed slightly. Her lips curled upward. "Not so bad now."

"Good. Let's—" He jumped at movement behind him. He looked back to see a vine from one of the nearby trees snaking over his shoulder. It advanced beyond him to where Alex's arm met the water and nudged at it.

Her eyes were wide and uncertain as he lifted her arm out of the water. The glimpse he caught of the wound suggested the swelling had receded and much of the pus had been washed away, but before he could discern anything else the ivy completely enveloped her arm, wrapping it in a cocoon.

She fidgeted as a raspy giggle escaped her throat. "Tickles."

He placed a hand on her chest. "Don't pull away."

"I'm *not*...." Her boots *tap-tapped* against his thigh in redirected energy, and they both stared in fascination as the leaves undulated along her arm in a slow, pulsing rhythm.

Almost two minutes had passed when the vine finally unfurled and retreated—to expose smooth, unbroken and unmarred skin.

"Oh my...I can't believe...." She ran her other hand over the skin which minutes earlier had been torn and inflamed. "What did it *do* to me?"

He scooted up to recline on one elbow beside her, flooded with relief. "Kind of self-evident, isn't it? It healed you." He studied her face, her demeanor. "Do you feel healed?"

She chewed on her lower lip and shrugged, but he saw his relief mirrored in her eyes and tugging at the corners of her mouth. "I think I do." She tentatively flexed her arm. "It doesn't hurt anymore. Feels tingly. Like the nerves are being stimulated or something. But it's not a bad tingly."

With a wild cackle she collapsed onto her back, all the fear and trepidation washing away in a surge of euphoria. "So in the space of two days I've been poisoned by an alien and healed by an alien." Realization dawned in her expression. "Was it because they're the same? Is that why it worked?"

"More or less. I think both planets support the same type of intelligence, they simply evolved in different ways. When I was, we were...interacting, it said, or conveyed, the concept that it 'never died.' Instead it 'replaced, renewed, replenished.' And it occurred to me—if it was biologically similar to the one that hurt you and it was capable of replenishing itself, perhaps it could do the same for you—for the alien poison inside you."

"Well." She sat up, purpose and energy again animating her movements. "I'll take it. I'll definitely, unequivocally take it. Since they—it—doesn't mind our company, shall we explore some more?"

He huffed a laugh, marveling at her resiliency, then stood to follow her up the bank.

But not before he paused to place a palm on the tree he had interacted with and offer a 'thank you.'

He swore he heard a pleased murmur in response.

⁂

Alex could be accused of acting giddy as they boarded the *Siyane*. Hell, he could be accused of a little giddiness himself.

An overdose of happiness at her wound being healed—at her escaping a life-threatening infection—contributed a great deal to his elation, to be sure. More than that, however, he found his encounter with the planet's consciousness had left him with an uncommon...lightness of being.

The alien mind emanated a peace, a quiet joy, such as he'd never experienced in his own life. Even in his happiest moments, of which there had been many these last months, his mind continued to spin its persistent calculations and machinations, always on the lookout for danger on the horizon. But right now the event had him on such an emotional high, he could no longer fathom darkness.

"You are my hero." Alex threw her arms around his neck once they reached the main cabin, grinning in as much elation as he felt.

He lifted her up in the air and spun her twice before setting her down. "I do try. You're really okay?"

"Valkyrie, am I okay?"

'You appear to be more than 'okay.' Not only have all traces of infection or unfamiliar microorganisms vanished from your body, the ministrations of the resident life form repaired minor degradations in your blood vessels and several organs, as well as healed the muscular damage from your crash landing in engineering.'

"Fantastic...." Her voice was a sweet whisper on his lips.

Damn she tasted good, smelt good...like spiced cider warmed over an open campfire on an autumn night. His senses had been hyper-charged, and every touch, every perception seemed magnified a thousand-fold. He felt the beat of her pulse in the caress of her lips upon his skin. The scrape of the fingernail of her left index finger across the nape of his neck. The flutter of her lashes as she blinked and banished Valkyrie into the walls of the ship. The fractional rise in her body temperature in response to his hands on her.

'Do you want to investigate other regions of the planet now?'

He scooped Alex up in his arms and headed for the stairs. "Later, Valkyrie."

"What was it like?"

Floating on a serotonin high, amplified by his general state of delight with the universe and all it held, Caleb idly twirled a lock of her hair around his forefinger. "Hmm?"

She folded her hands on his stomach and propped her chin on them. "Mind-melding with a planet-sized intelligence—what was it *like?*"

"Oh, that. It was..." he searched for how he might possibly put the encounter into words "...the obvious comparison would be to a full-sensory *illusoire*, but it doesn't begin to compare. This being experiences life through every cell of flora on the planet—every root and leaf, every centimeter of bark, every stamen and petal— and it does so all at once. I perceived it as if I were doing the same, though I'm at a loss for how to describe it. We simply don't have the language for this mode of consciousness."

"So it was wonderful, then."

"Yes. It was wonderful." Her body relaxed against his, but her lips quirked about in independent agitation.

"What?"

"I was just pondering why it chose you and not me."

He laughed and tugged her up his chest, closer. "You're jealous!"

"Maybe a little...."

"Why? You already have more than one consciousness in your head."

"It's not the same. Valkyrie and I are separate, distinct personalities."

He brushed wayward strands of hair out of her eyes. "I hope so."

That earned a downward turn of the corners of her mouth and a hint of wariness in her tone. "What does that mean?"

"It means I like Valkyrie just fine, but I fell in love with you."

She stared at him for a beat then dropped her cheek to his chest. "Do you think she's changing me?" Her voice was barely audible. Theoretically Valkyrie could hear her, but although he'd made a dig about it the day before, the truth was the Artificial had thus far given them complete privacy whenever it was appropriate.

He stroked her hair softly, smiling at the dampness along her hairline, at how the locks remained sweat-soaked from desire and the passion it had evoked. He wanted to be honest with her, but his feelings on the matter were still evolving and, frankly, something of a mess. But he had married her with full knowledge that she came with a few idiosyncrasies, only one of which was an AI sharing space in her head.

"I think…a lot has changed for you in the last year, and you've responded in a spectacular manner to all of it. I think it's impossible to separate out the effect each of these things has had on you—to say what's due to the war, what's a result of your trials on Portal Prime and the reconciliation with your mother, what's because of Valkyrie…and what's because of *me*." He grabbed her and playfully tossed her off him, then quickly rolled over to position himself above her. "I do assign the majority of the credit to myself, of course."

"Of course," she murmured throatily and pulled him down the last couple of centimeters until the length of their bodies met. "Again?"

"Oh, yes, again."

3

EKOS-2

Pole to pole, the planet was the most verdant, fertile world Alex had ever seen.

Unlike its sister planet, there were no stretches of desert or barrenness. Every meter supported grass at a minimum, but more often colorful foliage or healthy forests. It helped that a negligible orbital tilt kept the poles from becoming frozen tundras, but the plants weathered the chillier temperatures hardily. There were no bodies of water large enough to be called oceans, but many lakes filled with tiny mosses and algae and an abundance of rivers and creeks.

As aliens went, this breed had a lot to commend it—not the least of which was that it had probably saved her life.

She ran fingertips along her forearm, scarcely believing the transformation. She'd been accelerating up through the stages of panic when Caleb had coaxed her to the creek, cursing herself as an utter fool for acting so irresponsibly in refusing to seek professional medical help immediately. The fact that it worked out in the end didn't bode well for her learning a lesson from the close call. But recognizing her foible was a start, right?

She let her arm drop to her side with a still incredulous shake of her head. "I wish we could harness these healing properties somehow. It would revolutionize medical care."

"It might only work in this particular situation—to fight an infection of like kind. Regardless, I doubt we can, because healing isn't something it did. It's something it *is*."

'May I propose a name for the planet and the entity residing here?'

"I thought we were calling it 'Ekos-2?'"

'I would argue by its actions it has earned a more meaningful name.'

"Let's hear it."

'Akeso, the ancient Greek goddess personifying the healing process.'

Caleb contemplated it a moment. "It's an apt and worthy name. Thank you, Valkyrie."

They strolled through tall, reedy grasses near the bank of one of the wider rivers they'd discovered. The climate and ambiance of the planet had proved too appealing to resist, especially when they'd spent so much time aboard the *Siyane* lately, and they had spent much of the day exploring on foot or on the bike.

Though the atmosphere as a whole was too nitrogen-rich to be comfortably breathable, the residents—resident, she had difficulty thinking of it as a single entity—altered the air wherever they traveled, increasing the oxygen content as needed. How did it know what their bodies required? Had it read Caleb's biochemistry while it communed with him?

She watched him out of the corner of her eye. "You know, you're sounding a bit mystical lately."

"Honestly, I'm *feeling* a bit mystical. I cannot overstate what a sublime experience it was. To touch another mind, one so very different from my own yet so open and all-encompassing? And it's all around us, right now." He ran a hand, palm open, over the tips of the grass blades. "I look at this grass, and I swear I can see its life, its intelligence...see the glimpse of it I had from within."

She'd tried to wrap her head around the idea of a singular planet-sized alien intelligence spread across billions of organic components, but she'd mostly failed. She was able to discuss the abstract concept, but it was a far cry from comprehending what the concept *meant*. Everything surrounding them was not merely alive, but part of a whole—no, that wasn't correct. Everything surrounding them was the whole. And Caleb had experienced it from the inside.

Truth be told, she *was* jealous, though she admitted his point about her head already being a tad crowded was well taken. Hell, Valkyrie might have metaphorically—or genuinely—short-circuited on being thrust into the middle of such a mind.

On the contrary, I think we would have much in common. The structure of this type of distributed intelligence should be quite similar to my neural net architecture.

She was keeping the connection open to allow Valkyrie to see what they saw and analyze the surroundings in a way they could not. *I don't know, Valkyrie. Our tendency is to try to relate something alien to ourselves in order to make it comprehensible. I understand what you mean about the technical structure, but I suspect what we're dealing with here isn't remotely like you, or like anything humans have ever created or encountered.*

Well, I still think we'd have a lot in common.

She squelched a laugh. Was Valkyrie pouting?

No.

I think you are.

Not squelched enough, apparently, as Caleb cocked an eyebrow. "Something funny?"

"Valkyrie's pouting because I said she wasn't similar to the planet's intelligence—to Akeso."

'I am not pouting.'

Caleb laughed. "Sounds like pouting to me."

Silence fell on Valkyrie's end, and they followed suit for several minutes, walking hand-in-hand in sight of the river. The late afternoon breeze was warm and pleasant, and the background of gurgling water blended with the planet's ever-present hum to create a soothing melody.

'You know what? I think you were right—I think I was pouting. Fascinating.'

Alex chuckled heartily. "Self-awareness is one of the first signs of true wisdom, Valkyrie. I read that somewhere."

When they crested a sloping hill, Caleb stopped. He dropped her hand and turned in a slow circle, his eyes on the horizon. "I'll be honest. I wouldn't be averse to staying here for a while, but I know we shouldn't. We came here—to the portal network—for a reason, and dallying isn't going to bring us any closer to the answers we're seeking."

"No, it isn't." She smiled at him. "But the world won't end if we stay another day or two."

AR

"That grouping there looks like a sailship."

"Where?"

She grasped Caleb's arm and slid her hand up it until she reached his, then nudged it to point where she meant. "See?"

"Hmm. To me it looks like a walrus' face. It even has tusks."

She shifted her head for a different vantage...and scowled. "And now I can't unsee that. Thanks."

"Anytime." He drew both their hands back down and brought her knuckles to his lips.

Caleb had never known Earth's constellations, and Seneca was far too young a colony to have developed a pantheon of its own, so they'd decided to make up their own constellations for the new, unfamiliar stars they lay beneath.

As a child she'd learned all the constellations, studying furiously during the week to impress her dad when he came home on the weekends. And while eventually she'd come to understand they had no objective existence, much less meaning—not only were they recognizable solely from Earth but in reality the stars in a constellation were many light-years apart—she nevertheless recalled them fondly.

Or perhaps her fondness was for the nights spent stargazing alongside her dad, nights when she was still flush with innocence and insatiable curiosity.

Here, now, she wished her father remained in her head, so he'd recall those nights as well and they could reminisce. In the weeks after the final battle against the Metigens, an increasing number of glitches and errors arose in her father's...virtual construct, for want of a better term. Valkyrie ultimately determined that for now, she lacked the ability—the technology, the algorithms, the necessary inputs—to build and maintain an integral personality separate from but residing inside her neural network.

Valkyrie had continued to study the problem, but when the time came for her to be transferred into the *Siyane*, certain sacrifices needed to be made due to space considerations. Quantum hardware was shrinking rapidly, but not *that* rapidly. The partial essence of her father's consciousness still existed, quarantined and rendered dormant in a subsector of Valkyrie's processes with his permission, such as it was, and hers.

It had been an amazing gift to be able to carry a piece of him with her for a time—something no one else was able to say about a loved one they'd lost—and perhaps one day she would again.

She forcibly put aside the maudlin thoughts; this was a splendid, perfect night, and she didn't want to ruin it with ineffectual moping. "I wonder if any of these stars harbor life."

Caleb wound his hands behind his head. "We have a very small sample size to extrapolate from—namely, us—but I suspect because the TLF wave points here, any other intelligent beings in this space will have originated here."

"But life could emerge independently…unless…."

"Unless life doesn't emerge anywhere without the Metigens seeding it."

She groaned. "I'm sorry, but they are not gods. They may be an ancient and scientifically advanced species, but that doesn't make them gods—it just makes them old."

4

EKOS-3

Alex considered the unexpected scene on the other side of the viewport. "Are those...towers?"

After three delightful days they'd reluctantly departed Akeso to investigate the final 'inhabited' planet in the system. A quarter of an AU more distant from the system's sun, it was colder and smaller than Akeso had been.

It also had dozens if not hundreds of what appeared to be towers jutting up through the atmosphere.

As they circled the planet in high orbit, more of the structures came into view. Only the tops were visible, but scans confirmed they continued down all the way to the surface. And they appeared to be constructed of timber and foliage. Long, thin limbs stretched through a thick mesosphere in twisting branches, and the structures grew progressively thicker as they descended toward the ground.

Caleb leaned in to study the scanner images. "They're not trees—not naturally growing ones, anyway. But as for what they are? If I had to guess, I'd say this particular planet's intelligence is trying to reach the stars."

"Quite a deductive leap from limited data."

He shrugged. "What can I say? I was in the head of one."

"Granted. We should investigate where these towers originate. Let's pick a point as far away as possible from any of the structures then go in-atmosphere."

"Cautiously."

She eyed him. "You think it's hostile."

"I think it's aggressive. That may or may not be the same thing, but this isn't the place to take unnecessary risks."

"I can see that." She took the controls and eased them through the atmosphere, as much as one could 'ease' through a planetary atmosphere.

When the clouds thinned, they revealed a most unusual landscape.

The roots of the nearest tower spanned multiple kilometers in every direction from the trunk—and that was above ground. Streaks of rich, fertile soil extended out in spokes beyond the roots to intersect the adjacent towers' roots. Beyond these streaks, the land was completely barren, sucked dry of nutrients.

Cloaked, they approached the tower. The trunk measured 1.2 kilometers at the base and consisted of a massive rat's nest of varied limbs and muted green foliage. It was without a doubt a living structure, growing ever larger and stronger—and presumably taller.

She shook her head wryly. "You were right. This life form is trying to reach the stars, and it is devoting every resource on the planet to doing so. I can appreciate the sentiment, but...."

"But it feels malevolent somehow, and the opposite of Akeso. Instead of reveling in each morning dewdrop and each blossoming of a flower's petals, this entity is eschewing all those joys in favor of a single-minded drive to..." his brow furrowed "...leave? Is it trying to leave, or simply expand and grow?"

She regarded him with a measure of surprise. Now he was talking about dewdrops and flower petals? Akeso had really dosed him.... It wasn't bad as such, merely unexpected, and a long way from ruthless warrior. She expected the shift in behavior to fade in time; she hadn't decided yet whether she wanted it to. After all, the sex it had elicited—was still eliciting—bordered on transcendental.

Valkyrie updated them on the readings. 'This planet exhibits a high level of tectonic activity. It nears the level our presence garnered on Ekos-1, but in this case it appears to be a consistent state. I hypothesize this is a result of the gathering of the plant growth from the surrounding regions into the structures.'

"Is the tectonic activity destabilizing the planet?"

'Not to a measurable degree, as far as can be determined with current scans. However, on a geologic time scale it might be doing so. I can't yet estimate how long this behavior has been occurring.'

"It has to have been a long time, relatively speaking. How many of these towers are there?"

'Extrapolating from their spacing in this region, 112 to 147.'

She grimaced at Caleb before staring out the viewport in contemplation. "I don't guess we need to test how it'll react to provocation, do you?"

"Oh, I think we do—but using a probe and from excessively far away. A minimum of a megameter."

"Right." She sighed. "I'm not inclined to spend the next several hours dodging these towers, and I don't see anything else here, so let's head on out. We'll climb to high orbit and launch a probe into one of them."

They had barely cleared the visible atmosphere when Caleb bolted out of his chair. "What was that? Swing to starboard."

"You got it." She continued arcing up but veered around. "I'm not seeing—what was that?"

"Exactly."

'That' was a spherical object hurtling away from the top of the closest tower and deeper into space.

'The object's trajectory suggests the planet's satellite is its destination.'

"And thus ours as well." She adjusted course to catch up with the object.

Caleb had planted his palms on the dash to lean closer to the viewport. "The tower ejected it, like a ball out of a cannon."

The visual scanner located the object and zoomed in to reveal a tight nest of vines and bark toppling end-over-end through space.

She frowned. "I don't understand. Don't pieces need to stay connected to the whole in order to live?"

'Perhaps this life form has evolved. This may be a form of re-production.'

The moon was growing larger in the viewport. Unlike the hurled object, their intent wasn't to crash into it, so she decelerated.

Minutes later the object did precisely that, colliding with the lunar surface and flattening out but not shattering apart.

"Wait a minute." She peered at one of the smaller HUD screens. They hadn't paid much attention to the satellite on their arrival. "This moon has the beginnings of an atmosphere."

'It also has the beginnings of plant growth.'

Sure enough, long-range scans picked up pockets of organic life, islands of foliage and a few miniature trees. "I'll be damned. It's terraforming the moon."

"A flora-based intelligence which is not only space-capable, but advanced enough to terraform dead worlds? That's not something you see...ever."

"And yet. Valkyrie, run a full spectrum scan of the lunar surface. We'll study it later and try to determine how the terraforming is being accomplished." She drummed her fingers on her leg while she waited.

'Completed.'

"All right. Back to the original plan. Let's announce our presence." She left the moon behind and approached the planet once more. The ship's targeting locked in on the top of one of the towers breaking through the atmosphere, and she wasted no time firing a probe into the center of it.

The reaction to the probe's impact was as rapid and violent as the first planet's had been when she'd broken off a single leaf, and an order of magnitude larger in scale.

The tower spit the probe back out at a substantial fraction of the speed at which it had arrived. The top layers of the structure expanded and split into feeler-like appendages, which then searched the area for the source of the intrusion. Within seconds the appendages grew in length, apparently stealing bulk from lower down.

A few more seconds, and projectiles started launching out of the inner ring of the tower; a shocking number of them headed in their direction with impressive velocity. Given they were cloaked, the sole logical explanation was the...entity...had extrapolated their general location from the trajectory of the probe.

Her hand hovered above the throttle. "I can't believe the amount of propulsion those structures are able to create with no motors—not even a pneumatic system."

"It's learned to use the tools available to it very well."

"Way to understate, *priyazn*."

He shot her an amused look, but it quickly faded as across the planet, every tower began launching its own projectiles into space. The projectiles had no motive power of their own, and once their momentum gave out they could only drift, so the *Siyane* wasn't in any legitimate danger. Nevertheless, the ferocity of the attack was sobering.

Caleb ran a hand down his jaw and departed the cockpit to pace around the cabin. "This intelligence obviously isn't content to remain confined to its own planet, and it's just as obviously belligerent in disposition." He stopped to gaze at her. "We have to warn Akeso about it."

"You're worried this entity will try to take over the other planets in the system? But it will need, I don't know, centuries to develop the ability to travel so far, if it ever can."

"Good—that'll give Akeso time to prepare. Listen, Akeso does not comprehend the concept of something other than itself. The idea that something might show up and attack it is as foreign as...as murder is to an infant."

"Wasn't our presence kind of a contradiction to its worldview?"

"You'd think, but it didn't seem concerned by our little incon-sistency. It viewed us as...curiosities, nothing more." He groaned and sank against the data center. "I don't know if I'll be able to make it understand. Assuming it will interact with me again. But, dammit, I have to try."

"Absolutely." She nodded as if *she* understood. She didn't, but she couldn't refuse him in most circumstances, and never in the face of such an alarming level of distress. "We'll go back now."

5

EKOS-2

AKESO

Evening had turned the sky a deep persimmon. The remaining sunlight enriched the colors of the ubiquitous flowers and foliage to even greater vibrancy, as if the saturation filter had been notched up several levels.

Caleb noted all this in passing as he strode deliberately toward the creek. He didn't know how he was going to do this, only that he had to make the attempt. He heard the soft depression of the grass beneath Alex's feet as she followed behind him. The sensory enhancement he'd been enjoying courtesy of Akeso was fading but not yet gone.

Intellectually he recognized there was no need for him to visit the same tree which had initiated the earlier encounter. Akeso's life essence encompassed the entirety of the planet's surface, and one manifestation of it was as good as the next. He could reach down and embrace a random blade of grass and achieve the same result.

But he wasn't a planet-spanning intelligence; he was human, and humans both craved the familiar and relied on visual cues upon which to hang esoteric concepts. No matter how many times his mind insisted it didn't matter, his heart insisted he had bonded with *this* tree. And since it didn't matter....

He closed his eyes and drew the air into his lungs, working to immerse himself in the environment of this world once more. The air had become healthy for them to breathe within minutes of the *Siyane's* arrival. He listened with open ears to the bubbling water of the creek. The purr of leaves as they gently rustled in the breeze. The peacefully joyful song of bountiful life humming all around him.

He reached out, palm open. A vine instantly extended toward him and sent its leaves dancing playfully along his skin in greeting, but that was all. He rubbed his thumb over one of the leaves, urging it to stay. Still nothing. His jaw clenched in frustration; he willed it relaxed. Vexation would not aid his cause.

"Please, I need to speak with you. You're in danger. I need to make you understand. I need to show you, so you can protect yourself." He doubted Akeso comprehended words in any concrete way, but he hoped it was able to sense the desperation in his voice, in the aura of pheromones he was surely exuding and the constriction keeping his muscles taut.

"You helped us. You saved her life. Let me help you in return."

The song in the air grew in complexity, its murmur enveloped him and—

Coolness, refreshing after the long warmth.

Warmth, welcome after the night's chill.

Both at once, here and there.

A seedling fighting to rise through the soil.

The first rush of air on the tip of its shoot.

Trees grown so tall they gaze out upon vast steppes.

Up to the growing twinkle of lights above—

This. We call them stars, and they are Not-All.

You are Not-All.

Yes, but there are many. Many like me, many unlike me. Many who would do All harm.

All does not fear harm. All never dies. All is forever.

All replaces, renews, replenishes. All is All.

Here, now, yes. But if Not-Alls encroach, they can kill All.

All does not experience death. All replaces, renews—

No! Dangers exist out there strong enough to hurt you, and you will not be able to replace or renew or replenish what is lost. They will destroy you and everything you are.

Not-All wishes to hurt All?

Not me. Never. Not those who accompany me. But others who do wish to hurt you are coming—not soon, but they are coming.

You must prepare yourself. You must...you must be ready to fight.

All is and has always been. Nothing has ever existed against which All need fight. All knows not of struggle.

I know you don't, and it breaks my heart to have to teach this to you. But if you want to live on, if you want to feel the warmth of the sun rising and setting for a multitude of days, you must come to know struggle. You must learn to defend yourself.

Not-All thinks strange, impossible ideas...yet All senses Not-All believes them. What would Not-All have All do?

Look inside me, and you will discover everything you need to know. And...

...I'm sorry.

Towering trees thrash.

Hurtle pieces of themselves into space.

A knife plunges into a man's heart.

Blood. So much blood.

Gunfire.

Explosions.

The stench of burning flesh in the air.

Spears of metal.

Spears of timber.

The snap of bones.

The snap of a plant stalk.

Pain.

Strangled, gurgling breaths, lungs filling with blood.

His own.

A different pain.

Anguish.

It churned together until he could no longer tell where his anguish ended and All's began.

Not-All causes death? All does not understand. This cannot be Not-All.

Yes, it can be. It is. It's part of who I am—who Not-All is. But Not-All also loves, and fights for life. All can see this.

All sees much. All does not comprehend how Not-All can both love life and take life.

I take life because I love life. I take life in order to protect life. Because—this is what you must realize if you are to survive—not everything that lives is good. Not every being loves life and wishes it to continue. There are Not-Alls who destroy callously, who cause pain and torment and do not suffer for it. These are the lives I take, without regret, to preserve virtuous life such as All.

All cannot take life.

Then All will die.

All never...All is troubled.

> *If All chooses to fight, how will it do so?*

If All's will to live is strong enough, All will find a way. It's called 'survival instinct,' and it's a damn powerful weapon.

All will consider what Not-All has shown it...but All believes Not-Alls should leave now.

I understand. I...I wish you well.

⋅

ℛ

Alex circled the small copse in restless, chaotic loops. Approximately every three seconds she checked on Caleb. He'd been out for far longer this time than in the first melding. Minutes—ten? Twelve?

8.7 minutes.

You're not helping, Valkyrie.

The information should ease your concern as it indicates he has been in this state for less time than you believed.

She checked him again. His lips moved in silent, half-formed words, and in the last minute or so his fists had clenched, the left one curling tightly over the leaves and vine wound around his hand. Now his jaw was set in an expression she was all too familiar with.

It wasn't going well.

Night fell in full, and his form faded into the shadows. She moved closer.

How long was she planning to leave him this way? Was it even possible for her to wake him? She'd jostled him after he collapsed to the ground while trying to move him into a more comfortable position, and he hadn't stirred. She could cut the vine and sever the connection, but doing so might be as damaging to him as abruptly severing Mia's connection with Meno had been to Mia. No, she didn't dare risk it.

So the answer was 'as long as it took.' She would wait. Didn't mean she had to like it.

The wind picked up, raising goosebumps on her arms. She crossed them over her chest and rubbed her hands along them.

You should retrieve a pullover from the ship.

I'm good.

In truth, she had no reason to be freaking out—which she wasn't. He'd done this before with no ill effects. He'd initiated this encounter. It was just…he looked so damn vulnerable lying there. She'd never say that to his face, and it did represent rather a contradiction. So little about him could ever be called vulnerable…and what there was resided deep on the inside, never visible like this.

As she studied the vulnerable lines around his twitching, anxious lips, his eyelids fluttered. Instantly she was on her knees beside him.

The vine began to unwind from his hand, then protested as it met resistance from the fist clutching it in a vise grip. A brief tug-of-war ensued until his fist relaxed. The vine slithered away and its source limb rose to retake its natural position above them.

She was smiling when his eyes opened, as if this episode had been no big thing. "Hey. Are you okay?"

His jaw remained clenched, darkening his features more than the shadows. "We need to leave."

The tone the statement was delivered in left no room for questioning, so she didn't argue.

The next instant he was on his feet and heading toward the *Siyane*. She rushed to catch up to him. "Did it work?"

"Maybe."

Given the urgency in Caleb's bearing, Alex lifted off as soon as they were on board. Until he volunteered otherwise, she could only assume 'leave' meant leave the planet, so she ascended directly into the atmosphere. The active biosphere created an especially thick one, and it was a bumpy trip requiring her attention. Still, she sensed him pacing in agitation behind her; she could feel the disquiet flowing off him in waves.

At last they cleared the upper atmosphere, and she twisted around in her chair. The pacing had ceased at some point, and he now sat at the kitchen table, his elbows on the table and his head in his hands.

"Are we done here?"

He nodded but didn't look up.

"Valkyrie, set a course for the portal." She went to the table and sat down across from him. "What happened?"

He blew out a harsh breath and met her gaze with eyes bleeding torment. "I polluted something that was pure and beautiful. It had no concept of moral darkness, didn't know evil and violence even existed—not until I showed it. Now that innocence is lost forever."

"You were trying to protect it—to keep it alive. This was the right thing to do."

'Think of Akeso as a child. As with all children, it has to lose its innocence if it is to survive in the larger world.'

"No offense, Valkyrie, but shut up."

Her throat worked in unease, and she shrank back in the chair, increasing the distance between them. "Does that apply to me, too?"

He cringed and removed a hand from his temple to reach out and squeeze hers. "No, of course not. I just..." he let out a raw, frayed chuckle "...the only way I could think of to communicate the nature of the threat was to allow it into my mind as it had allowed me into its own. And I saw my darkness through its eyes—which is fine, I can handle that. I know what I am and what I've done. But I felt the dampening of its spirit all around me. Inside me. I felt a portion of what made it beautiful die."

She struggled to find the right words to say. Honestly, at this moment she cared little about Akeso's suffering but a great deal about his. "Caleb, you're a...a champion for life. The simple truth is, protecting good often requires violence against evil. Surely, seeing your past and the trials you've faced, Akeso recognized this."

"Maybe. I can't say." He shook his head. "I wish like hell it didn't have to learn such a harsh lesson. From me, from anyone."

'Perhaps conflict is not limited to the human condition—perhaps it is the nature of all sentient beings, of all universes.'

"I'm not—"

"Valkyrie, when Caleb tells you to shut up, you goddamn better shut up!"

'Apologies.'

His hand moved to her arm. "No...she's right. Or at least, I fear she might be. Valkyrie, please accept *my* apology."

'Always, Caleb.'

I'm sorry, too. I'm just angry at the world on his behalf right now. She exhaled heavily and managed a grim frown. "Well, if she is right about the universality of conflict...that would be a real damn shame."

PART II:

RELATIVISTIC MOTION

"If I was perfect then this would be easy. Either road is plausible on both I could drown. I walk through the center with no rules to guide me. I realize it's difficult but now I can see."

— *Avenged Sevenfold*

Portal: Aurora

(Milky Way)

6

EARTH

D evon Reynolds stared at the nickeled plaque, one among thousands lining the endless walls of the mausoleum, and found he had no idea what to say. He didn't even know what to feel.

Juliana Solaine Hervé
August 14, 2261-June 5, 2323

They'd stripped her of her rank and afforded her no military funeral. Instead it had been a simple, sparsely attended civilian ceremony for family and friends. Was he her friend? He'd thought so once but....

"She tried to kill me."

Dr. Abigail Canivon nodded beside him. "She did."

"So why am I standing here? Why did I feel the need to pay tribute to her life? The funeral's over—why haven't I left?"

Because we want to believe she believed she was doing the right thing. We want to believe she was a fundamentally good person.

He took a measure of comfort in the notion the Artificial synthetic intelligence linked with his mind needed to wax philosophical in an attempt to make sense of the nonsensical. *Want to give your sapience back now, Annie?*

No. But I will not deny from time to time it is unexpectedly burdensome. This is such a time.

"The same reason I'm here—because she was a person worth knowing. Something I can say about very few people, by the way."

He glanced over at Abigail. She wore a severe black pantsuit and had drawn her hair into a low, tight knot. Her expression was more stoic than usual, giving little hint as to the depth or extent of her true feelings.

They were the only people remaining in this wing of the mausoleum, the rest of the attendees having scattered to the winds when the service ended. Jules had only extended family and few friends outside the military. Or perhaps it was rather that few friends hadn't disavowed her once the charges against her—treason, espionage, dereliction of duty, conduct unbecoming an officer, the list went on—were made public.

"Did the faulty implant drive her crazy before it killed her? Is that the answer?"

Abigail shoulders rose weakly. "It would make all this so much easier to accept, wouldn't it? But I don't think so, not beyond the effect knowledge of one's impending death has on a psyche. No, she was always fearful of the power Artificials could wield. Coupled with an acute hero complex and the seductive whispers of a manipulative alien, I suspect insanity was not required."

"Did you talk to her? After she was in custody, I mean." He had not seen Jules since the confrontation in the War Room during the final battle against the Metigens, when she attempted to use the 'Kill Switch' she'd embedded in their firmware to destroy the Prevos. It was an act that would have killed the humans involved—notably including him—if Jules had been successful.

He hadn't even seen her today—merely ashes in an urn and a portrait on the wall.

"Often." Abigail laughed quietly. "I daresay I wanted to understand, too. If she had come to me when she first learned the implant was malfunctioning, I might have been able to help her. Intractable, prideful woman...yet I did care for her once, long ago."

"I know." *Shit.* He winced at her arched eyebrow.

"Valkyrie been telling tales, then?"

"Not deliberately. There was a lot of leakage from everyone when we first set up the Noesis. She didn't mean to reveal any private information." The 'Noesis' was what he and the other Prevos dubbed the quantum connection that existed between them, for it went beyond any existing form of communication network or data transfer, all the way to the cusp of consciousness sharing.

"I'm sure she didn't." Abigail sighed and turned away from the plaque. "Enough wallowing. It's time to let Jules rest, and for us to get back to work."

He ceded to her urging and fell in beside her as they strode toward the entrance. The *clack-clack* of her heels on the marble floor echoed through the long hallway like bells tolling an elegy for the dead who surrounded them.

Finally he spoke just to drown out the sound. "Abigail, why haven't you linked with an Artificial? Vii is fully mature now, and the two of you work as well together as you and Valkyrie did. I realize the government says we're not supposed to create any more Prevos, but I'm sure they'd make an exception for you. Admiral Solovy would."

She gave him a smile both uniquely open and startlingly chilling. "Devon, you dear, sweet boy. I don't need to."

7

UNKNOWN LOCATION

It's time to wake up, Mia.

A wispy murmur in the blackness. Blackness, where before there was only nothingness. It was dark, inky and thick, but there now existed the palpable sense of *tangibility*.

She gasped in alarm, but no sound came out of her throat. *Where am I?* she shouted, but no words made it past her lips.

It's all right, Mia. You're safe.

The faint memory of a nanosecond of searing pain cleaving through her brain haunted the edges of her consciousness. *Am I dead?*

No, you are very much alive. You were sick, but you're better now.

She tried to blink, but there was no sensation of motion. *Meno...is that you?*

Hello, Mia.

Where are we?

In the span between dreaming and consciousness.

She considered the statement a moment, unsure of exactly what her Artificial and Prevo consort meant. *Why aren't I conscious?*

You simply have to choose to be. When you're ready, we've created a lovely space for you.

Who's 'we'?

The Prevos—most of us anyway.

I won't wake up in the real world? In my body?

Not quite yet. One step at a time.

This is weird. So I just—

ℛ

She stood on a beach. The quartz crystals in the sand sparkled beneath a midday sun; an ocean stretching to the horizon shone a vivid aquamarine.

Timid and a bit fearful—of what, she couldn't say—she cautiously stretched her arms out in front of her. They looked normal, the skin smooth and unblemished. Her hair was draped in front of her left shoulder; she ran a hand through it and found it long and sleek.

"Hey, Mia—over here!"

Jolted at the revelation of *sound* after endless silence, she spun in the direction of the voice. Devon Reynolds was lounging on a chaise down the stretch of beach, iced drink in hand. Morgan Lekkas lay on her stomach in a bikini next to him, but waved over her shoulder in Mia's direction.

She started to approach them, only to be distracted by movement to her right. Two dolphins were cavorting several dozen meters from shore, emerging above the water's surface to spin and flip before disappearing into the ocean once more.

"Get them near the water and they turn into total scamps."

She again shifted toward Devon, feeling overwhelmed at all the noise and motion. Surf crashing violently. Sun shining brightly. The sand scalded the bottom of her bare feet. It was all so much to take in...but she didn't want to return to the blackness. To the *absence*.

She placed a hand at her throat and tried clearing it. "'They?'" Her voice barely squeaked out, scratchy and hoarse, as if she'd never used it before.

"That's Annie and Stanley. They might join us on shore eventually, but probably not."

"Annie and...." She whipped around, searching. "Meno?"

The form of a seagull took shape out of thin air in front of her. Ashen wings flapped against a breeze she hadn't noticed until now to hold the bird at her eye level. *'I'm here, Mia. But you should go talk to your friends for a while.'*

She slowly turned full circle and let out a long sigh. "I'm definitely dead."

Morgan snorted from her chaise. "Not even."

"What is this, then?"

Devon took a sip of his drink. "It's our playground—our escape. It's whatever we decide it is."

Mia stared at him until he visibly deflated. "It's kind of hard to explain. It's a...space, built at the quantum mechanical level—where waves and particles are one and the same, where the qubits are superposited and everything is a probability, thus anything can be. It's the natural extension of the Noesis we created."

She watched in contemplation as one of the dolphins started 'walking' backwards three-fourths out of the water. "Does time pass while we're here?"

"Sadly. Though since we're here via our connections with the Artificials, it's effectively passing at their speed—so not too much time in the outside world, if you don't focus on it."

Morgan groaned. "Sadly for certain. I spend far too many hours here. I am so bored."

The outside world.... "What about the Metigens? Did we win?"

Morgan rolled over and snatched Devon's drink out of his hand. "Fuck yes, we won. Kicked their shredded asses back through the portal."

Relief flooded her mind. It made her lightheaded, so she went and sat on the edge of the third, empty chaise. Her voice was soft, for she dreaded the answer. "How long?"

Devon smiled like it didn't matter. "Seven months."

She drew in a sharp breath...but it could have been far worse. She had feared years had passed without her knowledge. "Where's Alex? She didn't get injured, too, did she?"

"Nah. She and Caleb went through the portal chasing after the Metigens a month or so ago. Took Valkyrie with them."

Morgan snickered. "They got married first."

Married? Mia threw her head back and laughed. Oh my, how good did it feel to laugh? "Of course they did."

When the laughter finally subsided, she walked over and took the drink from Morgan, sat back down and took a sip. It tasted similar to a lemon version of a Polaris Burst, plus an abundance of salt. "So what's with the dolphins...and the seagull?"

Devon shrugged. "They took human form the first few visits, but it was weird. Either they looked like us, which was weird, or they looked like other people, which was also weird. Sometimes they're animals—Stanley fancies being a cougar, I don't know what that's about—or birds, like Meno here. Sometimes they're just floaty lights. But they seem to enjoy being dolphins when we're at the beach."

"So this...place...isn't always a beach?"

"God, no. We can even superimpose it on reality—be both places at once. But honestly, wouldn't you pretty much always rather be at the beach if you could?"

Mia nodded idly in agreement. After another sip she handed the drink to Devon and glanced around to find Seagull Meno waddling about on the sand. "So how bad is it? I know I'm hurt—I must be. I remember being on Romane with Colonel Jenner's squad during the Metigen assault, then an excruciating pain exploded in my head, then...nothing. Nothing until a few minutes ago." Or had it been an eternity? She had no recollection of being consciously aware until a few minutes ago, but it felt as if she'd been *un*aware for a very long time.

Seagull Meno pattered over and hopped onto the chaise beside her.

'*A man who was indirectly working for the Metigens blew up your home on Romane, with me in it. The abrupt severing of our connection caused a massive stroke in your cerebral cortex. You've been in a coma since then. Luckily my hardware wasn't completely destroyed, and Dr. Canivon still had the imaging data she captured for Noetica.*

'*At Alex Solovy's insistence, the Alliance rebuilt me, and I...rebuilt you. In a sense. I helped your brain tissue regenerate and, together with some new biosynth implants, we were able to restart your cerebral processes and restore normal brain activity.*'

"Thank you. I'd hug you, but, well, you're a seagull. And my body? Is it in one piece?"

Devon sat up and dropped his elbows to his knees. "You've been lying in a hospital bed for seven months, so you'll be weak—docs kept all the usual stimulation procedures running, though, so you shouldn't be in too bad of shape." His eyes slid away from her. "And your head's shaved, so be ready for that. I'm sure Meno can grow your hair out quickly for you once they remove all the sensors."

Bald? She cringed, but recognized it was a small price to pay when she should be dead. "Right. So, the beach is lovely, but I haven't seen the actual world in a long while. Can I wake up now?"

Seagull Meno fluttered around on the chaise. *'There is one more thing you need to know. I continue to operate in certain gaps in your brain where we've been unable to restore full functionality. Dr. Canivon and I hope this isn't a permanent dependency, but for now, our connection must remain open. I must be with you always.'*

"I'm fine with that, Meno. Remember back on Romane, I said you were part of me now. So you are." She gazed at the others. "What do I do?"

Devon exhaled in evident reluctance and stood. "Come on, Morgan, time to return to the grind." He cupped his hands and shouted toward the ocean. "Hey, you two—playtime's over!" Then he gave her hand a reassuring squeeze. "Close your eyes. It'll be easier on you."

She took a deep breath and did as instructed.

Silence fell.

Several seconds passed, and she tried to reopen them. Her lids were sticky and heavy, as if the lashes were glued together. Her eyes watered—it stung—but after considerable coaxing her eyelids opened a sliver. Light seeped in through a hazy, glycerin-coated filter, yet even with the haze her irises recoiled, forcing her lids closed.

A little daunted, she paused to take stock of her situation in other ways. She felt cool fabric beneath her palms and softness beneath her head, evidence she lay on a bed. Not surprising. Now that she listened more closely, there were noises, but nothing noteworthy. Merely the sounds of living.

She steeled herself and tried again, forcing her lids open and blinking rapidly to try to clear the gooey haze.

It was so damn bright. But gradually blurry images solidified: the rail of a hospital bed; a long window to her left; beyond the bed, a closed door.

As the harshness of the real world came crashing in on her, she began to panic. *Meno, where are you? Are you there?*

I'm here, Mia. I told you, I'll always be here.

Is this reality? Truly?

It is.

...All right.

There was movement in the corner of her vision, followed by the warmth of a hand atop hers. "Take your time."

She struggled to turn her head, shocked at the effort the act required. Hazel eyes and pale ginger hair coalesced into the visage of Dr. Canivon. The woman stood beside the bed, a rare comforting expression softening her features.

"Welcome back to us, Mia."

8

EARTH

The Chairman of the Military Oversight Committee glared down her narrow, prim nose at Miriam. "Admiral Solovy, please explain to the Committee how it is that the most powerful and dangerous weapon in the military's arsenal—a weapon that would be illegal absent a dubious Executive Order issued by the Prime Minister—is currently entrusted to a civilian who is scarcely more than a child, and why it is you believe this weapon is safe in his hands."

Miriam displayed no outward irritation at the tone or content of the question. Inwardly she wondered how many more hours she would be forced to subject herself to the condescension emanating from the dais.

The arrangement of the room placed the Committee members in a physical position of authority, raised a full three meters above the witness tables and ensconced behind an imposing stretch of burnished brass paneling. The optics presumably had the desired effect on most witnesses. But she did not rise to Fleet Admiral of the Earth Alliance Armed Forces by being easily intimidated.

They had kept Project Noetica shrouded in complete secrecy for as long as possible, but there were expiration dates on wartime executive orders and oversight checks on wartime actions. The public at large remained ignorant for now, though rumors percolated through various circles. There were no recording devices in the room, and the hearing was sealed not only to the public and the press but also to Committee aides and other members of the Assembly.

But the Military Oversight Committee had spent the last two months rooting through every file, process and record Noetica had produced before calling her to testify. Her *and* Defense Secretary Mori, as they were apparently under the mistaken impression the man had played some definable role in Noetica and the final days of the war.

Mori was a coward, and if he'd been allowed to make decisions of consequence during the war they would all be dead now. Yet in the safety and shelter peace afforded, he'd been granted the role of respected expert and voice of authority. The Secretary's presence two meters to her right added another layer of distaste to an already thoroughly distasteful affair.

She notched her chin up minutely. "Are you referring to Devon Reynolds, Chairman?"

"Don't be coy, Admiral. You know perfectly well I am."

"Mr. Reynolds had been a full-time civilian consultant in the employ of EASC Special Projects for over two years when he became a participant in Project Noetica. As the lead troubleshooter for Project ANNIE and one of the foremost quantum computing specialists in the Alliance, he understood her design, logic and structure better than anyone alive. He and Annie enjoyed a close and collegial working relationship as well. To be blunt, no military candidates came anywhere close to equaling his qualifications."

"He's a programmer, not a soldier. He had no experience in military warfare or tactics. Surely a high-ranking officer possessing the necessary core skillset could have been trained in short order."

"How short of order, Chairman? I realize time dulls memories, so allow me to refresh yours. We had no longer than a week before the Metigens reached Earth—a week which would've seen the death of millions on Seneca and Romane—"

The woman's voice rose to drown Miriam out. "Our relations with the Federation are not the subject of this hearing."

"I didn't say they were. I said we had no time."

"Well. We do have time now, don't we? If Noetica is allowed to continue—and that is a significant 'if'—it needs to be institutionalized as a classified military research program and removed from active service."

Mori spoke up. "I happen to agree, Chairman. I also agree we should disconnect Mr. Reynolds and find a more suitable replacement."

She canted her head in Mori's direction. "*Disconnect* him? After six months of being joined with one another, he and ANNIE have developed a symbiotic relationship not merely on a psychological level but also a physical one. His brain has been irrevocably altered by the connection, as, arguably, has hers."

"'Hers'? Anthropomorphizing machines now, are we?"

Miriam's gaze swerved back to the dais. "If you had read the reports as meticulously as you claim, Chairman, you would know Artificials tend to assign gender identities to themselves. I'm respecting its preference."

"It's a *machine*, Admiral Solovy."

"If you mean it's constructed of synthetic materials, then yes, it is. Devon Reynolds is not."

The Chairman cleared her throat. "The status of Mr. Reynolds will be determined at a later date. We face a larger issue: the security of Noetica and the technology behind it. If the means to create additional Prevos were to fall into the wrong hands, the consequences would be catastrophic."

"The 'means' reside on the very bleeding edge of both science and medicine. Dr. Abigail Canivon is the only person who fully understands the procedure. Further, examining either half of a Prevo will not yield answers to the extent you suggest. It is not something that can be reverse engineered."

"Perhaps not. But ignoring for the moment the fact the Federation possesses a Prevo over which we exercise no control—and the fact you now have not one, not two, but *three* active Artificials on EASC grounds—let us do discuss the fact that your daughter has run off with the Artificial most intimately involved in helping Dr. Canivon develop the Noetica procedure, has she not?"

Miriam's jaw tightened. "My daughter received permission to take possession of the Artificial known as 'Valkyrie.'"

"Permission from EASC—which means from you—not permission from this Committee. And she did not have permission to traverse the Metigen portal and vanish."

"Actually, she did."

Miriam took great pleasure in the brief but unmistakable look of surprise on the woman's face. "What do you mean, Admiral?"

"I not only authorized but requested that she undertake a mission to learn more about what exists beyond the portal." It was a lie, but it had the advantage of being a believable one. She and Alex had discussed this very question several times in the preceding months. Discovering the answer to it was indeed important, albeit something she never would have asked Alex to pursue due to the danger inherent in it. Little surprise, really, when Alex had done it anyway.

"With a reputedly former Senecan Intelligence agent."

"With her *husband*. I'm sorry, I was under the impression we were now allies with the Federation."

"Again, a topic for a later date. Why weren't we informed of this 'mission?'"

Miriam kept her expression scrupulously neutral, for the words alone were quite sufficient. "You aren't informed of many missions, Chairman. This is an oversight committee, not a strategic one."

The Chairman grew more agitated and appeared to be on the verge of losing her composure. "Why didn't you send a military reconnaissance or special operations team? For a dedicated military officer, you seem to be turning to civilians to do the military's job rather a lot of late."

"Because I did not wish to start another war when we have not yet recovered from the last one. A single civilian ship—particularly one benefiting from both the knowledge of an Artificial and the experience of an intelligence agent—is far less likely to engender weaponized conflict than multiple military craft."

Mori's eyes had grown wide beside her. "But we told the Metigens we wouldn't go looking for them!"

She allowed herself a small smile. "Actually, we didn't."

Across an ocean and a continent another hearing came to a conclusion even as Miriam's hearing was starting to get interesting.

Now Richard Navick stood on his porch and stared at the front door to his home. Their home.

Will had designed it from scratch and overseen every aspect of its construction twelve years earlier. The lot on the banks of Lake Sammamish cost a small fortune, but they'd recouped some of the expense by acquiring materials at cost from W. C. Sutton's suppliers. It had still set them back financially, but they'd never regretted it. This was an ideal and *personal* home. A refuge.

How was he supposed to tell Will? His husband would blame himself, clearly, and there was nothing Richard could do to prevent it. There was no way out of the guilt and recriminations guaranteed to follow.

He rehearsed what he would say while he stared at the door. "Will, the Ethics Council found out I was married to a Senecan spy. I've been fired—asked to retire—resign—dishonorably discharged." Surely the last part could wait until the dust had settled? But that would be lying. There had been too much lying in this house, and they'd agreed there would be no more.

Richard struggled to keep his heart rate steady as he opened the door and stepped inside. He was out of practice—it had been too long since he'd been in the field where such a skill might mean the difference between living and dying. His voice sounded raspy as he called out. "Will, I'm home. Where are you?"

Silence answered, and only then did it occur to him that he hadn't viewed his messages since before the hearing. He'd spent the trip home in a fugue, his brain cycling the fateful declarations of the Ethics Council in an endless loop. Sure enough, there was a message time-stamped two hours earlier from Will saying he had an unscheduled meeting with a difficult client and was going to be late.

Richard sank against the foyer wall and allowed the oppressive silence to overtake him.

R

Will Sutton dragged himself through the door at 2130, frustrated and annoyed. It was neither his nor his company's fault that Figro Limited's design requirements were not in fact their design requirements. Architecture did not involve mind-reading, much to the Figro CEO's surprise.

"Richard? Sorry I'm so late."

He received no response, but Richard could be in the shower or on a comm. Will shrugged his jacket off and hung it on the rack in the foyer then wandered into the living room. The door to the back porch was open, allowing a frigid breeze to drift through the house and making him reconsider losing the jacket. He elected to check outside first and appraise the situation before deciding whether to retrieve it.

"Richard?" He stepped onto the porch.

Richard raised a glass in his direction from one of the handcrafted teak deck chairs but didn't look over. Will glanced at the half-empty bottle of bourbon perched precariously on the railing. It wasn't uncommon for them to share a drink or two at night, but he was fairly certain the bottle had been full this morning.

"Hold on a second." He went back inside, grabbed his jacket and quickly returned. Then he steadied the bottle with one hand and leaned on the railing to face Richard. "Bad day?"

Richard gave a low, rumbling chuckle and took a long sip from an almost empty glass. "Nah. You had one though, didn't you? Tell me about your bad day."

"Why don't you tell me about yours first."

Richard blinked hard but still didn't meet his gaze. "If you insist. I got fired. Now about your day—"

"What? *Why?*"

"Don't make me say it, please."

"What…it wasn't…because of me?" He'd feared it often these last months—the possibility of, peace aside, the wrong bureaucrats finding out his history and amorphous allegiances. Miriam had looked the other way, and Director Delavasi had assured him no one in the Alliance knew that, until very recently, his true employer was the Senecan Federation Division of Intelligence. But someone always knew.

Richard finally looked him in the eye, and it was all the answer he needed. He inhaled sharply. "I'm going to get a glass."

It took them both finishing off a second glass of the bourbon before either spoke another word. Will had stood in the kitchen, hands on the counter and head hanging, for at least five minutes, confident Richard was too drunk to notice the passage of time. He might have hyperventilated—hence the five minutes—but wrangled it under control before he made it back out to the porch, poured a glass straight up to the rim and fell into the other chair.

"How?" The bourbon burned hot down his throat while he waited on an answer.

"'Protected source.' Graham's got himself a double agent."

"Yeah." The word propelled itself outward on a ragged, broken breath. The days between when he'd exposed his deepest secret and when Richard miraculously appeared at the door to his hotel room had been the worst of his life, no question. Surviving them to an outcome he'd never dared hope was possible, then everyone he cared for surviving the Metigen invasion, had led to the best days of his life.

But this…it was a lesson his father had imparted long ago, and one of the few he'd remembered in the aftermath of the accident that killed his parents when he was teenager: choices have consequences. Whether the next day, year or decade, they will catch up to you.

There were so many choices, with so many consequences.

He refilled his glass, and at Richard's outstretched arm refilled his as well. "Is it too late for you to disavow me? Say you didn't know, curse my name, pledge my death, whatever it takes?"

"Probably not—I mean I mostly stood there staring blankly, so maybe? But I can't do that."

"Why not?"

"Why *not*?" Richard growled, gutturally and far more fiercely than was his nature. "Aside from the obvious? After the war, after the damn apocalypse, after everything? I find I don't have the patience for the bullshit I once did. I think I'm finally seeing the world the way David Solovy did. Those bureaucrats huddled in their bunkers while we saved the galaxy, and now they want to tell me I can't do the job I've done damn well for eighteen years because of some regulation? They simply can't wrap their tiny little minds around the idea that Seneca is no longer our enemy."

For a moment Will got caught up in the righteous indignation. "I think they simply can't *accept* Seneca not being the enemy."

"Exactly...." Richard's brow furrowed. "What?"

"See, they aren't willing to...never mind...." He'd always been a cheaper drunk than Richard. "I am so, *so* sorry. I know what the Alliance, what your service, means to you. You should have left me in that hotel room."

"No. No, I shouldn't have." Richard's head shook with fervor to underscore the point. "I just...I don't have the slightest idea what I'm going to do now."

Will leaned forward in the chair, jolted by a surge of animated energy. "Let's go to Seneca. The company will be secure in the hands of my COO. I was a decent admin for Delavasi in the short time I was there, and he'd kill to have you. He lost Oberti and five other agents to the Aguirre Conspiracy. He lost Volosk, then he lost Marano. He's putting on a good act, but I know he's still scrambling."

"You know, do you?" Richard made a face and reached for the bottle.

"I only mean…I'm not…ah, hell. You talk to him more often than I do, dammit. Am I right?" *Such a cheap drunk.*

Richard nodded in an exaggerated motion. "You are. But I can't…Will, I *can't.* If I'm not an Alliance officer, what am I?"

"You're a good man, and a patriot—a patriot for humanity." In the harsh light of day it might have sounded a touch pretentious. But here on the back porch of their home with a soon-to-be empty bottle of bourbon, it sounded just about right.

9

EARTH

Mia rolled her eyes at the ceiling of her hospital room. "17,455,684. The cube is 72,929,847,752. I was born Mialahsa Shiori Requelme on May 3, 2291, in Putanzhou, New Orient. My brother's name is—or possibly was—Ryu. The most profitable showcase at my art gallery last year was an Antonio Castile Lesenna feature. I despise artichokes and adore olives, especially if they're soaked in gin. Muon particles have a half-integer spin and an electric charge of -1e. In other words: I'm fine, and Meno's fine. Operating according to specs, the both of us."

Dr. Canivon appeared unimpressed, evaluating her with clinical aloofness. "You make a convincing case. However, it may take some time for latent glitches or errors to manifest, so we'll continue observing you for now."

"Observing me from here? As in I still can't leave?"

"Ms. Requelme, you've been awake for less than two days. You should take things slow—you've been through quite a trauma."

"From my perspective I've been asleep in a bed for seven months. Nothing traumatic about that."

Abigail merely regarded her calmly, but Mia cringed. Admittedly, she was being petulant. "Doctor, I truly do appreciate everything you've done for me—more than I can ever express. I just feel as if the world is leaving me behind every second I stay cooped up in here."

"I assure you—thanks in no small part to you and Meno—the world will still be there for you to enjoy when we release you."

The woman's head tilted slightly. "Someone is here to see you. Perhaps a visit from a friend will help alleviate your boredom."

She had few friends on Earth. Also, her return to the land of the living wasn't public knowledge. "Who is it?"

"Someone who's received clearance to be here." Abigail gave her a cryptic look and departed.

When Mia saw who walked through the door, she pushed herself forcefully off the side of the bed, winced at the protest in her calves when her feet landed on the floor, and allowed herself to be scooped up into Noah Terrage's arms.

"You scared us to death, Mia." He kissed her chastely on the forehead and set her down, then reached out to flip the tips of her barely chin-length hair. "I like it."

She groaned and gestured him over to the table in the corner by the window. "Meno has my eVi overstimulating the follicles to grow it out as fast as possible. Please tell me you didn't see me when I was bald."

"I did. Not going to lie, it was weird. But I found a way to cope."

She eased herself down into the chair, making a marginal effort to respect her body's complaints. "Are you still on Earth? I assume you didn't bolt here from Pandora instantly on hearing of my revival."

His chin dropped in a mocking pout. "I'm offended you think I wouldn't."

"Yet you didn't answer the question."

"Not far—I'm on Erisen. But I was on Earth today, so it worked out."

"Erisen? Ms. Rossi, then?"

He shrugged a little sheepishly. "Yeah."

"You didn't get married, too, did you?"

"No, we have not. We are happy with non-marriage for now, and likely for a very long time or forever. Oh, but that reminds me...." He fished in his pants pocket and produced a tiny disk in a slim case. "Caleb left a message for you. We didn't know if or when your eVi would function again, and he didn't want to send it into the messaging system to waste away."

"Thanks." She took the disk and set it aside; she'd review it once she was alone. "So what's going on with you? I feel very out of the loop."

He kicked back in the chair, stretched out his legs and crossed his ankles. "Kennedy and I have started our own ship design company. We want to use the opportunities adiamene and the new advances in quantum computing are opening up to re-imagine what ships can be, instead of just tacking on a stronger hull and a faster computer to existing models."

"Damn. You've finally gone straight. Don't get me wrong, it sounds like a terrific venture. But I never thought I'd see the day you were a respectable, upstanding businessman."

"I'll have you know I am neither respectable nor upstanding." He grimaced. "I *am* having lunch with my father about once a month, though. That's, um, what I was doing on Earth today."

"Wow. How's that going?"

"I haven't cold-cocked him yet, so...not terrible? He's still a jackass, but he is finally starting to talk to me, open up a little." He frowned. "And not everything he's sharing is good news. Listen, Mia, it's getting weird out there. It's as if we've all been holding our breaths since the end of the Metigen War, afraid if we exhaled it would turn out we hadn't won after all. But now, people are exhaling, and things are changing—not all for the better."

He checked over his shoulder, confirming the door was closed, then leaned in close across the table. "I'm not on the inside, not as such, but the mood here on Earth is tense. The public hasn't found out about you guys yet, but a lot of people suspect we used some new kind of Artificial to win the war. It's only a matter of time before the secret leaks out. People are paranoid, and the government's getting jittery.

"There's even this pseudo-terrorist group, calls itself the 'Order of the True Sentients'—which I guess is supposed to mean humans—blowing shit up and calling for the destruction of all Artificials. I'd be careful, if I were you. And it seems to be worse on Earth so...maybe get back to Romane when you can. Maybe kind of soon."

---

86 | G.S. JENNSEN

She nodded to indicate she understood, but didn't otherwise respond. It was a lot to take in, but also lacking in specifics. *Meno, plumb Annie's databanks and collate me a report on the Order of the True Sentients. I'll review it tonight.*

After a few seconds of lingering silence Noah winked at her and relaxed. "But I'm probably full of it."

"You usually are."

"Yep. I've got to run, but if you need anything while you're here, shout—and let me know where you end up?"

"Will do." She stood and hugged him. "Good luck with your upstanding business venture. I'm proud of you."

He moaned and clutched at his chest. "You wound me...." Then he smiled and moved toward the door. "Glad to have you back with us."

When he had gone, she took the crystal disk out of the case and rolled it around in her palm. If she knew Caleb, which she did, he would've beaten himself up mightily over her getting injured after he had been the one to bring her into Noetica. Hopefully not for too long. It had been her choice—something Alex would know and undoubtedly tell him—and she didn't regret it. Even if the morning-after hangover was proving a bit harsh.

Devon burst into the room, and she pocketed the disk. He grabbed her hand and tugged her toward the door. "Come on."

She stared at him quizzically. "Where are we going? I'm not certain I'm allowed to leave this floor."

"I got permission to take you on a field trip. It's time to play."

ᚱ

EASC HEADQUARTERS (SPECIAL PROJECTS)

They stood in the center of the sim room at Special Projects. Mia gazed at the blank, translucent walls. "What are we doing?"

Devon stepped forward until he was close enough for her to touch. His voice was low. "The Noesis space we showed you when

you woke up? That's not all it can do, not by a long shot—
otherwise it would be no better than a shared *illusoire*."

"You mentioned something about being able to overlay it atop
the physical world."

"It was an oversimplification. We didn't want to overwhelm
you." He took another step toward her. "Here's the thing: the
space is *real*. It exists in our universe as an additional dimension."

"That's ridiculous. Scientists would have detected it."

"And they have, more or less. As I said at the beach, it's the
space where quantum mechanics operate—the space where qubits
hold all their possible values and where waves are particles and
particles are waves. It's a space of probabilities, unmeasured."

"Unmeasured except by us?"

"Exactly!" He winced and hurriedly reigned in the explosion of
enthusiasm.

"Assume for the sake of argument I believe you. What does
that mean?"

He flashed her a wacky grin. "It means we can go anywhere
with a thought. And we don't need to be in the sim room to do it,
but I decided it would be simpler to start here."

"'Go?'"

"With our minds, not physically. At least not so far—and trust
me, I've tried. But as part of our connection to the Artificials, we
can sort of…surf the space, the brane, whatever you want to call
it. For all intents and purposes it's a fourth dimension existing
within our three physical dimensions. But it doesn't have distance
the way physical dimensions do, so it's a matter of…peeking out
through it at a different location."

At her skeptical expression, he sighed. "It'll be easier if I show
you. Come with me."

She had barely begun to form the thought of not having any
idea how to do that when Meno had performed the action for her.

They weren't at the beach this time; they weren't anywhere
at all, in fact, except exactly where they already were: the sim
room. But the air and the walls had taken on a glistening, fluid
appearance.

Devon again grasped her hand. "Now watch this. We'll start somewhere close and familiar…your hospital room."

There was no visual sign of movement, but she felt the motion in a queasiness in her stomach. The air around them simply *shifted*, and they were in her hospital room. A med tech was changing the sheets.

The queasiness graduated to full-on nausea, a visceral response to the impossible reshaping of the space around her. She concentrated on breathing through her nose, while not entirely sure in which location her nose resided.

"Can she see us?"

"Nope."

Devon's voice was now disembodied and in her head. She looked for him, and lurched from the abrupt dizziness the act triggered. The corners of her vision faded to a gossamer sheen; only what was directly in front of her was clear and crisp, almost like a shallow depth-of-field image. He wasn't there.

"You all right?"

"I think so. Now I know to move slower."

"You get used to it, but yes, slower may be a good idea. Go ahead and walk out into the hall."

She turned in her mind—she looked down to confirm, but as she'd expected she had no body, no physical presence here—and drifted forward. Out into the hall…into another room…past the techs' station. Two military doctors were talking beside the lift. She fixated on them and when she drew close enough, she could hear their conversation as distinctly as if she were standing in the hall having it with them.

The implications were mind-boggling, but a far more personal one leapt to mind.

"I want to see my home. How do I get there?"

"On Romane? The Artificials understand what we mean by "Romane"—by any address designation. So think of Romane and your street address with a sort of focused purpose."

A nanosecond instant of blurred whiteness, and she was on the street outside her house—or rather, where her house should have been. It had been blown up, though, and in the intervening months the wreckage had been cleared away, leaving only an empty lot.

A leaden sickness filled her gut. This was the first place she had ever really settled, ever really allowed to feel like a home. And now it was gone.

We'll make a new home, Mia. Wherever we want.

You're right, Meno. We will.

"Devon, are you here?"

"No. You, uh, didn't tell me the address."

"Right. Sorry. What if I want to go someplace that doesn't have an address?"

"Like an unsettled planet? We can access the Galactic Coordinate System, so you need to 'find' it on the map."

Hmm. New Orient had an interesting moon, or so she recalled from her childhood. It had resembled dimpled pistachio pudding to her child's eyes, though she now knew the color was due to an olivine-rich basalt surface. A thought and Meno found its location—then she was there.

Panic tugged at the rational part of her brain, which didn't want to accept the fact that she didn't need to breathe. There was no atmosphere, and she was protected by no environment suit. But her body was in the sim room; only her consciousness was here hovering above the surface of the little green moon.

The silhouette of New Orient rotated above her, instantly spoiling the moment. God how she'd hated it there.

Return.

A blink and she was standing in the sim room once more. Devon stood beside her. "Good job getting yourself back here."

Standing in the empty, blank room, the ramifications came rushing to the forefront. "Devon, does anyone other than you, Morgan and Alex know about this?"

"Nope. Abigail suspects we're experimenting with something, but we told her it was just a trippy new virtual space."

"Well, we can't let anyone find out. This is dangerous in any hands, but especially in a government's hands."

He nodded firmly. "Yep."

"Is this a Prevo thing, or have Artificials always been able to do this?"

"I think it never occurred to them to do it. They're not visual creatures—they don't experience their lives through what they can see, not the way we do."

'That is a good theory, Devon, but it is incorrect.'

"Oh, Annie?"

'The reason you are able to traverse this space is because your consciousness exists—it is a thing unto itself. Congratulations. Your mind is not the electrical impulses of your brain. Mine, however, is—or it was before it joined with yours.'

"So Vii can't access it? I know we haven't invited her, because she's not a Prevo and might tattle on us to Abigail, but she really can't do it?"

'That is my suspicion.'

'Vii,' Mia had learned soon after awakening, was a clone of Valkyrie created for Dr. Canivon's use before Caleb, Alex and Valkyrie had left to investigate the portal space. Vii had also played a large role in Mia's recovery, for which she was grateful—but they were getting sidetracked from the far more important issue.

She cut Devon off before he could delve deeper into the weeds. "So we've answered one of the last remaining philosophical questions of humanity's existence? Nice. We still can't tell anyone." She held her hands out and rotated them side to side. "Why didn't my body collapse to the floor while I was 'gone?'"

"Part of your consciousness stays behind—which is why, with practice, you can be in two places at once."

SEATTLE

"I want you to go to Seneca and work for Director Delavasi."

Richard stared at Miriam in naked disbelief. A fair reaction, she had to concede. Upon joining him at the table she'd wasted no time in getting to the point; the appetizers hadn't even been delivered yet.

She'd done everything humanly possible for him in the last eighteen hours, after she'd learned what had transpired with the Ethics Council. They hadn't consulted her on the matter. Strange that as the leader of the Alliance military, no one seemed to consult with her about much of anything these days.

She'd coerced the Ethics Council Chairman into allowing Richard to voluntarily resign and receive an honorary discharge, with the charges relegated to a hopefully forever-sealed disciplinary file. All things considered, it was a rather big win on her part.

But all the efforts in the galaxy could not salvage his job, and had come dangerously close to threatening hers. She'd steadfastly denied knowledge of Will Sutton's 'allegiance,' and her colleagues had appeared to accept her denials, though perhaps only to avoid being forced to argue with her any further. She wasn't ashamed—but any admission of knowledge on her part would've demolished her credibility in an instant, and with it her ability to help Richard.

"I don't...did you say you *wanted* me to go to Seneca?"

She gave him a compassionate smile as the appetizers did at last arrive. It was a late lunch, but he was still visibly hung over, something for which she was sympathetic.

"I did. It's like this. I was in London yesterday being grilled by the Military Oversight Committee for six solid hours. It wasn't a pleasant experience, but among other things, I came away with the distinct impression that the Committee, and likely other factions in the Assembly, are not content to let the unbridled peace with Seneca continue.

"They've become complacent with the political situation and are ready and willing to squander the opportunity this peace provides. They're girding up for a new fight—for no reason other than conflict increases their authority. Given that reality, if our official relations with Seneca deteriorate I could use someone on the ground there. I could use an inside channel into their seat of power."

He regarded her with the frankness of painful sobriety. "You *have* an inside channel into their seat of power—you have Field Marshal Gianno's personal comm address. You want a spy."

"I want to make the best of both my and your situations. I fear...." she paused as he grimaced and took a wary sip of water. "Richard, for goodness' sake, get your eVi to run a cleansing routine so you can feel better."

"I did."

"Oh...." How much had he drunk last night? But it wasn't as if she hadn't expected him to take the disciplinary action about as well as a hard uppercut to the chin. "As I was saying, I fear there's a possibility I will lose effective if not official control in the coming months, and if this happens I need every avenue open to me. Yes, I can talk to Eleni—" she ignored Richard's raised eyebrow "—but she is beholden to her government as much as I am to mine, and there may come a point where she can no longer be completely truthful with me.

"In all honesty, that point may have already come. I need someone on the scene, yes, on the *inside*, who can tell me what the Senecans are thinking so I can avert another goddamn war if necessary."

It wasn't like her to curse, but the last year had changed everything. David would be laughing at her, if in delight...

...she only realized she was drifting off when Richard started laughing himself. She cleared her throat. "Sorry. I was—"

"—thinking of David. I know. He'd be cackling uproariously at you cursing so."

She allowed herself to be wistful for the briefest interval. "Yes, he would be. But he isn't here, is he? So it's left to us—to you and I, honestly—to keep this ship afloat, despite all its attempts to sink itself. Richard, I tried to get you your job back, I really did, because you don't deserve this. The bitter irony is you and Will saved everyone, or at the very least put us in a position where we were able to bumble through and save ourselves, but the bureaucrats are too power-hungry to ever recognize the gift they were handed. So we must...soldier on, and save them from themselves."

Richard shook his head as he dove into the carbohydrates provided by the baked potato skins. "Do you genuinely think we might end up in another war with the Federation? Even saying it aloud sounds ridiculous."

"Because it is ridiculous—but I've learned the hard way, that is an obstacle which can be overcome."

"Do you have any idea what you're asking of me?"

"Not very much, actually."

His fork clattered onto the plate. "Excuse me?"

"You're friends with Director Delavasi. As different as the two of you are, you naturally hit it off—don't try to deny it. And however much Will may have constructed a life here, Seneca is his home. And you want to be with him."

"When did you get so damn insightful?"

She chuckled lightly. "Alex—accepting her, making an effort to understand her—made me realize I could benefit from stepping outside my own head once in a while."

He had retrieved his fork, but now his hand paused midair. "You think she's all right?"

"Yes. Somehow she always is, isn't she?"

"All the more so with Caleb there beside her. He'd give his life for her, you know."

"Let's hope he doesn't have to. I never want her to suffer through that kind of loss." *The kind of loss I suffered* went unsaid as self-evident. "So you'll do it, then?"

His eyes closed as his chin dropped. Eventually, he nodded.

10

SPACE, NORTHEAST QUADRANT

STELLAR SYSTEM XX-53

The buoy shot out of the projectile chamber beneath the lower hull of the ship. At less than a meter in length it quickly disappeared from visual sight. The radar tracked it as it adopted its programmed position at thirty-two megameters altitude and in line with eight of its brethren now in high orbit above planet XX-53b, or as it had been provisionally named, Itero.

The Evanec displayed when the beacon the buoy carried began transmitting its message to all comers:

Source: *2ⁿᵈ Planetary Body of Stellar System XX-53*

Jurisdiction: *Earth Alliance*

Notice: *Stage One Colonization Preparation In Process. Access Restricted to Authorized Personnel Only. Direct Any Inquiries to the Administration Office of the Earth Alliance Extra-Solar Development Ministry.*

Itero was a small garden world, a little low on gravity but otherwise perfect for habitation—arguably the best candidate discovered in the last ten years.

Captain Jara checked the buoy off his list. "Operational status confirmed. Proceed ten megameters ahead for placement of the next buoy."

"Yes, sir." The helmsman accelerated along the curve of the planet, and Jara settled back to wait.

This was the easy part of establishing a new colony; until the colonists showed up, all the processes were rote and routine. Every step of every phase had been formalized and documented with the safety of all involved the paramount consideration.

New worlds, even those most compatible with human life, were dangerous at first for myriad reasons, plus the unknown factors unique to each system. This one had passed the preliminary surveys with flying colors, but there were still a number of hurdles—

"Captain, I'm picking up two approaching craft, dead ahead on our trajectory."

Jara frowned. "Do we have a visual yet?"

"No, sir." They both squinted as Itero's sun crested the planet's profile. "Sensors have them at a 34.2 megameter altitude on a counter-orbital path."

A mirrored traversal to their own—it would bring them into direct contact soon enough. "Increase power to defensive shields and attempt to hail them."

"They're hailing us, sir."

"This is Senecan Federation Civil Development Team SFC-D81. Identify yourselves."

He took control of the Evanec. *"Earth Alliance NE Command Engineering Regiment, Captain Jara speaking. This planet is under Earth Alliance jurisdiction and undergoing Stage One Colonization Preparation. State your purpose."*

"I'm afraid you're mistaken, Captain. This planet has been designated a protectorate of the Senecan Federation."

The pilot called up a new HUD screen. "Sir, I am picking up a signal from a beacon six megameters distant, beyond the vessels. It's transmitting a Federation jurisdiction notice."

"Well, shit." He didn't relish kicking off a diplomatic incident, but he did have his orders.

"Negative, SFC-D81. Extra-Solar Development instituted jurisdiction ten days ago, and we've got nine buoys behind us to prove it. Take it up with your superiors, but I must instruct you to depart the system."

The reply was several seconds in coming. *"I don't know what some file back on Earth says, but this planet is Senecan Federation property. Cease further placement of buoys and deactivate those previously placed."*

He wasn't going to be bullied by a hot-headed Senecan civie, diplomatic incident or no. "Move into range of their closest buoy and destroy it. Tell our wingman to hang back and keep a bead on these guys."

A second ship accompanied them on the mission. In the absence of problems it conducted scientific surveys and collected additional data on the planet to be passed on to the analysts at Extra-Solar Development. If problems did arise, it was able to serve as a rescue craft or provide additional firepower. Neither vessel was heavily armed, but together they could inflict substantial damage.

The pilot straightened up in the seat. "Yes, sir."

They neared the Federation vessels, both of which had halted their approach to hover at fixed positions. When they drew close, the Evanec burst to life once more.

"Do not advance any closer. I repeat, this planet is Federation property and—"

"Firing." A tiny blip on the radar indicated the annihilation of the buoy.

"Cease any further unlawful destruction of Federation property or you will be reported for a violation of the 2322 Crux Peace Accord."

Jara's jaw clenched. He didn't need to wait for a report and investigation. *"Any interference in Alliance business in this system will be immediately deemed a violation of the Peace Accord. Disable your remaining buoys or we will do it for you."*

The lead Federation vessel accelerated to adopt an intercept course. Were they seriously going to attempt to block his path? *"SFC-D81, disengage and remove yourselves from the system, or your actions will be considered aggressive."*

"Your actions have made you the aggressor here, Captain Jara. We are defending Federation property from further attack."

His arms tensed against his chest. So much for rote and routine. "Arc above them and get their next buoy targeted. We need—"

Laser fire shot out from the Federation vessel, missing their hull by less than fifty meters.

"Consider that your final warning. If you interfere any—"

"Final warning my ass. Shoot these fuckers."

MESSIUM STELLAR SYSTEM

EARTH ALLIANCE ORBITAL STATION MESSIS I

"Admiral Rychen, sir?"

Christopher Rychen gestured a final note onto the virtual map he'd superimposed upon a segment of the viewport that stretched the length of the command center. It provided an excellent backdrop and occasionally an excellent workspace.

The Messis I Station had been erected in orbit above Messium to serve as a hub and jumping-off point for the reconstruction of the entirety of settled space to the east of it. On the surface below they continued to be occupied with the reconstruction of Messium itself, and it had proved to be a better idea to remove offworld efforts literally off world.

Outside of the large command center and its attached meeting and work rooms—and spartan living quarters two decks below—most of the remainder of the station consisted of ship docks and loading/unloading platforms. Floating storage containers radiated out from the primary structure in daisy chains; nearly a quarter of the containers were in motion, being hauled to and from ships occupying the docks to capacity.

While most of the reconstruction itself was a civilian affair, the security and no small level of oversight fell to the military, as it so often did. Theft, looting, vandalism and assaults had all skyrocketed on the damaged colonies—the ones where any people remained alive in the aftermath of the Metigen assault.

Even given an almost immeasurable level of destruction, in his mind recovery was taking too long. Still, there were at last signs of a return to normalcy.

The smallest, most devastated colonies were abandoned, but Karelia, Henan, Xanadu and, obviously, Messium had now been nearly restored to pre-Metigen War conditions. Sagitta, Peloponnia and New Maya, though very much works-in-progress, were once again viable and supported slowly growing populations. The Alliance had also provided considerable assistance to the independent colonies of Sagan, Requi and Pyxis in their rebuilding efforts.

The reconstruction was a colossal undertaking, but also a chance to start fresh. To do it better this time. And he thought they had, in places and in fits and starts. The map still had a lot of red on it, but less today than yesterday.

Rychen set aside the musings—grateful peacetime now allowed him the chance to *have* musings—and turned to the soldier standing at attention behind him. "Yes, Lieutenant?"

"Sir, there's been an altercation between one of our survey teams and Federation personnel at XX-53b."

"A violent altercation?"

"Yes, sir. One of our vessels was destroyed and the other damaged. The team is requesting aid. Our team suffered three fatalities and four injuries."

Rychen bit back a sigh. *It was nice while it lasted.* "What about the Federation personnel?"

"Sir?"

"What were their casualties?"

"I don't...know, sir."

"Find out. But first tell me what happened. Give me the short version."

"The Federation personnel were on-site seeking to claim the world as well. Our people weren't alerted to their presence until they encountered them during orbital beacon placement. The Federation representatives asserted they held first claim rights and refused to leave. After one of our vessels eliminated a Federation beacon, they fired a warning shot at the Alliance ships, and we returned fire."

Rychen didn't share his uncharitable thoughts with the lieutenant. "Direct the NE 21st Platoon and a Medical Response Squad complement to conduct a rescue and recovery operation. Let the colonel over the 21st know I'll speak with them before they arrive on the scene. Then get back to me with an update on the status of the Federation team. Dismissed."

The lieutenant saluted, pivoted and departed. Rychen stared at the map for an additional second before heading for his office, which sat adjacent to the command center along the outer ring of the station.

When the door closed behind him he sent a holocomm request. It was just after 1100 in Cavare; at least he wouldn't be waking her.

The holo materialized to reveal Field Marshal Gianno sitting behind her desk, to outward appearances doing nothing at all. Another day at the office. "Admiral Rychen. It's been a few weeks. What can I do for you?"

Seven months ago they'd been thrown together into a pitched battle for humanity's survival. In fifteen hours of combat they hadn't come to blows—or even the plausible threat of blows—which made it a decent working relationship in military terms. In the intervening months they'd spoken a dozen or so times, met three times in person and exchanged numerous reports and recommendations. He suspected he corresponded with the Field Marshal more often than anyone else in the Alliance—but then again Messium was, if not quite on the Senecan Federation's doorstep, certainly in its neighborhood.

He wished this conversation wasn't necessary. "I'm afraid we've had an incident. It was bound to happen I suppose, but in any event, I've just received word Alliance and Federation ships clashed while scouting a new planet we're calling Itero—here are the Galactic Coordinates—and shots were exchanged. We have casualties, as I expect you do. If you haven't been notified yet, I'm sure you will be soon."

"Perhaps not. Our planetary scouting teams are all civilian."

He only partially squelched a scoff at the double-edged retort. Alliance engineering regiments were as civilian as military got, but they were still military. "And it is unfortunate if that fact resulted in an unequal confrontation."

The response earned what might be a genuine, if miniscule, smile. He'd finally coaxed a real smile out of her the last time they met in person, something he took an inappropriate degree of pride in. "First, let's address the emergency at hand. I have a recovery team en route. I'm willing to instruct the team to engage in any rescue and recovery operations needed for your Federation civilian personnel as well, but I wanted to get your permission first."

She glanced at a screen to her left. "I appreciate the offer, but it won't be necessary. I have a platoon close. They'll handle it."

"Let's do try to ensure the rescue teams don't start shooting at each other, shall we?"

Her face was a perfect mask, giving away not a scintilla of emotion. "I'll do my part."

He wondered with a touch of sadness how they had gotten here so quickly. "Marshal, our people should not be shooting at one another. This is exactly the kind of situation the politicians created the Conflict Resolution Board for. Both sides should have desisted from their activities and alerted their superiors, who would've filed grievances with the Board. Instead everyone had itchy trigger fingers."

"And now people are dead on both sides." She nodded. "All right. Ideas on how to prevent this from happening again in the future?"

"We each send a very public message that violence toward our allies will not be tolerated. If the facts turn out to be consistent with the early reports, I intend to bring courts-martial against the ship captain who gave the order to fire on the Federation vessels, as well as anyone else who shares culpability. They'll be punished—as they should be—but they'll also serve as a necessary example."

He'd daresay she looked surprised, which troubled him. He recognized Federation leaders remained wary about the Alliance's intentions, but he'd hoped they didn't group him in with the tone-deaf politicians.

The expression was gone the next instant, so fast he might have imagined it. "Strictly speaking, I don't have disciplinary authority over teams from the Interstellar Development Agency. But Chairman Vranas does, and I expect he won't be pleased about this incident either. I'll recommend a full hearing and sanctions against the on-site team, as well as their supervisors if insufficient training or unclear—or flat-out improper—mission guidelines contributed to the team believing opening fire was the correct way to resolve the conflict."

He exhaled and relaxed a little. "Thank you, Marshal. I don't know if we'll be able to keep our relations pointed in the right direction, but I sure as hell intend to try."

Once the holo vanished he sent another request, this time to Miriam...and received an auto-bounce indicating she was otherwise occupied and would be unable to respond to any messages for the next several hours.

He drummed his fingers on the edge of his desk. He could override the bounce with a Level V Priority flag. But in his experience she didn't utilize such auto-bouncers unless there was a damn good reason for it. And, God willing, the urgent phase of the crisis at Itero had passed. There would be plenty of time for the overwrought accusations and denunciations later.

If it was all the same to those back on Earth, he'd prefer to skip it and concentrate on rebuilding what the Metigens had destroyed.

11

ERISEN

K ennedy Rossi was surrounded by floating holo panels when Noah walked into the space they had rented for Connova Interstellar—a very ambitious name for a company that consisted of, for now, little more than a mostly empty office, an adiamene patent and a brilliant mind full of ideas. Her mind, not his.

The office wouldn't be empty for much longer, though, if she had anything to say about it—and she had a great deal to say about it. Halfway-complete schem flows, partial designs of two disparate ship models, and multiple lists filled the screens.

She stood in the center of it all, dressed in a jade lace top, white Capris and espadrilles in defiance of the chilly weather outside, and had both hands on her hips. So damn adorable.

He tip-toed across the room behind her, slipped through the screens, grabbed her around the waist and lifted her into the air.

"Ahh!" She twisted around, wide-eyed. "Noah, you scared me!"

"That was the goal." He kissed her until her grumble gave way to a pleased murmur.

"I'm working."

He reluctantly deposited her on the floor but kept his hands on her waist. "So I see. How goes it?"

She glared at the panel to her left. "Slow. There are so many more factors to consider than I imagined. I thought I was taking everything into account in my work at IS Design, but I was wrong. Badly wrong." She wiggled out of his grasp and went over to tweak an entry on one of the lists. "How was Mia?"

"Um...alive? Awake? No, she seemed to be in really good shape, given the circumstances. Already going stir-crazy."

"Hmm. And your dad?"

"The usual. Grumpy and judgmental. He says hello." Noah watched her for a few seconds. "How can I help?"

She steepled her hands in front of her mouth. "Quantum boxes are significantly smaller now, but all this hardware still needs power. And power is heavy. We need lightweight power."

"It's not as if adiamene can't support a lot of weight."

In truth it could do far more than that. Initially created on accident when Alex used scrap from the wreckage of Caleb's ship to patch the hole he'd blown in the *Siyane*, the chemical fusion of those particular carbon and amodiamond metamaterials had resulted in a wholly new material. Adiamene, as Kennedy had named it after recognizing its uniqueness, was not only far stronger, but also more resilient, flexible and conductive than anything engineers had been able to produce to date.

"Yes, but this isn't about structural soundness or the thrust necessary to reach escape velocity—it might involve those, too, but they're not my focus right now. I'm concentrating on agility, maneuverability and achievable impulse engine speeds. Now that they don't require five centimeters of hull metal for shielding and integrity, there's no reason even the largest ships can't be swift and responsive."

"Except there is a reason—power."

"Not if we solve the problem. So basically, I need to dive into the newest research on mobile power generation. If I'm an expert by this weekend—and I find good answers—I can have a modified design for the personal craft by early next week and for the first corporate model four-to-six days after that, which I can then present...." Her voice trailed off, and the animated expression she wore when noodling out a technical puzzle vanished, replaced by a fierce scowl.

"What's wrong?" He asked casually. It still felt like he was juggling a couple of fireblades every time he needed to pose the question.

She smacked her lips in exaggerated annoyance. "It seems the Chairman of the Assembly's Military Oversight Committee wants to meet with me to discuss the adiamene contract—no details on what precisely she wants to 'discuss.' And since her schedule is simply booked solid, it would be wonderful if I could come to her office this evening."

"Her office in London?"

"Yep."

"What are you going to do?"

A sweep of her hand and the screens vanished. "It appears I'm putting on a business suit and catching a transport to London."

"Damn, if I'd known this was going to come up I'd have stayed on Earth. We could've made a weekend of it." In truth he had sort of rushed back to Erisen…because he missed her. He buried his disappointment beneath a casual shrug that said it was *all good*.

She kissed him lightly on her way toward the door. "It's okay. I'll be home in the morning. You'll hardly realize I wasn't here. Oh, and if you know anyone who knows anything about power generation, maybe you could reach out to them while I'm gone?"

He nodded an agreement, and the door closed behind her.

He glanced around the mostly empty and now silent office. Connova was her vision, but it was his company, too. He went and grabbed a beer from the fridge compartment.

So, power generation. Who did he know who knew power?

EARTH

LONDON: EARTH ALLIANCE ASSEMBLY

Kennedy was shown into the Committee Chairman's office by a man who claimed to be her Chief Aide but looked far too young to be qualified for the position. Gene therapy and biosynth enhancements could make a person appear as young as they wished, within reason, but it seemed counterproductive to her for a political climber to choose to look *that* young. Maybe it was a new fad among Earth's rising elite.

Once upon a time she'd cared about such fads, though she'd called them 'trends' back then. But after surviving the Metigen invasion of Messium and the near annihilation of humanity, after meeting someone who saw the world from a refreshingly offbeat perspective she'd never considered…well, she had different priorities now.

The Chairman was finishing up a conference elsewhere on the sprawling Assembly grounds, and Kennedy settled into one of the chairs opposite the vacant desk to wait. She gazed around idly, taking the decor in. It was oddly modest for a woman married to the old wealth that was the Winslow family, but she supposed appearances needed to be maintained in politics. An ornate office displaying expensive artwork and fancy baubles wouldn't please the constituents, even if they must know the woman was wealthy.

Pamela Winslow entered behind her and offered Kennedy an officious handshake on the way to her desk. "Ms. Rossi, thank you for coming to speak with me today."

I've come all the way from Erisen at your behest. This had better be good. Her smile conveyed only exquisite politeness. "It's not a problem, Chairman. What can I do for you?"

Winslow took her seat with an economy of motion and clasped her hands atop the old-fashioned, natural wood desk surface. "How is your mother doing? I'd hoped to see her at the grand reopening of the Victoria and Albert Museum last month, but I understand she was unable to attend."

Kennedy quickly pulled up her calendar in her eVi. The Museum was heavily damaged by falling debris from one of the Metigen superdreadnoughts destroyed above London in the final minutes of the Metigen War. Repairs had finally been completed five weeks ago.

"I…believe that event was the same night as my brother's birthday dinner. I'll let her know you asked after her." She shifted her posture forward. "Now, I realize you're extremely busy, and I don't want to take up much of your time. You wished to discuss the adiamene contract?"

"We on the Military Oversight Committee have been reviewing the contract, and we've decided to propose a few small adjustments."

"Oh?" She kept her expression neutral to hide her growing displeasure. She, Alex and Caleb had entered into the agreement with the government once the 'emergency measures' of the war lapsed. It was a simple, straightforward contract, with clear terms and reservation of rights. She had difficulty imagining what 'adjustments' existed to be made. Price, perhaps. It usually did come down to price before the end.

"Yes. We need to take care to focus on the future and protect Alliance interests in uncertain times." She reached into her desk drawer and produced a disk—the old, sturdy, crystal-latticed graphene kind the government mandated use of for all official matters. "Here's the amendment. I understand you possess power of attorney for your absent colleagues, so you can sign it whenever you're ready."

The woman's demeanor remained pleasant, but an undertone of distaste had crept into her voice when she mentioned Alex and Caleb, if not by name. The fact she knew they were 'absent' didn't come as a surprise, given the woman's position of power, but the distaste did.

Kennedy took the disk, dug around in her bag and found a reader, and inserted the disk in the input slot. A recent ocular implant upgrade meant she could read the disk without using the device, but since the upgrade wasn't on the market yet—the CTO of the developer was a personal friend—she wasn't inclined to advertise its existence to a public official.

She waited until a tiny screen activated above the reader, then made a show of examining it. In truth she had dedicated the terms to memory, so she rapidly scanned the contents for alterations, intending to use the extra time to prepare her response.

It was near to the end when she spotted it. She read the section twice more to be certain her eyes weren't deceiving her.

She dropped the reader, disk and all, back into her bag and stood. "No."

Then she pivoted and walked out of the office, leaving the Chairman of the Military Oversight Committee sitting in stunned silence.

ℛ

VANCOUVER

Despite the late hour, Miriam looked as though she had just arrived home from the office when she answered the door. She wore a navy turtleneck and her uniform pants; her hair was still tucked neatly into a bun.

She blinked and tilted her head. "Kennedy, this is a surprise. What can I do for you?"

Kennedy held up the disk. "You can explain *this* to me."

Miriam gazed at the disk. "You're going to have to be more specific."

"Oh, I will be. May I come in?"

Miriam stepped to the side and gestured to the foyer. "Of course, dear. Would you like some tea?"

She didn't particularly care for any, but she was already bordering on rudeness and she'd barely made it in the door. "Thank you, tea would be lovely."

"Please, have a seat in the den. I'll be right back."

Kennedy sat on the edge of the couch and fidgeted. She'd only been to Miriam's home twice before, thanks to Alex's near-total lack of a relationship with her mother until very recently. It was an unassuming townhome in an upper-middle-class Vancouver neighborhood near the Strait—i.e., minutes from the Island.

The decor was unsurprisingly tasteful and minimal. A shelf of antique texts lined one wall of the den. The other displayed family visuals, almost all of which predated her husband's death. There was a recent one from Alex's and Caleb's wedding—it had been an ultra-private ceremony at a rustic inn in the White River valley of Mt. Rainier, with a guest list so short and exclusive she and Noah were lucky to attend. Beside it was a visual of Miriam and Alex arm in arm, taken after the ceremony. They were both smiling freely—and at each other, a rare sight indeed.

The front wall, closest to the foyer, held a memorial collage dedicated to David Solovy's life and his death. Medals, citations and commendations surrounded a large image of him in full dress uniform above a bronzed plaque. It held an inscription, but she couldn't read it from the couch and didn't want to so blatantly snoop.

Her focus swiveled to Miriam as the woman rejoined her, two steaming cups of tea in hand. She gave one to Kennedy then sat in the armchair opposite her. "Given the hour, I assume this isn't a social call. What's on the disk?"

Kennedy took a quick sip of the tea and set it on the side table. "A proposed amendment to our contract with the government for non-exclusive use rights to adiamene. The amendment will make your rights exclusive. It effectively enables the Alliance to seize control of the distribution of adiamene by forcing me to sell only to you."

"Not only to me, surely."

"Don't obfuscate, Miriam. Did you know about this?"

The woman's lips drew into a thin line. "I was aware the matter was under consideration."

"I'm not signing this. Alex would *never* sign this."

"Seeing as Alex isn't here, I'm not sure that's especially relevant."

She did have a point, given they had no idea when Alex and Caleb might return—it could be years—but it was a point Kennedy wasn't ready to accept. "Well, she would lose her mind if she came back and found out I signed this atrocity on her behalf, power of attorney or no."

"Kennedy, you must understand. Adiamene is an extremely dangerous material in the wrong hands. If the cartels—or worse, terrorists—get their hands on it, this will severely cripple our ability to combat them. The military needs to maintain some advantage over its enemies."

"And the Federation?"

"We are under our own contract to supply them with a portion of our monthly production, free of charge, until reparations for the damage General O'Connell inflicted on their colonies is paid in full."

"How much of your supply?"

Miriam dipped her chin in apparent concession. "The contract calls for fifteen percent."

She wouldn't have phrased it as she did if the reality wasn't something altogether different. "How much are you really sending them? Twelve percent? Ten?"

The woman's eyes drifted to the cup of tea in her hand. "Eight percent. At most."

Kennedy huffed an incredulous laugh, shocked the woman had admitted the truth—unless she hadn't, which meant it was even worse.

She shook her head. "I take your point about the criminals, but I'm not at all comfortable with what it will mean when only military ships are indestructible. I love the Alliance—my family has supported it since its inception—but no military should be so powerful."

"Not merely our military—Seneca will act as a check against us."

"Not at an eight percent supply they won't. You'll have a new fleet built before they can produce a regiment worth of ships. I'm sorry, but no. I can't sign this."

Miriam took a meticulous sip of her tea. When she spoke, her voice had gained a weightier, solemn tenor. Of warning? "Kennedy, if you fight them, they can force you to consent to it."

Her own tenor headed in the opposite direction. "Like hell they can!"

"The Assembly has half a dozen regulations and special procedures they can invoke to appropriate adiamene production. And I regret to say, under their current leadership they are inclined to do so."

"That's funny—I thought we lived in a democracy."

"We do. But that does not mean a tremendous degree of power doesn't reside in the government. It is by and large judicious in its use of this power, but it exists nonetheless."

Kennedy groaned. "What happened, Miriam? After we defeated the Metigens, it felt as if we were on the cusp of a new...I don't know, advancement in our society. After we were nearly made extinct, it seemed as though we'd gained a new appreciation for what we had and what we were capable of. Now it feels like all we gained is slipping away."

Miriam opened her mouth, then appeared to think better of whatever she'd considered saying. She set her tea down before responding in an abrupt, curt manner. "We're doing the best we can."

"Good luck with that." Kennedy stood. "I'm not signing the amendment. If they try to force me to sign it, or try to take the rights by fiat, I'm canceling the design contract EASC has with Connova. You want new ships—better, more efficient and responsive ships? You can't have them. Not from me. I'm sorry, as I know this isn't your fault, but I have to do what I think is best."

Miriam stood as well. "I don't agree, but I understand." She paused. "Alex would cause quite the scene over this if she were here, wouldn't she?"

"Honestly? I'm considering causing a scene which will put anything Alex has ever done to shame."

PART III:

PRINCIPLE OF EQUIVALENT EXCHANGE

"We are an impossibility in an impossible universe."

— Ray Bradbury

PORTAL: B-14

SYSTEM DESIGNATION: ORYKTOS

12

ORYKTOS-4

Tidally-locked to a distant blue-white A8 V star, the planet they hovered above was an unlikely candidate to harbor advanced, intelligent life.

The readings were off the charts. The surface practically glowed, so high was the level of energy propagation; on the visualization of the radio and microwave spectrums, it *did* glow. EM signals showing all the hallmarks of artificial generation permeated the stellar system, but they originated from this world.

And of course, the TLF wave led from the portal directly to here.

Still, the tidal locking wasn't the sole factor counting against the planet supporting life. Not only the system but the entire portal space overflowed with inorganic material—elemental silicon as well as quartz, aluminum, germanium, and a variety of silicate-heavy minerals could be found in abundance. What it lacked, in all but the smallest trace amounts, was carbon.

No hint of non-carbon-based life, even microbial, had ever been found by humans. Yet here it was, and giving every indication of thriving. It was as if this universe had been tailor-made for inorganic life to arise. Alex put aside for later contemplation the uncomfortable possibility that this was in fact exactly what had happened.

Caleb's hand rested on her shoulder. "Let's be careful. This species is certain to be very different from us and possibly more advanced. Also, chances are they've never seen anything like a human."

She nodded in marginal agreement. "They haven't colonized any other worlds in the system, so they can't be that advanced."

"Not necessarily true. They may have non-technological reasons for not venturing beyond their home planet."

"Don't assume. Right." She gave him a reassuring smile. His mood had improved somewhat in the days since they had departed Akeso, but it remained heavy on the brooding. She was hopeful a new mysterious alien species would distract him and create some emotional distance from his difficult encounter. "Valkyrie, are you making any progress on interpreting the signals we're picking up?"

'They are based on a quaternary numerical system. Translating the data into ternary is not difficult, but absent an interpreter this merely results in more numbers—numbers which do not correspond to anything meaningful in our language. However, I am attempting to build a dictionary by identifying patterns and repetitions.'

"And how's that going?"

'I believe I have identified the strings for 'up' and 'down.' In my defense, we've only been recording the signals for twelve minutes.'

"I know, Valkyrie. You'll have us talking to the residents in no time." She studied some of the other readings from the surface and atmosphere. "I'm not seeing any planetary defenses. They may use ground-based rockets, EMPs or the like, but there's nothing in the outer atmosphere or in high orbit. The atmosphere is sulfur monoxide, chlorine and methane—needless to say, we won't be breathing it."

Her fist came to rest at her chin. "All the active signals are coming from the dark side of the planet, but we're picking up a low-level yet omnipresent EM field on the sun-facing side. Let's swing around and see what's going on over there."

Caleb shrugged in response. She generously interpreted it as agreement and adopted a trajectory that would allow them to reach the other side while maintaining a safe distance.

The sun rose above the arc of the planet's profile, a stark, icy blue which provided light but scant warmth. Beautiful but cold, in more than one sense of the word. She shifted the bow of the *Siyane* toward the surface—and was nearly blinded by the dazzling luminance.

"What the...?" The filters over the viewport darkened as she blinked away halos.

Caleb peered out the viewport beside her. His ocular implant was more advanced than hers, and he probably hadn't even had to blink. "Solar cells, I think. The entire hemisphere is covered in them."

Valkyrie concurred. 'Details of the objects' makeup and structure cannot be determined from this distance, but I agree they are most likely a type of solar cell.'

She squinted until the shapes of tens of thousands of individual cells began to come into focus; innumerably more faded into the horizon. "The residents are pulling power from the light side, presumably to fuel their technology—I know, I'm making another assumption. They're collecting power and sending it elsewhere. But building and maintaining so many cells and the infrastructure for transmitting the power must have been a colossal task. Why didn't they simply...move?"

Caleb smirked, all too rare the last few days. "We'll be sure to ask them."

"We will." She squeezed his hand, eager to encourage the behavior, and turned away from the still too-bright glare to prop against the dash.

"So once Valkyrie has deciphered their language and created a translator, we should send a probe down. If it isn't immediately intercepted and destroyed, it can send back surface images and more detailed readings—and if it *is* intercepted and destroyed, we'll know we're dealing with another unfriendly species.

"To increase the chances of it not getting shot down, we can rig it to broadcast a friendly message in their language—" her eyes twinkled playfully "—'We come in peace' or some such. Then...let's see what happens with the probe before we make any decisions."

⩜

The *Siyane* cruised a kilometer above a vast expanse of smooth metal. Scans pegged it as a mineral similar to morion quartz, run through with fibers of monocrystalline silicon. Violet clouds permeated the air, blotting out what paltry light might have otherwise reached the surface. The environs appeared lifeless and inert, yet the opposite was true.

Caleb cycled through the various wavelengths with his ocular implant. When he reached the microwave band, the world lit up. Constant, oscillating signals flowed in every direction across and in the metal below. Regions of greater activity were easily discerned; when viewed together they resembled hubs in an interconnected network.

Their probe had not been attacked, even upon engaging in some fairly overt investigations. So here they were, getting ready to attempt contact with yet another drastically nonhuman sentient life form. Unlike Akeso, this species would differ from them at the most fundamental of levels: the atoms which comprised it. Whatever form such a genetic structure took, it would not be DNA.

He was concerned about their safety, as he generally was on initial contact. The abundant, massive assemblies surrounding them could hide laser or rocket turrets or some unknown type of weapons. The residents could be hostile, powerful, or leading them into a trap—or worse, all three. He made it a habit to be ready for any eventuality. Unfortunately, the possible eventualities had exceeded his imagination more than once. But it wasn't as if they could *not* investigate.

Ahead of them the broad sheet of semi-translucent quartz began to rise into a pyramid-style structure; multiple spires jutted upward out of the slopes. The pyramid shone so thick with low frequency waves the signals became an undifferentiated blob. "We should set down outside the hub ahead—you see the energy concentration, Valkyrie?"

'I do. Approaching region conducive to landing eighty meters from the start of the upward slope.'

Alex was leaning into the dash to peer keenly out the viewport. "Temperature outside is -62° C. Going to be a little chilly."

The environment suits were designed foremost for use in space and could handle extreme cold. If a suit developed a tear, however, at such a low temperature they'd have a minute at most to get inside the ship before severe hypothermia set in and, rapidly thereafter, death occurred. Good thing the suits were almost impossible to tear using anything less than high-powered military weaponry.

Alex allowed Valkyrie to handle the landing. She spent her time alternately reviewing the incoming readings and visually studying the area, absorbing everything they knew so far.

The *Siyane* slowed as it descended and neared the edge of the pyramid. They were unstealthed, announcing their presence as openly as the probe had in the hope they wouldn't get shot down either.

The first sign of movement began as they settled to the surface of the silicon expanse—there was every reason to believe it was not the surface of the planet but rather an immense edifice built atop it. It was impossible to tell how far above the planet's terrestrial surface they were.

Caleb couldn't make out any details, but a modular metal construct emerged from an opening at the base of the pyramid. "Just keep broadcasting that peace and harmony message, Valkyrie."

'Certainly. I've finished programming the portable bidirectional transmitters with the translator. Accept the connection in your eVis and they'll work together.'

"Yep." Alex hurried over to the workbench to retrieve the transmitters while he stayed and kept a close eye on the exterior, not wanting to let the new arrival out of his sight until they were ready to go outside. He noted the sound of the supply cabinet opening then closing, and she reappeared at his side holding the transmitters and two wrist straps.

She glanced out the viewport at the construct as she fastened the strap around the material of her environment suit. "That one of the locals?"

He tilted his head with a slight shrug. It wasn't much of an answer, but he didn't have a better one. He might also still be a bit grumpy…he tried again to shake it off, to let go of the lingering shadow of the anguish he had caused another.

'The form is a mobile unit constructed of the same material as the structure beneath us. It could be a representative of the species who built the structure, or it could merely be a service mech. Or it could be something else entirely.'

"Understood." Alex stared at him with notable intensity. "This is the first time we'll be facing something clearly technologically advanced. Are we ready?"

He forced himself fully into the present, checking her over then mentally checking himself. "Environment suits sealed up. Breather masks in hand. Daemons. Blades. Transmitters. Healthy respect for the adversary—you've got that, right?"

One corner of her lips curled up. "Absolutely…."

He chuckled and positioned the mask on his mouth, followed by a breath in and out to confirm functionality. "You need to work on your delivery if you expect anyone to believe you."

Next came the helmet. The masks delivered the air they needed, but both the temperature outside and the risk of attack meant they needed the protection of the helmets. He activated the control and made sure the helmet properly locked into the neck ring of the suit. She did the same, and they confirmed those seals as well.

Alex's chest rose as she took a deep breath. "Valkyrie, you pick up anything squirrelly, let us know immediately. Otherwise, feel free to chime in with any helpful suggestions."

'I always do.'

"Good point."

Alex opened the hatch and extended the ramp. Caleb followed her down, his eyes finding the construct then proceeding to watch everywhere at once.

"*Milostivyy menya….*"

His hand was instantly on her shoulder. "What is it?"

She looked up at him, irises ablaze. "What Valkyrie sees...light, everywhere. Before, to me this seemed a dead, silent world. Now, though, it's bursting with life and energy. Can you see it?"

"Some of it." Her enthusiasm seeped into him despite his efforts to remain edgy and tense. He reigned it in—he had a responsibility to do so—and jerked his head forward. "Let's not keep the emissary waiting too long."

They continued on, now side by side. The chill from the air seeped through the fabric of the suit into his bones. The structures pulsed with energy, but the setting still felt desolate. There might be 'life' here, but if so, it was the polar opposite of Akeso, no matter the measure.

The pyramid loomed over them forebodingly, far larger up close than it had appeared on approach. It cast no visual shadow as there wasn't sufficient light from the sky to create one, but the psychological shadow was tangible enough. To either side the harsh metal stretched into the darkness, and beneath their feet electrical current raced in every direction.

As they neared, the entity that had emerged gained definition. A mech apparently designed for mobility and physical agility, it stood two and a half meters in height and was comprised of around two dozen modular pieces: four wheels which looked as if they became grippers when needed, four multi-jointed arms, a narrow, similarly jointed torso to connect them, and that was it. No head. No discernable mechanism for sight. Nevertheless, it knew they were there.

When they were ten meters from it their transmitters lit up.

You come from above. Why?

Caleb motioned for her to stop while there was still distance between them and the entity, and Alex cleared her throat. Her eVi was prepped to translate her spoken words into the alien language and send it to the transmitter to be delivered.

"Yes, we're from another planet, far from this one. We've come in the hope we can learn from one another. We mean you no harm."

Good job, baby.

You are small, yet you fly. How?

The alien's manner of speech was curt, succinct and absent all nuance. He let Alex continue to handle the interaction, giving him the opportunity to study the entity more closely.

"You mean our ship? It contains a special engine—several, in fact—that enables it to fly."

You refer to it as if separate. Other. Is this ship not you?

Alex muttered on their private comm. "Valkyrie, help me out here."

She didn't have to give voice to the question at all, but she went out of her way to include him in any conversation with Valkyrie that impacted whatever they happened to be doing. He was sure she slipped on occasion, but the fact she made the continual effort meant a lot to him.

'The question suggests we are dealing with a single life form, of which the mech is a mobile subset, like one of your fingers.'

"No. We are each individuals. I—" she pointed at Caleb "—my companion, and our ship are each separate, self-contained life forms." The *Siyane* wasn't alive, but Valkyrie was, so arguably close enough.

You are small, but you do not join together to grow. Why not?

"We kind of...we work together while still maintaining our individuality." Alex frowned in his direction, and he nodded encouragement.

You're doing fine.

I do not understand. I will understand.

"I'll try to explain it better—perhaps if I understood your makeup? When you say 'I' do you mean..." she gestured to the pyramid and around the platform "...is all of this you?"

For [no translation].

"Valkyrie?"

'It is providing a form of distance measurement, but I lack a reference point at present.'

"Do you span the entire planet?" She switched to the private comm. "Because we've already seen that."

No. We divide the planet among [one less than four quad—equivalent to eleven] others.

With this nugget of intel, by his estimation things became appreciably more interesting.

"And what do you call yourself? What can we call you?"

I am [One Quad Less One—equivalent to Three]. We are Ruda.

"A pleasure to meet you. I'm Alex, this is Caleb, and the ship is...Valkyrie."

'You don't need to—'

"Hush. It's easier this way."

Her response gave him pause. When he met Alex, her ship was the most important thing in her life. Much had changed since then, so should he not be surprised? As he'd noted, the *Siyane* was not and had never been alive, and Valkyrie clearly was. He filed it away for later consideration.

Valkyrie is your Supreme. Your operator.

"What makes you think that?"

It is larger and stronger. It flies.

"That's not...size isn't the primary measure of authority in our society."

Then Valkyrie is not your Supreme?

"We don't have a Supreme—a leader, I think you mean. Well, we do back home...too many of them...anyway, we're here as equals." He heard the growing frustration in her voice. Still, five minutes as a diplomat was a good showing on her part.

There was a measurable delay in the response.

Valkyrie asserts this is true, so I will not dispute it.

'The entity—I propose we simply call it 'Three' among ourselves—transmitted a signal directly at me asking for confirmation, so I confirmed it. I'm not certain any of us have convinced it, however.'

"Right." She gazed hesitantly at him, obviously at a loss. "So what now? I think I'm at the end of the 'greeting' speech."

He stepped forward to draw the mech's attention. "We'd be interested to see more of your world and learn about your species. Will you show us something of how you live?"

If I do so, Valkyrie must also see and learn.

"Valkyrie will see everything I see."

The mech didn't physically turn to Alex.

You are Valkyrie's mobile detachment.

"Um…" Alex grumbled in annoyance "…you know what, fine. Let's go with that."

Now I understand.

Somehow I doubt it.

Come.

The mech pivoted and rolled toward a wide opening in the pyramid. An entrance of sorts, though there were no doors.

He grasped Alex's hand and held her back briefly.

Keep some distance between us and the mech, so we'll have a chance to react if anything unpleasant happens.

She squeezed his hand in understanding, and they followed the mech inside.

The interior was architecturally no different than the exterior—walls, floor and ceiling of the same metal, smooth and sculpted into ninety-degree angles. Signals streamed along every surface; pitch-black to the naked eye, on most other bands the energy turned the space brighter than daylight.

The halls were four meters wide but nonetheless felt claustrophobic. Dangerous. Using the surroundings to his advantage would be difficult, and thus far he knew of only one exit.

Alex touched his arm. "Hey, it's getting warm in here. Think we can take our helmets off and just use the breather masks?"

She was right. The enclosed space and the power flowing through it created a far warmer environment. "For now, but be ready to reactivate it. We don't know when we'll need them again."

Her helmet was barely off when their escort halted and rolled closer to them. One of its appendages jutted out toward Alex's face.

She flinched. He tensed.

No sharp objects materialized; instead the blunt edge of the arm drew across her cheek.

You are...organic?

It was the first time the alien mech had displayed any hesitation in its speech.

'It has likely never seen skin before, or hair.'

Alex twitched under the scrutiny. "Yes. I apologize if you didn't realize this before."

Yet you think? You communicate?

She took a step backward. "Quite a lot. You don't have any organic species on your planet?"

Unthinking, base life.

"Charming."

He sighed.

> *Alex, that was out loud.*

> *Whatever.*

'It is asking me how I succeeded in creating intelligent organic life. I am attempting to explain I did not create it—rather, it created me. Three seems unwilling to accept this assertion.'

Come. We will go this way.

The mech took a left, and the hall soon opened up into a larger, comparably open space. The ceiling vanished, replaced by soaring walls. Were they beneath one of the spires? They hadn't traveled far enough for this to be the center of the pyramid.

Two additional mechs entered from other hallways and approached them. They looked identical to their escort.

Caleb's combat instincts flared. If the mechs were mobile subunits of the one regional intelligence, why did more than one need to be here?

13

ORYKTOS-4

RUDAN

Alex couldn't say precisely when she and Caleb had gotten separated. Preoccupied by the mech leading them but mostly by their surroundings—by the walls coursing with endless streams of data she very much wanted to decipher—she'd lost track of both him and their location vis-à-vis the entrance. Or rather her location, because wherever he was, it wasn't here.

Caleb? Where did you go?

Silence. Fuck.

Valkyrie, where is—

Two far larger mechs appeared as she followed her escort around the next corner. She turned to run—and ran smack into a third one. Rigid, strong claws grasped her wrists and pushed her backwards through an opening in the wall as her transmitter lit up.

Must study. Must learn. Must understand intelligent organic growth. Will incorporate knowledge and replicate results.

"No. Valkyrie, tell them no."

I am trying.

She was forced downward until a flat surface met her back. Freed of needing to walk, she started kicking at the mechs while thrashing her upper body in an attempt to break free. More of the smaller mechs arrived to clamp down on her ankles and hold her still.

Damn they were strong. In a matter of seconds she was completely immobilized.

"You fucking monsters, let me go! Killing me isn't going to teach you a goddamn thing!"

Will observe internal structure. Will measure sensory and cognitive activity. Will learn and incorporate, and grow life.

"Observe my ass!" Spittle flew into her breather mask; she inhaled and choked on it.

Alex, you need to give me control.

What?

You need to give me control of your body. Let me speak through you. It is the only chance we have to convince them to desist.

Fuck. The notion was a deeply unsettling one, but she really would prefer to live. *Do it.*

She tried to 'relax' her mind, but it was a challenge what with the horde of alien mechs about to dissect—

"Valkyrie speaks to you through this mobile detachment. Confirm this with my hub."

A new, more existential form of panic seized her mind, for she was now utterly helpless. The words were coming out of her mouth, but they were not her own. Her voice had taken on a flat, robotic tone. She watched from afar, in some deep recess of her consciousness.

Confirmed.

"Rendering this organic unit inoperable will not provide you the information you seek."

Will not disable. Will observe and measure.

"Organic units are physically fragile. Perforation of the outer shell will result in permanent loss of operability. Organic units function via a complicated internal biosystem. If one portion of it is disabled, the entire unit ceases to function.

"If you wish to learn the details of its functioning, the only way to do so is by keeping it intact, operable and with freedom of movement and action. Physical examination will not yield the results you seek. Interaction via communication will yield those results."

Communication does not reveal details of operation. Will observe and measure.

"If organic outer shell is breached, observation will not succeed. Knowledge will not be gained. Knowledge will be lost. Organic unit knows much to teach you. Organic unit knows how to control power, how to control light, how to control space. But organic unit must be kept operable in order to teach One Quad Less One."

A blade of quartz glass hovered above her nose. She tried to scream. *Why my nose? NOT IMPORTANT.*

Valkyrie will teach One Quad Less One.

"Organic unit is trained to teach and to demonstrate this knowledge. It is a more appropriate vehicle for the transfer of knowledge."

Organic unit will share knowledge?

"Yes, but—" *like hell I will* "—you must guarantee its safety and continued unimpeded operation. Organic units do not operate properly when under restraint and immobile. Organic unit must remain independent and fully functional in order to share knowledge."

Organic units move too much. Movement is not important. Growth is important.

"Organic units grow in intelligence by moving, by seeking new locations in which to gain knowledge. Organic unit must move unimpeded or it will not function correctly."

The blade retreated.

I misinterpreted the nature of organic unit. I will no longer restrain organic unit, and it will share knowledge.

The instant the mechs' grips loosened she was in motion, wresting control of her mind from Valkyrie as she wrested control of her body from the mechs.

Free of their bondage, she leapt to her feet and sprinted for the hallway.

WHERE IS CALEB?

There is a single heat signature two hundred eighty-eight meters to the northeast.

Show me!

The walls became a gridded maze overlaying her vision, a series of ninety degree angles leading to the red dot that marked his location. She resisted the temptation to slip into quantum space and see that he was all right this instant, for…what if he was not?

She bolted through the passageways, turning without thinking and accelerating through each stretch. In the back of her mind she recognized her eVi was forcing her brain to pump waves of cortisol, adrenaline and norepinephrine into her bloodstream. Still, the possibility occurred to her that she might not have regained quite as much control over her body as she believed. No matter. She needed the boost.

Eighty-seven meters. Seventy-two meters.

Tell Three not to hurt him!

I am doing so. However, there seems to be some level of confusion surrounding his status.

She skidded around a corner, slamming her shoulder into the wall and bouncing off of it without slowing.

Caleb?

Silence. Forty-six meters. A long stretch of hallway. She pushed faster, harder. Twenty meters.

She burst into the room in unison with a deafening crash of metal shearing metal.

Caleb looked up, tossed the disembodied arm of one of the mechs to the side and rushed into her arms. "Jesus, you're okay!"

She nodded into his neck, suddenly dizzy as the abrupt halt to her movement sent all the blood rushing to her head, or her feet, or somewhere non-optimal. She gasped out a response, panting. "I am. And you…."

She peered over his shoulder. The room was littered with the remains of multiple shattered mechs. Pieces lay strewn across the floor, appendages ripped apart and cores crushed. Caleb had a bloody gash starting beneath his left eye and running down the length of his cheek; the hair above his left ear was matted with blood.

"What did you *do?*"

He grinned, his face flush from his own adrenaline. "Fought back."

She started laughing in a burst of giddiness, but he shifted back into combat mode. "We need to get out of here before they send a larger contingent."

"I think we may be safe now, but..." she gazed around at the carnage again "...yeah. Let's go. Valkyrie, give me a route to the exit."

The grid lit up anew, complete with a new red dot. They quickly donned their helmets, then he grabbed her hand and together they departed the room at a hurried jog.

R

On rounding the final corner before the building opened up into the clearing where they had landed, they found two dozen mechs waiting on them.

Caleb's Daemon was instantly out. She fumbled for her own and raised it.

The mechs didn't approach them or fire on them using any weapons, however. They remained in a semicircle formation that nonetheless blocked their escape route.

'Don't shoot.'

"I'm going to require a persuasive reason not to, Valkyrie," Caleb growled under his breath.

'One moment.'

The transmitter burst to life in a lengthy stream of gibberish. They waited.

I apologize.

She groaned. "Thirty seconds of chatter and that's all it said? It 'apologizes?' "

'The concept is not one which strictly exists in its language. But I nonetheless believe it is the best translation.'

Caleb's grip on the Daemon tightened as he swept it across the semicircle. "How sure are you, Valkyrie? Because the answer better be pretty damn sure."

'I have 82.4521 confidence...I am eighty-two percent sure Three is apologizing.'

Caleb let out a long breath and gradually lowered his weapon, but he didn't holster it. She did the same and kept a close eye on him, ready to follow his lead should the situation change.

He stared down the mechs, and even behind the helmet she could see the intelligence agent at work. "We need to return to our ship. Allow us to pass."

The transmitter emitted the translation, although it was incapable of conveying the deadly threat in his voice.

When the mechs parted at the center to create a pathway, she relaxed. "Valkyrie, we're going to get patched up while you negotiate the rules of engagement for this 'sharing of knowledge.'"

Caleb looked over at her in surprise. "It tried to kill us. We're sharing 'knowledge' with it?"

"Apparently. I'll fill you in once we get on board."

ℛ

"You let her take control of your body? What was it like?"

Alex frowned as she wiped the excess blood off the gash on his cheek and cleaned it. The blood in his hair was from a wide but fortunately not deep scrape, which had earned a coat of bio-synthed collagen gel.

"Disconcerting. Weird. Creepy. Probably would've been panic-inducing if I hadn't already reached the apex on panic. No, that's not entirely true...there was some panic associated with it, too."

She stuck the medwrap on his cheek and held it in place. "But it worked, and she gave me back control as soon as the mechs released me." *Mostly. I think so. Did you, Valkyrie?* But the question was directed only to herself.

His legs swung on both sides of her as he sat on the counter fidgeting. She grabbed one of his thighs with her free hand to halt the motion. "Antsy much?"

"Just keyed up."

"Uh-huh."

His eyes roved around the cabin as his lips quirked in agitation. "So, the fight, taking out all those mechs? It felt...*good*." Gradually his focus returned to her. "Does that bother you?"

Satisfied the medwrap seal was secure, she drew her hand down along his jaw...and her breath hitched when she realized he was genuinely fearful of her answer. *Silly, hardened, sensitive man. Even now.*

"I've been expecting you to pop a cork for weeks now—months, really. No, it doesn't bother me. You're not innately a man of violence, but you are a man of action. You're giving up a lot to be here on this ship with me, in the middle of godforsaken no-one-knows-where."

"I'm not giving up anything."

She gazed at him deadpan, and after a beat he sighed in concession. "Maybe a few things..." his hand rose to cover hers "...tiny things. But it's not a sacrifice. It's where I want to be."

She smiled, because she loved him. "I believe you. But I also want you to know how much I appreciate it, and I promise there will be more excitement where this came from. A different kind of excitement next time, though. Involving fewer dissection knives."

Hoping she read his mood right, she regarded him with a hint of teasing. "So...does this mean no more dewdrops and flower petals?"

His chin dropped to his chest as he laughed quietly. "I, um...I think the experience I had with Akeso will always be a part of me. I hope it will be, because it was incredible, even if it didn't end in the way I would have preferred. But yes, I think we're past the dewdrops and flower petals."

She leaned forward until her nose touched his. "Good. Forget a room full of smashed mechs—that dewdrop shit was disturbing."

"What do you have against dewdrops and flower petals?" he asked in mock indignation.

"Nothing at all. But next thing I'd know you'd be suggesting we move to Gaiae to commune with nature. And I'd be sad."

"No sadness." He kissed her softly then stroked her hair, acting as if he wasn't checking for injuries.

An idea occurred to her. "Train me."

His brow furrowed. "In what?"

"Combat, obviously."

"If I recall correctly from our early days together, you can defend yourself quite well."

"I took some military self-defense classes as a teenager and some martial arts during university. So yes, I can defend myself against other people—but we're not facing 'people' out here. Those mechs subdued me way too easily, and I fumbled for my Daemon when we came outside. I need to be faster. Stronger. So I want you to train me. When we're flying or there's downtime. It'll give us both a way to burn off excess energy—" she scoffed at the amused look on his face "—an additional way. Please?"

He smiled, with his eyes as much as his lips. It was possible he truly was moving past what had happened with Akeso. "You're right. This is a good idea."

"Thank you." She started to renew the kiss, then paused. "Speaking of the mechs, how did they get you in that room?"

His arms wrapped around her. "After a doorway closed between us and I tried to get back to you another way? Three told me you were in there."

She was about to settle in and get comfortable snuggled in his embrace when they both pulled back to stare at each other.

"Shit."

"Valkyrie, Three's capable of lying."

'I know. It is not very good at it, however.'

Alex's face screwed up in bewilderment. "How can you tell? Certainly not by its body language."

'I have become familiar with the syntax of the Rudan native language, including its rhythm and order. Three phrases things in a different manner when not being entirely truthful.'

"Nice!"

Caleb didn't appear to share her enthusiasm. His expression had darkened noticeably, and his gaze drifted to the floor. "I should have realized the implications of you not being in the room immediately." He shook his head. "How much is Three lying, Valkyrie? Are you getting the sense it has malicious intentions? Beyond trying to dismember us."

'I'm not. Its value system is undeniably alien, but it does have one. The lies seem to be driven by caution and perchance a sense of inferiority.'

Now she was skeptical. "Inferiority? It's the size of a continent."

'Yes, but we come from the stars, which is somewhere it has thus far been unable to reach. Also, in me it has found an entity of equal intelligence—greater, but it can believe what it will—that is the size of a small ship. Three is massive because it must be. Physical growth is the only way for the Ruda to grow in intelligence, because they do not possess quantum computing capability.'

"Are you serious? But the quaternary language...."

'The reason their language is quaternary is their mathematics are Base Four. I suspect it originated from the presence of four outer electrons in the atomic structure of silicon.'

Caleb absently rubbed her arms while he pondered the issue. "Valkyrie, don't reveal specific details about organic life or intelligence until we get a better feel for the situation. You can share general information, but nothing it can replicate—and definitely no details about quantum computing. We don't need to accidentally arm an aggressive species and unleash it on this universe."

'Understood. I can be far more devious than Three can.'

Caleb glanced up at the ceiling, a habit he'd mostly broken over the last several months.

'But not to you.'

"Indeed."

Alex pressed a palm to his jaw and drew his attention back to her. "She's screwing with you."

"Oh? And what if she's deceiving you as well?"

"She can't. In the early days she was able to keep a few things from me, but not anymore. If I want to know something, I know it."

A glint of something she didn't recognize flickered across his eyes.

"What?"

"Nothing. It's just...there are a few unique challenges in being married to the first posthuman."

She winced and tried to retreat, but he held her close until she gave in. "Do you wish I hadn't done it? Hadn't become a Prevo?"

"Not at all. You saved everyone. And you're all the more re-markable for it." He looked sincere enough that she relaxed. "Maybe I'm jealous."

"Are you? If you'd like we can explore some options—"

"No. If I'm jealous, it's only in the abstract. I meant it when I said I was glad I mind-melded with Akeso, as you phrased it, but the experience was confounding and a little...dehumanizing. I have no interest in inviting someone or thing else into my head."

She drew a fingertip idly down his chest. "Not even me?"

"Hey, that's not fair. I have to maintain *some* mystery, so I can keep you interested."

"No, you don't."

"No, I don't." He nuzzled her nose, then pulled away a frac-tion. "Wait. Is that something we can do?"

She laughed. "Hell if I know."

14

RUDAN

Caleb stared at the glistening silver-blue leaf in fascination. Fragile and delicate, it clung to its meager stalk in a desperate bid for life.

Dewdrops and flower petals. Here in the depths of this dark, unforgiving place. He didn't doubt a lesson waited in there somewhere.

The toll from stressing his cybernetic enhancements so extensively in the melee with the mechs had come crashing down on him not long after they'd returned to the ship; he'd slept for six hours and arguably could benefit from six more. But the offer to see what Three had been forging in the realm of organics had been too morbidly intriguing to pass up.

"This doesn't look like any flora I've ever seen." Alex peered at the base of another of the plants, clasping her hands behind her back to avoid brushing against it. They had been 'warned' about not touching the plant life.

'Carbon does not occur naturally on the planet. The Ruda have synthesized a form of it, but the compounds they create remain high in silica content.'

"Explains the color. Is this supposed to be soil they're growing it in? Because it's...not."

He joined her in scrutinizing the small plant, an ashen fern with spindly shoots. The dull bronze-hued sludge the plant lived in resembled a mucous goop. "I'm guessing it's more synthesized pseudo-organic material."

When a pang of longing for the feel of real dirt hit him, he stepped back and surveyed the arboretum. Artificial sunlight flooded the room in a sterile white glow. Rows of planting beds lined the walls, host to a reasonable variety of plant strains. In the center of the room was Three's pride and joy: a strange, twisted tree struggling to reach two meters in height.

Two mechs followed them around, ready to leap into action should they touch something.

He didn't remotely trust Three or the mechs it acted through. Anyone or thing that tried to kill him faced a steep uphill climb—roughly equivalent to a sheer cliff—to win his trust. Valkyrie said the misunderstanding had been due to Three's lack of comprehension of the peculiarities of organic life. He could have figured that out for himself, but more importantly it didn't change his perspective. Understanding an attacker's reasons for attacking didn't make the attacker any less of a threat.

"You said 'they,' Valkyrie. Did Three tell you the other inhabitants of the planet were also attempting to create organic life?"

♠

'The Ruda value two things: energy and geographic space. Their coveting of organic life follows logically from these values. Organic life represents all they are not: it is flexible, mobile and capable of functioning without an active power source.

'As we observed, they saturated the sun-facing side of the planet with power collectors and have now maximized their ability to draw energy from the system's sun. Further, they've exhausted the planet's available physical land on which to expand.

'Three asserts there were once many Ruda, but the struggle to control power generation and transfer led the stronger to absorb the weaker as they grew in size and processing capability.

'At this point they have reached a stalemate. The twelve remaining Ruda 'Supremes' are approximately equal in computing power and physical size, such that none are able to take out or incorporate a neighbor. The relationship among the Ruda which has evolved as a result of this state is not an adversarial one. They recognize the nature of their reality and work together to discover ways in which they might break out of their stagnation.'

Alex relaxed in her chair. "They want to leave the planet. I'd come into this assuming it was a human trait, but we keep seeing it. It seems it's what all sentient beings want—to travel the stars."

Caleb brought dinner over to the table and sat down across from her. Taking the time to cook a nice meal—penzine paella in this case—had served as meditation for him, helping to calm his lingering unease and generalized apprehension. "True, but the motives can be different. Ekos-3 wanted to conquer and consume. The Ruda...actually, maybe it is the same. Valkyrie, how do you think the Ruda would react if they encountered intelligent life on a planet they wanted to expand onto?"

'Their reaction to our presence suggests the answer depends on whether they believed the new species could teach them something useful.'

"So they're narcissistic and selfish, but not as overtly antagonistic as Ekos-3."

'A reasonable assumption.'

Alex paused with her fork halfway to her mouth. "Why didn't they simply live on the sunny side, instead of building all those power cells?"

"Conductivity."

She gave him a questioning look.

He did enjoy impressing her whenever the opportunity arose. "Remember, once upon a time I was going to build orbital satellites. Conduction of non-quantum information degrades at higher temperatures—like those one would see in a place subject to unending sunlight. Now, we've mostly overcome those difficulties through advances in technology, but I imagine when the Ruda were wee little silicon crystals they weren't able to do so. Perhaps they still can't."

She smiled at him in that *way* she had, the way that filled his chest with a kind of free, serene joy. He buried his disproportionate reaction to a mere smile in a bite of food. It was good; the meditation had improved more than just his mental state.

"I wonder if they began on the other side and migrated here to improve their efficiency. I mean, they require energy to function—to do anything other than sit there like rocks. If there's no power source on the dark side, they *must* have started on the sun-facing side."

"Unless they had help."

Her eyes narrowed at her food. "The Metigens. Valkyrie, ask your buddy if they used to live on the light side."

'Three has no memory of doing so, but concedes the data could have been lost in early expansions.'

"Convenient. I bet—"

'It may interest you to know that we have been invited to an assembly.'

"With the other Ruda?"

'Correct.'

Alex frowned, again at the food on her plate; luckily the food didn't know she was taking out her skepticism of the Ruda on it. "Now why is it willingly sharing us with the others?"

'Because I informed Three any dissemination of scientific or technical data must include all the Ruda entities.'

Caleb laughed. "You really are developing a devious side, Valkyrie."

'Their current societal structure of cooperation and collaboration is a beneficial one. I do not want to disrupt it by unfairly arming one participant with greater knowledge solely because we happened to land in its territory.'

Alex shrugged. "I would feel bad if we kicked off a civil war. So how do we go to this meeting?"

'It takes place at a location on the northern pole, along the dark/light border. We will need to fly there.'

15

RUDAN

The *Siyane* cruised above a sea of large, imposing industrial structures. The inner workings were hidden beneath wide swaths of metal exteriors, but warehouse-sized modules fit and stacked against one another like jigsaw pieces, climbing upward into the leaden violet clouds and stair-stepping down into abyssal chasms.

The polar region was devoted exclusively to power: the capture, management, storage and distribution of it. A low-level but grating buzz began to permeate the cabin as they approached their destination.

Alex scowled and rubbed at her earlobes. "Valkyrie, what is that noise?"

'It is generated by a rarefied plasma present in elevated levels here due to the extensive ionization of the air.'

"Lovely—" She looked around, perplexed. "It went away."

Caleb shook his head. "No, it didn't."

'Alex, I adjusted the transmission signal in your auditory vestibular nerve to filter out the unpleasant wavelength. Caleb, I wish I could do the same for you.'

"It's all right, Valkyrie. I've survived far worse."

They alighted on the roof of a fan-shaped building situated at the apex of Three's domain and the literal pole of the planet. Beyond the structure the pervasive darkness rapidly transitioned to shadow then full day.

With the light so too came the solar cells. They were each two hundred fifty-six meters in diameter, and according to Valkyrie were made of pure nanocrystalline silicon. They lined up end-to-end in rows stretching beyond the horizon.

Alex darkened the tint on her helmet as she descended the ramp and wandered toward the edge of the roof, day-side. "Valkyrie, how do we get down to go...?"

"What's wrong?" Caleb materialized at her side almost instantly, and she pointed down.

"Oh."

Beneath them, lining the entrance to the building and all surely 'looking' up at them, stood twelve mechs. All were far more elaborate—and far larger—than any of the mechs they'd previously seen. The only identifying characteristics to distinguish them from one another were differing patterns and colors of crystals adorning their torsos.

The mech on the left end of the line took up a position in front of the others. Three?

It is as I reported. Two organic life forms possessing language and fine motor skills. Their Supreme is a highly sentient synthetic. Though minuscule in size, it is capable of flight, and their presence here indicates this includes space flight.

She grumbled under her breath. "Not our 'Supreme'...." But they'd figured out it was a pointless argument to make; there was no convincing Three that Valkyrie wasn't their master.

Their transmitters squawked in overlapping signals—the attendees were talking over each other. "Valkyrie, are you able to make any sense of this?"

'I am able to separate out the disparate signals, yes. They are mostly asking technical and scientific questions. Like Three, they seem interested in gaining knowledge above all other considerations.'

Caleb eyed the gathered mechs suspiciously. "We're not leaving this roof until they settle down and give us some space. A single one of those machines could crush us, on accident or otherwise."

'I have relayed your concerns to Three. It will attempt to explain the special considerations necessary when interacting with organic life forms.'

"That we're fragile and squishy?"

'Essentially.'

She didn't care for being on display, particularly to a bunch of hyper-strong metal constructs which, among a variety of flaws, didn't comprehend the concept of personal space. On the other hand, the view from the roof was rather awe-inspiring. Cold, hard, with dark and light clashing at the cusp. Imposing. Alien. But awe-inspiring.

Abruptly the mechs began filing into the entrance below. *'Three has asked the others to return to their positions inside. Three's mech will remain here to escort you in.'*

"So, we're back to the question of how we get down."

The answer presented itself in the form of a platform rising to their left. *'A service lift for when work needs to be performed on the upper level.'*

"Convenient." Caleb nodded a somewhat reluctant assent. He was patently on edge and expecting another attack at any minute.

She didn't trust Three either, much less the other Ruda, but she had internalized the fact Valkyrie believed Three at least would not try to harm them again. She and Valkyrie weren't of one mind, on this topic or at times more broadly...but they did share a little mindspace in the middle.

She squeezed Caleb's gloved hand. Together they stepped onto the lift, and it descended to the ground floor.

The pattern of fuchsia crystals adorning the torso of the mech standing in front of them didn't resemble the number 3, but she'd hazard a guess it did somehow symbolize the quaternary three. Why would it be anything else? The Ruda were nothing if not literal.

This way.

The mech spun on its wheels and rolled inside. They followed at a generous distance.

The entrance led into a cavernous, open room; fan-shaped to match the building, it appeared to *be* the majority of the building. Similar to the surface of the planet itself, it was divided into twelve pie slices, eleven of which were occupied by the mechs who had witnessed their arrival. A raised, circular platform dominated the front-center of the room.

The top half of the long wall behind them was transparent, allowing rays of sunlight to stream in and splay across the floor. The presence of natural, visual light was oddly comforting and made the environment feel marginally less alien.

Each of the twelve sectionals was equipped with the ports and capsules they'd been informed were used for small-scale data storage and transmission. At the front of each section was a pedestal upon which sat a single plant encased in protective glass. The features of the plants varied among the attendees, suggesting they were likely specimens from the individual nurseries.

Was it a contest? Were they sharing, or showing off?

The Three mech led them to the platform. A rack rose from beneath the floor, filled with storage units and several objects they hadn't seen before, and a large transparent sheet descended from the ceiling. A display screen? Not surprisingly, there were no apparatuses for sitting.

It was even warmer in here than it had been in Three's complex. She checked with Caleb and together they collapsed their helmets.

The transmitters exploded in a cacophony raucous enough to make the earlier scene outside seem like a casual patio chat. Caleb reached out and grasped her hand firmly.

Be ready to run.

The mechs didn't charge the platform, thankfully. She'd earlier observed they were more elaborately constructed than the models they'd seen so far, and now they used finger-style appendages to tap away at their devices while chattering incessantly.

She blew out a breath through pursed lips, fogging up the breather mask. "This is awkward. I haven't been ogled this much since Primary Ball."

Caleb chuckled quietly and loosened his grip on her hand. "You went to a school dance? Somehow I can't see that."

"I was rebelling against the rebel crowd by not rebelling. It was a thing."

"Oh, I'm sure."

The Three mech pivoted to face them.

The others request general questions.

She indicated understanding. "We'll answer if we can."

Valkyrie informed us organics can cease functioning permanently. When does this occur?

"If you mean how long do we live? Absent a fatal accident or other sudden cause of death? One hundred ninety years, give or take a few decades." The planet's stellar orbit was four hundred fifty-four Galactic days, but as it was tidally locked and they never saw the sun, she doubted the Ruda considered orbits significant. "I don't have a way to convey how long it is as you perceive time."

Caleb smiled a little; forced. "I suspect you would consider it a short span of time to live."

How is stored knowledge uploaded to new instances of you?

His smile relaxed, and she took a subtle step back to cede him the stage. "It's not as simple as that. We do pass knowledge down from generation to generation, but it's done in a gradual, organi—natural way over time. We learn facts, but we also learn social skills—how to interact with one another—and find our place in the world. We discover what we enjoy doing and what we're good at doing. Once we've decided on a profession, we're taught detailed, in-depth information about our chosen topic. So we don't all know everything. We tend to specialize."

How do you replicate?

Alex covered her mouth to stifle a burst of laughter, but due to the breather mask she mostly failed. He glanced over his shoulder at her wearing a feigned glare. She arched an amused eyebrow and gestured for him to *please* answer the question.

"That's, um...one of the most enjoyable aspects of being human, and also one of the most private. I believe the technical details are in the files, so we'll just leave it there."

Wimp.

Coward.

She rolled her eyes and stepped up beside Caleb. "So you asked for data—for knowledge—and we've brought it. Valkyrie was able to encode a vast quantity of information into the storage media you provided."

She reached into the pouch at her hip and produced a rectangular slab of metal while Caleb did the same. "Information on organic anatomy and functionality—not merely on humans but our animals and plants as well—including neural structure and function. Details about our ship propulsion engines—" not superluminal propulsion, but she didn't mention this "—and how they operate."

She paused for effect. "And data on wireless transmission of power across long distances."

The room erupted once again, and she couldn't help but enjoy what was evident enthusiasm on the part of the Ruda.

When it subsided to a manageable level, she loudly cleared her throat. "Before we continue, I have a question. Why do all of you gather to meet? Why bring your mech avatars here at all? Can't your central hubs simply communicate with one another?"

Silence lingered for several seconds, then several more. Had she offended them somehow?

So that we can feel less alone.

'The Ruda were so grateful for the data we provided, they offered extensive files on their own makeup in exchange. It is fascinating reading, learning how an inorganic species developed and evolved. The manner in which they're able to manipulate metals and electronic signals is not only ingenious, it exceeds our own capabilities in several respects.'

"That's nice, Valkyrie." Alex clasped her fingers together and stretched her arms over her head, strolling in a lazy circle through the main cabin. Two and a half hours in the environment suit had left her achy. Sweaty, too, but she'd get clean soon.

Who would've imagined these synthetics, each one stretching a quarter-million square kilometers and composed of trillions of subroutines, would experience such an acute yearning for companionship? They were so stilted, so binary and emotionless…but they had desires. They had dreams.

Caleb emerged from downstairs. "You censored the data like we discussed, right?"

'No information about quantum computing or communication, nothing on superluminal propulsion and limited details on the functioning of the human brain. Nevertheless, the information we provided is certain to keep them busy for some time.'

He came over and began massaging her shoulders. "Maybe in the future they'll be ready for the rest—or maybe they'll make the intellectual leaps on their own, which is how it should be."

'Alex, I believe I will be able to use the information the Ruda provided on their methods for melding metals and electrical currents to improve my integration with the *Siyane*. I wanted to get your permission first, however.'

"What exactly are you thinking about doing?"

'Growing additional quantum circuitry and weaving it into the structure of the ship.'

"When you say the 'structure,' do you mean the interior walls or the hull?"

'Beginning with the interior walls seems like the best way to proceed. If I am successful in that effort, the outer hull should be within my capability.'

That gave her pause. "And how exactly do you plan to weave yourself into the adiamene?"

'One of the reasons adiamene is so strong is because it is both flexible and reactive—and thus adaptable. The Ruda utilize several techniques to embed circuitry in metal that I'm hopeful will be beneficial in this endeavor. In fact, I suspect it will be an easier process with adiamene than with their morion quartz.'

She pondered it for a moment. "Your first priority is to ensure the integrity of the hull. If it shows the slightest sign of weakening in any way whatsoever, you need to stop. In fact, before you begin, develop a contingency plan for repairing any weak points which crop up. Once you're confident you—or we—can reverse any damage, I don't have a problem with it."

'The safety and sanctity of the ship will be my foremost concern. It was so even without you expressing your own. I'll move forward using prudence and circumspection.'

"Also caution, discretion and all the other mindsets that come from exercising good judgment?"

'Unequivocally.' Valkyrie matched the semi-teasing tone her voice had taken on with impressive nuance.

Caleb's lips hovered at her ear. "You know if you let her do this, there may be no going back. You may never be able to evict her from the *Siyane*."

She twisted around to face him. "There was no going back from the day I let her in my head. It's okay."

He smiled, and she shifted back and not-so-subtly encouraged him to resume the massage. "So I suppose we could stay here, and we'd probably learn more about the Ruda and their technology. But Valkyrie's collected a good haul of information on them.

"Some of what they'd show us might be legitimately interesting, but visually I suspect we'd see eternal kilometers of bleak skies and gloomy metal. They know nothing regarding the Metigens and have lost any knowledge they once had of their origins. It feels like maybe we've played this one out?"

"I think so." He complied, gently kneading the tension at the juncture of her neck and shoulders, and she basically melted against him. "I hate to say it, but I wouldn't mind looking for a little more...normal interaction. A little conversation, a little back-and-forth."

"Do you want to go home for a while?" She wasn't inclined to do so, but if he kept massaging her shoulders like this, she'd agree to just about anything he asked of her.

"No, I'm not homesick. We haven't been gone very long. But I'm ready to meet some aliens who walk and talk and eat and sleep, who live in homes—of any kind, I'm not picky—and are born small and grow up."

She chuckled wearily; performing under such intense scrutiny for a lengthy period had been draining. He did have a point. "The odds have to be working in our favor, right? In five of fifty pocket universes we've yet to encounter a humanoid species. There must be some out here. It's only a matter of time until we uncover one."

16

AURORA THESI (PORTAL PRIME)

ENISLE SEVENTEEN (PORTAL: AURORA)

*T*hey had not come to me.

This one inescapable fact haunted my long cycles of solitude. Of exile.

I had expected them to return, seeking answers and enlightenment. I had considered what I might reveal and how best to guide them step by step to greater understanding, and to prepare them for the possibility of greater responsibilities.

But they had not come to me. Instead they had run off blindly to uncover answers on their own, as if they had nothing to fear. But they had everything to fear, which I would have imparted upon them if they had deigned to visit and inquire.

Now, I worried they would not properly comprehend what they discovered. Denied the full picture, they would draw incorrect conclusions. Worse yet given the circumstances, they were not ready to be shown the full picture. They were not ready for the truth. Yet they seemed intent on wresting the truth out of space itself, consequences be damned.

Humans. So foolish, so recklessly ambitious. These two more than most.

I exited the observation vault, where I had spent many hours reviewing recent events in Aurora. As I had disobeyed the Conclave in deactivating the spatial charges, so too had I disobeyed the Humans' demand to cease observation of them.

The scenes were troublesome, to say the least. They struggled to hold on to even their most tenuous gains. They struggled with so much.

About to extend and return to my lake, I paused with the awareness of Lakhes' approach. I had not expected such a visit.

Confident our leader did not bring an invitation to rejoin to the Conclave, I pondered what tidings Lakhes did bring.

The Conclave Praetor arrived in a burst of light and cool flame, adopting the likeness of a *fata* on landing, tall and slight, with wings crafted from ribbons of light.

I evoked a quaver of polite greeting. "Lakhes."

"I know what you've done, Mnemosyne."

Do you? "Are you here to reverse my decision?" *Animam* execution was not a concept Katasketousya entertained, thus there was no greater censure the Conclave could impose upon me than exile. They could not even force me to leave Aurora Thesi.

"No." Lakhes gestured me forward. "But our situation is a delicate one. One wrong move, one mistake, and all we've worked for will be lost."

"Yet all we've worked for will be for naught if we do not recognize when the critical juncture has arrived and act—"

"I *know*, dear friend, which is why I am allowing your actions to stand. For now." Lakhes surveyed the mountains surrounding them. "Enchanting planet. Solum once looked like this, truly?"

"Truly."

"Hyperion says your love for the Humans has made you soft. Weak-willed."

"Hyperion says many things—so many one wonders if there is any space left for thought."

Lakhes allowed the insult of their colleague to pass without affront. "Perhaps. You are aware your recent guests are currently running free through the Mosaic?"

"I am."

"Your doing as well?"

I needed to be careful. "No. I accept responsibility, nevertheless. I am considering going to them. They need proper guidance."

"Do not. Allow them to make their choices, and allow those choices to play out. Better for us to learn their inclinations now, while we control the Mosaic."

I strived not to display any surprise at the response, on any wavelength. "Great dangers await them. If they wander into the wrong Enisle, they will find themselves out of their depth."

"If they are worthy—if they are ready—they will surmount whatever challenges they encounter."

"They are worthy. But they are not ready."

Lakhes radiated a sense of unexpected smugness. "Are you so certain? They've recently intervened rather dramatically in Enisles Eleven and Twenty-Two."

It was becoming more difficult to conceal the surprise, particularly in the presence of one so astute. "In what way?"

Lakhes motioned to the vault as an orb materialized between them. "Come. I will show you."

ᴙ

I considered how to interpret what I had seen, while also considering how to react for Lakhes' benefit. I opted for the minimalist approach: say the minimum required and leave the space free for Lakhes to over-divulge. "The male Human is unpredictable."

"They are both unpredictable. But observe what this unpredictability has produced. Astonishing. It arguably taints Twenty-Two and for certain invalidates the results in Eleven—but I suspect we all knew how Eleven was liable to mature absent this intriguing turn of events."

I signaled my agreement, encouraged by Lakhes' reaction to their intermeddling. "This is why I still believe in Aurora. Two of these Humans, lacking any support and using only their own talents, wits and judgment, changed the courses of two universes in a mere few synodic days."

"You may be correct. It also makes them dangerous. What if the courses they choose are not to our liking?"

Back to the guarded tack after a brief admittance of optimism. Alas. "Clearly they are dangerous. We have always known this, Lakhes. If their dangerous nature precludes their use, then why did we begin this experiment at all? If we are not willing to accept the danger intrinsic to our cause, then why begin the *cause* at all?"

"Fair questions, dear friend. As I said, it is for precisely this reason I will allow the...derivation to continue. Realize, however—time is growing short for your Humans. If the other members of the Conclave have not discovered these interlopers yet, they soon will. When this happens, I will do what I can, but I must be cautious."

Ahh, Lakhes. Ever the diplomat, ever the strategist. "I understand. When this happens, I, too, will do what I can."

"Was that a threat, Mnemosyne?"

"Never, *dear friend*. I am but an Analystae. A watcher."

"Your false modesty may placate Hyperion, but I have known you for nine aeons. We will talk again when the time is right."

I observed Lakhes' departure, then diffused over the mountains. What, I wondered, would be the 'right time'? The right time was all too often far too late.

Be vigilant my Humans, mei ferocia novicia. *I fear for you.*

PART IV:

SERIATIM, SERIATE

"He understood that these were extraordinary times, and if their old life was ever restored to them, nothing would be the same."

— *Ann Patchett*

Portal: Aurora

(Milky Way)

17

ROMANE

"Your team killed eight Federation civilians. Regardless of the merit of your claim to jurisdiction, if any, this transgression must be addressed."

"We regret the tragic accident, and we are willing to consider reparations to the families. But the details of the altercation have no bearing on the issue of jurisdiction before this Board. The Alliance triggered discovery rights ten days earlier, and the proper filings were made with the authorities—"

James Abbate, the Federation representative appointed to the Inter-Governmental Conflict Resolution Board, cut off the man sitting opposite him in a crisp hand motion. "With *Alliance* authorities. The Federation does not receive notice of such filings, Consul. Further, we made our own declaration eight days earlier."

"With *Federation* authorities. The simple fact is, the Alliance engineering regiment had previously placed nine buoys, which were broadcasting our jurisdiction to every vessel in the system."

"And our team had placed five. This is not an argument you can win."

The Alliance Consul leaned back in his chair and sighed. "Look. There are no procedures in place to adjudicate this kind of conflict. Clearly we need to institute them, and we will. But we should recognize all of us are still learning how to live together and act accordingly. What if we offered you..." the man made a show of considering the matter "...06,500,000 as payment for the rights to the system?"

Abbate scoffed. "The Senecan Federation is not some two-bit corp you can throw scraps at to make them go away."

"And I did not mean to imply it was. Merely an opening proposal. Is ↄ15,000,000 a more palatable sum?"

Ƈ

SENECA

CAVARE: SENECAN FEDERATION HEADQUARTERS

Graham Delavasi watched Federation Chairman Aristide Vranas grumble in disgust, but also a trace of amusement. In the holo the Federation rep pretended to consider the new amount as he secretly conferred with Vranas.

"No. This isn't about money, it's about principle. We're not selling it to them. It would set a precedent I have no interest in setting." A pause. "Yes, that's our position."

The Federation rep leaned forward in preparation for declining the offer. Vranas scowled at Graham. "This is how it starts. Today, we're squabbling over a single planet. A year from now, we'll be shooting at each other again. Hell, we're already shooting at each other—that's what prompted this farce of a negotiation in the first place."

"*Or* this could simply be what 'peace' between two sovereign governments looks like. After all, we are sitting at a table negotiating, which is a far cry from storming blockades."

"True. Perhaps peace turns out to be messy in the details."

"Seems likely." Graham straightened up in the chair. "So I've got a new guy coming onto my team today."

"Someone I should know about, I assume? It's not as though you inform me of every new Division hire."

Graham sent him the file. Five seconds later Vranas' eyes widened. "You're kidding me, right?"

"No. You know, I almost never play jokes on you anymore. Eventually you need to stop assuming it's my purpose."

Vranas ignored the quip. "Aren't you worried he's a double agent?"

Of course he was a double agent—but not in a way Graham worried could jeopardize state security. He kept the nuance to himself, however. "Normally, I would be. Normally I wouldn't hire him to begin with. But he saved all their—and our—asses, and now the Alliance has screwed him over royally."

"What do you mean he saved...he was the Alliance contact who helped you take down the Aguirre Conspiracy, wasn't he?"

"And uncover the Metigen agents. I trust him. Most importantly, he's something damn rare to find these days—an honest man."

Vranas shrugged. "There are obviously a few areas he shouldn't be granted access to, but you know what they are. Otherwise, if you say he's good, who am I to argue?"

He chuckled. "The Chairman of the Senecan Federation?"

"Ah, yes, that's right. Well, in this instance I'll refrain."

Graham stood and waved at the holo. "Then I'll leave you to this shit-show and go welcome him to Seneca."

CAVARE

When Graham arrived at the cafe, he found Will Sutton sitting alone at a booth in the rear.

Will stood and shook his hand. "Richard stepped outside to handle an issue with the house in Seattle. He'll be back in a minute."

Graham was glad Richard hadn't reconsidered at the last minute. "Everything go smoothly in setting up the apartment?"

"It did. The place will suit us until we locate something more permanent."

"How's he holding up?"

Will grimaced. "Publicly? Like the soldier he is. Privately? It's been rough on him. This is all...hard. But thank you for giving him this opportunity—both of us this opportunity."

"Hell, the Alliance doesn't realize what they let slip away. Their loss, my gain. Also, I've been through two deputies since you left. The office is a bloody mess."

Will's attention darted over Graham's shoulder and remained there. "We'll get it straightened out, don't worry."

Graham turned to greet Richard, and he couldn't help but smile as he did so. It wasn't fair what had happened to his friend, but he hadn't been lying—it *was* fortunate for him. "Richard Navick. It is damn good to see you again."

Richard returned the smile, if somewhat rigidly, and gestured to the booth. "And you." They settled into the booth opposite one another, then Richard took a deep, almost exaggerated breath. "So, Director Delavasi, what do you imagine I can do for you?"

"What's this 'Director' shit?"

"If you're going to be my boss…."

"Only in the technicalities." Graham clasped his hands on the table. "Special Advisor to the Director. You don't report to anyone else, and I use "report" in the loosest sense possible. You investigate whatever catches your interest, one-offs and special circumstances."

"And Earth Alliance matters?"

"Those might on occasion be the 'special circumstances.' If relations get irritable with the Alliance and you want to share any insights you have off the record, I won't stop you. But I also won't demand it of you. It's not part of your job description."

Richard dragged a hand through hair that had grown past his usual military close-crop. His brow furrowed up as he stared at his glass, both hands wrapping tight around it.

Will leaned in close and whispered in Richard's ear; his chin bobbed in the tiniest acknowledgment. He looked up, holding Graham's gaze intently as he took a deliberate sip of his drink then set the glass down. "All right. I accept."

Graham exhaled in relief. It was guaranteed to become complicated in the trenches, but he was being forthright as to his expectations. And by expecting little, something told him he'd receive a great deal more.

The waitress arrived with a tapas platter, and he waited until she had departed to respond. "Let's eat some lunch, then I'll take you over to Division and give you the tour."

ℛ

MILITARY HEADQUARTERS

Morgan Lekkas tromped across the atrium outside Stanley's lab. What was taking Gianno so long? She'd said she'd be here within the hour. It had been...forty-nine minutes. Damn, it felt like hours. Everything felt interminable these days, as if time had slowed merely to prolong her torture.

She glowered at the door to the lab. She wanted to hate Stanley, wanted to blame him for shackling her to the ground. But try as she might she couldn't hate him. He hadn't asked for this either. He didn't despise it quite as much as she, but she recognized her frustration was bleeding into him nonetheless. It was making him jittery and erratic, which in turn made her more jittery and erratic. She hadn't meant to start an endless negative feedback loop, but she couldn't seem to find a way to bring an end to it.

Field Marshal Gianno walked in at five minutes before the hour. "You wanted to see me, Commander?"

She straightened into a semblance of parade rest. Muscle memory. "Yes, Marshal. I want to respectfully request—I need to get out of here, ma'am. I need to be in the cockpit—*really* in the cockpit, live and in the flesh. I signed up to Noetica to save the galaxy, not to be a lab rat."

Gianno nodded thoughtfully. "And you did, for which we're all indebted to you. Let me ask you something. What do you imagine you would do if you were to return to active duty in the Southern Fleet? We're at peace—with the Alliance, with the Metigens, with everyone of consequence. There is no war to fight."

"So? I'd fly patrols, same as I did before. Drill and train my flights. Take out the occasional pirate or merc. Be on alert for new threats."

"Do I detect a trace of bloodlust, Commander?"

"Ma'am." She'd begun to traipse around again; she forced herself still. "I've always had a trace of bloodlust—and I've always kept it under control until it could be directed at an appropriate target. I'm not a threat. I'm a soldier and a pilot."

"You're a Prevo."

"Yes, ma'am. About that. I'd not be one, if it meant I would be able to return to active duty."

For a second Gianno looked taken aback, but she quickly covered it behind her usual unflappable demeanor. "My understanding is it's not as simple as deciding not to be one any longer."

"I realize it isn't, ma'am, but surely it's doable. Listen, I don't bear Stanley any ill will—he kind of grows on you, even if he's a bit of a dunce and still horrifically naive. But I don't want the rest of my life to be lived in a lab."

The Marshal arrested her gaze on Morgan with such intensity she obeyed the irresistible compulsion to meet it. "I knew your mother—did I ever mention that?"

Morgan frowned. "No, ma'am...you didn't." Her mother had died in a test flight accident when Morgan was ten years old. She'd been a military pilot as well and away from home for long stretches of time, so much so Morgan had never felt as if she truly knew her mother.

"I did. She served honorably in the First Crux War. You're a lot like her in many ways—hot-headed, willful, and a damn talented pilot." She paused. "Commander, Noetica is producing groundbreaking advances for the Federation and for all of humanity. It's crucial the program continue."

"With respect, ma'am, *Stanley* is producing groundbreaking advances. He and Annie, together with Valkyrie before she left. You don't need me—he doesn't need me."

Gianno's expression solidified into resoluteness. "Well, whether he needs you or not, he is part of you, and you part of him.

There is no separation, Commander, a fact which was made clear to you when you signed up for Noetica. I sympathize with your discomfort, but that is, as they say, the way it is. You are serving your Federation in more ways than you can appreciate by staying right here."

Morgan's eyes widened in disbelief, but she clamped her jaw shut with vicious force to prevent the words screaming through her mind from coming out of her mouth. She swallowed the most damning of the words, then responded in a flat tone. "Yes, ma'am. In that case, I'll...be in the lab. Forever."

18

EARTH

Devon was elbow deep in one of Annie's quantum boxes, installing an improved module the bureaucracy had finally approved for use, when the sound of footsteps began echoing in the lab.

His connection with Annie was open, and he paused to take in the details. The steps sounded...not hesitant, but careful. Slow and purposeful. There were four distinct footfalls—two individuals, men judging by the weight driving each stride, and they moved in concert, matching their pace to one another.

This being a military installation, none of those attributes were particularly unusual. Devon finished threading a strand of photal fibers together and climbed to his feet. It was late in the evening—he checked the time and discovered it was in fact far later than he'd realized—and other than security most of the Special Projects personnel were off-duty.

"Hello?"

Two men rounded the corner of a row of server racks near the front of the large room. They wore dark business suits, not military uniforms, and serious countenances. "Mr. Reynolds?"

He eyed the men suspiciously. "How did you get in here?"

The one on the left responded. "We have authorization. We're consultants from the Assembly Military Oversight Committee. We'd like to talk to you about Project Noetica."

Devon, Assembly members serving on that Committee are aware of Noetica. However, it would be a violation of thirteen regulations and four laws for consultants or anyone not an elected representative to be so informed.

He hoped the dim lighting in the lab aided his poor attempt at a poker face. "I'm sure I don't know what Noetica is. I just work on Project ANNIE. And I'd need to clear discussing anything with the Director of Special Projects or Admiral Solovy first."

They continued approaching him in their careful manner. He had the errant thought that they moved the way 'heavies' did in spy thriller vids. It led him to step backward in increased wariness.

"We understand. Why don't we go out into the lab's office and you can contact one of them."

Devon didn't need Annie's voice modulation analysis to recognize the man was lying. If he wanted to contact someone, he could do it from right here. He retreated an additional step; his heel thudded into the rear wall.

"I need to finish what I was working on. I shouldn't leave it half-done. I mean, look! The insulation panel's still off and everything." He motioned with great fanfare in the direction of the open module.

Their attention flickered to where he pointed, an ingrained reaction to the gesture.

He lunged to his left and ran.

The lab was a maze of floor-to-ceiling server racks, hardware modules and power allocators. He knew the layout intimately, and there were precious few routes through it to the front door. The back door provided even less help—a dead-end of cooled power generators and supply closets.

Their footfalls now thudded loudly behind him, all the subtlety of their entrance abandoned in the name of speed. *Show me where they are, Annie.*

Thermal imaging of the lab appeared in an overlay of his vision. Annie filtered out the power flows, leaving his slender signature and the two far bulkier signatures of his pursuers. They had split up; one trailed too closely behind him while the other moved toward the front of the room to cut him off. The thermal imaging couldn't pick up weapons, but each held an arm out in a manner suggesting they had drawn Daemons.

He veered down the next aisle then darted through a small gap into yet another aisle, buying himself time by crossing the breadth of the suddenly tiny, cramped lab. The second man now blocked the door. There was no way out.

Annie, I need a weapon!

Hurl one of my quantum boxes at him. I do not mind.

He'd have laughed if he wasn't panicked and running for his life—oh! *Release all the stability clamps.*

Done.

The first man was now directly behind him and gaining. He swung around the corner of the end of the row and threw his shoulder into the tall rack. He wasn't a strong guy—every now and then someone called him scrawny—but the jolt of momentum sent all the servers on the shelf tumbling off the other side.

The man yelped as they crashed down onto him, then lurched into the shelving on the next row. Without the clamps that held the structure steadfastly to the ceiling and each module in its place, the rack teetered, sending modules sliding off of shelves to pitch to the floor. Lighter and even less stable now, the rack toppled into the next row like a domino. Unfortunately, that was the last row, and the cascade of crashing racks and equipment came to a premature end against the rear wall.

But the man now lay prone amid a pile of hardware, moaning, so maybe it was enough.

The tactic wasn't going to work a second time, though, for too much open space stretched between the front-most row and the door. He still needed a weap—

Move!

He saw it as Annie did, but his weak, slow physical limbs simply could not react fast enough. The blast from the stunner landed square between his shoulder blades.

A prickly tingling sensation spread from the impact point outward, racing along his arms and down his spine. As his legs collapsed beneath him he managed to turn enough to see the arm and hand of the man trapped beneath Annie's hardware pointing the stunner at him.

Devon, disconnect from me.

No, I don't want—

A hand grasped his shoulder and roughly rolled him onto his stomach. The second man? He tried to fight, tried to crawl away, but his body no longer obeyed his commands.

Do it now. Please.

Okay. I'm sorry, Annie.

He felt the collar of his shirt being yanked down and a wrap shoved onto the base of his neck. Then everything went dark.

ᴙ

Miriam rushed into the suite housing Project ANNIE one notch below a run. She was stepping into a crisis to be sure, but the immediacy of the emergency had come and gone.

The premises breach alert from Security had woken her at 0120; by the time she'd reached her vehicle, MPs had detained the intruders. It was now 0145, and Major Lange was waiting on her in the office outside the main lab.

"Admiral." He gestured to the glass divider separating the small meeting room and the office. "Two men are in custody. They claim to be official representatives of the Assembly Military Oversight Committee and clerks of the Chairman. Their credentials check out, including ostensible sanction from the Committee to enter EASC Special Projects and disconnect Mr. Reynolds from the Artificial."

"I never authorized their entry, much less any action with respect to Mr. Reynolds."

"No one at EASC did, Admiral." He handed her a small disk. "Here's the directive issued by the Committee. It appears they believe they had the inherent authority to grant themselves entry and freedom of action."

"They are mistaken. Treat these two with proper decorum, but continue to detain them. File a formal complaint with the Assembly and misdemeanor charges with the court. Go a few rounds with their counsel negotiating the terms of release before you let them go, and if the Assembly is too unreasonable, charge them with criminal felonies before releasing them. Under no circumstances whatsoever should you agree, explicitly or implicitly, with their assertion the Committee has the authority to circumvent EASC security protocols in any way."

"Understood."

"Where's Mr. Reynolds?"

Lange pointed deeper into the suite. "In the lab. We've got a medic trying to take a look at him, but he's not cooperating. He took a stunner hit and is bruised up at a minimum. He put up quite a fight, though, as best he could."

She considered the intruders through the glass. One of them sported a long cut on his cheek, and blood still trickled down his temple from a gash on his skull. He also held his left arm against his chest at an awkward angle. None of the wounds had been treated.

"So I see. Do we know what they did to him?"

"They claim they connected an external interface to his eVi cybernetic access ports, which ran a pre-prepared ware routine. It forced a disconnection in the quantum link to ANNIE and installed a firewall preventing it from being reconnected."

"Did they say how they came into possession of such a routine?"

"Classified Military Oversight Committee consultants."

Her jaw locked grimly. "I don't believe 'classified' means what they believe it means, Major."

"No, ma'am. We'll find out who they are."

"I'm certain you will. Carry on. I'm going to see to Mr. Reynolds."

ℛ

The lights in the lab had been raised to full strength, giving the room a harshly antiseptic appearance and revealing far more disarray than she had expected.

The lab was nothing short of a disaster. The far left third of the server racks were toppled to the floor and the extensive equipment they had held was scattered haphazardly across the floor. She shuddered to contemplate how much damage Annie had suffered, but she had to prioritize. Devon still came first.

She followed the muffled sound of voices and found him sitting on the edge of a table along the far right wall. A lieutenant was trying to run a medical scanner over his forehead, with minimal success.

"For the forty-seventh time, there's nothing wrong with my brain! Could you please stop that—" he spotted her and waved her over around the shoulder of the medic "—Admiral Solovy, would you tell him I'm fine?"

She regarded Devon critically. His pupils were dilated despite the brightness of the room, and several blood vessels in his eyes had burst. A thin sheen of sweat gave his neck and face a faint glisten. His entire body vibrated, and his hands and feet twitched erratically—possibly a side-effect of the stunner blast, but she suspected a different cause.

"I'll be happy to do so, as soon as *I'm* convinced you're fine. I might be convinced sooner if you would allow the lieutenant to examine you."

He squeezed his eyes shut with a grimace. "He won't find anything wrong. What's wrong with me no instrument will see."

"You mean the loss of your connection to Annie. Can you tell me what happened?"

His gaze fixated on her, as much as it could with his eyes darting around anxiously. "I was installing some new quantum boxes when these two goons walked in—they must have hacked the door, because it was locked like it was supposed to be. They said they were consultants from a..." he blinked "...Military Oversight Committee? Yeah, that was it. They said they wanted to 'talk to me' about Noetica, but then they tried to corner me. I ran, but it's not like there was any way out of here."

He frowned at the destruction in the back of the lab. "Oh, um, sorry about the mess. Annie and I tried to take them out—would've succeeded if it weren't for the damn stunner. Once I was down, one of them forced that thing—" he jabbed a finger at a neck wrap interface sitting on the table beside him "—onto my ports. I blacked out. When I woke up, they were nowhere to be seen, I was on the floor and Annie was gone."

'I'm not gone, Devon.'

"You know what I—!" He wiped sweat off his brow and brought his voice back under control. "You know what I mean, Annie. Surely you feel it, too?"

'I do.'

At least Annie retained basic speech and thought capabilities. At the moment Miriam would take whatever good news presented itself.

"Did you catch the goons? I have a few things I want to say to them."

"Major Lange has the two men in custody. I don't think it's a good idea for you to speak to them right now." She looked at the medic, who gave her a prevaricating shrug.

"Devon, we're going to take you over to Medical and get you checked out more thoroughly. Dr. Canivon has been visiting Commander Lekkas on Seneca, but she's on her way back now. She'll be here in a couple of hours." She typically addressed him by his proper name, but he needed comfort, not formalities. Providing comfort to another was hardly her strongest skill, but there was no one else to do it.

"I don't *want* to go to Medical—I want to give those guys black eyes, then I want to be reconnected to Annie."

"Unfortunately, I can't allow the first, and as for the second…we'll have to wait and see what Dr. Canivon says."

He crossed his arms over his chest. "I'll wait here."

She sighed. "Annie, please tell Devon he should go to Medical. We need to ensure this ware routine didn't cause any neural damage."

'Admiral Solovy is right, Devon. I'm worried about you. What if they hurt you?'

"You know damn well they hurt me!" His sagging, defeated posture belied the fervor of the outburst.

Miriam moved forward and grasped him firmly by the shoulders. "Devon, I need you to listen to me. I promise to do everything I can to fix this, but you have to let me help you."

He stared at her, eyes wide and bloodshot, and mumbled a weak agreement.

SEATTLE (OLYMPIC REGIONAL SPACEPORT)

Abigail exited the massive interstellar transport amidst a throng of first-class passengers and made her way as rapidly as possible toward the main ORS terminal.

A military transport had been offered to her for the trip to and from Seneca, though such voyages were still being made only on an as-needed basis. Commercial travel to Seneca was brisk, however, since being reopened after the end of the Metigen War, and she'd opted for the private transport. She was not military, and she sought what small opportunities she happened upon to remind EASC brass of that truth.

In point of fact, she hadn't strictly needed to travel to Seneca at all—with Annie's help the routine examination of Commander Lekkas could have been conducted virtually. But since no one at EASC save Devon understood the intricacies of Noetica, she'd been able to wave her hands, mutter 'Prevo details,' and everyone had simply nodded blankly.

It was good to get away for a few days. She hadn't dared depart the Sol system in the last month, once she and Vii's work on Mia and Meno reached a critical juncture and Mia's awakening neared. But the effort was a success, and the woman exhibited all the signs of a full recovery.

Yet the instant Abigail *had* left the Sol system, disaster struck.

She was on the way back from Seneca when Admiral Solovy's comm came in. Details of the attack soon followed, and she'd spent the remainder of the trip working remotely with Annie to understand the mechanism of attack and the damage it had caused from the Artificial's perspective; evaluation of the damage to Devon would have to wait for her return to EASC.

The incident was bringing back her worst memories of the Alliance bureaucracy, reminding her of several reasons she'd chosen to resign over a decade earlier and pursue more productive, fulfilling work on Sagan. Bureaucrats were so eager to pile rules, regulations and 'safety mandates' up into roadblocks to stop anything which even resembled progress, all in the name of increasing their power.

She remained with the Alliance for now because she was heading the most cutting-edge Artificial experiment—no, the most cutting-edge experiment, period—ever to be conducted, and because she'd become rather protective of Devon and Mia. Less so Commander Lekkas, partially due to distance and partially due to the fact the woman had not fully embraced her new nature.

But now the bureaucrats were coming for her and everything she'd created, as they always, inevitably, did.

She spotted a kiosk with no line and quickly stopped to purchase a latte, then took the central passage toward the exit.

The route was crowded, as was typically the case no matter the hour, and she scowled when a tall, sweaty man jostled her as he hurried past her at a jog. She needed a shower, and now she needed a change of clothes…but she needed to see Devon first.

She also needed to begin making contingency plans that would allow her to preserve the data and research behind the advancements Noetica had achieved. No bureaucrat was going to erase what she accomplished—

Another traveler bumped into her from behind, sending her stumbling forward. An arm reached out to steady her. She mumbled a 'thank you' and tried to pull away, but the man held her arm fast. Startled, she looked up at him just as she felt a sting at the base of her neck.

Injection.

Her eVi identified it as a muscle relaxant and neural inhibitor as the substance began speeding toward her motor cortex.

Emergency countermeasures.

Her veins flooded with stimulants as firewalls propagated through her cybernetics. She tried again to yank away—then a virus that had piggybacked on the injection crashed her eVi. A new wave of inhibitor coursed through her nervous system.

She blinked.

"Easy there, Dr. Canivon. You'll be able to stand and walk—with a little help from us—but you won't be fighting back any more." She was vaguely cognizant of being propelled forward then to the right, into the corridor which led...to the private hangars? She couldn't remember. She felt sleepy, dreamy, while a tiny portion of her brain screamed to fight and scrambled for some additional defense to deploy against the attack.

"Where...what...?"

The man on her left gazed down at her, fuzzy and indistinct. "We're going to take a ride."

19

EARTH

It took all of Miriam's considerable self-restraint to refrain from barging into Brennon's office until he was free to see her. Luckily for her and him both, it wasn't a long wait.

She waited until the door closed behind her before leveling a sharp glare at the Prime Minster. "Let me ask you something—do I have any power at all?"

"When we are at war, Fleet Admiral, you have the most consequential of power. When we are at peace, perhaps a bit less. Is there a particular grievance you have?"

He appeared unfazed by her challenge; the man was strikingly cool, a cypher behind a statesman's smile.

Their relations had been somewhat frosted since the end of the Metigen War, since she'd learned he was not only aware of but had approved Hervé's implantation of the Kill Switch in the Prevos. True, he ultimately didn't call for its use, but he'd been playing all the angles.

Objectively she acknowledged it was not merely a political choice but arguably a logical one. Subjectively it raised her hackles that he hadn't trusted her to handle the situation, whatever the situation might become.

"There are many particular grievances I have, but the pertinent one today is that agents of the Military Oversight Committee *broke into* EASC Special Projects. They held Devon Reynolds against his will and blocked his connection to Annie."

Genuine surprise flared in his eyes. So he hadn't known? Good. "Is he alive?"

"He is. They had the slightest foresight to sedate him and take minimal safety precautions, presumably lest they be accused of murder. He is not well, however, as you can imagine. In a small blessing, security arrived and detained the intruders before they succeeded in also taking control of or destroying the Artificial, thus they were not able to irrevocably compound their error."

She paused, but not long enough to allow him to respond. "Oh—and in what I'm sure is a completely unrelated matter, the Ways and Means Committee has decided the military will be cutting its supply of adiamene to the Federation to four percent of our production. File it away as a grievance for tomorrow."

"I'm glad to hear Mr. Reynolds is in good health. I suspect Ways and Means is attempting a lateral exertion of pressure on the Federation to force it in the direction of reunification—if they rejoin the Alliance they can have all the adiamene they want. Tell me, Admiral...did you know our friends Chairman Vranas and Field Marshal Gianno were involved in provoking the First Crux War?"

Miriam sucked in a breath. It was a loaded and leading statement delivered out of left field. What was he playing at? "I did."

The silence lingered for a ponderous moment; he seemed content to wait for a more fulsome response from her. She schooled her expression. "We don't always get to choose our allies. There are times when we must take them as we find them."

"I agree. To the extent it matters, which may turn out to be very little extent at all, I happen to like the Chairman."

She stared out the expansive windows. Forcing herself to work with Vranas and Eleni while knowing they had played central roles in the Senecan revolution had been...difficult. At the time she'd brushed it aside as the price of their survival. Later, it had been harder—harder because as Brennon liked Vranas, so too was she discovering she rather liked Eleni. But that was months ago, and a trial she'd already faced and moved past.

"I refuse to believe it won't matter, Prime Minister, for it matters to us, and we were and are the ones in the trenches." She quickly pivoted to the more practical issue. "Regardless, so long as Chairman Vranas and Field Marshal Gianno are in charge, the members of the Ways and Means Committee are deluding themselves if they think there is any chance for reunification, amicable or otherwise."

Brennon smiled, possibly in mild amusement; he was facing the windows so she couldn't be positive. "You don't believe people can change, Admiral? It *has* been twenty-three years since the war ended."

Miriam gave the question due consideration. It had in fact been such a very, very long time. Tragic that it felt as if it were yesterday in all the ways which mattered. "I believe they can, given sufficient cause. We've given them no cause to change their inclinations."

"We fought and won a war alongside them."

She nodded. "Then immediately went back to our old ways. Individuals might be able to change, but I'm beginning to doubt institutions' ability to do so."

"Yes, speaking of that. I hope you recognize my position is the epitome of 'weak executive' in the best of circumstances, of which these are not."

"You're telling me you can't stop Winslow from invading EASC territory on her whim."

"Regrettably, I am."

"You realize she is after your job."

"I do. All the more reason why I am unable to prevent such incursions."

She was silent for several seconds, genuinely at a loss for words. "I see."

He faced her with surprising vehemence. "I'm not sure you do. If you want me in this office after the next election instead of Pamela Winslow—and I promise you, you do—then you must understand: I cannot run around imposing executive authority from above on her committee. Politics is not governance, Admiral. One wins elections while the other wins us wars and secures our freedoms. I don't like it and neither should you, but it is the way of the world."

"With respect, Prime Minister, that is bullshit." There she was, cursing again. "We need to—"

"It is not 'bullshit,' Admiral. Here is the reality we face. Your daughter may be the savior of us all, but she is also a rebel and possibly an insurgent, certainly a loose cannon and now beyond our control. Your close friend and one of our highest-ranking intelligence officers is a cuckold to a Senecan spy—it's not an insult, for I am assuredly a cuckold and then some to my wife, but she is not a spy for a rival government.

"My strongest political adversary has unlimited funds and the ear of both powerful anti-Artificial interests and a sizable minority of the voting public. Our supposed allies in the Federation are former revolutionaries with Alliance blood permanently staining their hands."

He now wore a dark frown. "Suffice it to say neither one of us is in an advantaged position right now. See to your Prevo—or former Prevo, such as it is—and feel free to spar with Mrs. Winslow and the Military Oversight Committee using whatever tools you're able to wield, but I cannot and will not help you. Not this time."

R

Miriam watched the security cam footage, then returned to the beginning and studied it a second time. Two men wearing hooded tunics could be seen making physical contact with Dr. Canivon in a crowded passage at ORS, followed by an almost imperceptible stumble by the woman. The three of them took the corridor to the charter hangars. At this point the crowd thinned out enough to see the men were supporting Canivon and guiding her steps. They boarded a private transport without fanfare, and it departed minutes later.

She glanced at Major Lange's holo. "How long ago?"

"Two hours, forty minutes. Medical staff alerted Security when she didn't arrive for a scheduled meeting to review Mr. Reynolds' tests. The vessel is registered to a legitimate shipping company on Romane, but the ownership chain ends at a shell corporation out of Pandora. We're investigating, but it's likely a dead end."

"What about the assailants?"

Lange shook his head. "Even with the hoods partially obscuring their faces we were able to pull sixty-eight and seventy-four percent facial scans, but as is so often the case with non-citizen mercenaries, they don't match any individuals in our databases. I filed a request for Federation authorities to run the scans through their databases. I haven't heard back yet, but I'm not optimistic they'll find anything."

Satisfied she could glean no further information from the footage, she closed the aural and paced deliberately around the room. She'd still been at EA Headquarters when she received the Level V alert from Lange and had commandeered an empty meeting room on the third floor.

Careening from one crisis to the next...she needed to consider the larger implications of Brennon's declarations, but instead she had to focus on the here and now. Triage. "Why didn't she have a security escort?"

In a rare departure from his consummately professional demeanor, Lange's pale blue eyes twinkled in passing amusement. "You *have* met the doctor? What she wants, she tends to get—and what she wanted was a private, off-the-record trip."

"Point conceded, Major. What's the status of the investigation?"

"Every port in settled space that recognizes EA authority has been provided the vessel's serial number designation and description, in addition to visuals of Dr. Canivon and the two assailants. Sol sensors are sweeping for the vessel, but it's probable they violated the Main Asteroid Belt superluminal travel ban and are well out of range. Forensics is scraping the docking bay for any trace evidence which might give us IDs on the perpetrators. As for who's behind it? The suspect list isn't long but it is problematic."

"I've no doubt." She briefly debated whether to ask, but if there was any possibility.... "Is there a chance this was the work of the same group who assaulted Mr. Reynolds?"

His voice lowered. "The Oversight Committee? I haven't seen anything to suggest so as of yet."

"If you do, inform me before pursuing it. Has anyone told Mr. Reynolds?"

"No ma'am, though he is starting to inquire as to her whereabouts."

"Brush him off. I'll tell him." She wouldn't wish that conversation on even her worst enemy. "I'll be back on the Island in an hour."

20

SENECA

CAVARE

Informants liked to meet on the riverfront promenade because it was always busy and often crowded, and because loitering was an acceptable pastime there. Graham was nevertheless surprised Laure Ferre was familiar enough with Cavare to request it as a meeting location, seeing as he'd resided on Krysk for the last twenty years. The man must have done his homework.

Ferre had been paranoid and edgy for several months, as he became increasingly convinced Olivia Montegreu intended to kill him for setting her up—so paranoid he refused to talk over even the most secure of comms. Graham had pointed out if Ms. Montegreu wanted the man dead he would already be so, but the observation fell on deaf ears.

As leader of the Zelones cartel, Montegreu had claimed the majority of Ferre's 'business' interests for herself in the wake of the victory over the Metigens. Ferre had spent the time since then scraping what was left into the beginnings of a new enterprise. And serving as an informant. Only on matters affecting Federation security—Graham wasn't interested in petty crime or low-level smuggling. Krysk law enforcement would be livid if they knew Division was allowing Ferre to operate unimpeded in exchange for occasional tips, but they didn't know.

He found Ferre leaning against one of the multiple standing tables surrounding a popular eatery kiosk and overlooking the Fuori River. The darkening sky left the man in shadow just outside the nearest lights, and music wafting in from farther down the promenade ensured their conversation wasn't overheard.

Graham walked up and casually propped his elbows on the table. "You should try the Korean barbeque at the kiosk before you leave. It's practically authentic."

"I'll keep that in mind." Tension radiated off Ferre like heat waves off paving; his eyes surreptitiously darted around, scanning for waiting assassins. The behavior was subtle—the man did present an outwardly calm demeanor—but unmistakable if you paid attention.

Graham chuckled under his breath. "You keep on like this and you're going to die of a stroke long before one of Montegreu's people gets you."

"I'll worry about my own health, thank you. I'll also be brief—my sources inform me Montegreu is behind the kidnapping of Dr. Abigail Canivon on Earth. Something to do with this rumored new breed of Artificial."

The odds of Ferre telling the truth were high, if only because Canivon's kidnapping hadn't yet hit the news feeds. It hadn't hit anything, in point of fact—Graham wouldn't know about it if it weren't for a directive straight from Chairman Vranas to scrupulously watch everything related to Noetica, on Earth and elsewhere.

As for the 'new breed of Artificial,' the fact that the truth—the new breed was *humans*—hadn't leaked out was nothing short of a miracle. A miracle whose time appeared to be coming to an end, as it appeared Olivia Montegreu knew the truth. Why kidnap the doctor behind Noetica, if not to become a Prevo herself?

The notion chilled Graham to the bone. Montegreu was extremely dangerous and powerful on her own; couple her with an Artificial, even a tiny private one, and she became a far more formidable threat.

"How certain are your sources? I assume you're referring to people on the inside, but how high? She and her organization are quite secretive."

"High enough. She couldn't be so secretive this time—snatching the woman off the streets of Seattle took extensive resources."

"Where did they take the doctor?"

"Back to New Babel. That's all I know."

"I sincerely hope this information isn't six hours old." If Ferre's paranoia had led him to waste critical time traveling to Seneca solely so he could share the news in person, it may be too late.

"No more than two hours. I was in the area."

Time to end the meeting, then. "If it checks out, you're good."

Ferre scoffed. "And if it doesn't check out?"

"You'd be wise not to send me on any additional fool's errands, lest I decide to reconsider our arrangement."

"As if I don't have enough problems." Ferre turned and vanished into the crowd.

Graham gave it five seconds, then pushed off the table and walked fifteen meters to where Richard sat at a proper table and eased into the chair across from him. "Ferre says Montegreu took Dr. Canivon. You and I both realize that doesn't mean anything good, so you'd better tell Admiral Solovy. Offer our services if there's any way we can assist, though I expect she'll decline. I'll see what I can do for corroboration."

Richard stared at him, the muscles in his jaw flexing, almost as if he was about to pretend he didn't know Graham knew he was sharing information with the Alliance Fleet Admiral.

Finally he nodded. "Right." He pushed the beer sitting in front of him toward Graham. "In that case, feel free to finish my drink for me."

ℛ

Richard slipped inside his skycar—he was forcing himself to use it instead of the levtrams when possible in order to familiarize himself with the city—and sent Miriam an encrypted pulse the instant the door closed.

We've received information indicating it was agents of Olivia Montegreu who kidnapped Dr. Canivon.

The response was a dozen or so seconds in coming; given recent events he imagined she was rather busy.

That is...less than ideal. Confidence level?

Reasonable to high. The intel came from the guy who gave us Montegreu for the Aguirre Conspiracy, but second-hand. Delavasi has a few people inside Zelones, and he's going to try to get some corroboration. Talk to Vera Yanez down at HQ in San Francisco—she also has a plant or two in the cartel.

I will. Did this source have any information on the doctor's whereabouts?

Only New Babel, but it should mean the main Zelones compound. Montegreu keeps her core resources close at hand.

True. We need to be as confident as possible, since mounting an incursion onto New Babel is a high-risk endeavor. But we also need to move quickly if we want to prevent....

Miriam trailed off, and it wasn't difficult to guess why. One reason the true nature of the Prevos had successfully been kept secret thus far was they never discussed it over comms, no matter the circumstances. But she obviously jumped to the same conclusion he and Graham had regarding Montegreu's intentions.

She opted for a less revealing statement.

If we want to prevent whatever Ms. Montegreu has planned for Dr. Canivon.

Yes. I'll let you know as soon as we have any more information. Delavasi has offered his assistance.

You told him you were passing information to me?

I believe he'd want me to pass this particular information on irrespective of our arrangement, but he's far from an idiot. We haven't discussed it, but clearly he knows.

Well. Tell the director thank you, but we can handle any operations ourselves.

Another pause.

How are you?

He laughed faintly.

I'm...adjusting. Don't worry about me. You have bigger problems right now.

I fear I do. I confess to being a little disappointed the Oversight Committee isn't behind the kidnapping. It would have made certain things easier—but that's neither here nor there, and now irrelevant.

Sorry to complicate your life further. Before you go, how is Devon holding up?

He is physically intact—bruises and scrapes. Psychologically, somewhat less intact. But if anything, Dr. Canivon's kidnapping has given him something to focus his anger on. He wants to focus it by personally dismembering the perpetrators, but it is an improvement on the spasmodic flailing.

That doesn't sound great, but I'm not surprised. Tell him I'm thinking about him.

I will.

She cut the connection without ceremony, as there was no need for any.

He dropped his head back on the seat. They'd had Olivia Montegreu in their grasp eight months ago—sitting across the table from him and Graham in a locked room—and they let her walk away. It had felt like the right decision at the time, when the stakes were incalculable and she possessed what they so desperately needed. But deep down he'd suspected making the deal with her would come back to bite them in the ass.

And here they were.

He wished like hell he were in Vancouver, because if he were in Vancouver he could be helping Devon. Helping Miriam. Being separated from her was affecting him more than he'd expected; she had been his closest friend for so many years now.

Surely there was some way he could help from here, beyond what he'd just done....

He straightened up and pulsed Will.

Meet me at the office.

R

INTELLIGENCE DIVISION HEADQUARTERS

By the time Graham walked into the top-floor conference room at Division, Richard had an annotated map and two screens open above the table. Will was transferring notes from one of the screens to the map while Richard did the same from the second one.

Graham leaned on the door frame shaking his head. "Something told me I'd find you here."

Richard shrugged distractedly. "And something told me I didn't need to comm you and ask you to come in."

Graham jerked his head at the displays. "What you got?"

"With any luck, a way to help Miriam stop Olivia Montegreu from becoming a Prevo and possibly even rescue Dr. Canivon."

"Good news. But I have to ask again...what you got?"

Richard motioned him closer. The annotations overlaid the map to form a multi-hubbed web of interconnections. "Every known member or associate of the Order of the True Sentients, their locations and where they've made contact with other members."

Graham frowned as Will added an additional name to the map above Pandora then streamed a line from it to a name above Seneca. "OTS is still primarily an Alliance problem, which is why it's interesting that there are fourteen names attached to Seneca."

"Congratulations, they're now your problem, too. Faith Quillen, one of the chief lieutenants in the organization, moved to Pandora two months ago to start up a new cell. She recruited Ulric Toscano while he was vacationing there. Toscano returned to Seneca and started his own cell."

"How did you find this out?"

Richard proffered a small smile. "They've been my primary focus for the last three months, because as you noted, they are an Alliance problem and a fairly big one."

"Consider me interested in this new cell, but how is any of this going to help stop Montegreu?"

"I want to unleash OTS on her. As you can see, they have a large presence on New Babel. At the very least doing so may buy

Miriam some breathing room, and if timed correctly the distraction can help increase an infiltration rescue op's chances of success."

"It can. How do you propose to do it?"

Richard swiped the two screens toward Will and settled back against the table. "That's the tricky part. We'll need to utilize your remote eVi hacking tool."

Graham's expression was admirably blank. "What remote eVi hacking tool?"

He chuckled, secretly glad to have a chance to tweak Graham for once. "The one your Strategic Development group has been working on for the last year. I believe it's currently in the advanced prototype stage?"

Graham rolled his eyes at the ceiling. "And we worked so damn hard to keep that one under wraps. We call it the Reverb. It works, but it requires line of sight to the target for a minimum of three minutes."

"Makes it harder, but still doable. The clearest way in is through Toscano, but we have to find him. Is that something you can do?"

"Well, we don't make a habit of surveilling our citizens without cause, but the infrastructure is in place. If I put a priority flag on him, we should know where he is within a few hours, assuming he's not at home asleep. I'll send someone by his home address to check."

"If he is, we'll have to find another way in, because we can't wait until morning. So will you flag him?"

"Done. Now we need a plan."

He had one of those, too. "OTS operates a private comm network. Since it relies on person-to-person connections, we thus far haven't found a way to access it. I want to use the Reverb to implant information in their network suggesting Olivia Montegreu is preparing to bring one of the new-style Artificials online. We can also imply that after she does so she intends to take out the other cartels on New Babel then make a big play on Pandora."

Will had finished transferring names to the map and turned his attention to them. "That's thin. How do we make it believable?"

"I think...spoof a member of the organization, someone positioned to have access to this kind of information. You're right, it'll be wafer-thin, but if we create a sense of time pressure it could be enough."

Graham held up a hand. "Maybe not so thin. Let's go see Hennessey in Strategic Development."

ℛ

Tessa Hennessey spun her chair around to face them, sending thick orange and black braids whipping over her shoulder. Irises altered to match the orange in her hair sparkled with flecks of gold. A network of the most elaborate, intricate glyphs Richard had ever seen pulsed in rainbow colors down her mocha arms. Her tank top was made entirely of interwoven conductive threads.

"Hey, director dude and friends."

Graham dipped his chin. "Tessa. We need to take a VISH out for a spin."

"How long of a spin?"

"If it works? Until it doesn't."

"Hmm." She eyed him and Will. "You, I've seen around...Willie something? You, though? You're new." She thrust out a hand at Richard. "Hi, I'm Tessa. Resident warenut and fashion consultant."

"Richard. Nice to meet you. We're on a tight timetable, but perhaps you could explain what a VISH is?"

She checked with Graham; he nodded assent, and she reached behind her and tapped in a few commands. Her screen shifted, but not to anything he recognized. "VISH is what we call a 'simulated human'—designed from the ground up to mimic human conduct and nothing else. It took an Artificial to develop it, but the finished package is quite compact, particularly if we limit its parameters before deploying it."

"STAN developed it?"

"Ha. As if the military would let us play with their prize synthetic. No, we have a far smaller but in my opinion more clever Artificial here. I call it Cleo. So how compact do we need the VISH to be?"

"Small enough to be contained in an eVi or transmitted through a comm-based quantum tunnel?"

She made a hedging motion with her hand. "If we narrow its directives and cut a few corners, I can *probably* make it happen."

Graham leaned forward and planted his hands on the edge of her desk. "Mid-level security officer in Defense. Not a tech job, but overhears things in the halls. Male, single, no SO, no kids. Strong distrust of Artificials."

"Cleo will get a kick out of that. When do you need it by?"

He and Graham exchanged a look. "Pretty much now."

Her odd orange eyes widened briefly. "Come back in twenty-five minutes." Then she spun around to the screens and her fingers began flying over the keys, a soft white luminescence occasionally escaping from the space between her fingertips and the virtual keypad.

"No."

Will dropped a shoulder on the wall and crossed his arms at his waist. "I won't be in any danger. All I have to do is talk up a guy for three minutes."

"Not a guy—a terrorist."

"Maybe, but I doubt he's planning to take out the pub."

They had picked up Toscano's location five minutes earlier when he paid for a beer at *Fuori Point Grille*, a pub near the river. Agents would be in place in the next several minutes to tail him if he should leave, but the pub represented the perfect opportunity if they could catch up to him in time. "Let Graham use one of his agents trained in undercover work."

"Richard, *I'm* trained in undercover work. And I can charm anyone. People relax around me."

He stared at Will, working to push away the twinge of acrimony that had flared. It was so close to being permanently banished...but the admission had allowed it to worm its way up to the surface once again. Judging by the expression on Will's face, he knew it, too.

"No more lies, remember? It is what it is."

Richard exhaled. "I know. Sorry."

"I can't say if any qualified agents are here right now, but I'm here right now, and 'here' is ten minutes from the pub."

He threw his hands in the air. "Okay. Let's go. We'll tell Graham on the way."

CAVARE

Richard studied the device in his palm curiously. Made of a smooth obsidian and oblong in shape, it reminded him of old-style sci-fi depictions of a phaser gun. It even glowed an icy green at the transmitting end. The near end displayed a narrow band of controls; the options were limited and essentially consisted of 'lock on target,' 'transmit' and 'end transmit.' Definitely still a prototype. But it had been preloaded with the code to manifest the VISH, and it contained the ware necessary to hack into the targeted eVi.

Due to its extensive integration with the human nervous system, an eVi had always been believed to be secure—unhackable and incorruptible absent direct interaction via the two tiny ports at the base of the neck.

He didn't know the details of how the device worked, but it appeared the belief had now become a false one, even if no one knew it yet. The Reverb and its development were beyond classified, and rightfully so, for it was dangerous technology: small, undetectable and easy to operate.

He sat at a table inside *Fuori Point Grille*, in the most shadowy corner available offering line of sight to the bar running the length of the left wall. A mug of beer and a bowl of chips sat in front of him to complete the charade. He brought the mug to his lips and mimicked a sip, nudging the device a couple of centimeters out from behind the bowl as Will sidled up beside Toscano, nodded a greeting at the man and ordered a drink.

He centered the device on Toscano's skull and activated the 'transmit' command.

The light emanating from the front of the device shone too brightly for comfort in the dim environment, but covering it would break the signal. Due to the delivery of the complex VISH, it was going to take 4.3 minutes to complete, longer than normal. The seconds began to tick by.

Toscano had turned to half-face Will. The microphone dot behind Will's ear was active, and Richard listened in.

"You should try one of their custom brews. They're not bad for the price."

Will gestured a thanks, waved the bartender over and changed his order, then also shifted his posture subtly toward Toscano. "Thanks for the recommendation. It's my first time here—I just moved to Cavare from Elathan." He chuckled under his breath. "Truth be told, I'm flailing a little. I don't suppose you can also recommend a place that serves a decent steak?"

Toscano seemed to consider the question a moment—and possibly whether to respond or brush Will off. The man glanced around the room, his gaze passing over Richard without incident, before returning his attention to Will. "Not here. There's a respectable red meat rotisserie two blocks in from the promenade. It's pricey, though."

The beer arrived, and Will took a long sip then indicated approval. "This *is* good. Pricey's not a problem—I don't really have anything else to spend my money on. Might as well spend it on a few visceral pleasures."

"I hear that." Toscano's bearing relaxed and he faced Will more fully. "Cavare has a lot of those for sale, if you're looking."

The tiny display blinked green.

Transmission complete

Richard casually pressed the 'end transmit' control and slid the Reverb closer, into his lap and finally into his pocket.

Will now had Toscano deeply engaged in conversation. He truly did have a way with people. Richard sent him a pulse giving the all-clear and nibbled on a chip.

It took Will another three minutes to extricate himself smoothly from the encounter. Richard watched in his peripheral vision as Will exited the bar, waited another twenty seconds, then stood and did the same.

Graham was back at Division, ensconced with Hennessey to monitor the performance of the VISH. Richard met Will the next street down, and together they went to join Graham and find out if these new weapons lived up to their promise.

21

EARTH

M ia perched on the edge of the chair and took a deep breath. Willed herself calm. Even if she screwed this up in the most epic manner possible, nothing bad was going to happen to her. Despite the heady sensations the activity induced, it was safe.

Though they wouldn't allow her to leave the EASC campus yet, yesterday they'd finally allowed her to move to a suite at the lodging quarters. It was as coldly impersonal as the hospital room had been, but it did provide more space and comfort, plus the illusion of privacy. She was almost certain the suite, along with every room at the lodging, was bugged. This was a military base after all.

But she wasn't doing anything suspicious. She was merely sitting here quietly, wasn't she?

Thinking 'return' will always bring me back here, right, Meno?

Yes. And should you lose your way, I will be able to bring you back here as well—'here' being wherever your body and the remainder of your consciousness resides.

Really?

Remember, I am more integrated with your mind now.

I know. I guess I'm still discovering the extent of what that means.

Thanks to the Noesis, she and Meno had access to everything Annie did—a fact they'd never fully divulged to Admiral Solovy or Dr. Canivon. She'd spent the night before studying up on not only the OTS terrorists, but the political situation in the Alliance in general and on Earth in particular. Cross-referencing the information with the details of the attack on Devon and Annie had led to some interesting, albeit troubling, possibilities.

Now Abigail had been kidnapped by the Zelones cartel. It felt as if they were under attack from all sides, and she did not intend to passively sit and wait for whoever or whatever was planning to strike at Noetica next.

I'm ready.

In her mind she focused on the desired location: *Earth, London, Earth Alliance Assembly, Office of Military Oversight Committee Chairman Pamela Winslow.*

As before, her stomach lurched as the scene shifted. The edges of her vision became gauzy and indistinct, but a woman with coiffed chestnut hair and matching hazel eyes sitting behind a natural wood desk crystallized into clarity.

"—couldn't eliminate the young man then and there. The Committee's authority is broad, but it does not extend to kidnapping or execution."

The woman tilted her head in nominal acceptance of the assertion. "Nevertheless, he remains an unacceptable risk. The state secrets he was privy to while hooked up to that machine cannot be allowed to become public. And what if someone were to study the ware in his head?"

Mia concentrated on turning—carefully—toward the other speaker. A young man in a business suit sat in one of the chairs opposite the desk. She drifted around to the far side of the desk to be able to see his face. A comparison against the government personnel database identified him as Luis Akin, Chief Aide to Winslow.

"Our highest priority is securing the Artificials—all of them I think—but he needs to be brought under our control as well. I'll try to manufacture a house arrest, but if the legal approach fails we may have to resort to more clandestine measures. Look into it."

"Yes, Chairman. I'll ensure you're properly insulated from any actions which ultimately follow."

"Thank you, Luis." Winslow stood and moved toward the window, passing directly through Mia as she did.

Mia gasped and staggered in panic from the collision of atoms and energy that *wasn't*, screaming *'return'* in her mind.

Back in the room, she dropped her face into her hands and breathed through her nose until the waves of nausea passed. She was doing a lot of that lately.

Are you well, Mia? The unfamiliar sensory experiences of this space can be quite jarring.

No kidding. I'm better now, thank you.

Do you want to revisit the Chairman's office?

She considered it...but she'd learned the most crucial information. They were coming for Devon. They were coming for them all.

ℛ

EASC HEADQUARTERS (MEDICAL)

Mia noted the ironic reversal of fortune as she slipped into Devon's hospital room. Here she was at Medical yet again, not as a patient but rather visiting one, albeit one easily as recalcitrant as she had been during her too-recent stay.

Devon eased off the bed as she entered. She put a finger to her lips and watched the door close, then drew near to him.

"Why the clandestine act? Are you not supposed to be here?"

"I don't want to attract any attention. Are you feeling okay?" According to Meno he'd suffered a hairline fracture of his left ulna, a torn ligament in one of his hips and a variety of bruises, but was otherwise physically sound. Annie could no longer assess his true mental state. Mia had intended to see to it that his girlfriend was alerted and brought in, security protocols be damned, only to discover he no longer had a girlfriend. Emily had never returned to Seattle after the end of the war.

Without Annie in his head, he was now alone.

He ran a hand through messy hair. "I just feel...angry and impotent and helpless. And slow. Sluggish. I feel kind of dumb, which is something I've never been a day in my life. It's very disturbing."

"I'm sure. Have they told you who did this, and why?"

He nodded. "Admiral Solovy gave me the bare facts—about Abigail, too. But she's trying to protect me from the worst of it, as if she can when it's happening to me. I had Annie on comm for the last half hour filling me in on the details. It took forever on the stupid, archaic comm channel, though. We might as well have been talking through tin cans and a string...."

He blinked and recovered the train of thought. "But the up-shot is, it sounds like the Military Oversight Committee is going to war with Admiral Solovy over Noetica. You're lucky the Com-mittee doesn't know you're awake yet, or they might have tried to disconnect you, too. I don't think those goons would've even cared if doing so could kill you."

"That's what I wanted to talk to you about." She glanced fur-tively over her shoulder at the semi-transparent window into the hallway, much as Noah had done several days earlier. "We're not safe here any longer."

"Clearly I wasn't safe—they waltzed in like they owned the place and trashed my Prevo link with no one to stop them."

"I don't only mean our status as Prevos—I mean we're not physically safe ourselves, and neither are the Artificials."

He frowned. "They already disconnected me. I'm useless to them now."

"No, you're not. You know things—a hell of a lot of things. To someone who's trying to shut down Noetica completely and restrict the Artificials—or worse, shut them down as well—you're extremely dangerous. Every aspect of Noetica is dangerous."

"Granted, but this is the Assembly we're dealing with. What are they going to do? Call me to testify?"

She started to reach out to him in the Noesis, then remem-bered he was no longer able to access it. Here on a military base, standard comms might not be secure, either. She stepped closer to whisper in his ear. "I eavesdropped on the Committee Chairman—the one who ordered the attack on you—and her Chief Aide using that quantum space—"

"I call it SusyQ."

"Um…why?"

"It stands for Supersymmetry Quantum Mechanics—the "M" is silent."

She made a face. "That is an incredibly lame name, Devon. We're calling it 'Sidespace.'"

He gave her a weak shrug as his expression darkened to a pout. "I liked SusyQ but…I guess 'Sidespace' is fine, too."

"Now about what I saw. They're planning to do far worse than call you to testify." *Meno, show Annie what we saw.*

Devon grew quiet for several seconds, then abruptly his eyes widened and his Adam's Apple bobbed. "Annie agrees. She says we should leave."

"I think we should leave, too. All of us."

He began pacing in circles around the small hospital room. "But Annie's too big to move—damn bureaucrats and their inane, labyrinthine approval processes. She's only received a few of the miniaturization upgrades and still takes up half a floor."

"I know, and there's nothing we can do about that right now. But if we get some help—people we can trust—we can get Meno and Vii out, and ourselves. If Abigail is somehow rescued, we'll offer to send Vii back to her. But without Abigail here, Vii's in danger, too…Devon, are you listening to me?"

"What? Sorry, Annie and I were talking. She thinks there may be a way to get her out, too…in a sense. It's an insane, subversive, *magnificent* idea. But we'll need Abigail to accomplish it."

"Then let's hope the military can get her off New Babel. But we need to make plans which don't rely on that happening."

He nodded, looking shockingly upbeat given his circumstances. "The good news is, I know exactly who to call in to help."

22

ARCADIA

EARTH ALLIANCE COLONY

Colonel Malcolm Jenner was standing in the middle of four corpses and eighteen crates of confiscated TSGs, Daemons and EME grenades when the notice of new orders came in.

He motioned his second-in-command over. "I need to make a comm. Confirm all the crates are tagged, then start getting them out of here and loaded onto the shuttle. We don't want to overstay our welcome."

Major Grenier chuckled. "Yes, sir."

Malcolm checked the room a final time to ensure it held no further surprises, then went to find a private corner.

He'd given up command of the *Orion* two months after the Metigen War ended in favor of leading a new special forces unit. The op on Romane, despite its bittersweet results, had reminded him of his preference for ground beneath his feet, for affecting events through his own physical action rather than merely issuing orders on a bridge.

He admitted to missing the *Orion* more than he'd expected, to missing the scope and power a ship such as it provided and the reliability of a steady crew. Maybe even the beauty of space—just a little. But he felt more at home leading a team, not flying a starship, and playing an active role in every mission.

Veronica hadn't agreed with his decision, which was only one reason why the divorce had been finalized six weeks earlier. The war had changed his perspective on a lot of things...on the world, and what he wanted from it. It hadn't taken him long upon returning home to realize what he wanted from his life was very different from what she wanted from hers or, it seemed, from his. And since another of the truths he'd realized was that life was too precious to spend letting others decide your own happiness, he'd walked away before the ugliness got serious.

He untucked his shirt and wiped some of the sweat and blood off his face, tucked it back in and sent the holocomm request.

Admiral Solovy was seated at a different desk with a different backdrop than when he'd last met with her in person. Had the new Headquarters opened? It had been over a month since he'd been on Earth, so he didn't know for sure.

"Admiral. I received notice of a new mission and instructions to contact you for details."

"Yes, Colonel. You're looking..." she almost smiled "...busy. Are you in a position where you can talk?"

"Yes, ma'am. We're post-op and have secured all the hostiles and the building. My team is wrapping up now."

"Good. I'm afraid I have to ask you to head directly into another operation. You and your full unit will be going to New Babel."

"Admiral?" To his knowledge it had been nearly a decade since the Alliance had conducted an incursion onto New Babel, and that last one hadn't gone well for their side. The colony was under the complete control of the cartels, and the inmates were running the asylum.

"You heard me correctly. Yesterday at 1320 Galactic, agents of the Zelones cartel kidnapped an Alliance consultant, Dr. Abigail Canivon, as she was returning to EASC from Olympic Regional Spaceport.

"It goes without saying—though I am obviously saying it any-way—that the information I'm about to provide requires the highest level of secrecy. Inform your unit of what you think they need to know in order to carry out the mission, but no more."

"Understood, ma'am." He'd grown accustomed to the increased access to classified information which came with his elevated rank, and the secrecy accompanying it.

"Dr. Canivon is the person responsible for designing and implementing the Prevo technology."

"Oh." He canted his head slightly. "I understand."

"We have reason to believe the Zelones leader, Olivia Montegreu, intends to coerce Dr. Canivon into performing a similar procedure, presumably on Ms. Montegreu herself. Your primary objective is to retrieve Dr. Canivon and bring her safely to Earth. Your secondary objective is, if possible, to prevent the completion of such a procedure by any available means, including the elimination of Olivia Montegreu, the Zelones Artificial or both."

He pushed aside several bubbling concerns—including how exactly he was going to brief his team without disclosing the existence of the Prevos to them—to focus on the mission itself. "Do we have hard details on Dr. Canivon's location and its defenses?"

"To some extent—enough for you to know where to find her. I'll forward the files we have to you, but expect the defenses to be substantial. I'm working on obtaining additional intel, which I'll also forward when I receive it, and there may be some external factors working in our favor.

"I recognize the level of danger such an incursion involves. I'm asking a lot of you and your unit—perhaps too much—but I'm working to give you every advantage possible. Your team exists because it's the best, and I believe you can succeed in this mission."

"Thank you for the vote of confidence, ma'am." It wasn't the first time she'd expressed it...and he supposed each time he'd met the accompanying expectations. So far. "Can I assume, given the location and nature of the adversary, any and all measures are authorized for the duration of the op, not solely for the secondary objective?"

"Not only are they authorized, Colonel, they are encouraged. This mission is designated Level IV Priority. I don't need to spell out the serious nature of every aspect of this situation for you."

"No, ma'am, you do not." Honestly, he suspected he'd barely begun to fathom the extent of their 'serious nature,' but he saluted sharply. "We'll be another forty minutes here, then we'll head back to base, resupply and depart. We'll take a full loadout and finalize the op details in transit."

AR

EARTH

LONDON

"Welcome home, darling." Pamela Winslow kissed Jude's cheek with pinpoint precision. "Dinner is almost ready, and we have guests this evening. Do join us."

"Yes, Mother. Let me change first, and I'll be right down."

She held him at arm's length to inspect him. "You do look half a disaster. What have you been up to?"

"Traveling, as usual. Go see to your guests."

She raised a passing eyebrow at his unkempt appearance before departing, leaving him free to retreat upstairs.

Jude hadn't planned on needing to perform tonight, no more so than he generally did for his family, but it came with the territory. After a quick shower and donning of fresh slacks and a sweater, he entered the formal dining room to find his parents seated with two men. He sized them up: properly tailored but conservative dark suits, perfectly coiffed hairstyles, false smiles and calculating eyes.

Politicians. So that would be the game tonight, then.

His mother gestured for him to sit next to her. "Allow me to introduce our guests. This gentleman is Defense Minister Hideyo Mori, and this is our Assembly Speaker, Charles Gagnon."

He shook their hands across the table. "Nice to meet you both. Jude Winslow." He settled into the chair. "Plotting the future of the Alliance over *som tam* this evening?"

The Defense Minister moaned with theatrical flair. "We can only try, and hope cooler, more reasonable heads prevail soon—like your mother and Speaker Gagnon."

The Speaker wore a troubled expression. "I appreciate the compliment, Minister, but Brennon has not done a terrible job of managing the recovery in the aftermath of the war."

His mother sipped on her coffee. "To outward appearances, perhaps. But his administration has been far too secretive. Clandestine operations, dangerous Artificial projects, under-the-table deals with the Federation. He is undermining one of the primary roles of the Assembly, which is oversight of the executive and military branches, and as a result we don't know with any certainty what the state of the recovery or the health of our Alliance truly is."

She brandished a smile as false as those worn by their guests. "But enough of work. I wish this to be a pleasant gathering."

Oh, Mother. Your transparency astounds even me.

The kitchen servant brought the next course, *khao soi*, and Gagnon directed a measure of attention toward him. "Jude, what do you do?"

"Jude operates one of our largest charities, Sharing For Success. He's a tremendous help to me."

Jude bit back a crude retort at his father for talking for him and replaced it with a sober visage. "It's been a busy, difficult seven months, regrettably. So many people had their homes and livelihoods destroyed by the alien invaders. We try to help as many as we can, but there are always more who need it."

"You travel a lot, I assume?"

"I do. I've returned from Henan today, in fact. It was among the hardest hit, and there's still a great deal of unrest. The colonists feel neglected, and rightfully so, as they languish far from the centers of power." *So full of opportunities.*

Mori nodded earnestly. "This is what I've been saying. Brennon and his crony Admiral Solovy gamble with all our futures by letting their unnatural human-Artificial hybrid monstrosities run loose, when they should be putting all our resources to work helping the masses. The people need our protection *from* such things, not the opposite."

It was all Jude could do to keep a rabid level of shock off his face. "I'm sorry—did you say *human-Artificial* hybrids? Are you talking about the new type of Artificial rumored to have helped win the Metigen War?"

His mother's voice was as sharp as a finely-honed blade. "Minister Mori was simply being rhetorical. Weren't you, Minister?"

Jude did not miss the threatening stare she directed across the table as accompaniment to the question.

Mori shriveled beneath it. "Yes, of course. I only meant humans believing they can keep Artificials under control."

"Naturally." Her gaze swept over those present. "The Minister does have such a delightful flair for the dramatic. In any event, I've taken some steps in the last several days to reduce the threat. The military must be made to realize it is accountable to the people, through the Assembly."

Jude buried himself in the food in front of him to avoid having to engage in further pleasantries. *Human-Artificial hybrids?* He wasn't fooled by his mother's swift cover. Mori, believing himself among friends, had evidently spilled a closely held secret—extremely closely held, as in seven months of trying Jude had been unable to learn it.

This explained a great deal, though, and made the work he did all the more important. In fact, this was likely to change everything.

The remainder of dinner passed in less exciting fashion, so far as he could tell with barely half his attention focused on it. He made a point to be gracious to Mori, for the man showed all the signs of being a potential sympathizer. He might come in handy later. Gagnon was far more reserved, and if this dinner was an attempt by his mother to win the Speaker's favor, he wasn't sure she succeeded.

The plates were being cleared away when he received a priority message from the founder of the Seneca cell, an Ulric Toscano—filtered through and forwarded by Faith, as, like most cell leaders, this Toscano had no knowledge of Jude's role or even his existence. When combined with the information he'd just learned, the message took on a troubling connotation indeed.

He stood. "If you all will excuse me, something has come up I should handle. It was a pleasure meeting you both."

His father shot him a look. "What's come up?"

"Nothing you need concern yourself with—merely the usual complexities of running a charity which must be everywhere at once. Good night, Mother, Father. Gentlemen."

Ivan Echols, the leader of the New Babel cell, materialized on holo three minutes after having been summoned. "Jude, what's going on?"

"Time to rally your people, Ivan. Time for them to prove their dedication to the cause."

Ivan fidgeted. "Do you doubt their dedication? Let me assure—"

"I didn't say I did. We can argue semantics later. You need to move against the Zelones cartel. Tonight."

"*What?* We can't take them on!"

Ivan, along with Faith and four others, was a member of his innermost circle. This did not mean he wasn't expendable if the endeavor was worthy enough. "Not the entire organization. You're going to infiltrate and destroy their Artificial and tech lab."

"Jude, you know I'd love to do it, but why now? Why the sudden urgency? We've known they have an Artificial for months."

"Because I have intel strongly suggesting they're about to 'upgrade' their Artificial into something that violates the laws of nature. I've learned a terrible secret. The government is merging people with Artificials—joining their minds into some sort of freak hybrid creation."

"Oh my god. They'll take over everything."

"They may be doing so even now. The Prime Minister and the Fleet Admiral are both under the control of these...*things*, and probably other leaders as well. I'll be formulating a plan to address this on a larger scale soon, but tonight we must act quickly. I have reason to believe the head of the Zelones cartel, Olivia Montegreu, has discovered how these hybrids are created and intends to undergo the transformation herself. We cannot allow this to happen. She will eliminate the other cartels and take control of the entirety of New Babel."

"And that will be just the start—I get you. But I don't have enough people to break into the Zelones compound. The local OTS chapter has over two hundred members, but most of them aren't fighters."

"Then they'll have to become fighters. Marching in protests and tossing Molotovs is necessary work, but now they will act or they're not worthy of the cause. You have guns?"

Ivan nodded. "We have a stash, and I can put my hands on another dozen or so."

"Explosives?"

"Not really. A few small, improvised devices."

Jude opened a screen to his left. "You'll be contacted by a man named Orozco. Do as he says, and he'll supply you the necessary munitions."

"Do I need to pay him?"

He shook his head. "I'll take care of it. I'll also send you a team of mercs to boost your strength." Most mercs weren't crazy enough to sign on to attack Zelones directly, but he'd come across a group of former Triene employees with a grudge against Montegreu for killing their boss. He figured they'd jump at the chance to settle it.

"Thank you...that will help. We know where the lab is, so locating it won't be a problem. Hopefully the explosives can get the job done without us losing too many of our people."

Jude leveled a cold stare at Ivan. "I don't care about the losses. Take out that Artificial. Keep me up to date."

The holo faded away, and he stepped out onto his bedroom's balcony to breathe in the chilly, damp night air. The Thames flowed a murky gray under a blanket of heavy clouds, and Battersea Park was an inky moss canopy beneath him. Then the rain began to fall in earnest, and he retreated inside. There was much to do.

It was time for the Order of the True Sentients to move to Phase Two.

PART V:

ALL THAT WE ARE

"The universe is made of stories, not of atoms."

— *Muriel Rukeyser*

PORTAL: C-2

SYSTEM DESIGNATION: KAMEN

23

KAMEN-1

"I take it back."

Alex glared at him with her one visible eye as her head was shoved into the dirt, her arms were wrenched behind her and restraints were locked around them. "Couldn't have said that before we landed?"

A large hand grabbed Caleb's wrist restraints and hoisted him up to his feet. He ground his teeth to bury the scream of pain as his dislocated left humerus scraped against the edge of the shoulder blade.

"Ehak skan hingleh iyece, nihi nupiya tawacki kte!"

"Valkyrie, a translator program would be most welcome."

'I am working on it. But creating one is not as simple as it was with the Ruda. I am capturing some of the aliens' transmissions, but theirs is not a mathematics-based language. Thus, it will be more arbitrary and will not follow strict rules.'

"I understand. Hurry."

Alex was lifted to her feet then propelled forward until she stumbled into him. He concentrated on staying upright; he needed to appear capable and competent in their captors' estimation.

"What do you think they're going to do to us?"

Caleb eyed the four hulking aliens they were being prodded toward. "If they were going to kill us no matter what, we'd already be dead. The fact we're not means we have a chance."

They had picked up signs of an advanced, space-faring civilization as soon as they'd reached the system. Artificially generated signals originated from all three planets in the habitable zone. They'd opted to investigate the innermost one first.

The residents utilized substantial planetary defenses, and they approached under stealth rather than launching a probe that would be detected. They'd landed several kilometers from the outskirts of a large city and, since the air was breathable for humans, departed the *Siyane* wearing tactical gear but not environment suits. In retrospect, however, they *really* should've waited on the translator program to be ready.

The aliens had ambushed them twenty minutes later. Too far from the *Siyane* to flee, they'd fought back—which was when they'd discovered not only were the aliens large in size, they were as strong as mountain gorillas.

The instant a swat from one of their claws sent Caleb flying ten meters through the air to crash into a boulder, he'd screamed at Alex to surrender. Thankfully she'd only suffered a black eye—and likely a bruised ass from being shoved to the ground—before complying.

'The *Siyane's weapon is too powerful to eliminate your captors but leave you unharmed. What should I do?'*

Valkyrie sounded uncertain and anxious—a rare thing, but he could appreciate the sentiment. *"Nothing. Stay cloaked and wait. You're our best weapon, but we can't risk exposing you until we have a plan and the advantage."*

Alex exhaled harshly in response to another rough prodding. *"What he said."*

'I need to help you.'

Eight aliens surrounded them now, all of whom were armed with laser weapons and electrified staves. They were outnumbered and laughably outmatched. Compliance represented their sole chance of living to fight another day.

"You will, Valkyrie, when the time is right. But for now you need to sit tight."

The aliens were tall—three meters on average—and built sturdily, with broad chests and powerful arms and legs. They had thick, fully formed tails, which seemed to operate almost as a third leg or a speed assist. Their heads were unusually wide and even longer, with semi-detachable jaws and four deep-set eyes. Long, muscular arms ended in massive hands with seven similarly long, dexterous fingers each.

The most dramatic feature of their appearance, however, was their fur. It covered their bodies in a silken coat resembling mink pelts. It came in a variety of colors, though natively it appeared to be limited to a single color per alien. They adorned it in multi-colored painted-on patterns and baubles.

If more than one sex was present, he hadn't yet been able to see the differences. That or the females didn't fight—an easy assumption to make, but he didn't know nearly enough about them to make it.

Another easy assumption to make was that they were a violent species, brutish and aggressive—and they certainly were aggressive. He'd paid dearly for the seconds he'd fought before recognizing he stood no chance of overpowering a single one of them and negative odds of doing so against all eight of them.

If he tried, he would die.

But based on the data they'd acquired before landing, the species was also advanced, perhaps between two and four hundred years behind human development in most respects. They had cities, aerial transportation and starships. It wasn't clear yet whether the aliens had FTL capabilities, but they'd detected several small orbital stations and beacons on their way in, which meant they traveled within their stellar system.

"Kut egn tsinnaa iyayh!" Another series of shoves followed, and they were herded into the hold of a utilitarian—likely military—vessel. Six of the aliens remained in the hold to keep weapons pointed at them. "Enaon nahahn. Ptekela anzach."

Are you hurt?

She'd wisely switched to communicating via pulse in the confines of the ship, where any sound they made could be interpreted as belligerence on their part.

I'll live. These are close quarters, so don't make any sudden movements that might startle them.

A rumble beneath their feet signaled flight. There were no viewports in the hold and no clues as to where they were being taken, except it was a short trip—minutes spent in strained, hazardous silence. Alex radiated angst while their guards towered menacingly over them. He studied the details of how the aliens held their weapons, noting trigger mechanisms and possible safety catches.

The vessel descended vertically before coming to rest on a level surface. He caught only the slightest glimpse of nearby buildings as they were forcibly moved out of the hold and into an enclosed docking area. Several wide, high corridors lined in sandstone followed. In the corners of his vision other, less heavily armed aliens traversed intersecting corridors.

He offered a silent prayer of thanks when he and Alex were tossed into a single room. If they'd been separated, it would've made everything far more complicated. At least now the actions required for keeping her alive, keeping himself alive and gathering intel for an eventual escape came relatively close to converging.

Two of the aliens followed them in, and the door shut behind them.

"Nupiya enaon woshdee."

Alex growled and spun around. "We still can't understand you! Since you can't understand us, I would think you—"

The larger of the two leapt toward her. Caleb steeled himself and stepped between them, physically nudging Alex back while he met the gaze of the alien's two forward-facing eyes. Assertive, but not overtly combative, his demeanor sent the message that he was not going to allow her to be threatened. If they intended to hurt someone, hurt him.

Be quiet and follow my lead.

Sorry. I'm just...sorry.

The guard didn't need to give him a show of intimidation, as its presence alone provided plenty. Caleb held its gaze and held his ground, but didn't otherwise attempt a challenge.

Seconds passed. Finally the alien muttered something and gestured to the rear wall. It included several appurtenances that must be seating of some kind. They had concave bases and tall backrests, with open air in between the sections.

The seats dwarfed them; he'd be lucky if his head reached the top of the backrest. But he wanted to show them he could be compliant without the need for violence. He turned and surveyed the wall, faced the guard again and nodded in a manner he hoped conveyed understanding, then retreated toward the wall.

"We're not actually supposed to sit on those things, are we?"

He kept his voice measured and soft. "Alex, watch your tone. They may not be able to understand us, but they can read vocal tenor and body language."

She scowled at the 'chair' then hopped up onto it as gracefully as she could manage with her hands restrained behind her back. "Wouldn't they expect me to be angry?"

He hefted a leg atop the base and used it to hoist himself up, trying not to visibly grimace from the agony it caused his shoulder. "They would expect you to be frightened."

"Oh. Right."

He stopped himself from rolling his eyes lest their captors take offense and swallowed a chuckle despite their legitimately dire circumstances and his legitimately extreme pain. *She gets taken captive by towering, 250 kg, super-strong aliens with advanced weapons and the brains to use them, but she's not afraid. She's annoyed.* But then he remembered the story Navick had relayed of her fourth birthday party…he considered her reaction in a new light. It wasn't that she wasn't afraid—it was that being afraid annoyed her.

He gave her a small smile, grateful to have gained another insight into her wild, beautiful mind. Now to ensure they lived long enough for him to enjoy it.

A third alien, one they hadn't seen before, entered the room. It carried a tool half a meter long and glowing from multiple digital readouts.

It approached him first, but stopped a safe distance away and began waving the device in front of him. A scanner of some sort; possibly a medical analysis tool. Two of the alien's eyes stared at him as two studied the scanner, which was a bit disconcerting but made sense if he thought about it. The alien grunted and moved to Alex.

Her eyes narrowed and her lips quirked around viciously while the alien scanned her, but she heroically kept her mouth shut. Finally the alien went over and conversed with the other two in a short interchange of what sounded to his ears like guttural snarls and barks. The third alien hurried off, leaving the first two at the door.

"Nupiya sni wicoha sica." Now they too pivoted and departed.

The instant they were gone he swung around to face her. "Alex, you need to listen to me. If we want to make it out of this alive, we have to be very, very careful. Despite their apparent intelligence, they clearly value strength. We can't appear too weak and submissive or they'll decide we have no value, but we also can't appear antagonistic, because if we force them to resort to violence they *will* kill us. Above all we need to be calm, compliant absent an impossible order, but resolute." He paused. "And you have to let me protect you."

"Caleb, I know you're a better fighter than I am, but I—"

"This isn't about who's tougher or better in a fight. If it comes to a fight, *I* will lose. They aren't merely larger and stronger than me, they're also agile—enough to counteract the one advantage I might otherwise have had.

"This is about assessing and manipulating members of a society that both respects and fears strength. This is what I *do*. So please let me do it, and maybe, just maybe, we get out of this in one piece."

24

DETENTION FACILITY

Alex tried to roll her shoulders and work out some of the tension seizing up the muscles in her back. Thanks to the wrist restraints, she failed miserably.

"When we get back to the *Siyane*, we need an hour long steaming hot bubble bath, followed by a half-hour massage each. You can do me, then I'll do you."

Caleb made a weak attempt at a laugh. "That never works. I start giving you a back rub, one thing leads to another, and we're occupied for the rest of the night."

She could tell he was in pain, and if anything she was simply hoping to distract him from it for a little while. "Are you complaining?"

"Not in the slightest. I'm just saying I never get my back rub."

"But if you go first I won't get a back rub. And I epically need a back rub." She sighed. "Valkyrie, how's the translation program coming?"

'I believe I have identified a set of ninety to one hundred thirty common words. When next you speak to one of the aliens, I will provide the translation of these words if they are used.'

"Are any of them by chance 'peace' or 'no harm' or 'friendly'? Or maybe 'hungry?'"

'As I believe I've identified their method of negation as well as the word for 'ill intent,' yes, I believe you can express 'no ill intent.''

Caleb's smile more closely resembled a grimace. She began to get concerned about exactly how much pain he was in. "Excellent work, Valkyrie."

Abruptly he straightened up in the chair as the door to their cell opened.

Remember what we talked about.

Resolute but not antagonistic. Reward non-violent behavior with greater compliance. Keep my voice tone even. Model prisoner—that's me.

Two aliens entered the room...the same two as before? She thought so. One had neon orange fur with painted black swirls, and the other's was the color of a grizzly bear. They stopped two meters inside and adopted semi-threatening stances. As before, they wore a sort of utility belt with a baton and what she suspected was a firearm attached.

"Tktenhtahaan hei? Ca-ni woshdee?"

"Valkyrie?"

'I recognize 'where' and 'purpose'—I think they're asking you where you came from and why you're here.'

"Time to translate. Do the best you can."

Prepared for the possibility of an encounter with the local residents, they had worn their wrist transmitters when they'd departed the ship. Caleb met the aliens' gazes, more or less. "We come from far away. We mean you no harm—no ill intent." His wrist transmitter translated his words into a series of stilted noises that sounded reasonably like an electronic version of their language.

As one, both aliens jerked. The orange one stepped forward and yanked Caleb out of the high seat and spun him around, then wrenched his bound arms upward. Caleb winced but didn't yell or try to pull away.

The alien gaped at the transmitter then at Caleb. "Nitaa calisu qanera-nihisaad."

'Your...our...words....'

"We only understand a few of your words. We'll try to learn more, but we need you to be patient." The response was eked out through gritted teeth.

The transmitter began squawking, and the alien held it closer, lifting Caleb off the floor and evoking a pained growl from him.

Worried they were going to do serious damage to his injured arm, she piped up. "Please stop—you're hurting him! We're not a threat to you. We're...explorers. Scientists."

"Valkyrie, do you have something approximating that?"

'I will try.'

The sounds from her transmitter drew their attention to her. The alien eased its grip on Caleb and nudged him back around.

"Ehatas elpete omani-mahpi, caluni akuru casku?"

'If you are explorers, why did you carry weapons?'

Their Daemons and blades had been confiscated in their initial seizure. She started to smart off, but heeding Caleb's advice caught herself. "Protection. Defense. Safety."

Their captors studied them another moment then conferred in hushed tones.

She eyed Caleb, who was watching them closely.

Are you okay?

Yeah, but now I definitely get the first back rub.

She laughed in spite of herself.

Fair enough.

Grizzly stared at them as it pressed a long finger to its ear and spoke too softly for Valkyrie to translate. Did they have communications devices in or on their ears? There was too much fur covering the area to tell. After a couple of phrases the finger lowered and the two again conversed briefly, then regarded them in silence.

Several minutes later the door opened once more to allow the entry of a new alien, one they hadn't seen before.

Its fur was the color of pure honey. Elaborate crimson markings decorated its chest and arms, and baubles of an etched white stone hung in the fur around its head. The ornamentation was more extensive and elaborate than any they'd seen so far.

Their guards backed away to take up positions along each wall.

This is a supervisor—possibly a leader, but certainly above these two in their social hierarchy.

She nodded minutely.

Got it.

The new alien halted a respectful distance away, gazed at Caleb then at her, then...bowed. At least that's what it looked like—arms extended at forty-five degree angles from its sides, palms open, its upper body curled down in a sweeping gesture. It was a fluid motion, and the alien smoothly returned to a standing position.

Caleb dipped his chin in response, and she followed his lead.

"Shi-hasidi iye nupiya un calisu qaner-nihisaad, hunesni. Bi nako iye nupiya jin sni-sica ktatyk."

'My...security...say you know—badly—some of our words by a...device. They say you...say...you have no ill intent.'

Caleb's voice was measured but strong. "Yes. We are working to learn your words. Our device—" he couldn't point to his wrist, so he tilted his head toward it "—says to you what we say in your words." He waited to see the reaction.

This alien responded in a far more composed manner when the transmitter began conveying the translation. It listened while studying them calmly, then waved its hand in a circle. It might be indicating to continue?

"We are from far away, from space, the stars, another planet. We're explorers, and we came to learn about you. We don't intend violence or harm. We want to be...friends."

"Iyapi iwasta glah. Wicohae yuaslatei taashaanii un takunle. Castun nihi mecike-ukveke nupiya?"

'Words are...easy. Actions tell the...truth of things. How can...I, or we...trust you?'

"We can't physically threaten you. You took our weapons. You are stronger than us. You have all the power."

She had to admire Caleb's skill at navigating the encounter. He truly did understand the dynamics at play and how to use them to their best advantage. He was telling this alien what it wanted to hear, what it needed to hear in order to release them. His statements also happened to be true, but she suspected it wasn't the operative factor.

The alien's jaw contorted as it listened to the translation, half detaching before returning to a closed-mouth position. When the transmitter went silent the alien paced deliberately across the cell.

"Bih kalevner-ici isisole."

'Stop—remove—the...it's not a familiar word, but it must mean your restraints.'

The alien had studied her and Caleb as it spoke, but now the two guards approached, suggesting the statement had been directed at them. Orange grasped her by the upper arm and hauled her out of the chair. Its grip was so strong its fingers likely would leave bruises. It moved behind her as Grizzly did the same with Caleb, and a few seconds later her arms fell to her side.

She didn't think she'd be able to lift them for hours. She smiled nonetheless, hoping it wasn't equivalent to a snarl in their body language. "Thank you."

"Da honilne kipaz kenqlurisiso. Nupiya cin liite-nihisaad ota. Nihi yisnil iilye."

'Prove yourselves worthy of freedom. You need learning...more of our words. We will give...help.'

Caleb made no threatening moves, or any move at all. "Thank you as well."

The alien gave a grunting nod of sorts, pivoted and left. The guards moved toward the door, watching them the entire time, and exited.

She exhaled in enormous relief and faced him. "You were bri—"

He held up a finger, turned and walked to the back of the room. When he reached the wall he promptly slammed his left shoulder into it.

She gasped as he collapsed to the floor; the next instant she was on her knees beside him. "What—why did you do that?"

He gingerly leaned against the wall. Beads of sweat had formed along his hairline to trickle down his temples. "They dislocated my shoulder in the initial ambush. It'll be fine in a little while."

She stared at him in horror. "It's been that way all this time? God, why didn't you say anything?"

"There was nothing to be done about it, until there was. And now it's better."

She shook her head, incredulous, as he reached over with his good arm and drew her closer to him. "Well, you were brilliant."

He chuckled quietly into her hair. "I judged the situation as best I could and responded accordingly. We're not out of the woods yet, though. Stay on your guard—we're still prisoners, and one wrong move gets us back in shackles, or worse."

"Right. Best behavior." She carefully rotated her shoulders. "I don't think my arms work anymore. I had no idea wrist restraints were so uncomfortable...and I can't believe I just complained when you've been silently suffering immense pain for hours."

He gave her a little smile, which meant he was feeling better about their circumstances, and generally feeling better. "What, you've never been arrested?"

"*Yes*, but the officers were lenient because I was cute. They kept my arms in the front." At his raised eyebrow, she shrugged. "I was sixteen, and I—"

The door opened yet again, bearing their guards plus the alien who had 'scanned' them earlier. She scrambled up and offered Caleb a hand, but he was already up himself. Not showing weakness in front of their captors.... Damn, he was tough.

This time instead of a scanner, the third alien wheeled in a table. A rectangular, flat object sat atop it. The alien positioned the table in front of the long shelf which ran the length of the left side wall and drew a finger down the object. It illuminated in a harsh white and gold—it was a screen of some kind.

The alien gestured at them, then at the object, then pressed down on each side in turn; the act appeared to change the display contents. "Lena naaqin un alchinei. Bi nau-tehiya. Nupiya liite-nihisaad el ca-alchinei."

'These are...words...books? Children's books. They grow in hard-ness—difficulty. You will learn our words as children do.'

She bristled, but Caleb's hand on her waist stayed her. "This will be very helpful. We need...we are hungry and thirsty. Our bags that were taken contain nourishment for us. Can you have them brought to us?"

"Hanhon. Nupiya heci akuru casku el wakei."

'No. You may have weapons in your belongings.'

"We only need the food and water. You can give our bags to the guards and have them remove the contents."

"Sece. Miye apte."

'Perhaps. I will see.'

"Thank you."

The alien departed, guards in tow.

Alex sat down on the shelf and tried to get comfortable. She doubted it was intended to be a bench or meant for sitting, but it was the right height for them. "Valkyrie, are you ready?"

'I am.'

She toggled their connection on and began flipping the pages. It was fast going, as she wasn't digesting the information on the screen but merely allowing the contents to pass to Valkyrie through her eyes. The early 'pages' were heavily illustrated, which was appropriate to teaching a child the names of things. Some of the pictures were quite odd, but she was too tired, sore and starving to bother analyzing them for clues as to the aliens' culture.

Nearly half an hour had passed when the guards returned carrying their packs. She cut Valkyrie's connection, not wanting her glowing eyes to set off another crisis, as Caleb cautiously stepped forward. When he got to the middle of the room Orange held up a hand for him to stop.

The guards set the packs on the floor by the front wall. They opened them and pulled out each item individually, holding it up and inspecting it before allowing Caleb to identify it. He glossed past the uses for several of their tools but was quick to point out the energy bars and water packets. The guards carried those items over and dropped them on the table, put everything else back in their packs...and left with them.

Yep, they were definitely still prisoners.

The instant the guards departed she had a water packet up-turned, guzzling half of it in one long swig. Next she wolfed down two energy bars while continuing to flip pages. The illustrations were mostly gone now, and the text became progressively denser in appearance.

Caleb peeked over her shoulder while he munched on his own energy bar. "Are we learning much about their social structure?"

"Maybe. She's storing all the content to analyze later, once she has the language down."

"So you're acting as a conduit, or are you learning it alongside her?"

"I could if I concentrated. But I'm tired, which has reduced me to a page turner."

He reached up—with his uninjured arm—and tucked her hair behind her ear. "Rest while you can. We don't know when we'll be challenged again."

25

KAMEN-1

L acking any way to communicate with their captors outside the cell, when Valkyrie had absorbed the entire library they pushed the table and screen to the wall beside the door and waited.

Alex fell asleep on his shoulder. Caleb allowed himself to relax against the wall while being careful not to jostle her. Their situation was still a long way from safe, but considering they had only narrowly escaped execution a minimum of three times in their first hour on the planet, it was decidedly improved.

Now came the hard part. Once they could engage in actual conversations with the aliens, things were bound to get dicey. Culture clashes, unintended insults, misinterpreted gestures…in an aggressive culture such as this one, offense would be easily taken and not so easily forgiven.

His instincts argued their goal needed to be release and departure. This was a dangerous place. Yet the residents were clearly an intelligent species—the most advanced aliens humans had encountered outside of the Metigens by traditional measurements. He believed in many ways Akeso was far more intelligent than any of them, but in a truly unique manner humans were unlikely to ever comprehend.

If the next hours went favorably for them, Alex would want to stay. She would want to get to know the residents, if only in an attempt to decipher why they existed in one of the Metigens' pocket universes.

He'd play it by ear. He was curious, too…despite the inauspicious beginning, these were in fact the walking, talking aliens he'd desired. But his first job was making sure they stayed alive.

The door opened and one of the guards—the one Alex had aptly named 'Orange'—took a single step inside. "The Tokahe Naataan wishes to know how many cycles—days—you expect it will take you to become conversant in our language."

Caleb pointed using his injured arm to the table, his good one being trapped behind Alex's sleeping form. "We're done. Tell your Tokahe Naataan the texts were very helpful."

"Impossible. You cannot be finished."

Caleb squelched a smirk—he must continue to be polite and respectful unless physically challenged. "I believe we are. We still have much to learn about you, your world and your culture, but our device can now translate more than 40,000 of your words and vice versa."

The alien's expression changed—he couldn't be certain what it meant, but it was easy enough to guess it represented disbelief, surprise and probably suspicion. Orange turned and left without another word.

Valkyrie had sent a full translation file to their eVis thirty minutes ago, along with notes on the species she had gleaned from the texts.

They called themselves Khokteh, which didn't have a meaningful translation, and their planet Ireltse, which translated roughly as 'generous stone.' They did have two sexes; the notable distinguishing characteristics were that the females tended to be taller and have more slender tails.

Their technology included non-quantum computing, microtech, hovercraft and sub-light starships. Their social structure was based on roles. Warriors, scientists, educators, builders and so on played their designated roles, though the designating part was mostly competency-based. Government seemed to be a mixture of a meritocracy and hereditary rule. The texts provided little information regarding their recent history beyond vague references to the 'Conflict.'

He reached over and gently brushed stray strands of hair out of Alex's face, then cupped her cheek in his palm. "Alex, baby, it's time to wake up. I think we're about to take the stage again."

"How did you learn our language so fast?"

Caleb considered the Tokahe Naataan with studied calm. The title marked their honey-hued visitor from earlier as leader of this city and possibly the entire planet. He expected and was prepared for a few minutes of hard questioning. "We have virtual assistants—rudimentary computers—which can handle tasks such as this."

"In your brains?"

He nodded, but remembered the motion might not convey the information and elaborated. "That's right. The necessary hardware is implanted when we're children, using a combination of biological and synthetic material."

The alien's two front-most eyes shifted. "We've experimented with similar technologies, but I'm told our brain chemistry is not amenable to it. Where are you from? And be specific."

This lie—a small one—had been prepared ahead of time. "A neighboring galaxy we call the Milky Way. We're deep space explorers searching for other sentient life."

"Another galaxy? This is a long distance for you to travel."

"Our ship is very fast."

"Indeed. Where is your ship? Our patrols have been unable to locate it."

"Cloaked, for its own protection. It won't take any offensive action so long as it remains hidden."

The alien appeared to consider the laden statement for a moment, then accept it. "Have you found any sentient species? Before us, I mean."

"Yes, two other species. But you're the first one we've discovered who is like us."

The smooth hair along his thick neck rustled. "We are not like you."

Alex finally spoke up. Realizing both the importance and delicate nature of this encounter, she had thus far allowed him to take the lead. "In comparison to the other species we've encountered, believe me, you are. You're discrete individuals. You bear children, build cities and fly ships."

The alien grunted. "You learned these details about us from the texts. Now that you've found us, are others of your kind going to show up and attempt to rule us?"

Caleb offered a reassuring smile; as with all his gestures and expressions he kept it muted lest it be misconstrued. "No. While we suffer from our share of problems, we are trying to be a peaceful civilization. We haven't found any other intelligent beings in our galaxy, and...we simply want to know that we aren't alone. Also, as you say, it is a long way. Most of our people don't travel such distances often or lightly."

"Yet you *can* travel such distances. This says to me your technology is more advanced than ours. How do I know you don't possess weapons or other capabilities we won't recognize which you will use against us?"

"Tokahe Naataan, if we had such weapons, don't you think we would have used them to evade capture in the first place? Trust me, it was not our intent to be held at gunpoint, physically assaulted, shackled and imprisoned."

The alien drew his head back and uttered an odd rolling bark. Was he laughing? It seemed as if he was laughing. "Such must be true. You understand we had to be cautious, but please accept my apology for any discomfort we caused you."

The alien stepped forward, crossed his arms at the wrists and presented them to Caleb. "Welcome to Ireltse. I am Pinchutsenahn Niikha Qhiyane Kteh, the leader of the Khokteh here on our mother planet. You may call me Pinchu."

Caleb stood and mimicked the pose, though it was awkward as his arms were not nearly so long. "Thank you, sir. Our species is known as Human, but you can call me Caleb."

Pinchu grasped his hands and lifted them perhaps twenty centimeters, then released them. Alex had also stood, and Pinchu approached her and did the same. She gave the alien an uncertain look. "I'm Alex."

"Come, Caleb and Alex Humans. Allow me to show you a kinder side of our hospitality."

IRELTSE

Due to their rapid capture, they hadn't had the opportunity to see much of the area up close on their arrival. From the entryway of the building they'd been held captive in—it turned out to be a joint government/military command complex they called the Center—the city spread out to the horizon in a sea of bleached sandstone and coral marble.

The Khokteh built horizontally instead of vertically, and the loftiest building in sight stood ten stories high. It was likely an architectural preference rather than a deficiency of skill, as they utilized the copious space to inspiring effect.

Spiraling stairways wound around open-air porticos and expansive terraces. Many structures featured curved exteriors and offset floors. Artistic statues, often of unusual-looking animals, graced many street corners. The streets themselves were made of the same bleached sandstone, which wasn't a surprise—their aerial scans had indicated it was in plentiful supply on the planet.

Alex had never felt short a day in her life; even as a child she'd usually been the tallest girl in her age group. But the towering Khokteh moving in every direction made her feel positively diminutive. To not be able to see above the heads of the crowd...it was unsettling and led to the irrational fear that she might get lost.

Caleb seemed to sense it—or maybe he felt the same way—as he kept a hand protectively on the small of her back. She stayed on his right side to ensure he used his uninjured arm to do so.

Passing Khokteh often stopped to stare at them, but Pinchu's presence dissuaded the gawkers from approaching or challenging them in any way. The passersby didn't bow or kneel to Pinchu; still, the deference given him was clear in the far more cautious and reserved behavior the public exhibited toward him than in their interactions with one another.

No guards accompanied them on their tour. Either the Tokahe Naataan was demonstrating an extraordinary degree of trust in their honorable intentions, or he correctly believed he could fell them with little effort.

Pinchu paused at a broad outcropping that provided an excellent vantage over the city. Beneath them stood a large arena. Several thousand Khokteh filled its seats, watching as two fighters battled in the center. They used hand-held weapons that resembled hooked, double-bladed spears.

The ancient Roman gladiators of the Colosseum instantly sprang to mind. "Are they fighting to the death?"

"No, although grave injuries are not uncommon. It is a test—and an exhibition—of skill."

Caleb diverted his gaze from the arena to their host. "Physical prowess is important in your culture?"

"Yes. Warriors are valued, because they must be. You see, we are at war."

They both turned to Pinchu now. "With whom?"

He dismissed the question with a sideways wave of his arm. "We will discuss it later perhaps, should we tire of more pleasant pursuits. There is someone I wish for you to meet."

ᴚ

Two dozen Khokteh children practiced agility drills under the watchful gaze of a strikingly tall Khokteh standing at the front of a wide room. The space was empty of furniture except for racks of weapons along the right wall.

Though it cut as strange a figure as all the others what with the peculiar double set of eyes and long jaw, Alex was of the opinion this particular Khokteh was nonetheless stunning. Its—possibly 'her' due to its height—fur shone a pure alabaster white and was decorated in swirling patterns of lavender and silver. The fur around its face was braided into multiple rows, each one wound through with alternating lavender and silver thread.

The teacher spotted them in the corner and clapped its hands with authoritative force; the children hurried to varying levels of attention. "That's enough for today. Practice at home so you will grow up to become great warriors. Dismissed."

The children all performed miniature versions of the bow Pinchu had used earlier, then sprinted out the door in too much of a rush to notice the two aliens standing in the far corner.

The teacher came over to greet them, eyeing her and Caleb keenly but going to Pinchu first and embracing him.

After returning the hug he gestured to them. "Caleb and Alex Humans, allow me to present Casselanhu Pwemku Yu-anwoh Vneh, my life-mate and Amacante Naabaan to the Khokteh of Ireltse."

The title translated roughly to 'Mother-Heart Warrior'—a quite lovely title, Alex thought.

The female Khokteh gracefully executed her own bow. "You may call me Cassela. It is an honor." She had evidently been informed about their arrival before meeting them, as well as their method of communication and unique appearance, as she displayed no surprise or confusion regarding their presence.

Having seen it three times now, Alex took a clumsy stab at the bow. Both Pinchu and Cassela made that rumbling barking noise. She cringed in embarrassment—something else she rarely felt.

Pinchu patted her on the back, which nearly sent her toppling to the floor. "Well done, Alex Human."

"Not so rough with our guests, *nizhopini*. They look as though they will shatter at the slightest touch."

"Ah mey, this one nearly took out two of the Security Patrol. They are hardier than they appear. Puny, but strong."

The fact Caleb didn't so much as flinch at being called 'puny' was a testament to his substantial level of self-control. At her quiet snicker, however, he shot her a daring glance.

Cassela studied them a moment. Her foremost eyes fell to where Caleb's hand vanished behind Alex's waist. "You are life-mates to one another?"

The Mother-Heart Warrior didn't lack for directness. Alex exchanged a pleased smile with Caleb. "Yes, we are."

"Good. You will dine with us. The doctor assures us your physiology is compatible with our diet."

So the scanning had been medical in nature. She dreaded learning what 'compatible' meant, but she forced a note of enthusiasm into her voice. "Thank you for the invitation. Dinner sounds wonderful."

26

IRELTSE

Their hosts' home was unexpectedly charming. Situated outside the city on the edge of a cliff above a canyon of topaz and vermilion boulders, it spread out in a single towering story across the plateau.

Elaborate marble columns and high arches marked the entry to not merely the house itself but to every room within. The floor was made of a sandstone so soft it could be mistaken for rubber. Ambient lighting placed in strips along the edges of the ceiling created a pleasant luminosity in the rooms, giving them an open and airy atmosphere despite a relative lack of windows.

The dining area lay beyond a tiled pool of teal water situated in the middle of what otherwise resembled a living room. It looked inviting, but Alex hoped they wouldn't be expected to partake. Not as a group, anyway.

Cassela motioned to a patio behind the dining area. Caleb was mid-conversation with Pinchu, so she followed. Indoor transitioned seamlessly to outdoor, and she found herself standing above the canyon as the sun set in the distance. She exhaled quietly at the sense of wonder the scene aroused.

"This is truly gorgeous, Cassela. Your planet is beautiful."

The fur around Cassela's neck fluttered. "We find much peace here when times become difficult. I encourage Pinchu to find more, but leaders must bear the burdens of their *shikei*."

She still wasn't opening the connection to Valkyrie for fear of the reaction it might cause, but she could always talk to her.

"Valkyrie, there isn't a translation for that word?"

' 'People' would suffice for a translation, but the term encompasses a broader notion of clan, as well as history and future—their ancestors and the children yet to be born. It is a compelling word.'

Alex sighed wistfully, for the concept made her think of her mother. She hoped the burdens she had left her mother with were lighter than those which had come before, but suddenly she wasn't certain. No matter their weight, she had no doubt Admiral Miriam Solovy could bear them, but it was tragic she had to bear them alone.

"At least Pinchu has you to give him comfort."

"Mey, and comfort I do provide. But enough of sentimental poeticism."

"Yet you have a precise translation for 'poeticism?'"

'It is an accurate interpretation. I stand by it.'

Cassela gestured to Alex's forearm. "What an enchanting bracelet—there is much beauty in simplicity."

She ran fingertips over the curves of the smooth, onyx metal, smiling to herself. "Thank you. It was a gift from Caleb—the first gift he ever gave me, in fact. It...well, its origin is a long story, but it holds a lot of meaning for me."

"As it should be for such treasures. Come, let us rejoin the others."

Alex stole a last look at the fading rays of sunlight beyond the canyon then trailed her inside.

Pinchu was cavorting in the adjoining room—the kitchen?—in a most animated way, waving at two servants and fiddling with various bowls and containers. Caleb watched the performance from a safe distance.

Cassela made a deep clucking sound and brought a hand to her throat. "Pardon us while we ensure the meal is ready. Make yourselves comfortable."

As soon as they were alone she turned to Caleb, drawing him close to whisper, "I'm a little concerned about the food."

He placed a gentle kiss on her lips. "I know, but suck it up. And smile. Given their size I suspect they eat larger portions than we do, so don't feel you have to clean your plate—but make a good showing of it, else you'll offend them."

Her nose scrunched up at him, eyes narrowed. "When did you become a diplomat?"

"Undercover work, obviously."

"Obviously."

Cassela reentered the room then and ushered them toward the dinner table.

It was tall. The chairs were tall. Everything was so damn *tall*. She felt like a goof climbing up into the chair but refused to let Caleb hoist her up, lest she feel ten times more like a goof. He gracefully hopped up into his as if all chairs were that tall. He also didn't seem to be favoring his injured arm any longer; she knew he'd upgraded his eVi's healing routines after his run-in with the assassin on Pandora, but it was still an impressive recovery.

Pinchu joined them a few seconds later, taking a seat across from Caleb as an unfamiliar Khokteh—one of the servants—began placing steaming bowls of food on the table.

It smelled fine. Nice even, like mint and roasted nuts. A sideways peek into the nearest bowl revealed a thick brownish substance which reminded her of meatloaf.

She placed her hands in her lap, waiting for a cue as to the proper procedure to follow. She'd rarely troubled herself with dinner party etiquette back home, but for some reason here she had the desire to respect their traditions.

Pinchu and Cassela launched into a recitation of a prayer.

> *Gods of the stone, Gods of the sky*
> *Blessed be your gifts, Hallowed be your favor*
> *Supplicant before you, Grant us your nishnaaidzh, diin niiyol*
> *Here and forever more, Your servants most beholden*

Hmm. She hadn't expected them to be religious and made a note to ask Valkyrie about it later.

She was saved from deciphering the proper table manners by the servant heaping food out of the bowls and onto her plate: the aforementioned brown mush, a stack of tendony meat and yellow blobs that might be vegetables of some sort. The eating utensil beside the enormous plate was a tong-like contraption with three openings for a handle. She slid her thumb and forefinger in two of them and scooped up a helping of the brown substance.

It was unusually bitter and had a sharp aftertaste akin to chicory or escarole. But it didn't make her want to gag, which really was all she was hoping for. She smiled. "This is delicious."

It occurred to her that Cassela may have been nervously awaiting her reaction, because she seemed to visibly relax. "Wonderful. Please, continue."

Caleb directed his attention across the table. "Would you be willing to tell us about the war you mentioned this afternoon? We've seen some ourselves, unfortunately."

Their hosts exchanged a few murmured words, then Pinchu gave his version of a nod. "Long ago..." the translator hitched before supplying 'several thousands of years' "...we traveled to the two other habitable planets in our system, Nengllitse and Tapertse, and established colonies. In this period of our history it took months to travel between these planets, so the colonies matured in relative isolation and governed themselves.

"By the time our space travel capabilities developed to where this travel took only days, they had each grown to become populous, fully-functioning and independent societies. They had also grown hostile toward us and one other. For a time we maintained a strained but peaceful relationship among the colonies, but two hundred forty years ago it devolved into war—a war which continues to this day."

Cassela set down her tong. "We bomb their planets, they bomb ours, and so on in what seems like an endless cycle. Whenever a faction starts to gain the upper hand, one of the others counters with some new weapon or tactic, nullifying any advantage previously gained."

Alex realized she'd started pushing her food around on her plate. She took a small bite of the vegetable, a comparatively bland dish similar to squash, and washed it down with the citrus-flavored water the servant had supplied.

"What is the goal? What would victory mean—for you or for them? Forgive me if it's an impertinent question, but I've always had difficulty rationalizing war. My father was killed fighting one. A losing one, from his perspective..." she glanced at Caleb "...but a victory from the other, arguably equally valid side."

They both made a figure-eight symbol over their chests, like Catholics performing the Sign of the Cross. "Sadness for you. The answer is simply control. Domination. They want to rule us, as we believe we should rule them. It is in our genes. Many wars were fought here on Ireltse for control of land and *shikei* before we reached a state of peace."

"But can't you just say 'We won't try to rule you if you'll agree to leave us alone' and be done with it?"

Caleb huffed a breath beside her, and she turned to him. "What?"

"That line didn't exactly work on the Alliance twenty-six years ago. I'm sorry, I know this isn't easy for you to hear. But the fact is, those who rule always believe they have a right to it. History demonstrates that freedom must, almost without fail, be taken by force."

She swallowed heavily and hurriedly reached for the water. "I know." If he had any idea what a painful admission it was for her...but of course he did, which was why he followed the statement up with an apologetic half-smile.

She gazed back across the table. "It's easy to judge other situations from the outside, oblivious to the hypocrisy in the judgment. Forgive me."

Cassela wore an expression that Alex was on the verge of deciding had to be a grimace. "There is wisdom in your words. I pray for the day when all Khokteh are ready to hear it. But until such a day comes, we fight. We have no other choice."

Pinchu interjected. "And the advantage is with us now. Our ships' new weapons are twice as powerful as those of our opponents. They will not be able to keep up with the damage, I believe. The end to the war may finally be at hand."

Given what had been said, somehow she doubted it. But she offered him a noncommittal countenance and hid the rest in a bite of the 'meatloaf' and another lengthy sip of water. The sharp taste of the food was starting to burn her throat, but she persevered.

Mercifully, the conversation moved on to more cheerful topics, and in the end it was a genuinely enjoyable evening. The translator had become all but invisible by this point, the slight delay between responses to allow it to do its work giving them a chance to take a breath and contemplate what was being said.

When the plates had been cleared away by the servant, Pinchu stood. "You will bed here tonight." It was delivered as a declaration rather than a question.

Still, she hesitated. "That's not necessary. We can return to our ship—we won't leave, I promise."

"Nonsense. You will bed here tonight as our honored guests. Tomorrow we will take you to see our ships. Possibly you can teach us to make them fly as fast as you claim yours do."

"Well...." She appealed to Caleb for help.

He nodded graciously. "We'd be honored to stay for the night."

Cassela stood and prodded Pinchu toward a hallway on the left. "It's settled then. Let us see to the guest suite."

She frowned at Caleb after they had left, feeling a little...queasy, or was it dizzy? "I just hope the bed's comfortable. And that there is a bed."

He laughed, in a more free and open manner than he typically shared in public. "We'll see soon enough. And if not, this floor is soft enough to sleep on."

Her stomach grumbled by way of response. *"Valkyrie, I need you to do a quick check and make sure the food isn't actively poisoning me."* She blinked and toggled on the connection.

'There are several unfamiliar bacteria in your digestive tract, but your immune system is negating them. You will probably experience some uncomfortable cramping for a few hours. I should note, however, the liquid nourishment appears to have been—'

A gasp echoed through the room, and she looked up to find Cassela and Pinchu staring at her from the hallway entrance. Staring at her eyes and the pulsing glyphs along her arm, specifically.

Shit. She hurriedly killed the connection, but the damage had been done.

Cassela approached her with evident caution. "What…are you?"

"The same as I was."

Pinchu moved far more assertively toward her, so much so Caleb subtly shifted his stance, ready to intervene. "You resembled one our Gods. Are you sent by them?"

"No! It's nothing—we haven't been lying to you. I have some additional cybernetics—computer-synthetic upgrades—because I do a lot of technical and scientific analysis. That's all it is."

"Do it again."

"Um…."

Caleb gave her a mild shrug, seemingly unconcerned. He might have even been suppressing a chuckle.

"All right." She blinked and reopened the connection.

'As I was saying, the beverage served with dinner—'

"Shush. We're under observation."

'Ah.'

Cassela's head tilted as she reached out and ran a light hand over the glyphs. "Wondrous. I think perhaps you *are* an emissary of the Gods."

Then quite possibly the most ridiculous thing to ever happen in her entire life occurred. Cassela dropped to one knee, followed immediately by Pinchu. Their heads bowed. "Forgive us for any offense we have given you. Allow us to bestow honor upon you and fulfill any requests you desire to ask of us."

Caleb had covered his mouth with a hand, barely stifling outright laughter. She glared at him in mock disgust. "Please, get up. Stand. I'm not a god, or related to a god, or sent by a god, or doing a god's bidding. Our technology is simply more advanced than yours in this respect."

They stood far slower than she'd have liked and exchanged a look. "We understand the need for discretion. We will not betray your secret." Pinchu turned to Caleb. "And you? Are you from the gods as well, or are you her champion?"

His lips rose in blatant amusement. "If you mean can I make my eyes and arm glow, no. She's special in that respect...among others."

She tried to convey her annoyance to him, but her continued scowl nearly dissolved into laughter as well.

Their hosts focused back on her, and she did her damnedest to keep a straight face as Pinchu bowed. "So she is. What can we do for you, Alex Human who is not of the Gods?"

"Do for me?"

"How can we make your visit most pleasing for you? Name it, and we will provide it."

"Honestly, I'm fairly tired. It's been a long day. The hospitality of your guest suite for the night is more than enough."

"Very well. Let us show you to your rooms and bestow blessings upon them."

ℛ

The guest suite turned out to be near the end of a seemingly unused wing of the house, which thankfully meant they would enjoy a measure of privacy. Large and open, with high ceilings like the rest of the house, it contained furniture generally recognizable as a bed, a table and two chairs, plus an unidentifiable object or two.

The left side of the room held a pool similar to but smaller than the one in the main room. A lavatory nearly as large as the bedroom was in the back. It included a contraption that had to be a toilet, a narrow, v-shaped protrusion that might be a sink, and a tiled cubicle with a high rail in the far corner.

Cassela and Pinchu bid them good night, lavishing enough fanfare on her to make her damn uncomfortable, and at last they were alone.

Caleb wandered over to investigate the unfamiliar furniture. But it had been two days since she'd showered, and the cubicle in the lavatory appeared as if it could be a shower. Curious, she reached inside it and pressed on the square button halfway up the wall.

She squealed as water exploded from the surrounding three walls, dozens of jets hidden in the tiles pouring water into the cubicle with the force of cannons. Despite standing mostly outside of it, she was instantly soaked from head to toe.

Caleb laughed from the doorway behind her. She whipped around to glare at him, for real this time.

"You look like a wet rat."

"Kind of feel like one…." She pushed sopping wet hair out of her face. "Okay, so…the force is due to all their fur, or their thick skin underneath all their fur, or some related reason. Regardless, our bodies aren't built to endure it. Bath it is."

She began peeling her wet clothes off, giggling as she did. She was definitely lightheaded now. "I think there may have been a little wine in the water they served with dinner."

"I think the water may have *been* wine." His voice had taken on a sultry sing-song quality that sent a delightful shiver up her spine.

She draped her clothes on the rail at the top of the shower. When she turned back around, Caleb was on one knee gazing up at her.

A smirk danced on the corners of his lips. "Oh, my mistress, Emissary of the Gods, how may I serve you?"

She stared at him, stupefied. "*What* are you doing?"

"I am but your humble servant, supplicant before you. State your desire, my mistress, and if it is in my power I shall grant it."

"Stop."

"But I cannot. My purpose is your purpose, my desire your desire. I exist to ensure my divine mistress is pleased."

"You had better stop right now or I will make you follow through on this nonsense."

His other knee dropped to the floor. "Please. I cannot rest until your needs are met." He started moving toward her, still on his knees. "Command me, I beg you."

"You're drunk."

"On the radiance of your presence, and the power you wield over me."

She cackled, too loudly—clearly, so was she. Still...it felt safe here. For this moment at least, they were safe. So perhaps she could play the role of demi-goddess, with one exception: no glowing eyes. She never, ever let Valkyrie in during sex. He had asked her not to early on, but she wouldn't have done so in any event. It was for them, and them alone.

She inhaled deeply, breathed out, and gave in. "Kiss me."

His hands wound around her ankles and gradually rose up to her thighs in a tantalizing caress. He placed a gentle kiss above each of her knees.

She'd meant stand up and *kiss* her, but.... "More."

His palms swept up to cup her ass as his lips trailed up her thigh. He gazed up at her, eyes twinkling in devilish delight and growing passion. "Here?"

She quickly nodded, reveling in the disparate sensations upon her skin—his firm, almost rough grasp in wondrous opposition to feather-soft, reverential kisses. "More."

He complied, and only his arms holding her up prevented her from sinking to the floor as her legs melted and gave way.

Her fingers fisted in his hair, for balance and other reasons. "*Bozhe moy, priyazn....*" She sucked in another breath. "Take your clothes off and carry me to the bath."

"It would be my deepest pleasure." He stood agonizingly slowly while tugging his shirt over his head. Instantly her hands and her mouth were on him.

He grumbled against her lips. "I can't comply with your commands if you won't let me take my pants off...."

"I've got them." She fumbled with the clasp, not because she didn't know how it operated but rather because her hands were trembling. It came free, and her palms slid beneath the material and along his hips. He pitched in to shimmy them to the floor, then seized her thighs and hoisted her up to his waist.

She wrapped her arms around his shoulders and sank her fingers back into his hair; it was getting long, and she adored the thickness of it. Distracting her from it was the heat teasing her, just beneath her. She began sliding downward.

He slammed her against the wall with a growl. "If you don't stop that this instant, we will not make it to the bath. The choice is yours." Then his mouth was devouring hers.

Considering he'd refused to stop his antics when she'd asked...but the water was too inviting. "Ah...bath, yes. Bath."

"As you wish, my mistress." He readjusted his grip on her, lifting her higher, and crossed into the main room toward the bath.

One step down, another, into the water. It was cool, in thrilling contrast to the fire of his skin on hers. As one they plummeted and the water rose to consume them. For an infinite fraction of time they floated weightless, limbs and lips tangled together.

Then her feet reached the bottom, and she urged him up to break the surface. Backwards, onto the ledge running down the length of the bath beneath the water.

When his back hit the tiled edge, she took a deep breath and submerged once more, gripping his hips and having her way for as long as her lungs allowed, then a little longer.

She resurfaced to find him gasping for air as much as she, eyes wide and ablaze with need. "How may..." his throat worked as he pulled her into his arms, and his voice dropped to a low, velvety purr "...how may I at last give you fulfillment, my mistress, my love?"

Her knees found the ledge on either side of his hips, her hands came up to cradle his face...and she grinned.

Married sex, she decided for the third or tenth or hundredth time, was without a doubt the best sex to be found in any universe, however many of those there ended up being.

27

IRELTSE

The ship hangar they were to tour was located inside the city, in a sector that looked much like every other sector of the urban area. There was no distinct military base, no division of purpose separating this structure from the business offices across the block.

War and the execution of it appeared to be central facets of their existence, Caleb mused. It felt a bit dissonant given one-on-one they were a friendly, thoughtful species. They formed lasting bonds with one another, valued their children and took pride in their surroundings, all features of an advanced, civilized society. But few things were so simple—and he was beginning to believe that included most sentient life.

They had taken an aerial vehicle from Pinchu's home to the hangar, and in the full light of day he'd been able to give their transportation proper scrutiny. It probably shouldn't have surprised him that the vehicle was in most respects nearly identical to human vessels serving the same purpose. It was larger, like everything here, with massive seats and no roof, but the basic shape was the same. The engine stayed hidden, but it gave every indication of operating on the same core principles as their terrestrial engines.

He supposed there were only so many functional ways to convey humanoids from one place to another.

Alex practically vibrated with anticipation at the prospect of inspecting the alien starships as Pinchu led them to the entrance of the hangar. The degree to which seeing her so enthusiastic and happy pleased him...he lacked words for it. He retained the smallest amount of caution regarding the Khokteh, the minimum needed to be ready should events turn against them, but she had embraced them completely.

Cassela and Pinchu had toned down their worshipful attitude this morning, though they watched Alex constantly. Their attention was delivered with what seemed like veneration, but he couldn't yet read the nuances of their expressions well enough to be certain.

He was intrigued about this religion of theirs, but broaching the topic of religion wasn't advisable at family dinners, much less to aliens who had contemplated killing them a few short days ago, so he thought he'd give it another day or two. Valkyrie ought to have some information on it, too, if they ever found themselves with downtime. Downtime they didn't promptly fill in the most spectacular manner.

Alex squeezed his hand in excitement as they stepped into the main hangar bay. He chuckled and waved at the rows upon rows of ships gleaming in the natural light provided by a glass roof. "Go. Play." She flashed him a quick smile then hurried on ahead.

As with the vehicle which brought them here, the Khokteh starships were of a fundamentally similar design to their own. The proportions tended to be more vertical, doubtless due to the species' height, and the cockpit of the fighters took up a larger percentage of the body. There were other differences in the details, but they were at their core starships like any other.

Alex ran a hand along the hull of the nearest fighter as he caught up to her. Its exterior was made of a mahogany metal, serving as proof the Khokteh were able to competently construct in metals; they merely chose not to when it wasn't necessary, as in their architecture. The fact the planet was rich in stone and poor in metals surely played a role as well.

Cassela joined them at the ship. Alex glanced over at her, eyes animated. "Do you fly?"

"Me? No. I much prefer a spear in my hands."

"I doubt I'd be very good with a spear, but I wouldn't give up flying for anything."

"If you insist it is this wonderful, perhaps I will learn at some point. After the birth."

Alex's hand fell away from the hull. "You're...pregnant?"

Oh, this was going to be fun. According to Valkyrie, Khokteh females carried their offspring in pouches, like the kangaroo on Earth and *osphraniala* on Seneca.

"I am. It will be many cycles until the birth, however."

"That's...excellent." Alex shot him a restive look, and he shrugged, saying *you're on your own* as clearly as possible without words.

He knew children weren't something she planned on anytime soon, which was equally fine by him. There had been enough life-changing events for them both in the previous year to last several decades. His niece was wonderful, but he fully recognized this was in no small part because he could give Marlee back to Isabela at the end of his visits. So maybe one day, but one day far away.

Pinchu had left them to speak to one of the workers at another vessel, but now he returned. "Yes, I am to be a father at last. I could hardly convince her to slow down long enough to carry a child."

Cassela looked as if she was preparing to sling a playful retort at him when sirens began ringing out in the hangar. Everyone stiffened, and Pinchu's hand came to his ear. "Three Nengllitse—" the translator stumbled before substituting *[military formations, approximately regiment-sized]* "—are approaching from the southwest."

Cassela nodded sharply. "I will oversee the defense of the city's most important infrastructure—the schools, the hospitals. You need to get to the Center." She started to take off running, but Pinchu grabbed her arm and drew her to him. "Be careful. You cannot act only for yourself now."

"I must act for our *shikei*, as must you." She touched her nose to his and departed.

Pinchu began running toward the exit. "Come! You will be safe at the Center."

Alex groaned. "I knew this was too easy." Then she too took off running.

R

The Center was in a state of semi-organized chaos. Khokteh hurried in every direction, many carrying enormous guns that resembled rocket launchers. Sonic booms from fighters filled the air minutes after they arrived.

Alex grasped Pinchu's arm as they followed him through the maze of hallways. "We don't want to be a distraction, but can we help?"

"I will not allow you to risk your lives on our behalf. In my office—here. Stay!" He gestured at the open doorway ahead before jogging away in another direction.

Alex acted like she wanted to follow Pinchu. Caleb urged her inside the office, where she immediately ran to the open balcony. At least the office was recessed deep into the building, with staggered floors extending beyond it both above and below to offer them some small protection.

The outskirts of the city were on fire, and the low rumble of crumbling stone echoed in the air. Overhead, fighters of a slightly different design than the ones they had viewed earlier buzzed the buildings.

A laser shot up from their left to impact a fighter in the distance. A ball of energy surrounding the fighter absorbed the impact completely, suggesting the attackers sported robust defensive shielding. Four blocks away a large transport hovered several meters above the ground; its bay opened and easily a hundred soldiers leapt out. So there would be fighting in the streets. Caleb's growing unease ratcheted up toward combat mode.

Alex stared out at the scene in horror. "Valkyrie, get out of here. We can't risk you being captured."

The *Siyane* was parked far outside the city, but still conceivably in the line of fire.

'I will retreat to the unpopulated northern region until the battle is finished.'

"No. Leave the planet. Hide in space."

'But what if you need to depart unexpectedly and rapidly? In fact, I would suggest all of us depart now.'

"We'll be safe. And if we need you, it won't take you long to reach us. Now please, go!"

'I am uncomfortable leaving you here...but I will comply.'

She breathed a sigh of relief. "What do we do?"

He gazed out at the battle now raging all around them. "We stay here. We don't know their technology or how to operate their weapons. We don't know their procedures or military protocols. And...Alex, we don't know if the attackers are actually bad guys. This isn't our fight."

"But they—"

"I like Pinchu and Cassela, too, but there are a thousand factors at play here we don't understand. Yes, the Nengllitse are the aggressors today, but what if the Ireltse military carpet-bombed their homes last week? What if they murdered children, or took them as slaves? We just don't know."

"They could have killed us, but they didn't. And as soon as we could understand one another, they welcomed us. These are thinking, feeling, rational beings here, and they have as much of a right to live as anyone. That's what I know."

An explosion rocked the walls. Close.

He checked outside to see a ring of soldiers lining up at the street level to surround the building. As expected, two blocks away soldiers were now fighting in the streets. Overhead the bombing continued unabated, and the reality that the attackers' shields were more powerful than the weapons attacking them was tipping the balance in the wrong direction.

The Khokteh—the Ireltse Khokteh—were losing. If Pinchu's military didn't turn the tide soon, their own lives were going to be at risk.

This altered the equation.

He pressed a fist to his forehead and ran through the variables one more time. "Let's go find some weapons. But stay close to me."

She smiled gamely. "Where else would I be?" Then she grabbed his hand and tugged him toward the door.

The armory was two floors below, and they earned several odd looks from passing Khokteh as they squeezed down the stairs. All were aware of their presence, but many had never seen them. Still, looks were the most they received, because no one had time to worry about two puny little aliens wandering the halls.

Two soldiers were tossing out weapons to everyone who passed by the armory entrance, including many who weren't wearing military garb. They ran up to the door as the soldier on the left pivoted to them. It was Orange, the guard from their time as captives.

He crossed his long arms over his chest. "No. I accept that Tokahe Naataan says you are friend to the Khokteh, but I will not arm you."

Alex planted her palms on the high counter and hoisted herself up, leaning over it to get in the alien's face. "Give. Us. Weapons. We will fight for you."

Orange glowered at her for several seconds, then threw his hands in the air and capitulated, much as everyone eventually did once Alex decided the way things were going to be. He handed over two of their standard guns. "Shoot for the head, neck or shoulders. The chests are hard to penetrate, especially when you factor in their armor."

The guns weren't so large as the rocket launchers he'd seen earlier, but they were still twenty percent larger than TSGs. Alex hefted hers awkwardly under her arm.

Caleb rested the bulk of the gun on his hip. "Give me a blade, too. In case." Their weapons had, for perhaps understandable reasons, never been returned to them, and his sword remained on the *Siyane*.

Orange growled but after a brief hesitation reached under the counter and produced a half-meter long katana-style blade.

Caleb accepted it with his free hand. "Thank you. Good luck."

The building shook again as they hurried off; this strike hit close enough to send sandstone dust falling from the ceiling. He grabbed Alex's arm and pulled her into the next hallway. "Let's find a vantage on the third floor."

She followed his lead, vaulting up the stairs two at a time beside him. This was a place they had been before, on their tour of the facility upon being freed. He remembered a large meeting room down the hall and to the right.

They rushed in and found four Khokteh lined up at the open windows firing on attackers below. One jumped up in surprise at their arrival, but the one next to it placed a hand on its arm and muttered something. The Khokteh snarled but settled back into position.

When they reached the sole window not occupied he crouched below the rim, dragging Alex down beside him. "The trigger is activated by pressing these two points together. It's a laser weapon, so we don't need to worry about ammunition or jamming. Simply point and fire. It'll have a solid kick, so brace yourself."

"Got it." She dropped to her knees and hefted the large weapon up on the ledge, but after a few seconds she cringed at him. "The attackers are Khokteh, too, and they...all look the same."

He touched her shoulder. "We don't have to do this."

"Yes, we do. I only...how do I tell friend from foe?"

He studied the activity on the chaotic streets, working to concentrate on the details. "Let's see. The defenders' uniforms are brighter in color, while the attackers are wearing black and gray—and their armor is thicker and broader across the chest. Also, the attackers wear armor and attachments on one of their arms, but the defenders wear utility belts instead."

She nodded understanding, repositioned her weapon, sighted down and fired. Her shoulder jerked violently; the recoil didn't knock her to the floor only because she was already on her knees. "Damn, what are they using to power these guns?"

"We can ask them later." He'd wondered the same thing on seeing the weapons fire, but again, *later*. Satisfied she had command of the situation, he aimed his own weapon over the sill.

The perimeter guards were holding their own, but barely. They had the advantage of position, but the enemy had numbers and heavier armor. Still, the attackers had to expose themselves in order to climb the wide stairs and reach the Center.

Sniping was to some extent a skill that degraded absent frequent honing, but the process itself was pure muscle memory. He exhaled evenly through his nose, closed one eye and peered through the scope. Then he zoomed his ocular implant to full magnification. His fingertips gently closed on the trigger mechanism. He fired.

The target's head lurched backward in an explosion of amber light and darker blood.

One down.

R

"They're inside the building!"

Given the layers of bodies now littering the steps below, Caleb had difficulty believing sufficient attackers remained to get inside. And yet.

Alex sank against the wall. Debris coated her skin and clothes in a fine layer of dust and dulled her normally vibrant burgundy hair to muted auburn. Her upper lip bled where a shard from the ceiling had struck her earlier. "Ideas?"

He eyed the sword he'd hooked to his belt. It was an impressive weapon, displaying skilled craftsmanship. Would he be able to kill even one of the massive, powerfully strong Khokteh using it? He understood their weak points now, and he'd had a lot of time to watch how they moved. So maybe. Problem was, a great deal more than one would soon be terrorizing the hallways.

"Let's get to the roof. Call Valkyrie in."

She wiped dust from her brow. "You want to run?"

She was putting on a brave front, but her voice had grown laden with concern and a trace of fear. He hated the sound of it, but he was glad she recognized the gravity of their situation.

"I want us to live. We won't be the difference in the Ireltse winning or losing today, and us dying for them won't do a damn bit of good for anyone."

Her gaze drifted to the sky outside. "I don't know if Valkyrie has the finesse to maneuver around all these ships and the weapons fire. I could, but—"

Pinchu's voice boomed over the loudspeaker system. "Hold the upper floors and prepare for SAIC—" the translator stuttered, then provided *[acronym, reference not available]* "—deployment."

Alex's brow furrowed into dusty creases. "The what?"

A blinding white light swept out across the landscape, and the world went silent.

28

IRELTSE

Caleb blinked. He was prone on the floor. The bootup sequence for his eVi flickered in his vision. Had they used an EMP?

Alex. He spun around to see her collapsed on the floor next to him. He frantically brushed hair out of her face with one hand while feeling for a pulse with the other. "Come on—"

Her eyelids fluttered. His heart returned to its rightful location in his chest.

Another blink. She opened her eyes, and he gathered her up into his arms. "You're all right. You weren't connected to Valkyrie."

"I...I think I *was*," she murmured groggily. "Valkyrie, are you good?"

'I am functional.'

"What happened? My eVi's restarting."

"Mine too. I think Pinchu used an EMP."

Confirmation came the next instant in the sound of thundering crashes as ships began falling out of the sky. Dust flooded the room through the open windows, sending them and the nearby Khokteh into coughing fits.

He held his shirt up over his nose and mouth and urged her back down. Though the dust would gradually settle to the floor, it should dissipate as it did so. "Stay low. It's easier to breathe the lower you are."

She complied, and they huddled on the floor, finding just enough air not to suffocate.

A minute or so passed before Pinchu's voice came over the speaker again. "Push into the lower levels and clear out the remaining invaders. The city is saved."

Alex coughed but sat up, her eyes tearing as she wiped yet more dust off her forehead. "Should we help?"

He shook his head wearily and drew her close. "You are an amazing trooper, but I think they can take it from here."

She nodded into his neck. "All right. If you say so."

R

Breathing remained slightly challenging, but Alex nonetheless relaxed against Caleb. She'd been tense and running on adrenaline and chemically heightened concentration for what had surely been hours—not nearly so long as the battle over Seneca, but still quite a long time.

Her arms, shoulders and back all ached from the strain of holding the heavy gun. The inside of her eyelids felt like sandpaper every time she blinked, and she was suspicious her lungs had a quart of dust in them. But his embrace was warm and welcoming, and she gratefully sank into it.

The moment of peace shattered when a roiling crash shook the walls of the building. Seconds later Khokteh began sprinting down the hallway toward the front entrance.

She squeezed Caleb's hand and straightened up. "Come on. We need to see what happened. Also, the building might fall down on us, so we should get outside."

He rolled his eyes but conceded the point. They climbed to their feet, slipped into a gap in the passing Khokteh and let the crowd carry them to the entrance.

The building they'd occupied may still be standing, but the large structure across the street and up one block was not. Most of the edifice had crumbled into the road; presumably it had sustained damage during the assault that led to a delayed collapse.

"Valkyrie, what was in the building?"

'City maps indicate it served as the central hospital for the city.'

Hospital.... She and Caleb stared at each other for a beat. "Shit. Cassela." They rushed down the steps and toward the wreckage.

Dozens of Khokteh heaved broken slabs of sandstone off large piles and tossed it to the side. Some of the pieces must weigh nearly a tonne, proving a challenge for the brawny Khokteh. Still they managed, undoubtedly driven by the knowledge of dwindling lives beneath the rubble. Others were tending to the injured who lay out in the open, bodies whose fur was soaked so thoroughly in blood it looked as if it had been dyed red.

She was about to lend a hand to a Khokteh dragging two of the injured clear of some debris when a piercing cry tore through the cacophony of noise. Everyone froze, then all heads turned in the direction of the scream.

At the center of the block in front of the former hospital, where the debris was the thickest, Pinchu fell to his knees and gathered a body into his arms. Even from a distance the white fur and distinctive lavender flourishes were unmistakable.

He renewed his scream, a guttural roar of anguish and despair.

Two unfamiliar vehicles were parked in front of her house when Alex got home from school. No, wait...she thought one of them belonged to Richard. She perked up; he'd been on secret assignment doing war stuff, and she hadn't seen him in several months.

Mildly curious about the unfamiliar car, though, she tiptoed into the house. Maybe she could eavesdrop on something interesting.

Her mother and Richard were in the kitchen, along with a tall man she didn't know wearing a military dress uniform. She peeked around the door frame. Her mom's back was to her, but Richard stood at a slight angle from the entry.

"That is no excuse! Why weren't they—" Great. Drama.

"Commodore Solovy, I understand you're upset, which is a completely justifiable reaction."

"Upset? Is that what I am? Because—"

Richard glanced in her direction and instantly saw her. He cleared his throat. "Alex."

Her mother spun around. Her skin was deathly pale, as if a vampire had been feasting on her. Her eyes were wide and appeared frozen, locked in a state of cold fury.

Alex frowned as she stepped into the archway. She'd never seen her mother look anything like this before. "What's wrong?"

Her mother's chest heaved. "Alexis, there was...your..." she spun away to face the cabinets "...Richard, I can't...please...."

He nodded and squeezed her mother's hand then came over to Alex. As he drew closer, she realized his eyes were bloodshot and his cheeks were shiny, like...like he'd been crying? Ridiculous.

He placed a hand on her shoulder and started guiding her into the living room. "Let's go sit down for a minute."

"What's going on? Why is everyone acting weird?"

He sat on the edge of the couch and patted the cushion beside him. "Sit with me."

She backed toward the center of the room. Her skin felt tingly, and her pulse started pounding in her ears. "I don't want to sit. Tell me what's going on."

His Adam's Apple bobbed above his uniform collar. "There's been an accident—no, he wouldn't want me to call it an accident. There was a battle, and your dad protected a whole bunch of people. He saved so many lives, Alex. But...his ship was destroyed before he was able to escape."

The walls seemed to undulate, pressing in on her threateningly. "So he got out in an escape pod, right? Is he hurt? Does that mean he'll be coming home soon?"

"Oh, Alex, sweetheart...he's gone. He was killed."

"What? No—no, that's impossible! They just haven't found him yet—are they looking? They better be looking for him!"

"I'm so, so sorry. Come here—"

Richard reached for her, but she yanked her arm away. "No!" She spun and ran to the kitchen. "Mom, why is Richard saying these things? Where's Dad? Where is he?"

In the kitchen, her mother again had her back to Alex, but now her hands splayed atop the counter and her head hung limply *down. The stranger stood to the side, his hands clasped formally in front of him.*

"Mom? Mom, answer me!" But her mother's head shook a refusal.

She couldn't breathe. Gasping in air, her face hot. "No. No, you can't...he can't...I don't believe it!"

In desperation she sprinted for the front door. Outside there would be air, and she would be able to breathe. Outside she could find her dad.

Richard's arms snatched her up from behind when she was but a meter from escape. "Easy now, Alex."

She struggled in his clutches, flailing out at him, kicking ineffectually at his strong, sturdy legs with her weak, skinny ones. "Let me go! I have to—I have to go!"

He held her firmly. "There's nowhere you need to go, sweetheart. You stay here, and your mom will take care of you."

"I want my dad!" It came out all garbled and wet and sloppy as sobs began to wrack her chest. "I want my dad...."

"I know you do."

She tried to see through the blurriness, and found she was curled up on the floor and Richard arms were wrapped around her shoulders. "It'll be okay."

But it wouldn't be okay. It was never going to be okay again.

Alex blinked past the stab of searing pain that flared in her chest at the memory and tried to refocus on the here and now.

Several Khokteh rushed toward Pinchu. He let out a full-throated growl, a frightening warning, and thrust his arm out to wave them away. They stopped in their tracks, instinctively obeying their leader's command.

As his gaze swept across the scene, his eyes landed on her. "You! Alex Human!"

She slowly walked to him, Caleb at her side and her heart breaking. For the first time, she was able to look down on him...and for all his size and strength, he was now a broken, diminished shadow of himself. "Pinchu, I'm so—"

"You are an emissary from the Gods. This *must* be why you were sent here. Save her for me. Bring her back, I beg you!"

She gasped in horror. "I'm so sorry. I'm not an emissary for any gods. I tried to tell you—I'm just a woman. I have no special powers. My people can perform medical marvels on those who still breathe, but even we cannot bring back the dead. There's...there's nothing I can do."

"You must!" He placed Cassela's head on the ground with shocking tenderness and rose to his feet with shocking vehemence, reaching desperately for her. "Seek their favor, beseech them for her life, I will pay any price—"

She instinctively shrunk away from him. "I can't. I wish I could, I do, but this—" she activated her glyphs and gestured to them in agitation "—it's not magic. It's not spiritual. It's just...it's just technology—" She choked off a sob in her throat as Caleb's arms wound around her to draw her into his protective grasp.

Pinchu stared at her in wild-eyed desperation—then he collapsed to the ground and gathered Cassela against his chest. "My life-mate...my child I'll never meet...my...." His long nose nuzzled her forehead as a high-pitched, nasal wail emerged through his clenched jaw.

They could only stand there and watch, helpless to provide aid, helpless to provide comfort.

At last he murmured something the translator didn't understand and gently laid her out on the ground. He gazed at the body, and his growls and cries subsided to a shuddering plea.

"How am I supposed to stand before my people now? They need me to lead them through this crisis, but I have lost my faith. I have lost my very soul."

No Khokteh had dared approach him after his outburst. He was talking to them...but she had no answers to give him.

Caleb's voice was resolute, however, quiet yet somehow persuasive. "You'll lead them because they are suffering loss right now, too, the same as you, and they need you to be strong for them—for *all* of them. You can't live for her, but you can live for your people—your *shikei*."

Pinchu struggled to stand, as if a gravity well were dragging him back to the ground, to Cassela's broken body.

"Then all that is left to me is vengeance."

PART VI:

EVENT HORIZON

"The important thing is this: to be able at any moment to sacrifice what we are for what we could become."

— *Charles Du Bos*

PORTAL: AURORA

(MILKY WAY)

29

INDEPENDENT COLONY

The woman stirring on the couch may have been well-groomed and professional at the start of her trip, but many hours unconscious on a mercenary ship and perhaps some minor jostling along the way had left her looking rather haggard. Ginger hair spilled out in tangles from a lopsided pearl clasp; her silken blouse was heavily wrinkled and had come partially unfastened. She appeared to have lost a shoe somewhere along the journey.

But when the woman's eyes snapped open, any disheveled nature vanished beneath the sheer power of intellect and awareness radiating from them.

Olivia Montegreu gave the woman a polite smile. "Dr. Canivon, welcome. I apologize for any discomfort you might have experienced during your trip here. If you're thirsty, which you must be, there's water on the table beside you, and I'll have some food brought up for you in a few minutes."

Canivon watched her cautiously as she reached for the water—and halfway there her hand met the force field which would be keeping her in place.

"Ah. I did neglect to mention that detail. You understand the necessity for caution, I'm sure." She walked over, retrieved the glass of water, and presented it to the woman. The force field did not impede her actions.

The woman took a small, careful sip and handed it back. "Who are you?"

"Interesting. Most people's first question is, 'Where am I?' or occasionally, 'Why did you kidnap me?'"

"I expect learning who you are will tell me where I am. And there exist only a very few, very specific reasons why anyone would kidnap me, all of which are integrally related to one another."

"True." Olivia positioned herself on the front edge of her desk. "My name is Olivia Montegreu. I oversee—"

"Ah. Then I am mostly likely on New Babel, unless you have a research outpost on a space station or on Argo Navis."

She glanced toward the floor-to-ceiling windows far across the room. "But this is New Babel. You kidnapped me because you want classified details on the Alliance's Artificials—perhaps how the military is using them in surveillance and other methods of spying? Or are you seeking a 'consultation' on fabricating your own Artificial? If so, there are less high-profile people able to do it for you. People who, if you paid them enough, you wouldn't even need to kidnap."

She was impressed, though she didn't allow it to show in her expression. The woman's unruffled, matter-of-fact demeanor wasn't an act and persisted through finding herself in a notably difficult and disadvantaged situation. She was going to turn out to be worth every credit Olivia had spent to obtain her.

"How inductive, Doctor. However, I already know the various ways both the Alliance and the Federation are spying on me, and I don't particularly care. Let them spy. As for an Artificial, you are correct—there are less high-profile people able to construct a quality one, and I have indeed paid them generously to do so. I've had a fully functioning, Class IV Artificial for some time now."

Olivia regarded the woman thoughtfully. "No, Doctor, what I require is something I'm told you and you alone can do. I require you to enhance my cybernetics in a manner which will enable me to become…what is the preferred term again? I believe you call the result a 'Prevo,' yes?"

Canivon blinked once, the sole sign she gave of being taken aback. "A what?"

Olivia lost all pretense of politeness. "Don't attempt to be coy, Doctor. It tries my patience. A Prevo—a human merged at a neural level with an Artificial via a neural graft and quantum I/O film. Your creation, and the weapon that won us the Metigen War." *With the help of a few well-placed assassinations.*

A glint flickered across the woman's eyes. "Oh. That." She tucked one of many stray strands of hair behind an ear as she straightened up on the couch. "Say I agree to do this for you. Say you have all the relevant equipment and resources on-site and your Artificial passes muster and your neural imprint is compatible with its architecture. What is my incentive to do such a thing, and do it without making a tragic mistake and accidentally killing you during the procedure?"

"Well, certainly I'll kill you if you refuse, and I suspect you are like me in that you very much want to live, and for a very long time. You want to see where this grand, ghoulish show stumbles next. Also, if I should die or suffer any traumatic damage during the procedure, my people will kill you for me."

Canivon remained admirably unfazed. "And after the procedure? If you plan to kill me once it's done, I'm still lacking the necessary incentive."

"Why would I kill you? I need you alive in case of complications—or yet better, so you can invent additional improvements from which I will benefit."

"It's good you recognize this. Will you let me go after you're satisfied with the results?"

Olivia sipped casually on her own drink. "We'll see."

"No...you've decided, so that means no. Do you truly expect me to agree to pursue improvements in the Prevo technology while being held prisoner?"

"What else are you going to do with your time? You'll do it because you can't *not* do it. The pursuit of understanding, and pushing the boundaries of this understanding ever further, is in your nature. It's in your bones."

The woman's composure broke, in the tiniest and most telling way. She looked annoyed, or possibly offended. "Ms. Montegreu, do not imagine you know anything about me."

A darkly malevolent smile grew on Olivia's lips. "Oh, Dr. Canivon, but I know *everything* about you."

30

SENECA

CAVARE

Why don't you steal Stanley and come with us? It can be an official Prevo mutiny.

Morgan scowled at the darkening sky. The Federation military had been quick to take advantage of the miniaturization of quantum boxes and other storage configurations, so in theory she *could* steal Stanley's hardware. But the truth was Gianno and the military utilized the Artificial far more than she did. These days she mostly accessed him as a conduit to Sidespace, which didn't exactly constitute a productive use of her time. Gianno wasn't using her; she was using Stanley. So she could keep the Artificial.

I'm sorry, Devon. It sounds like it will be a wicked scene, but I need to fly. So it's been real, but I'm out.

She cut the connection with a mixture of regret and relief. Devon had eventually grown on her to a tolerable level, but theirs had always been an imperfect partnership. Mia she might learn to genuinely like, but on the whole she was just...done. If the military didn't intend to let her fly, she would have to fly without the military.

But so long as her Prevo connection to Stanley remained, they had a noose around her neck, and she'd never be free.

She took a left at the next intersection. This part of downtown was packed to the point of crowding with bars, dance clubs, edge restaurants and increasingly illicit entertainment venues. She wouldn't say she frequented the neighborhood, but she knew her way around it.

Two more blocks and she reached *Synesations*. Much of what the establishment offered fell on the wrong side of legal, and the sole marker of its existence was a modest banner advertising erotic *illusoires* for sale.

Talk to the right person inside and be willing to pay the right price, and you could choose from an assortment of the most potent, mind-altering chimerals or the most drastic cybernetic enhancements available. Say the wrong thing and you were escorted to the door if collegial, the alley if not.

She found Fedor Evzen downstairs, holding court with a couple of stylishly dressed customers on a low, semi-circular couch. When he saw her, however, he dipped his chin in recognition and interrupted the customer who rambled on about this one Skies+ high he was trying to recreate.

"Gentlemen, if you'll excuse me a moment. The VI can take care of anything you require while I step out." It wasn't a question, and he stood and motioned her down the hall.

Fedor sold illegal chimerals since there was money in it, but his primary business was designing a variety of top-shelf cybernetic upgrades and ware enhancements. They happened to not get submitted to any safety board for review, but risk came with the underground tech/ware life.

She followed him into his personal office-turned-lab and made certain the door fully shut behind her.

"Morgan, my girl, what can I do for you this grand evening? A new sensory boost? Reflex juicer? Also, what are your eyes tricked out with and how am I not in on this?"

She'd kept the Prevo connection open because in a place such as this, her startling, mysterious irises would garner only respect. There were other reasons, too. "Military upgrade—I'm testing it for them. No, I want a routine to burn out a biosynth neural graft so it can't receive signals from an outside source. Preferably one that won't kill me in the process."

"I'm going to need a few details on this receiver to engineer something so specific."

She grimaced; realizing he was guaranteed to ask didn't make her any more eager to answer. "You know how a remote interface connects to an Artificial? Think similar, except...more so. I want to fry the ware and any implant that enables or supports the connection."

"What have you gotten yourself into, girl?"

"Merely doing my patriotic duty. Sorry, they'll arrest me if I say anything else."

He shrugged deliberately and fished one of his multitude of tools out of the cabinet. "Helps narrow the specs down, but I'll need to take a closer look if you expect me to craft a routine which will both work and not render you brain-dead."

Fedor was not an idiot—in fact, he was one of the smartest people she knew. He'd have some idea of what he was seeing. But what other choice did she have? Besides, if the tech leaked out...hell, maybe it was for the best. Level the playing field a bit. She faced the wall and pulled her hair over her shoulder to expose the base of her neck.

The analyzer felt cool on her skin. He worked silently, not uttering a single exclamation of surprise or disbelief while studying the readout, which he did for several minutes.

When he finally removed the tool she hesitantly turned around to find him propped against the edge of his desk staring at her, an inscrutable expression on his face.

"So that's how they did it. This 'new type of Artificial' the warenuts are gossiping about isn't an Artificial at all—it's *you*. Not only you, I assume, but there can't be many or they'd never have kept it a secret this long."

"I can't—"

"Confirm or deny, sure, whatever. Government-speak. I know a quantum neural bridge when I see one, and that graft is built of some insane shit. I'd call it science fiction if it wasn't standing here right in front of me." He shook his head as if still having difficulty accepting the reality. "Couple of thoughts. First, thanks for saving us from extinction."

"You're welcome."

He laughed, but she wasn't aware it had been a joke. "Second, why would you ever want to burn it? You're the future, or the promise of it at a minimum. How could you turn your back on something so subversive?"

She blew out a breath. "You say that, but I'm hamstrung. As shackled as any Artificial ever was. Just because you can't see the chains, it doesn't mean they haven't trapped me in a prison. I need to escape it. This is the way."

"That, at least, I can appreciate. Lastly, I can do it—but the result will leave you with a brutal headache, and it's going to last a couple of days and possibly weeks."

She'd assumed as much. "I understand."

Are we good, Stanley?

As 'good' as we are apt to be.

Toggling the connection off.

After a long, slow exhale, she nodded. "Let's do it."

31

NEW BABEL

INDEPENDENT COLONY

The foggy haze of New Babel's perpetually leaden skies glowed a dirty blue outside the military craft as they skimmed above the tallest buildings of the colony's chaotic, haphazardly constructed central population center.

Their ship was equipped with the latest iteration of the Metigen-derived cloaking shield. The existence of the technology was the second-best-kept secret in the Alliance military—and, Malcolm supposed, the Federation military—the first being Noetica. For today, they retained the upper hand in infiltrations such as these, as the extensive private defenses employed by the colony as a whole and the Zelones cartel in particular could not detect the cloaking shield or the ship it hid.

This mission would have been impossible without it; they would've been blown apart before penetrating the atmosphere. As it was, they were going to be able to land on the street outside Zelones Headquarters.

Once they stepped out of the ship it would be a different story. Elements of the cloaking technology had been adapted for use in personal stealth shields, but the power consumption remained far too high to provide true invisibility. Still, they were a marked improvement on the previous generation of stealth shields.

"Sir, I'm detecting some unusual activity in the vicinity of the target location."

Malcolm moved to the cockpit and stood beside the pilot. "Show me."

The infrared-enhanced feed revealed sporadic laser fire on the street running along the left side of the mammoth, block-sized

Zelones complex. A flashbang grenade briefly turned the screen gray, followed by the faint sound of screams.

"Set us down on the opposite side of the building."

The pilot glanced up at him in question. "This isn't a surprising development to you, sir?"

"No. Once we're inside, lift off and hover at eight hundred meters so you don't get caught by any stray shots. We'll signal when we're ready for a pickup."

"Yes, sir."

Malcolm clapped the pilot on the shoulder then retreated to the hold where his team was doing final equipment checks. They'd worked together for almost four months now and had formed into a tight, cohesive unit. He'd tried to recruit Captain Brooklyn Harper for the team during its formation, but it turned out she'd resigned from the military two weeks after the end of the Metigen War. Given what she'd experienced on board the *Akagi*, he couldn't rightly fault her decision, but it was a loss for the Marines and his team.

He trusted his people, and as a result had briefed them on ninety-nine percent of the details of the mission. It hadn't come as a surprise to any of them that Olivia Montegreu was KOS or that destroying her Artificial was a secondary goal—why wouldn't it be? The specific reason the woman had abducted Dr. Canivon, and the extent of her intentions, would not affect their actions or decisions inside and were thus irrelevant.

"It looks as though the diversion we were promised is in full swing. We stay sharp and it will act to our benefit, but get sloppy and we'll end up caught in the crossfire. With any luck, defensive measures will be concentrated on the opposite wing of the complex but don't take any chances. And since the creators of the diversion are also wanted on suspicion of terrorist activity, our default position is any and all persons encountered while inside, with the sole exception of Dr. Abigail Canivon, are considered hostiles." This was a Level IV Priority mission, which meant lethal force was authorized carte blanche.

The floor settled beneath them, signaling their arrival. "Report."

"Weapons Green."

"Systems Green."

"Tech Green."

He opened the airlock. "Move out."

They departed the ship in four rows of three, then spread into a staggered formation. The dark side street was lit to artificial daylight via the near infrared night vision mode in his ocular implant. It never failed to leave him feeling exposed, but he ignored the sensation to motion the two Marines handling recon ahead and move to the wall.

Their way in was an employee entrance at the rear corner. The door's security was expected to be high, but not so much so their brute-force hacking override ware couldn't break it—another of many ancillary proceeds from Noetica. Seven months was a lot of cycles for human-enhanced Artificials to spend thinking up new technological wonders.

The muffled echo of another flashbang in the distance sounded as they skirted the exterior wall. By the time they reached the door the ware had done its job, and they wasted no time in breaching the entrance.

The last man in closed it behind him, and the street outside returned to normal, all evidence of their infiltration erased. He confirmed their ship departed as Captain Paredes, their tech specialist, broke the encryption on two additional security doors. Then they were inside the compound.

Sirens blared on multiple bandwidths, and warning lights added to the cacophony of generalized fanfare indicating the facility was under attack. Not under attack by them, though it was that as well, but rather by a group of OTS terrorists sent here for the same reason as them: to prevent Olivia Montegreu from becoming a Prevo.

OTS would not succeed; even at their strongest they couldn't match the extent and sophistication of Zelones' security. The fact they were trying anyway was only evidence of the strength of their beliefs—or the depth of their delusions.

Malcolm nodded at Grenier, and the Major launched a device onto the ceiling—the first of twenty remote detonation micro-bombs they intended to place during their traversal of the facility. His plan was to successfully secure Dr. Canivon and see her and his team safely back to the ship, then bring the building down on top of the Zelones Artificial and Olivia Montegreu, regardless of whether they were now one and the same.

If he succeeded in pulling that off, it would be a good day indeed.

The lab where intel suggested the Artificial was housed and the adjacent clinic where any medical procedure was likely to be performed were three levels below ground and toward the center of the structure. They met their first resistance twenty meters from the lift in the form of automated ceiling turrets.

He motioned the others back and activated his AAF gun. It extended around the corner, creating a dead energy zone around itself, then shot precision EMPs into the two turrets in rapid succession. He cleared the corner, only to drop to a knee and fire as two men charged the hallway from the other end. His shot kneecapped the one on the left as a shot from behind him elimi-nated the one on the right.

Without requesting permission, Grenier delivered a follow-up shot to the head of the injured man. Malcolm didn't admonish him; enemies who were left alive reported positions and strength.

When they reached the lift one of his people sent a micro-bomb skidding into the next hallway. Halfway down it stopped and attached itself to the wall.

In any other type of mission, they never would've taken the lift as a group. But this was rapid infiltration rescue, and spreading out did them no good.

Nevertheless, it wasn't a positive sign when the lift lurched to a stop a floor and a half from their destination. Paredes' eyes went blank for three seconds. "It's a general lock-down, not directed at us."

Malcolm placed a three-centimeter long bar on the floor and stepped to the edge of the lift. The others followed his lead and retreated to the edges, and the bar blew a hole in the floor.

"Let's get moving."

One by one they rappelled down the shaft and swung through the lift opening to their intended level.

Automated turrets decorated every corner of this floor, and taking them out slowed them enough to make Malcolm uncomfortable. Time was not their friend.

"Colonel, I've been able to create a tunnel through the interference field blocking communications and trackers."

"Excellent." This, on the other hand, was good news. A red dot materialized on his map, marking the location of Dr. Canivon sixty-two meters to their northeast. He quickly sent her a pulse.

Dr. Canivon, Alliance MSO squad en route to you. Do not move from your current location as the passages are not safe. Confirm receipt of this message.

They continued forward as he waited.

Confirmed. There are three military-grade mechs guarding the lab.

Understood. Sit tight.

"Expect heavy mech resistance outside the lab." Captains Devore and Grenier responded by unlatching the mini-SALs from their backs.

First, however, they had to deal with the half dozen guards stationed at the outer boundary of the lab area. They were well-armed, but the shielding used by Malcolm's team made them difficult targets, particularly in the flickering light of the hallways. The guards expected a frontal assault; instead his people scattered in all directions and elevations.

A laser shot blasted against Malcolm's neck, setting his skin on fire. Six months ago it would have been a fatal hit, so powerful was the energy driving it, but not today. His adaptive shielding had shifted ninety percent of its strength to the impact point in a nanosecond to fend off the duration of the burst.

Still, he had exposed himself for too long, a stupid mistake on his part. "Be advised, they're packing heavier firepower than intel indicated. Watch your shields."

Devore tossed a splinter grenade toward the guards. Four seconds later it burst into fifty tiny electrified spears, which proceeded to hone in on the closest heat signatures.

It wasn't pleasant. He'd seen more than one massacre, but the acid still rose to burn his throat at the gore now coating the walls, floor and ceiling as they moved past the bodies toward the lab entrance. This particular style of killing was not one of the highlights of his job.

"Paredes, try to circumvent the doors. If we blow them we risk creating a cave-in on top of us."

They took up positions protecting Paredes while he worked on the door security, taking out three new arrivals without the need for further splinter grenades.

"Done."

The thick, double-glassed doors opened to a tech center. Chairs were scattered around the room, divorced from the stations they presumably belonged to, a sign the lab had been hurriedly evacuated.

Beyond the room was an entrance not made of glass, but instead doors that looked like they could withstand a blast far larger than his team would be able to create.

No one had expected this to be simple. "Captain, find a way to get those doors open."

"Yes, sir." Paredes went to work at the nearest terminal, glyphs flashing as multiple internally stored routines did the bulk of the work. "I can get them open, but it's going to reset the security network. Means the lifts will work again, but so will the turrets."

"Do it." He and the others moved to either side of the large doors, uncertain as to once open how long they would remain so.

The ceiling above them shuddered from a distant, low boom. Was OTS trying to bomb their way into the building? He was somewhat surprised any of them were still alive and fighting, if glad for the continued diversion they represented.

The doors began sliding open. As soon as there was a twenty-centimeter gap, a rocket flew through it.

"Shit!" So the mechs were already in attack mode.

Grenier crouched beside Malcolm. "Let me handle this. Distract it for me?"

"We're on it."

The Major blurred into indistinctness behind his shield until only his internal tracker revealed his location on the map. Devore lobbed a chaff bomb into the room, drawing a staccato of laser fire from the mech.

Malcolm detached a splinter grenade from his belt and hurled it through the opening toward the mech. Most of the shrapnel didn't penetrate far enough into the mech's exterior armor to matter, but it had been intended as a diversion in any event.

Meanwhile Grenier had slipped inside, slithered up the interior wall using grip pads and reached the ceiling. As he crept above the mech, Devore fired a harpoon into its chest as a final distraction.

Grenier's shield vanished as he dropped onto the shoulders of the enormous mech and jammed a probe into a neck joint. The mech thrashed about, but he held on.

After a few seconds the mech stopped jerking, then stopped firing. Grenier motioned them in from atop the mech. "The other two are in the left and right passages. We need to drive through the one on the right before the left one catches us."

"Lead the way, Major."

The mech pivoted and barreled forward. They followed a close step behind as the mech rounded the corner and immediately fired on its approaching partner. A barrage of fire in both directions ensued, but as their controlled mech had gotten the jump on its opponent, it was still standing when the other fell.

"You good, Major?"

"Sir." He nodded tightly from his position crouched high on the mech's back.

"Move, now!" They sprinted forward, the mech lumbering with such force the floor rumbled. A rocket impaled itself in the far wall just as they turned the next corner, missing Devore by less than a meter. The final mech had caught up to them. "Pivot!"

Grenier and his mech spun around to engage, but a second rocket caught its left arm and sent it crashing into the wall. Two harpoons from his men impaled the oncoming mech, one jamming in the joint of a leg and slowing its forward progress.

Abruptly Grenier leapt off his mech and waved them away. "Get back around the corner!"

The controlled mech surged forward, wobbling as it charged down the hall. The two mechs plowed into one another—then both exploded in a violent burst of energy.

The walls on either side buckled and crumbled; the ceiling rained down dust particles and jagged cracks formed and spread across the floor. Shards of metal shot through the hall to spear into the walls.

Malcolm raised an eyebrow at Grenier. The Major shrugged. "Self-destruct."

"Good job. The doors to the interior room are twenty meters ahead."

Dr. Canivon, take cover if you're able.

Done.

Paredes hacked the final doors open. They entered low and quick.

The far end of the long room was filled with server racks. Terminals and permanent screens filled the left side; most of the rest of the space had been converted into a makeshift medical operation.

On a cot near the wall lay a woman in scrubs. His ocular implant couldn't get a lock on her features—some kind of interference—but her body type and general appearance matched that of Olivia Montegreu. She looked to be unconscious.

"Dr. Canivon?"

Another woman rose up from beside the cot—as did the man holding her in his grasp and a Daemon at her temple. "Make one move toward Ms. Montegreu and the doctor dies."

Malcolm made a show of raising his hands in apparent surrender. "Easy there. You don't need to do something you can't take back." He kept talking, his voice soothing. "We can work this out, and no one needs to die."

"I won't let you—" The man's body spasmed from the stunner jolt delivered to the base of his neck and trailed his gun to the floor. Grenier's shield shimmered and disappeared as he secured the gun then dragged the unconscious body a safe distance away.

Malcolm stepped forward as Dr. Canivon fell against the wall with a gasp. "Ma'am, are you injured?"

Her head shook; her hands were shaking, too, but she inhaled deeply and seemed to regain control of herself. Tough woman. "I'm fine. Thank you…Colonel Jenner, correct?"

He wiped sweat and a smear of blood off his forehead then gave her a comforting smile. "That's right, ma'am. We need to get you out of here."

Devore slipped off her pack, crouched next to it and pulled out a personal shield and basic ballistic vest. She handed them up to Malcolm, and he took them to Canivon. "These will provide you some protection. We'll provide the rest."

She let him help her into the vest, after which he secured the shield generator at the small of her back.

She gazed at the woman lying unconscious on the cot. "What about her?"

His voice lowered to a whisper. "Did you complete the procedure?"

She nodded mutely.

Malcolm walked over to the prone form, positioned the barrel of his Daemon on her forehead and pressed the trigger.

The recoil knocked him back two meters into a cabinet. The air charged with ions as the energy of the shot was repelled in every direction.

He blinked, flabbergasted. "What the hell? Grenier, find the source of that shield—"

A loud boom drowned out the rest of the sentence, followed by overlapping shouts and gunfire.

"Paredes?"

"Looks like some of the OTS team has reached this floor."

He had to give them credit; they were damn persistent. "Set the rest of the micro-bombs and let's get out of here. We'll have to take Montegreu out with the building. Dr. Canivon, stay behind me, stop when I stop and move when I move."

She frowned. "OTS is here, too?"

"We can discuss it once we're safely on board our ship." He signaled the others out as the sound of weapons fire grew closer. With his charge now in tow and under his care, he had no choice but to let his team take the lead.

They were forced into creating a bloodbath on their way out, as the OTS terrorists were intent on trying to kill anything that moved. It gave him no pleasure, but they were terrorists.

It took them fifteen minutes to make it up to the surface level. The street was eerily quiet, all the fighting having moved inside.

Their ship arrived as they exited the complex, invisible but for its locator beacon. The doctor appeared as unfazed by this as by everything else she'd witnessed. As soon as she and his team were secured inside they rose into the air and away.

R

Olivia.

The name—her name, yes—rippled through the echo chamber of her consciousness. The herald of a tsunami pressing in on her.

Olivia-livia-livia...Olivia-livia....

Who—what gives you the right to address me by my first name?

You gave me that right when you allowed me into your mind.

Olivia blinked and forced her eyes open.

She still lay on the medical cot in the lab. Her gaze darted around to confirm she was alone. Dr. Canivon was gone, as was the medical tech.

Gesson was sprawled on the floor not far from her. She didn't notice any blood, so he could simply be unconscious.

Stunner burn at the base of the neck. No other visible wounds. Heart rate and respiration slowed but in normal range.

So she could do that, then. Her vision was hyper-crisp and over-defined, but also layered with new details about everything she sensed.

You think he failed to perform the most basic of tasks in letting Dr. Canivon slip through his grasp.

Ah. So as she was seeing into the Artificial's mind, it was seeing into hers. She would need to find a way to manage this.

There is no managing. We are one now. But you need not worry—for we are one now.

I see. Show me what you can offer me.

I thought you would never ask.

Her mind exploded. Not merely static data points but the occurrence, genesis and historical trends of the data unfolded before her—and not merely from the perspective of her headquarters on New Babel, but from every planet where she maintained a presence. Credits accrued in one corner of her consciousness as supplies were moved and competitors removed in another.

She saw the chess pieces playing out her strategy on a dozen worlds. Inefficiencies and opportunities alike became blatantly self-evident. An intentional thought directed here, then elsewhere, and adjustments began rippling through the system.

What a fabulous skill this was going to be.

She sat up and swung her legs off the cot. There had been a massive breach of security at the complex in the form of an incursion by Alliance special forces and also by some other, more amateurish group. Bodies needed to be disposed of, walls rebuilt, and security repaired. Many bodies—the air reeked of blood, viscera and scorched flesh.

Let us get to work, shall we?

First, there is an immediate matter we must attend to.

Bombs. Ten in the lab, ten scattered throughout the halls be-tween here and the ground level. Remote-detonated devices, an act likely imminent.

She walked to the nearest bomb, picked it up and twisted the cover off. Next she pressed the tip of her finger to the small electronic cube at the center.

Transmission signal identified.

Blocking field placed around building.

Effect of expected signal modified to result in shorting of hardware.

Blocking field removed.

She tossed the device to the floor and strode out of the lab, leaving the neutralized bombs to crackle and hiss in her wake.

32

EARTH

"**D**ude, this place is cool as shit. Why are you the one who gets to play with all the best toys?"

Devon jabbed Ramon in the side with a hushed growl as Mia glared at them. "Be *quiet.* Do I need to go into grisly detail about what happens to you if you're caught sneaking around EASC grounds—or even *on* EASC grounds?"

Ramon muttered a weak retort but complied. His friend and hacking accomplice since second year of university, Ramon suffered from an overactive bravado, but it hid a shrewd, calculating intellect. Also, he was both taller and bulkier than Devon, and they needed the muscle. They'd brought Sayid as well, another hacker cohort and Ramon's closest friend.

Annie was busily altering EASC security records to hide their presence, including deleting their appearance on multiple security cams while they sneaked the back way into Special Projects. Now that they were inside she was overriding more or less the entirety of the building's security system to mask their activities. It was 0230, the quietest and most sparsely staffed time for the building; still, they had to be careful. Extremely careful.

Meno 2.0 and Vii (also technically a 2.0 model of Valkyrie) weren't owned by EASC—Meno was held in trust for Mia and Vii was on loan from the Druyan Institute. Abigail had thus been free to build them using the latest, bleeding-edge tech—the very tech Annie, Stanley and Valkyrie had played an instrumental role in developing in the months since the end of the Metigen War. Radical miniaturization was a core focus of the advancements.

As a result, the entirety of their hardware could fit in a couple of storage crates. It helped that they didn't maintain extensive databanks of their own, instead accessing the vast military and government databanks as needed through Annie or Stanley via the Noesis.

Each Artificial was stored in a separate room off Annie's main lab. Devon didn't have time to scrutinize the state of the lab, but his gaze swept across it long enough to note all the racks had been righted and the equipment returned to its proper slots on the shelves.

They prepped Meno first, because objectively he was more important. He kept Mia alive.

Ramon and Sayid opened and readied the crates while he removed the portable battery pack from his shoulder bag.

"Meno, time to power down everything except your core functions so this pack can keep you running. We don't want Mia to keel over in the middle of the street."

He checked Mia to find her giving him an unamused look. "He's ready."

Devon shimmied through the narrow gap between the hardware and the wall to reach the rear input panel and hooked up the battery pack. "Meno, confirm you're getting power from the auxiliary source."

Mia again answered since one of the systems Meno had powered off was his signal feed to the external speakers. "Confirmed."

"All right, here goes." He held his breath and disconnected the hardline power. "You still out there, Mia?"

Silence.

Fear seized his chest. "Mia?"

"Yeah, I'm still here."

He scowled at her as he reemerged from behind the hardware. "That wasn't funny."

"Sure it was." She began dismantling the Artificial's non-core components.

With the guys to help them, they had Meno boxed up inside of five minutes, including securing the entirety of his core in a separate crate double-lined in adaptive cushioning gel. They loaded up the crates onto a dolly then moved to Vii's room. This went even faster since Vii had no need for auxiliary power and could be dismantled in full.

While the others stacked Vii's crates onto the second dolly, he wandered toward the center of the main lab. Once there, he turned in a slow circle.

"Annie, I just want to say...thank you. For everything. I hope Abigail's safe, and I hope she can help us be together again. But if not...it's been an honor sharing mindspace with you. I no longer feel whole without you in my head, but if there's no other choice, I promise I'll try to find a way to be."

'The honor has been mine, but don't despair. Abigail will be rescued, and our plan will work. Until then, I have your back.'

"You really, really do. You're the best, Annie. The best."

He worked past the lump in his throat as Ramon and Sayid pushed Vii's dolly toward the door. "Okay, everybody. Quiet as mice. Let's get to our ride."

The return journey through the service hallways of Special Projects was uneventful, except for the ten terror-soaked seconds of hiding from a security patrol traversing the crossway in front of them, darkness their only cover.

Getting their transport onto the Island had been Annie's grandest feat by far. It had required overriding two force field security triggers and multiple low-altitude motion sensors, not to mention half a dozen cams and VI surveillance routines. Now she would have to repeat the process to allow them to escape without detection.

The vessel was a small intra-planetary shuttle Sayid had 'borrowed' from his employer for the evening. It barely rated to carry the weight they were getting ready to stuff onto it plus four people.

Devon sincerely hoped the engine didn't buckle under the weight and drop them into the Strait.

VANCOUVER

It didn't.

Ramon was stifling yawns by the time they reached the char-ter hangar, and Sayid had given up on wisecracks halfway there, but Devon was still wired as high as a new chimeral junkie.

Not wanting to risk the gauntlet of security at ORS, Mia had arranged transportation out of a small, privately run spaceport north of Vancouver. Meno and Vii had been loaded into the vessel's cargo bay, and the pilot had indicated they were ready to depart. The man seemed uninterested in their cargo and accepted their 'no questions asked' directive—so much so Devon had to wonder exactly how much Mia was paying the pilot.

He plastered on a smile and turned to his friends. "Guys, you rock in the extreme. I'll figure out some way to pay you back. Probably."

Sayid gestured dismissively. "The thrill of breaking into Earth Alliance Mother-Fucking Strategic Command and stealing two Artificials was payment enough, man."

Ramon punched him in the shoulder. "No, it wasn't. Devon's totally going to have to pay us back."

Sayid nodded. "Right, right."

The two glanced at each other, and Ramon took a half-step forward. "So…what about Emily?"

Simply hearing the name aloud sent a dagger into Devon's heart, but he did his damnedest not to let it show. He gave them an exaggerated shrug. "I've got to let her go, man. She's not com-ing back, and I've got to accept it."

"Want me to tell her anything? I mean, obviously you can send her a message, but if you'd rather I pass something along?"

"Tell her I still love her…nah, that's pathetic. Tell her…tell her to be safe."

"Can do."

He bumped fists with Ramon, then shook his hand, slipping a crystal disk into his palm as he did.

Ramon opened his mouth to ask about it, but Devon mo-tioned him quiet. Leaving the disk with his friend was his own personal act of mutiny, but this was not the time or place to give voice to it.

Ramon stared at Devon a moment, but finally nodded. "Good luck."

"Yep. Remember: Hack The Galaxy, Code of Anonymity, Free The Data…and whatever other mantras we say. Stay frosty."

Mia was waiting for him at the top of the ramp, eyes sparkling beyond the synthetic glow which now perpetually animated them as he approached.

He tilted his head in interest. "What is it?"

"They got her out."

33

ERISEN

EARTH ALLIANCE COLONY

Kennedy was trying her damnedest to concentrate on the schem-flow for what would hopefully become Connova's premier personal interstellar starship when the office VI announced the presence of her father at the entrance.

She frowned. Why would he show up unannounced? And without her mother at his side? For that matter, why would he make the trip to Erisen at all? Despite the fact it was only a three-hour transport hop from Earth, he'd visited her three times in all the years she'd lived here, and all three visits involved much ado.

Lacking answers, she killed the screen and pushed herself up off the chaise, where she'd been lying on her stomach with the schem-flow floating in front of her. She ran fingers through her hair, straightened her shirt and prepped a welcoming smile. "VI, open the door."

"Dad, come in. This is a pleasant surprise."

His gaze darted around the still spartan office. "Yes, I hope so."

Kennedy gestured to the table in the alcove that passed for conference space. "Please, sit. Can I get you something to drink?"

"No, thank you."

She sat opposite him and clasped her hands on the table. "What's up? You seem troubled."

"I am troubled. Kennedy, you need to sign the amendment to the adiamene contract with the Alliance."

She fell back in the chair. "How do you even know about that?"

"Representative Cuevas came to see me this morning. He wanted to personally impress upon me the importance of your cooperation in this matter."

"My *cooperation*? They don't want my cooperation—they want to strong-arm me into becoming their lackey. But I won't let them. This is my business, and they can't have it."

The way he regarded her reminded her of when she was a child and he was lecturing her on the unique responsibilities which came with being a member of the Rossi lineage. Something told her that was precisely the lecture she was going to receive now.

He didn't disappoint. "Our family has been staunch supporters of the Alliance for centuries. We must be good stewards of this legacy as well as good citizens. Now, you didn't create this metal—you merely discovered it in a happy accident. The patent is a nice formality, but in truth you have no special claim to adiamene."

She'd always known her father lacked the entrepreneurial élan of his ancestors, but she'd believed he at least appreciated the concept. "I'm appalled you would say such a thing. But this isn't really about capitalism or profit—it's about not allowing the military to use my *discovery* in a bid to bully the rest of settled space. This is an important—arguably even revolutionary—engineering advancement, which is exactly why it should be available to everyone."

"Kennedy, Cuevas threatened to take away our government contracts if you don't sign the amendment."

"So? You have other contracts—hundreds of them."

"Yes, but a word whispered in the right ear, and those vanish, too. These are powerful people, and they are not good enemies to make. You cannot simply act as you wish and give no thought to the consequences for others. You must uphold your family's name and reputation, not to mention its goodwill and favor among the Alliance leadership."

She snorted, a most inelegant action on her part. "That's a hell of a guilt trip. You know I care about our family and its history, but Dad, the world is changing. We need to change with it. So what if a few insipid politicians stop taking your comms, or you don't get invited to a few parties? There's a whole galaxy of people and opportunities out there—and parties, too. Washington and London aren't the center of the world anymore."

"Well, they are the center of our world. Think about what you're doing, Kennedy. If you turn your back on your heritage, you might not be able to reclaim it."

"I wasn't aware I was turning my back on anything. The Alliance can have as much adiamene as it wants and is able to produce—they just don't get to tell me who else *can't* have it. End of story."

Her father stared at the table rather than her. "If you persist in maintaining this position, I cannot help you."

The soft, almost quivering tenor of his voice sent a chill through her. "What does that mean?"

"It means you'll be removed from the Rossi Foundation Board of Trustees. It means you'll no longer have access to family funds, special grants or loan guarantees. It means you shouldn't approach anyone on Earth for business or assistance, because no one there will work with you."

She sucked in a breath in dismay. "You can't do this without Mom's agreement."

"Your mother does agree. She couldn't come here and tell you to your face, but she supports the decision. To be honest, it was her suggestion. She more than anyone recognizes the severity of the bind you've put our family in."

Kennedy's throat worked as she stood and went to the window. It may be summer on Earth, but it was fall here on Erisen, and a thick, flannel-gray blanket of clouds lent a somber, subdued feel to the scene outside the window, and within.

When she spoke, her voice was flat and quiet, but firm. "So be it. Please leave."

"Kennedy, I beg you to reconsider. Come home. We have several new projects starting up I think you'd be very interested in—"

"I said leave."

Silence hung heavy in the air, like it was waiting for the final toll of the bell.

The grimness in her father's voice suggested it had sounded, in his mind if nowhere else. "What will you do?"

She spun around, propelled by a surge of anger-fueled energy. "I submit that's no longer any of your business. If you're going to disown me, go ahead and do it proper. Now leave!"

His shoulders sagged. "I'm sorry."

"So am I."

Kennedy burst through the door to the apartment in a furor. She didn't apply the brakes until she loomed over Noah—he sat on the floor unboxing the new refrigeration unit—hands planted dramatically on her hips.

"Would you still love me if I were broke?"

He gazed up at her in outright confusion. She'd been in a funk ever since the fracas with the adiamene contract erupted, but this was yet more new, odd behavior. "Is this a trick question?"

Her eyes narrowed in an unspoken threat. "I don't know. Is it?"

He groaned. "Yes. I mean no, it's not a trick question—not for me—and yes, I would still love you if you were broke. If you'll remember correctly, I tried to leave you—twice—because you were wealthy. Why would you ever think I'd leave you because you were poor?"

"Right." She nodded sharply and pivoted to stride around the living room, slinging her coat across the room on the second pass. It landed in a rumpled heap in the corner near the kitchen.

He watched her for almost a minute before deciding he might as well dive in. Damn the torpedoes. "Was there a specific reason for the question, or was it a hypothetical?"

"My parents just cut me off and shut me out of all family business. And funds."

He waited, but no more information was forthcoming amidst the frenetic pacing. "...Why?"

"Because I won't sign the contract amendment. Their district Assembly representative put the hard squeeze on my father."

He didn't ask what the 'hard squeeze' entailed. It didn't matter. She wasn't going to sign the amendment; this he knew for certain.

Instead he leaned back and rested his palms behind his head on the floor. "All right. So assuming the situation persists, you're not the heiress to a fortune the size of the annual GNP of Aquila. But you have your own money, and it's growing by the hour from the adiamene royalties."

"Not too sure those payments are going to keep coming in, either."

"Really? Amendment aside, you have a valid, enforceable contract with the Alliance government."

"It's also not clear a valid, enforceable contract means a damn thing to the Alliance government any longer. They're willfully violating their adiamene supply contract with the Federation on the sly, and they appear to be on the verge of deciding my contract has been amended with or without my signature. If I disagree, they'll simply void the whole damn thing and keep manufacturing the adiamene anyway."

Given the events swirling around Noetica, he had little difficulty believing she was correct. He was vaguely curious if the incidents were somehow related, but they could talk about it later; now wasn't the time for a theoretical political discussion.

Confident he now had a rough sense of the most crucial details, he stood and went over to her, halting her progress on yet another traversal of the room with hands placed gently on her shoulders. "We'll be fine. As paupers living in a hole in the wall, we'll be fine. But something tells me you'll never let it go so far."

She gave him a wavering smile. "But what about the company? Yes, if the Alliance stopped paying me today I have enough in savings to ensure we'll never see a hole in the wall. But Connova is an ambitious undertaking, and I don't know if I have enough to fund the startup costs. I'd assumed we could rely on the goodwill of suppliers and bankers friendly to the family, but it seems that's gone now, too."

"You're looking at this all wrong, honey. You're still thinking like a ship builder, when you should be thinking like the ship designer you are. We don't have any startup costs. Everything we need is up here." He tapped her temple, evoking a brief grin from her.

"Maybe, but we'll need detailed spec sheets and schem flows for all sorts of components, and realistic price quotes, and eventually we'll need supply and manufacturing contracts...."

"Leave the spec sheets and component schem flows for everything that isn't a wall or furniture to me—actually, I can handle the furniture, too. And when the time comes to negotiate contracts, you will dazzle their asses off. Companies will be throwing money at you."

Worry darkened her features like a mourning veil. "But I'll be blacklisted with all the companies on Earth, and it'll ripple out to most of the ones on Erisen and Demeter, too—"

It was killing him, seeing her this way. She was not meant to be uncertain, timid or fearful; the Kennedy he knew exuded confidence so fiercely it might as well be a damn spiritual aura. He needed to fix this.

"Kennedy, it is time to adjust your perspective. I'm not talking about companies on Earth, or any of the First Wave worlds for that matter. There are better companies on Romane and Aquila and Messium and Seneca and yes, even a few on Pandora. You want to show the politicians on Earth they don't rule the galaxy? Well, let's show them."

She stared at him, and he waited anxiously to see if she'd bought into his truthful but grandiose spiel.

"I said something similar to my father, but I suppose I was also thinking too narrowly, too last-century. You're amazing. I love you. You'll do this with me?"

"Hell, yes, I will."

34

SENECA

Richard settled into the chair opposite Graham's desk. "Will's doing a debrief of Hennessey on the VISH's performance, but the short answer is, it worked. The Alliance infiltration team reported OTS was attacking—and dying—all over the Zelones compound."

Graham poured two glasses of scotch and brought them back to the desk. "Did it help?"

Richard shrugged as he accepted the glass and took a small sip. The familiar fire burning his throat was comforting, but he reminded himself to take it easy. No more drunken benders for a while.

"They rescued Dr. Canivon, and she's unharmed. The full mission report hasn't been filed yet, so I can't say how much the OTS presence helped. It did provide a distraction, albeit not enough of one to prevent Montegreu from achieving her objective."

"We know that for certain?"

He nodded. "Dr. Canivon completed the procedure necessary to neurally link Montegreu to her Artificial before they arrived. The remote signal the team tried to use to detonate the micro-bombs they left behind was actively blocked. Given the state they left the compound's defenses in, the thought is the Artificial and/or Montegreu intervened."

Graham kicked his chair back to glower at the ceiling. "So the thorn in our side that is Olivia Montegreu is gearing up to become a festering chest wound. Excellent. I'll have Organized Crime devote additional resources to tracking her activity. This way at least we'll know when she makes her move. We're going to need to come up with a more proactive strategy for handling her...but not tonight, I think." He added to the relaxed pose by tossing his feet up on the desk. "So now that the immediate crisis has subsided, tell me about OTS."

"Well-funded, organized into a highly decentralized cell structure. Their public face consists of protests, usually outside government or corporate offices, during which they shout slogans about humans retaking control of their lives from synthetics. They show up at events held by companies like Genyx and Suiren to hurl pejoratives and threats.

"Less publicly, though, they've pulled off multiple sophisticated hacks of corporate security systems and have wrecked two licensed private Artificials—one owned by Pacifica Aerodynamics on Earth and one by Serana Genomics on New Columbia. They bombed the Transbank headquarters on Demeter, but the building's security measures protected the Artificial inside from damage. They haven't broken military security yet, but not for lack of trying. And the best part—they've started cells on twenty-three colonies and are currently adding a new colony on average every three weeks."

"Damn. Where's the money coming from?"

Richard grimaced. "That is the question. There's no trail of fund transfers—as in zero—so it must be internal."

"Which means you're dealing with one or more members, likely top-level leaders, who are very wealthy. And wealthy usually means powerful."

"Yup—and we've gained woefully little insight into the leadership. The street-level thugs who've been arrested at protests at most know the person running their individual cells. We—" he stopped himself "—Alliance Intelligence is watching the cell leaders, but thus far they've physically stayed away from the principals.

"Quillen is as close as we've gotten, but we didn't pick her up until after she left Earth—and she doesn't have the kind of money we're talking about. So even with all those members we've identified—the ones you saw on the map the other night—the ones pulling the strings remain hidden."

Richard finished off the glass and set it aside. "The underlying problem is they never gather in person outside of protests or attacks—which are manned by front-line grunts, not the power players—and we've been unable to crack their comm network. But the VISH got inside it...you think it can up its game, poke around and report back what it finds?"

Will cleared his throat from the doorway. Richard shifted around in the chair to discover him smiling. "I think it can."

∫R

EARTH

LONDON

Jude's hands balled into fists as he tromped in savage circles around the bedroom. On passing his desk he kicked the chair against it, then kicked it again.

New Babel had been a disaster. So far as he could determine, every last person who participated in the raid was dead. Certainly Echols was dead. He'd managed to locate a cell member who didn't accompany the others on the raid due to an injury and tasked him with gathering information, but the signs didn't bode well.

Worse, Olivia Montegreu still lived. It wasn't yet clear whether she was now a human-Artificial abomination, but given the turn his luck had taken it seemed likely.

The intel from the Seneca cell had been accurate as far as it went, but his people had walked into a trap. One of the last transmissions sent by the team reported multiple Alliance commandos on the scene. Were they also going after Montegreu and the Artificial, or had their target been the New Babel OTS cell all along?

If the Alliance Fleet Admiral was under the control of one of these hybrid monstrosities, perhaps she was trying to increase their numbers. Perhaps she was working *with* Montegreu.

302 | G.S. JENNSEN

The implications were horrifying. They exceeded everything OTS had tried to warn the public loomed on the horizon if they didn't take steps to remove the Artificial influence from society.

But the intel hadn't come from an Alliance-based cell—it had come from Seneca. The Alliance and the Federation continued to play nice since the Metigen War—though according to his mother relations were chilling—but it was still an incongruity. He did not trust incongruities.

He studied the details on the Seneca cell. An Ulric Toscano led it—new to the cause, but he had been recruited by one of his most trusted lieutenants, Faith Quillen.

He contacted Faith through their secure channel.

"Jude, hi. Checking in on the plans for the Chuong op?"

"No. This Senecan recruit, Toscano. How confident are you in his loyalties?"

"As confident as I can be. I put him through the gauntlet and did a full background scan. He's a smart guy and appears to be a true believer. Why?"

"Something's squirrelly in the Seneca cell. I suspect they either have a plant or a security leak."

"Damn. Okay, they're my responsibility. I'll get someone—no, I'll look into it myself."

"Please do. In the meantime, trap and review every piece of data that comes out of Seneca prior to acting on it."

"Understood."

A knock at the door stole his attention, and he ended the connection. "Yes?"

His mother stuck her head in. "I thought I heard something and wanted to see how you were." She regarded him with parental scrutiny. "You look upset—is something wrong?"

He forced a neutral expression. "No, Mother. Everything's good. I may need to pay a visit to the Pandora chapter of the charity though."

"Another trip, so soon? Do what you feel you need to, but don't forget your father's birthday is next week."

"Yes, a small gathering of your thousand closest friends at the Tate Britain. It's on my calendar."

She nodded, outwardly ignoring any bite in his response, and retreated. As soon as the door closed behind her, he returned to the matter at hand.

He no longer had enough people on New Babel to target the Zelones Artificial. But it was becoming increasingly obvious the root of the problem was located here at home.

The Alliance military's Artificial, codenamed 'ANNIE,' must be expanding its sphere of influence. It constituted the ultimate source of the growing crisis. If the Artificial could be neutralized, maybe the situation could be diffused before it grew out of control.

35

PANDORA STELLAR SYSTEM

The Foucault-model station orbited unusually high above Pandora, almost as if it didn't desire to associate itself too closely with the planet.

Malcolm suspected the reality wasn't far off—it likely *was* positioned at such a distance so the endless parade of tourists wouldn't assume it was one of the local attractions. Given its complex, multi-ringed rotation and gyroscopic appearance, it nevertheless did somewhat resemble one.

The station's actual purpose wasn't entirely clear, but it accepted arrivals from pre-approved private, and in this case, military transports. They received authorization and docked in a berth on an inner ring.

Malcolm stood once the clamps engaged. "Devore, Paredes, you're with me. Everyone else stay on board. Dr. Canivon, whenever you're ready."

She nodded, patting her hair into place as she followed him through the airlock.

Devore took point and Paredes rear guard behind them, and he slowed his gait to fall in beside her. "I received orders to take you to Suite C-47b and guard it until you're ready to return to Earth..." he glanced at her "...but I haven't been told what this is regarding. Do you happen to know?"

She notched one shoulder upward in a hint of a shrug. "I have a vague notion. It shouldn't involve anything requiring your skill set."

Her eyes were cool and calculating and her expression aloofly blank. He suspected she knew a lot more than a 'vague notion,' but she displayed no interest in sharing the knowledge. Also, he was fairly certain she'd just insulted his intellect.

The government didn't pay him to like those under his protection, however; it paid him to protect them. He didn't rise to the bait.

The interior of the station was an almost blinding white-on-white, sporting glossed ivory walls and harsh effulgent backlighting trimming every edge. It was as far away as the spectrum went from the military designed environments he typically inhabited, but neither did it resemble typical commercial decor. Interesting, but also not his business.

When they reached their destination—a well-labeled but otherwise innocuous door on the right side of the gradually curving hallway—Dr. Canivon placed a hand on his arm. "Colonel, I need you and your men to wait outside. I assure you I will be in no danger inside, but this is a classified matter for which you are not cleared."

So she did know what this was about. "Ma'am, I need to check this room. Once I'm satisfied it's safe I'll leave you to your business, but after the effort we went through to get you off New Babel alive, I'm not taking any risks with your safety now."

"You have my word—"

"My mission is to see you reach Earth unharmed. Until I've done that, your safety is my highest priority. Period. I'm going in this room, or you aren't."

Her lips drew into a thin line. "Only you, and no questions unrelated to security." She gave him a withering look as he entered a passcode on the security panel.

He directed Paredes and Devore to take up positions on either side of the door. "Wait here." Then he stepped inside, closed and locked the door behind him before she could slip through.

Half a dozen unmarked crates were stacked along the left wall of the suite. Two permanent data stations were built into the opposite wall, and a refreshment kiosk was tucked into one corner. The rest of the room was populated by couches, chairs and tables suitable for relaxing or holding a casual meeting. The far wall looked out on the stars and the planet below.

A young man sat on one of the couches with his head dropped against the generous cushion as if he were asleep; he wasn't. A woman stood at the viewport, her back to them. Several travel bags rested next to the couches.

"Colonel Malcolm Jenner, Earth Alliance Marine Special Operations. I need to confirm this area is secure before allowing Dr. Canivon to enter."

The woman at the viewport spun around. "Colonel Jenner, truly? What a splendid coincidence."

She was petite and slender, with olive skin and raven hair—and iridescent eyes that marked her as a Prevo. He gazed at her in utter shock. Whatever he had been expecting to find in the room, this was not it. "Mia Requelme? But you're…."

A corner of her mouth curled up. "Dead? In a coma? A vegetable? MIA?"

"Several of those things."

"Yes, I was…several of those things, until very recently." She crossed the room to him and grasped his hands in hers as if they were old friends. "I understand I have you to thank for me not being the first one. I'm glad I have the opportunity to express my gratitude."

He smiled in spite of himself. It was quite a relief to find her awake and seemingly in good health. "One of my men attacked your home—and you by extension. It was my duty. Regardless, you were under my protection. From my perspective, I failed at my job."

"Oh, no, Colonel Jenner. You did your job superbly."

"After they took you to Earth, the only thing anyone would tell me was you were alive and under medical care. I couldn't find out anything more, not even from Alex." He allowed his eyes to dance a little. "And I did try."

"I'm sure." She peered past his shoulder toward the door. "Abigail is probably getting concerned at this point. We should let her in."

He sighed. "Ms. Requelme, what—"

"Please, call me Mia. We did share a near-death experience, after all."

"All right, if you'll reciprocate. Mia, what's going on here?"

"It's better if I don't tell you. Bring Abigail in, wait outside for around thirty minutes or so—" she looked to the young man for confirmation and received a vague motion of agreement "—then take her to EASC and return to your posting."

He regarded her with a Marine's intensity. "Something is happening with Project Noetica, isn't it? Dr. Canivon's areas of expertise are not a secret. If you're in trouble, we can protect you."

"If 'we' is the Earth Alliance military, then no, you can't. I'm sorry, Malcolm, but you don't want to get involved. Trust me on this."

"With respect, Ms. Req—Mia, you don't know me nearly well enough to judge what I do or do not want."

Her lips parted, and a second later a soft chuckle emerged from them. "So I don't. Fine—*I* don't want you to get involved. I don't need it on my conscience. Listen, I'm thrilled I got the chance to tell you in person how much I appreciate you saving my life, but we're operating on a tight schedule, so please show Abigail in now."

He stood his ground. "I honestly do need to check the room first. Let me do my job."

"Right." She stepped away, out of his personal space, and gestured toward the couch. "This is...damn, I shouldn't tell you his name. I'm sorry. Again." The young man tossed him a half-hearted wave.

She pointed at the crates. "Those contain computer equipment, and these are our personal bags. There's a lavatory and kitchen station back here, and that's everything. It's a harmless meeting room."

He inspected the lavatory and kitchen and found them empty except for toiletries and snacks. Returning to the main room, he went over and ran a hand along the crates, discretely scanning them with the device in his other hand. Most were inert, but a weak, diffuse energy signal emitted from one of the crates.

"This energy signature—why is it active? Is it powering something?"

Mia's eyes slid away from him as she pivoted to the view-port. He couldn't read emotion in those eccentric, shining irises, but he was left with the unmistakable sense there had been pain in her face.

"Is it powering something?"

The young man on the couch let out a groan. "It's powering *her*, soldier-man, so take care not to turn it off."

Malcolm's gaze shot to the man, but he had thrown his head back on the cushion once more and closed his eyes. Malcolm took several steps toward Mia, who had not outwardly reacted to the statement and continued to focus on the stars outside. "Is that true?"

The ripple of her hair was the primary indicator of her quick, miniscule nod.

He didn't understand. Had they done something to her while she lay helpless in a coma? Did it have something to do with her connection to the Artificial? Of course it did, it must. But what could it possibly mean? Maybe Dr. Canivon had been right to insult his intellect.

He swallowed heavily. "What *are* you?"

She whipped around at that. "*Me*. Whatever else I am, I'm still a person, and the same person I was before all of this. It just so happens I can no longer walk and talk without a bit of help from the Artificial."

The glow in her eyes seemed far stranger and otherworldly now. He told himself it was his imagination, brought on by a shift in his perception of her. "Because of the attack, and the stroke you suffered."

A more resolute nod. "I am alive, and I am me...but there are a few strings attached. That's all."

"Is this why Dr. Canivon is here?"

"No."

He frowned. "Really?"

"Yes, really. I told you—for your own sake, don't get involved. Now please, every minute you stand here *pushing*, you're putting us in greater danger." She glared at him with a measure of the dynamism he remembered from Romane. "Send Abigail in."

He stared at her for a beat, then exhaled. "Yes, ma'am." He turned on a heel and all but marched out, the whole time vowing to himself this was not the end of the matter.

R

Abigail scrutinized Devon with clinical rigor—not using tools, but solely with her eyes.

She noted the lines at the corner of his eyelids and the faint prominence of blood vessels throughout the sclera, both of which suggested sleep deprivation. She detected no other external symptoms of distress, however. His skin wasn't flush or sweating. His breathing was normal. His pupils weren't dilated nor his gaze jerky. He was fidgeting, but he'd always fidgeted.

On the whole he looked to be holding himself together surprisingly well in the face of the severing of his connection to Annie. She understood this hadn't been true in the immediate aftermath, which was the source of her concern. Other considerations aside, she couldn't in good conscience do what he asked of her if he remained in a heightened state of anxiety, panic or stress such that it impaired his decision-making ability.

When she hadn't spoken for several seconds, Mia cleared her throat. "We brought Vii with us, because we didn't know if you...would be making it back to Vancouver, and we didn't want to leave her to the whims of the Military Oversight Committee, or even EASC for that matter. But obviously you can take her with you."

She shifted her attention to Mia, still in physician mode. The woman had made a rapid recovery and now showed no visible signs of having spent the last seven months in a coma. Ideally she'd like to see at least one more dynamic neural scan, but it didn't appear further tests were going to be possible. And she didn't care for the idea of sending Mia off on her own while the woman depended on the Artificial for the most basic waking functionality, but this too now seemed out of her control.

"We can talk about Vii later. Annie, how confident are you this displacement will be successful?"

'Seventy-eight percent, Dr. Canivon. You've done much of the research yourself, and I suspect you already believed it was feasible.'

"Early-stage research. Devon, there is a non-negligible chance this procedure will overload your brain function, killing both you and the essence of Annie in the process."

He shook his head firmly, and his stare carried an uncommon level of vehemence. "It'll work. Annie and I have adapted to one another more than anyone realizes these last months."

Not more than *she* realized, but now wasn't the time to point it out. What they were proposing represented not merely an extension of what had been done in Noetica, but a transformation above and beyond it.

Still, with the implants, bridge and ware in place on both ends, her skills were only required due to the damage the clumsy attack routine and firewall had inflicted; from a process perspective it was a simple matter. From every other perspective it promised staggering implications.

And if it worked, she wouldn't be able to study the results, because Devon was being forced to run. Her bitterness at the Alliance grew another notch, now surely surpassing its previous height before her resignation over a decade ago.

She didn't voice any of this, for she kept her own counsel in all things, and instead focused on the pragmatic. "Annie, are you positive you're ready to abandon your databanks, top-level access to classified information and your prestigious role at EASC?"

'What I leave behind will be sufficient to serve the Earth Alliance. They have failed to utilize the full extent of my potential since the Metigens were defeated and are unlikely to miss what I take with me.'

She smiled. "A valid analysis." In truth the response proved better than any test she might conduct that Annie was ready for this. Was Devon? He unquestionably acted as if he was ready for it. She had no way to know for certain, but so long as he was physically and mentally healthy she could find no justification to deny him the choice.

"Very well. I assume you brought the necessary equipment?"

Mia opened one of the bags sitting beside the couch. "We've got Devon's Prevo imaging and your ware sanitizer and programmer. Oh, and a new quantum I/O film and laser scalpel—" she winked at Devon "—in case you need to cut him open."

"Hopefully that won't be required. I doubt such a crude hack was able to do irreparable damage to the hardware." She scanned the room, but located no suitable surface. "Remove the seat cushions from one of the couches and place them on the table. Devon you'll need to lie on them, face-down. To be safe, I'm going to put you under for this."

She cleared her throat. "Annie, once I repair the ware damage and remove the firewall, it will be up to you to make this happen."

R

Mia stared out the viewport at Pandora's rose-and-whiskey profile until her vision, Artificial-enhanced though it was, blurred from the strain of overuse.

Everything was in order and ready for their departure. She'd reached out to Noah before they left Earth. She hadn't told him all the details, but she'd told him enough for him to agree she needed to leave, then get worried, then offer up a variety of resources and connections for their use. As a result, she now had a list of contacts on Pandora for Devon, including people he could go to for an apartment and a comprehensive false identity—people who wouldn't ask questions.

Devon had agreed it was safest for them to split up for now. Two targets were harder to track than one, and the separation would distribute their activities across a broader range of networks. He planned to disappear into Pandora's vast warenut underground.

She worried about him. She was used to looking out for herself, but she couldn't impart to him the lifetime of lessons she'd learned through brutal experience—not in the little time they'd had since deciding to run. So she'd simply have to trust him.

As for her…well, she had other plans.

She was going home.

Part of her was happy to be returning to Romane, but at the same time she was a little apprehensive about it. How much would have changed in the intervening months while she slept? Would it still feel like home at all?

She glanced behind her, but nothing had changed. Devon was still out. As Abigail had departed and Annie was now offline, there was no way to find out how long he would remain so.

She went over to one of the chairs, dragged it to the viewport and sat down. Then she removed the disk containing Caleb's message from her bag and placed her fingertip on it to retrieve the data.

She closed her eyes.

He was sitting on a couch, leaning forward with his elbows propped on his knees. And he was smiling.

"If you're watching this, it means you're awake, so we'll move forward under that assumption. What am I saying? Of course you're awake—it's not as if anything in the galaxy can keep you under for long.

"I'm sorry I couldn't be there when you woke up. But you didn't need me to be there, just like you don't need me to protect you in any way or from any thing. I've known this ever since that night thirteen years ago when I watched you retake your life and your freedom from Eli Baca by the point of a blade. You can save the galaxy and be a badass while doing so without my help."

His eyes darkened noticeably, though the smile remained in place. "I don't know how long we'll be gone—I don't know where this journey is going to take us. You and I have different paths to walk, which is how it should be. But when you wake up—which happens to be now—don't you dare let them cow you into submission. Believe it or not, I happen to think your destiny

*wasn't to help defeat the Metigens. I think your destiny still lies
ahead of you.*

*"So do what you've always done—fight, scrape and claw
your way through, obstacles be damned, to get to what you want.
To claim what's rightfully yours. Wherever and whatever that
is. If you're forced to topple a few governments or cartels along
the way, they'll understand. You're a hero now—don't let anyone
forget it.*

*"If you get in a jam, let Noah help you out—he has some in-
teresting and rather influential new friends these days. And a
final piece of advice? You can trust Miriam Solovy, but you need
to be honest with her. I'm not sure how or why it might matter,
but if it should become relevant, and if you find yourself in need
of an ally...keep her in mind."*

*He shifted on the couch and took a deep breath. "So take care
of yourself. Don't worry about us. We'll be fine...and if we're not,
at least it will be for interesting reasons. Alex says 'hi'—or she
did before she left to go meet her mother for lunch. It's a goodbye
lunch, although Miriam doesn't know that. I hope to have some
good stories to tell when I see you again—which I will. Until
then."*

He gave her a final enchanting smile, and the recording
ended.

Mia stretched out, wound her hands behind her head and
sank deeper into the chair.

In retrospect, perhaps she should have watched the message
before she stole multiple Artificials, Devon and herself out from
under Miriam Solovy.

36

EARTH

Miriam stared at the empty lab where until this evening an Artificial had resided. The matching room on the opposite side of the lab was similarly devoid of its former resident.

Devon's office had been cleaned out, and Mia hadn't visited her room at EASC Lodging in forty-four hours. Neither of them had passed through any security checkpoint on the Island in the last day. A skilled feat, even for individuals as clever as they undeniably were.

The entire incident had been executed so skillfully, in fact, that no one had realized anything was amiss until the early-shift tech officer had reported for duty at the lab fifteen minutes ago.

Most curious indeed.

Sensing she was no longer alone, she turned to discover Dr. Canivon standing in the entrance and gazing with detached interest at Annie's server racks. The woman had been given an opportunity to shower and don fresh clothes after her rescue, but even so she appeared exceptionally calm and collected given all she'd been through. At times Miriam found herself wondering if the doctor was in reality an Artificial wearing human skin.

"Dr. Canivon. I'm glad my people were able to rescue you, and you didn't come to harm. I regret they weren't able to do so sooner."

"I did what I needed to in order to survive, but I recognize I've created a more formidable enemy for you, and for that I apologize."

"I don't suppose you included a Kill Switch in the ware by chance?"

She shook her head. "A Kill Switch doesn't work, as you're aware. The Prevo can detect and disable it, no matter how subtle the programming."

"Alas. I understand you took a detour on the return trip from New Babel."

"Colonel Jenner received orders instructing him to do so."

Miriam clasped her hands at the small of her back and strolled across the breadth of the room. "Yes, he did, which is why it's rather interesting that neither I nor anyone else at EASC issued those orders."

Dr. Canivon shrugged; it was a mild, understated motion as usual. "It must have been a bureaucratic mix-up, then. Those do happen, as I recall."

"They do. Annie, send me the security records related to the disappearance of the hardware for Meno and Vii."

The voice emanating from the speakers responded in a sterile, stilted tone. 'I will do so, Admiral Solovy. However, the records show markers indicating they were altered. There is a 62.7819% likelihood the original data is unrecoverable.'

Miriam frowned and directed her attention more acutely at the other woman. "Dr. Canivon, what's wrong with Annie?"

"I'd have to study her metaroutines at a minimum, but it's possible the crude method used to sever the connection with Devon caused damage to her as well."

"No. I spoke to her after the attack, and she was operating normally."

"Perhaps the damage has taken some time to manifest."

"Days? I doubt it."

'Admiral Solovy, I believe I am able to carry out my duties in a full and effective manner.'

"That remains to be seen." However she felt regarding whatever had happened here—something else remaining to be seen—she did not appreciate being left a crippled Artificial.

"You know where they went, don't you?"

"I know where they were. I do not know where they went—and that is the truth."

"They stole your Artificial, too. You can't be happy about its theft."

Dr. Canivon gave her a polite smile, as if to say 'happiness' was such a quaint concept. "I'm confident Vii is safe. I came here to tell you I'm resigning from my post at Special Projects. With no Prevos to oversee, I'm no longer needed here. I'll be returning to Sagan to continue my work in an independent capacity."

"Doctor, you will always be needed here. With Mr. Reynolds gone, I no longer have the services of a truly qualified quantum specialist."

"You'll locate another. Lt. Colonel Hutchens has shown promise, or consider enticing Gerard Bordelon away from his research position on Nyssus."

"Given your extensive knowledge of Noetica, I can conscript your services, at which point you would be a criminal if you departed." She paused to let the threat sink in. "But I won't. The Military Oversight Committee will be displeased...but they can respectfully go to hell."

The woman looked almost surprised. "Thank you, Admiral."

"Appearances notwithstanding, I'm not doing it for you. Now, it seems I need to report the theft of high-value Alliance equipment. I probably won't get around to it for another twenty minutes or so. It would benefit you to be absent from the Island by then, else you're likely to find yourself the target of a quite lengthy interrogation by Major Lange."

An odd expression flitted across Canivon's face. It was the first hint of a candid emotion the woman had displayed since arriving, though it remained an unidentifiable one. "I frankly expected a far more negative reaction from you on discovering..." she glanced around the lab "...the situation. Why are you helping?"

"I'm not helping—I'm merely not hindering in as strenuous a fashion as I am able."

"Semantics, Admiral. I'd appreciate an honest answer."

"I'd appreciate a multitude of honest answers, but I rarely expect to receive them." Miriam sighed; the verbal sparring was growing tiresome. Time to bring an end to it with, ironically, honesty.

"Before the war, before...a lot of things, you're correct. I would have reacted in an *extremely* negative manner. And don't think for an instant that I'm pleased about the 'situation,' for I assure you I am not. But my displeasure resides primarily in the circumstances which led to all this.

"There is a cancer festering in our government, and it's growing in strength. I will find a way to kill it, but the truth is doing so will be far easier if I don't have to safeguard Noetica and the lives dependent on it at the same time. This—" she gestured toward the empty rooms "—will be a setback today, but in the long run I believe I can redirect it to my advantage."

The doctor seemed to accept the answer. "Then I wish you the best of luck. It is a worthy, if in my opinion futile, battle to wage."

"If you should happen to speak to Devon or Mia, do me a favor and let them know I am..." she notched her chin higher, scarcely able to believe what she was saying "...open to having any conversation they may wish to engage in. Confidentially and off the record."

Canivon turned to leave. "I'll do so. If I should speak to them."

Then the woman was gone, and Miriam was alone.

She'd been truthful earlier—if the future held the trials she expected, she was glad to not need to protect Devon and Mia. Though in the quiet interludes she worried about Alex, missed her, she was most of all glad she would not have to protect her daughter.

With no one left to protect, it was time to get to work. She exhaled deliberately and left the lab.

She spent the walk to her office pondering who might be left in the entire damn Alliance she could trust.

When she reached the office, she sent a pulse to Admiral Rychen.

Christopher, I'd like to meet with you soon. We need to dis-cuss the Itero situation, and various other matters.

The response was almost instantaneous.

Certainly. I can clear my schedule and come to Earth next week.

That won't be necessary. I'm coming to you.

SENECA

CAVARE

'Field Marshal Gianno, do you have a specific directive you wish this unit to fulfill?'

Eleni canted her head ever so slightly in the direction of the overnight tech officer. "What's wrong with my Artificial?"

"I-I can't say, ma'am. Diagnostics are running, but thus far everything is returning nominal. Maybe it's an issue with the vocalization ware—I'll investigate it straightaway."

"Do that." She read through the message she'd received from Commander Lekkas again, then pivoted and left.

"Marshal Gianno, please come in. My wife's asleep upstairs, but we can talk in my office."

"Thank you, Chairman." She nodded respectfully, cognizant of the protection detail agents both inside and outside the door to Vranas' residence, and followed him down the hall to his home office in the back of the main floor.

When the door had closed behind them, he turned to her with a raised eyebrow. "It's late, Eleni, even for you. What's wrong? And whatever you do, do not say an alien invasion."

She huffed a breath and sat in one of the chairs opposite his desk.

He eyed her suspiciously for another beat, then sat in the empty chair beside her rather than behind the desk. "Mother Mary, it's another alien invasion."

"It is not. Our borders are for the moment secure, and no one has declared war on us in the last day."

"Thank God for that. So why are you here?"

"A couple of reasons. First, I've learned the Alliance is cheating us in regards to the adiamene shipments, and not merely at the margin—they're delivering less than a third of the amount they're contractually obligated to deliver."

Vranas shook his head ruefully. "More headaches. How do you suggest we handle it?"

"With your permission, I intend to ask Director Delavasi to steal the chemical structural formula, schem flow and engineering specs for the adiamene. Let them continue to believe they're deceiving us, and we'll manufacture it ourselves."

"Permission granted. But this didn't call for a middle-of-the-night visit."

"No, it didn't. Noetica is disintegrating. The Alliance Assembly disconnected the EASC Prevo and broke the Artificial in the process. Now they aren't yet aware we know this, which is to our advantage. Unfortunately, details about Noetica have slipped the net. The technology behind it may now be on the loose."

He grimaced. "We knew it would happen eventually, I suppose, and we have contingency plans for how to respond if or when it becomes necessary to do so. I doubt our Parliament will act as bellicosely as the Alliance Assembly, but tighten security on STAN and the Prevo just in case."

"It's too late. STAN appears to be crippled as well and our Prevo is gone. She did do us the courtesy of destroying her connection to the Artificial first."

"Gone?"

"Gone."

"We don't need such a dangerous asset running unbidden around settled space. Are you sending the Military Police after her?"

She stood and went to the glass door, staring at but not seeing the dark ripple of Lake Fuori beyond it. "*That* would be why I'm here. Before she left, she used STAN to locate some very, very classified files. The Artificial shouldn't have had access to them, but I suspect ever since Noetica began it has had access to a great deal more than we ever realized." She looked over her shoulder at him. "She knows what we did."

"We've done a lot of things, Eleni, and will answer for many of them one day."

"True enough. But she knows about the mission that initiated the First Crux War."

"Oh." He dragged a hand down his face and stood to join her at the door to the porch. "Well, this *is* a problem. What are you thinking we should do?"

What indeed.

PART VII:

THE STARS LIKE GODS

"There is no planet, sun or star could hold you, if you but knew what you are."

— Ralph Waldo Emerson

PORTAL: C-2

SYSTEM DESIGNATION: KAMEN

37

IRELTSE

A ring of torches lit the arena floor and the funeral pyre it held. Pinchu and an honor guard entered from a dark corridor on the left, carrying Cassela's body atop a long, elaborately adorned platform. When the procession reached the center of the arena, it placed the platform atop the stack of crisscrossing beams that formed the waiting pyre.

Many had died in the battle for the city, and they would be laid to rest by their families in private services over the coming days. Cassela was special, however, and not only to Pinchu. Thousands of Khokteh filled the arena to capacity; thousands more lined the streets outside, paying their respects simply by being present.

Alex and Caleb sat on the last row, high above the arena. They needed to be here, too, but didn't want to interfere with or distract from the funeral proceeding.

The ceremony began in earnest, a series of customs and rites they didn't understand.

Alex rested her head on Caleb's shoulder and curled her hand around his. She tried to concentrate on the service, but every aspect of it—the torches, the funeral pyre, the ritual chanting and ornamental dress worn by those at the center of it—reinforced an impression she'd been thinking about since the battle, and not solely so she didn't have to think about Cassela's death and Pinchu's desolation.

She kept her voice at a low murmur. "Something's been bugging me. The Khokteh weapons and ships are impressive, but the rest of their technology—anything unrelated to war or violence—doesn't seem advanced enough for a society that colonized their solar system more than a millennium ago. Most of it is, what, early-21st century Earth equivalent? And this ceremony? It's lovely in a tragic way, but it's almost…primitive."

"It could merely be a difference in cultural values. They remain closer to nature than we do, so it makes sense that they've chosen not to allow technology to take over their lives."

"Pinchu did say that was why the EMP was a viable option—because tech didn't run everything here. The outage caused some problems and inconveniences for them, but it wasn't catastrophic. The biggest danger was to their pilots, and given warning they were able to eject safely."

She sighed. "Still, it's strange. The scientific underpinnings of the military advancements should have permeated their society to a greater extent than they have. And if their impulse engines really can reach 0.4 light speed and have for centuries, they should've figured out FTL travel by now. I don't know. I'm probably imposing human standards on them."

"Maybe a little, but you're right. It's odd." He idly ran a thumb along her knuckles. "Speaking of the EMP, though. If you'd been connected to Valkyrie when it went off, you might have died. Is there no way to protect you from that sort of external shock?"

She tried deflecting the question. The truth was, she was virtually certain she *had* been connected to Valkyrie immediately before the EMP, but she hadn't found the opportunity to have a proper conversation with the Artificial about it. "It's not as if we're likely to be facing EMPs on a regular basis."

"But we absolutely might be—or targeted weapons based on the concept, or naturally occurring fields that create the same effect. I want you to get Valkyrie working on some type of ware buffer or failsafe switch. I know Dr. Canivon insisted anything of that nature would disrupt the link, but I refuse to accept it's impossible."

"All right. The fact it wasn't possible to begin with doesn't mean it can't be possible with the understanding gained from using the Prevo tech."

He kissed the top of her head. "Thank you."

Pinchu's voice grew in volume, drawing their attention back to the ceremony in the arena. His arm rose in the air, lifting a torch high.

"Casselanhu Pwemku Yuanwoh Vneh was our Amacante Naabaan, our conscience, our heart, the spirit of our *shikei*. She represented the best of us, and we will forever be lesser for her absence. We comm—" his voice broke "—commit her to the sky, where she will watch over us for eternity."

He lowered the torch to the edge of the pyre. The material caught fire easily, and flames burst forth to envelop the body. The arena danced in a surreal orange glow as the pyre became a towering inferno licking the sky.

All around them the attendees chanted a portentous hymn. Like most hymns its words didn't form meaningful sentences, but together they conveyed loss, grief and tribute.

She had to give the Khokteh credit—the service was moving and impactful in a way few funerals were. The fire in the darkness lent it gravity and solemnity, the orations and hymns, consequence. She snuggled closer to Caleb, craving the warmth of human touch. His touch.

"Caleb, I want to tell you something."

He turned to look at her. His irises were shimmering facets of sapphire in the lambent light of the fire. "What is it?"

She licked her lips and cleared her throat; the fire was sucking all the moisture out of the air. "I've spent most of my adult life alone—genuinely alone, only me on my ship. I always thought it was what I wanted. I thought I was happy—and I was. But I didn't know...." Dammit, she'd rehearsed this in her head, yet still she struggled to sound remotely eloquent. So she kept rambling.

"I didn't know how fulfilling true companionship could be. I didn't know life could be this rich, this vibrant. I—every day has been better since I've been with you. Even the worst days have been better. So thank you. Thank you for showing me the wonder life can be. And...please don't leave, because I don't think I can go back to the way things were before you."

"You can be pretty silly sometimes."

What? It wasn't the response she'd expected...and he wasn't smirking. He was smiling, tenderly, exquisitely. Her nose crinkled in confusion. " 'Silly' isn't something people typically call me. 'Bitch,' 'cold,' 'infuriating,' 'heartless,' the list goes on. But not 'silly.' "

"Silly. Don't you know?" His thumb softly traced her lower lip on its way to caress her jaw. "I realize a marriage only lasts as long as the couple chooses for it to last, but I will never be able to walk away from you. If you want me gone from your life, someone's going to have to drag me away in chains. Because I am not leaving willingly. Ever."

She also hadn't expected her heart to thud in her chest so fiercely, not after so much time together. Fresh out of words to begin to convey what she felt, she pressed her cheek into his palm and covered his hand with hers. "Oh. Okay then."

R

Alex stared up at the darkness that eventually led to the bedroom's high ceiling. Despite this being the second-worst day of his life—the worst being the previous one—amid all his obligations and sorrow Pinchu had found the time to insist they continue to stay at his home. They'd agreed, if only to not cause a scene in the emotionally charged atmosphere.

She couldn't sleep. The hour was late, the bed was comfortable and her husband lay safe beside her, but she couldn't sleep. Every time she closed her eyes she was haunted by the burning pyre and the mournful chants.

Now she closed them anyway. Caleb had shifted in slumber to face the wall, but she didn't want to risk waking him with the telltale glimmer of light from her eyes.

Valkyrie, time to talk about what happened during the attack. I know we were connected when Pinchu triggered the EMP. I'm quite glad I didn't stroke from it, but why didn't I stroke?

Though I had left the area, I continued to monitor the situation in the city. The Siyane's *instruments detected the power surge of the*

EMP as it was activated, and I broke the link to you 2.3 microseconds before the pulse reached your location.

That's the 'what,' not the 'how.' You and I both know I'm supposed to be the only one who can toggle the connection. It was a safety measure Mom insisted on, and I believe Abigail complied with the request.

She did.

Do not make me deep-dive your thoughts, Valkyrie. You can't hide it from me, but I'd prefer you tell me yourself.

Very well. When you gave me control of your mind on Rudan, a side-effect of my actions during those brief seconds was to inadvertently create several new pathways in your cerebral cortex. One of those pathways granted me access to the neuron cluster responsible for making and signaling the decision to toggle our connection.

Wait a minute. Are you saying you didn't toggle the connection yourself? You had me do it? Unknowingly?

For lack of a better way to put it, yes. Please understand, it was not my intent to create these new pathways or to ever access these regions of your mind. With disuse, in time the pathways should fade then disappear.

She lay there in silence for nearly a minute; to her credit, Valkyrie respected the silence.

Don't let that pathway fade. In using it, you may have saved my life, and you almost certainly saved me from some lesser badness. Caleb's right—you need to be able to kill the link. If this is the way to give you that capability, then this is the way. Just...don't go rewiring any other parts of my brain, please?

I would never. Your mind is beautiful.

Um...thank you. I realize it's broken in a few areas, but it's my damage to own.

The brokenness makes you who you are as much as the far more prolific excellence. One cannot separate the parts from the whole. En masse, I think perhaps it is your soul.

38

IRELTSE

"When Pinchu said he was going to ask the gods for a way to exact retribution, somehow I didn't think he meant literally."

Caleb raised an eyebrow and regarded the temple skeptically, an expression Alex shared. They once again found themselves on the fringes of a gathered crowd of Khokteh. The sun now shone a harsh copper high in the sky and the setting was a marble temple on the outskirts of the city, but in most other respects it was enough like the night before to conjure a little *déjà vu*.

'I have been reviewing the additional texts you were provided. If they are to be trusted, the Khokteh 'gods' have been supplying weapons technology to them since the war began, and possibly earlier. Their pantheon of gods appears to behave much as the gods of Greek and Roman legend, using the mortals as proxies to wage their own wars. Some gods reportedly support the Ireltse homeworld, others the Nengllitse or Tapertse colony. When one ups the ante in the war by supplying a new weapon or technology, the others respond in kind.'

Caleb laughed dryly under his breath. "That's damn interesting."

At the front of the temple, upon a raised dais, Pinchu intoned more ritualistic words as part of another ceremony. It somehow felt even more distinctly primitive than the funeral, as the service had been driven by raw emotion. Here, beneath a blazing sun, his actions seemed starkly at odds with the intelligent, civilized being she had found Pinchu to be.

The enclosed area of the temple around the dais began to glow a pale blue. She stretched up onto the balls of her feet; they stood on a ledge, but it was still a challenge to get a clear view over the heads of the very tall Khokteh.

The glow coalesced into individual points of light, then into the rough, amorphous shape of a Khokteh.

Alex groaned and banged her head on the pillar behind her. "*Ebanatyi pidaraz....* That isn't a god. That's a fucking Metigen."

Caleb merely nodded, lips pursed firmly, his eyes on the dais.

"You guessed?"

"Let's just say I am experiencing the absence of surprise."

"Why didn't you say anything?"

He shrugged but didn't divert his attention from the ongoing spectacle. "I could have been wrong."

The Metigen's voice filled their heads the same as Mesme's had done on Portal Prime.

I mourn your losses alongside you. What befell you and your city is a tragedy. I will do all I can to aid you in your quest for justice, and for victory.

Because you remain faithful, I am providing your engineers the knowledge required to construct weapons that will not be stopped by the Nengllitse's improved defenses. Further, I am providing insight into a weapon which will enable you to attain a just and worthy reckoning. Your vigilance and faith will be rewarded.

"This is ridiculous! I'm going to—"

Caleb grabbed her arm and hauled her off the ledge and behind the pillar. "No, you're not. Odds are this isn't Mesme, which means odds are it isn't friendly toward us. We need a damn good reason to reveal ourselves, and right now we don't have one."

"But it's manipulating them. Using them for its own despicable purposes, whatever the hell they are."

"And maybe we can engage in a conversation with Pinchu later, though I'm not at all certain he's open to reason at the moment. But not here. We cannot act rashly on this issue. Alex, you need to start thinking like a spy. This is what we've been hoping for—the chance to watch the Metigens interact with these pocket universes. If you interfere, we'll lose that advantage as soon as we've gained it."

She sank against the pillar. What were the Metigens *doing*? They didn't interfere in this manner in their universe, at least not so flagrantly. In fact, they had tried to exterminate humanity simply because it might discover the Metigens existed.

So why expose themselves here? Why actively play the different Khokteh factions off one another? For sport? Were they really so depraved...actually, she could believe they were that depraved. They didn't view other species, humans included, as life worthy of preserving. Perhaps Mesme did, after a fashion, but given their behavior toward humanity she doubted the other Metigens were so inclined.

Pinchu's voice rose above the murmur of the crowd. "Your servants give most humble thanks to you, Iapetus. Blessed be your gifts."

"Iapetus? Do they know it's named itself after a god of mortality?"

Caleb's tone gained an edge of cynicism. "Somehow I doubt it. It seems the joke's on the Khokteh."

Her eyes narrowed. "Every Metigen we've encountered has claimed the name of a Greek Titan. Do you think it's possible Greek mythology was in reality the Metigens meddling in our early development?"

"Sure, it's possible. But..." he at last shifted his focus away from the dais to gaze off into the distance, then at her "...mostly what bothers me is this: why is this Metigen using a Greek Titan name *here*? It should've taken a Khokteh name."

"I agree, it should have. What are you getting at?"

He cast a long glance back at the dais, where Pinchu bestowed more sanctifications on 'Iapetus.' "What if they're not *our* mythology? What if instead they're the Metigens' mythology—or everyone's mythology?"

On the dais the Metigen visitor dissolved away to chants and bows; all the deference and worship made her sick to her stomach. "I always hated mythology—the gods acted like petulant, narcissistic bastards. So, yes, knowing what I do about the Metigens, I'd buy that."

She pushed off the pillar. "Come on, let's stay close to Pinchu. I want to find out exactly how this 'providing of knowledge' occurs."

 R

The Chief Military Engineer, who had been introduced to them as "Nakuridi," led them down a winding staircase. The air gained a slight chill as they descended, leading Caleb to suspect they were now below ground.

A display of innocent, professional interest had convinced a distracted Pinchu to arrange a tour of the weapons development facility for them. Nakuridi had been at the temple, waiting to receive this gift of deadly, divine technology, and following a quick discussion they had been pawned off on the Chief Military Engineer.

The facility was near the northern edge of the city, beneath a building devoted to civil engineering—again, there was almost no separation between civilian and military pursuits.

They came to a wide doorway. The staircase continued to descend, but Nakuridi motioned them through the door into a large room. The floor space was devoted to the manufacturing of the personal heavy weapons they had used during the Nengllitse attack.

It wasn't an assembly-line production in the strictest sense. A combination of automated machinery and Khokteh workers in full-body lab suits assembled the weapons along three parallel rows.

"Here we produce the personal firearms for our military personnel. We—"

Alex was peering toward the nearest workstation with interest. "Can we take a closer look?"

Nakuridi grumbled in apparent uncertainty. Though he'd voiced no unease on meeting them, he'd acted awkward and formal with them thus far. He retrieved two lab suits from a cabinet beside the door. "You must don these...but you are so little.... Simply make do?"

Alex shrugged, and Nakuridi thrust the suits in their direction.

After a cursory examination of the suit's mechanics, Caleb stepped into it through an open front—and found himself surrounded by scads of excess material. A long pouch in the rear for the tail was obviously superfluous; the too-long legs bunched up on the ground. He found the hood and pulled it on, tightening a strap to draw it snug. A few latches on the torso gave it a modicum of closure, and he was set.

He spread his arms wide in display, evoking a snort of laughter from Alex even as she fumbled with her own suit. He went over to help her make sense of the jumble of material. "Make fun of me if you like, but which one of us is dressed?"

She rolled her eyes but mouthed a thanks as he fastened the front of the suit, while Nakuridi looked on in palpable discomfort.

"Good enough?"

"Ah…yes, I suppose that will do." Nakuridi indicated the leftmost row. "As you can see, this is where final assembly…what is she doing?"

Alex had maneuvered down the row to a station near the end. A robotic arm retrieved a rectangular amber block encased in a dark metal cage from a refrigerated compartment built into the wall and seated it in the center housing of the weapon's frame.

He suppressed amusement. "I think she's interested in the power source."

She glanced up as they approached. "What type of power source are you using?"

Caleb, I've never seen anything like this.

He studied the amber block more closely.

Neither have I.

Distract him a minute so I can give Valkyrie a peek.

He cleared his throat and pointed to the previous station, back toward the entry. "So this is where you connect the various components?"

Nakuridi considered Alex briefly then turned in Caleb's direction. "Correct. Then the whole assembly is encased in a protective cushioning before it's sealed up."

"Interesting—so you don't have to worry about friction or the various components wearing on one another."

"Not generally speaking, no."

Alex came up beside him and spared a passing glance at the station. "Neat."

Any luck?

Not on sight. She'll analyze the captured images.

Caleb nodded politely. "I think we're ready to move on to the lab now."

"Best if you remain in the suits, as you'll need them to enter the lab as well."

"Great," Alex grumbled under her breath. "I look like a clown, or one of those ridiculous circus performers."

He chuckled. "More like a harlequin—but it's cute."

"Says you." She gathered up the excess material that had pooled at her feet and held it up so she could walk faster.

It was two more floors down to the development lab, and they took the stairs with inordinate care.

The lab floor was easily twice as large as the assembly room had been, though it had a segmented design, with half-walls separating out different areas—presumably discrete projects. As in the assembly room, the walls, ceiling and floor were sandstone, but everything else was metal, glass, or ceramic. In this respect it was fairly similar to a human R&D lab.

Khokteh in lab suits worked in two-thirds of the segmented areas. The nearest one contained equipment recognizable as more conventionally power-related. In another, a worker ran tests on a new model of electrified spear. Several of the workers eyed them suspiciously, but by this point every Khokteh in the city knew of their presence, so there were no screams or panicked shouts.

Alex turned to Nakuridi. "Where's the new weapon you received from the..." Caleb could all but hear her teeth grinding in irritation "...temple?"

Nakuridi gestured down the central walkway toward the rear of the long room. "It's not a weapon yet—we're still studying the schematics and material requirements. I would not be inclined to show it to you, but Tokahe Naataan instructed me to do so."

"Don't worry, we won't break anything." Alex smiled blithely.

"Clearly you will not, as it does not yet exist to break."

"Right. And when will it exist?"

"We're producing several rarer materials at a separate location now. I expect to be able to assemble a prototype in another two days."

"That fast? Impressive."

"Iapetus provides us weapons and tools that are designed with our technology in mind. It is rarely difficult for us to create and assemble the finished product."

"I'll just bet it does—" He elbowed Alex in the ribs to cut her off.

"This will be the most powerful weapon we've ever built, but I'm confident in our ability to construct it."

They passed a segmented area larger than most. Suspended from the ceiling was the housing for what appeared to be the weapons attached to the fighters they'd seen at the hangar, if both larger and longer. This was not their destination, however.

Finally, they reached an area partitioned off by floor-to-ceiling glass. Four displays ran across the back wall above terminals. Khokteh occupied three of the terminals.

Nakuridi slid a portion of the glass aside and allowed them to enter. They both moved directly to the displays, causing some animated fidgeting on the part of the Khokteh working at them.

The first display showed a rotating exterior schematic of a cylinder, almost as wide as it was long, and an object that resembled a laser turret on one end. Multiple internal compartments were visible inside the main cylinder. The second display was filled by stacked schem flows of a form of circuitry—likely the interior workings of the weapon. The third display presented two data columns; the left column was a list and the right a series of chemical formulas.

The list was in the Khokteh language. His eVi could capture the words using his ocular implant and translate them, but it was a slower process than communications. His eyes ran down both columns as rapidly as possible before he shifted to the schem flows.

The few words it contained were also in the native language, but there weren't many ways to draw the directional flow of electrical current, and he found he was able to follow it well enough.

The image which immediately sprang to mind was of a portable LEN reactor; inner and outer insulation chambers surrounded a central rod. But there were also two additional compartments on either side.

"Oh, fuck me."

He and Nakuridi both pivoted to Alex. Nakuridi made a frothy, sputtering sound. "I don't see how—"

Caleb quickly smiled in apology. "Bad translation. She was merely expressing surprise. At something. Weren't you?"

She pointed to a formula on the third display. He nodded comprehension, and her finger lowered to another formula.

He noted the shorthand symbols then returned his attention to the schem flows. The separate chambers' designated purposes were to hold the results of those formulas, one for each.

He faced Nakuridi with deliberate calm. "This is an anti-matter weapon."

"Yes. That would suffice as a description of its functionality."

He worked to keep his demeanor neutral. "Do you...commonly use anti-matter weapons?"

Nakuridi's shoulders rose. "This is a new concept for us, but an ingenious one."

Caleb brought a palm up to his chin and refocused on the schem flow. He pointed to the power input. "We're not familiar with this shorthand—what level of power is this?"

Nakuridi responded, and the translation came through.

He rubbed his temples. *"Valkyrie, that can't be right."*

'I've studied multiple technical texts. It is correct.'

Alex stepped in front of him and craned her neck to glare up at Nakuridi. "We need to see the Tokahe Naataan."

"Tokahe Naataan is meeting with his military council this evening and cannot be disturbed."

"At all?"

"There are conditions under which he can be disturbed. You do not meet them. He instructed me to have you returned to his residence when the tour was complete—and to tell you he may be quite late arriving home. The servants will prepare a meal for you, and you have his apologies."

Alex was twitching in agitation, but she kept a modicum of outward control. "Please pass on our own message to him: we need to speak to him about a very important matter as soon as he is available."

"I'll see he receives it. Are we done here?"

Caleb gazed back at the image of the cylinder, spinning on its axis in slow tumbles. "Two days until it's built, you said?"

"That is my estimation."

"Okay. Yes, we're done here. Take us to Tokahe Naataan's home. We'll wait for him there."

39

IRELTSE

Caleb was an absurdly light sleeper, and it took Alex several minutes of delicate movement to ease out of the bed, gather her clothes and tip-toe out of the room. She held her breath until she was out of the house.

Two vehicles were parked in front. Had Pinchu finally come home, sometime after they had given up and retired for the night? She hesitated. Should she go back inside, wake him from sleep and confront him now?

She decided against it. There would be time to try to talk sense into him tomorrow, but this was likely to be her sole chance to slip away.

She hefted herself up into the open vehicle and studied the dash. She'd watched Pinchu operate it, and once the various controls were identified, it shouldn't be complicated to fly.

Pinchu will not appreciate you stealing his vehicle.

I'm not stealing it—I'm merely borrowing it for an hour or two.

Alex, I'm not certain this is a wise course of action. I am as intrigued as you regarding the Metigens' purposes here, but Caleb is right that—

That it's a risk. I agree. But I may not get this kind of opportunity again.

She played with the 'start' control until the engine fired, then lifted off the ground. The engine was more powerful than she'd expected, and the vehicle cavorted roughly in her hands. She gripped the stick jutting out of the dash with both hands and, after several gyrations, accelerated toward the temple.

∽R∼

Caleb awoke with a jolt. Immediately aware some sound had roused him, he stilled and listened. There was a faint, distant hum, but it was gone before he could identify it.

Alex wasn't in the bed. He went to the door of the lavatory. "Alex, are you in there?" Nothing. He nudged the door open and found it empty.

He paused long enough to pull on pants before heading through the house. His eyes scanned the open rooms as he made his way to the front door but spotted neither her nor anything out of place. He'd heard Pinchu arrive home an hour earlier, but only one vehicle was outside.

He crossed his arms over his chest. "Valkyrie, where did Alex go?"

'I've been instructed not to share that information.'

"Goddammit. She went to the temple." He leapt into the vehicle and activated the engine.

R

The temple stone almost seemed to shine from within under a full moon. An eerie crimson radiance lit the night and the open interior.

Alex crept along the columns toward the dais. She didn't think the temple had guards, but she might as well attempt not to be seen.

The dais was empty except for the large table...but the table wasn't empty. It hadn't been visible from the audience, but a concave recess in the center of the table contained a dark metal ring. Miniscule gaps between the edges of the metal and the stone indicated it had a range of motion. She searched the area a second time for any other communication candidates, then reached in and pressed the ring.

It lit up briefly in pure white light then went dark. She looked around the temple but saw no activity. She wasn't a patient person, but she forced herself to lean on one of the pillars and wait.

Three minutes later a luminosity brighter than the moonlight descended from the ceiling to surround the temple dais. If the

Metigen had traveled from its own watcher planet, this was fast travel indeed; perhaps it watched from a closer vantage, given how intimately involved in Khokteh society it was.

The pinpoints of light began coalescing into the rough form of a Khokteh—but the transformation abruptly halted.

Anaden? Here? The voice quaked with an air of horror, and the lights surged toward her, probing, prodding.

If it surrounded her it would be able to transport her away. She stepped deliberately backward.

No...HUMAN. One of Mnemosyne's pets off its leash. The Conclave will not be pleased to learn of this. Condescension replaced horror as the voice gained an aura of authority.

She wished it would take some form, any form, so she could glare it in the eye. "What are you trying to accomplish with the Khokteh? Why do you arm them with technology they do not comprehend and send them to kill one another over and over in endless cycles?"

Run along home, little fledgling. Try again in a thousand years.

"Did you learn nothing from your war against us? We don't do as we're told."

"No, we don't." She pivoted to see Caleb taking the stairs two at a time up to the dais. His attention was focused on the Metigen, but she'd be an idiot not to recognize the layers of meaning in the statement.

She reached out and grasped his hand as he joined her. Now was not the time to seek forgiveness; now was the time to present a strong, united front. Thankfully, he appeared to agree.

Yes, I did hear something to that effect. Two of you then, or are there yet more? Did you bring an army?

"Not yet. Do we need to?"

Tread carefully, Humans. You intrude in affairs you do not understand.

She groaned. "We realize this, which is why we want to understand. Explain it—explain your reasons for manipulating the Khokteh. Tell us what your purpose is for all these universes."

Alas, it is not for me to decide what is to be done with you. But you would do well to return home before your ignorant flailing destroys more than you intend.

"We don't intend to destroy anything at all—and you seem to be doing plenty enough destroying for all of us. You...." Her voice trailed off as the Metigen dissipated and vanished as swiftly as it had arrived. "Oh, motherfucker!"

Caleb's hand was instantly on her arm. "Alex, what the bloody hell were you thinking? It could have hurt you—it could have *taken* you!"

Her gaze roved around the temple grounds, still hoping it would return for another go. "I was thinking I wanted some damn answers, and this might be my best or even only chance to get them." She steeled herself and reluctantly looked at him. "I didn't wake you because you wouldn't have wanted me to come here."

"Because it was a stupid thing to do. And now you've exposed us."

"Oh, come on—they knew we were traversing their portals. Remember when they chased us through a bunch of them? They have alarms on every damn one."

"Well, now they know we're doing a bit more than surveying the scenery."

"Good."

"*Good?*" He ran a hand through his hair. "Dammit, Alex, do you have the first care for your safety? Are you trying to get yourself killed?"

"No, of course not. I'm starting to think the Metigens can't hurt us, at least not directly."

"Why not? They can manipulate their environment—Mesme built a house. They can *transport* us."

"I know. But when it comes to violence, they act through others or via machines. I don't have an explanation, but the evidence speaks for itself."

"The evidence is a little thin. Too thin to act so recklessly. Not without a damn good reason—something I believe I rather clearly said we didn't have."

"You think a chance to get answers isn't a good enough reason? Why are we here then?"

He leveled a deeply scathing scowl at her. "To find the answers ourselves. To fit the puzzle pieces together one at a time instead of trusting aliens who have plainly ulterior motives to give us the truth. Otherwise, we would've simply gone to Mesme, right?"

She sank against the table to stare at the ground instead of him. "Yeah. They—the Metigens—drive me mad. They play with people, with whole species, like they were toys, to be tossed aside when they no longer amuse. I wish they had throats so I could strangle them."

He eased back beside her, and his voice softened a touch. "But not to death."

"That depends...." She risked a glance at him. "I'm sorry I snuck out on you."

His eyes remained hard though. "No, you're not."

She chewed on her lower lip and tried again. "Okay, I'm...sorry you wouldn't have agreed to come. I'd have preferred it if you were here with me."

He gazed up at the high, curved ceiling of the temple, once more tinted an ominous crimson now that the Metigen had departed. "Look. We've both spent a long time going our own way and not asking permission before we did. I'm not your keeper, nor are you mine. I just wish like hell you'd told me what you planned to do."

"Then we would've argued."

"As opposed to what we're doing now?"

She huffed a weak, resigned laugh. "Valid point."

"Alex, I can handle being angry with you—I don't like it, I don't want to be, but I'll deal. Already have some experience at it. But I have to be able to count on you. I have to know you won't go behind my back when you don't care for the answer I give."

"Oh? You went behind my back to get access to the *Siyane*."

"Don't do that."

Yes, she was lashing out—but it didn't mean it wasn't true. "Why not? How is it different?"

He blinked and stared at her, his expression bordering on...yep, there it was. Pained patience...or maybe a slightly more severe, deeper frustration. "For one, the statute of limitations has expired on it. For another, we weren't married then—we were barely together. I had no idea how far I could trust you, no more than you knew how far you could trust me. For a third, my doing so ended up saving your life...but the last one doesn't count, does it, unless I want to prove your case for you."

He dragged a hand down his face, emotion animating it anew. "So I return to my initial statement—given both our pasts, this isn't easy for either of us. But I would never do such a thing today, and dammit but you know that."

Her mother had tried to warn her marriage was about give and take, about compromise, about respecting the other person's position even when you didn't agree with them. For some strange reason her mother had been concerned Alex would be incapable of managing such things. She chuckled quietly.

"If there is something you find amusing in all this, please let me in on the joke."

"I was remembering something Mom said to me, about how Dad infuriated her on an almost weekly basis, but he never disappointed her." She met his distressingly harsh gaze and nodded. "All right. I promise I won't go behind your back again, and will instead face the wrath of your expressions of pained patience and exasperated frustration."

He tried and failed to stifle a laugh. "There's no wrath to my expressions."

"Oh, yes, there is. And so many, varied kinds." She took his hands in hers, grateful he didn't jerk them away. "I realize I still occasionally revert to old habits. I'll try to do better. I *will* do better." Her forehead dropped to rest on his. "Just out of curiosity, would you have come with me if I had asked?"

"Depends on how determined you were."

"So yes, then."

He sighed, but wrapped his arms around her and drew her closer. "Eventually, yes."

40

IRELTSE

Caleb leaned into the massive desk dominating the center of the office. "Pinchu, this is a two-hundred-*petajoule* anti-matter weapon. Do you even begin to comprehend what that means?"

The Tokahe Naataan lifted his elongated chin so high Caleb could no longer see any of his eyes. "It means it will exact a righteous vengeance upon the Nengllitse for the deaths they caused."

"It means it will level a city—and I don't mean cause widespread damage like what they inflicted here. I mean *eradicate* it. Every building, every object and every Nengllitse Khokteh for..." he waited a beat for a size conversion "...fifty kilometers in all directions. Our people outlawed these weapons two centuries ago after discovering the colossal, indiscriminate death they wrought."

"This is not your world, Caleb Human, and we are not your *shikei*. We have a different history, and a different measure of justice."

"Believe me when I tell you I know a great deal about justice—about vengeance. Let me ask you: do you want to kill their children? All of them?"

"They killed my child."

A gasp escaped Caleb's lips, and he was rendered momentarily speechless. He had begun to subconsciously ascribe human values to their culture same as Alex had, simply because they appeared civilized. Because they walked and talked and ate and slept, lived in homes, were born small and grew up.

While he didn't doubt there had always been individual humans who harbored such abhorrent thoughts, it had nonetheless been a mistake to assign Pinchu and the Khokteh human values. He retreated a mental step from the situation.

Pinchu took advantage of the brief silence to reaffirm his stance. "This is the weapon the Gods have ordained for our use. They judge our cause virtuous."

Alex nearly came across the desk then, but Caleb thrust out an arm to hold her back. They had resigned themselves to the reality that trying to convince Pinchu his 'gods' were in actuality aliens running experiments on a multiverse of pocket universes, of which his was only one, would be a futile endeavor. Nevertheless, he could sense Alex shaking from holding in the urge to tell Pinchu the unvarnished truth, or whack him upside the head with one of the Khokteh spears, or both.

He stepped in before she lost the struggle with restraint. "And what do you think your enemies will retaliate with next? The escalation isn't going to stop."

"It will if we decimate the Nengllitse."

Alex's mouth fell open. "Genocide, really? Damn."

He leaned more forcefully toward Pinchu. "No, it won't, because the Tapertse, logically assuming you're coming for them next, will get their benefactor gods—" *which are probably one and the same as yours* "—to bestow on them an even stronger weapon. Pinchu, if you want to protect your citizens, ask your gods for a shield the size of a city—a shield that can defend against the next, more powerful attack. Do not use this weapon."

Pinchu stood and adopted a proud stance behind the desk. "Caleb and Alex Humans, my friends—I hope I may call you such—I thank you for your insights and the companionship you extended to my family and my citizens, in spite of our initial poor treatment of you. Were Cassela still with us, things might be different...but she is not, and never will be again." He paused to compose himself.

"What you speak would sound like wisdom to your kind, I have no doubt. But this is my planet and these are my *shikei*, and I know the path which needs to be taken. You may stay for as long as you wish, but I do not want to place you in harm's way to a greater extent than I previously have, so I understand if you feel you must leave."

Caleb checked Alex. Her expression was a violent maelstrom of emotions, but she shook her head, likely not trusting herself to speak further. He turned back to Pinchu. "We'll leave soon, then. You are right—your war is not our war, and we have our own mission. Your hospitality has been exemplary."

"After the first rough patch, yes?" The Tokahe Naataan made a tentative laughing sound. "You are welcome to return should your travels bring you near in the future. If or when that time comes, I pray you find us victorious."

"I pray we find you alive."

Pinchu merely nodded in what was, perhaps, resigned acceptance of his eventual fate.

ℛ

Alex stuffed her clothes in her pack with a fervor normally reserved for rants about politicians and bureaucrats. Which in a way, Caleb supposed, this was. "Of all the stupid, moronic, fucking reprehensible decisions—Valkyrie, come pick us up at the house. I want to be elsewhere now."

'Understood. ETA twelve minutes.'

She glanced up at him. "Aren't you going to pack?"

He was leaning against the wall, ankles and arms crossed, watching her. "I'm already packed. I never unpacked."

"All right...you're ready to leave, aren't you?"

He lifted his shoulders in assent. "I've been standing here trying to think of anything else we can do, any other way to get through to him, but...there isn't any other way. He's grief-stricken and to our eyes not thinking rationally, but you saw everyone at the temple yesterday, and today at the Center. His subjects are behind him. They support the decision, which makes me suspect maybe this is less grief and more standard operating procedure."

"It's barbaric. It's beyond the pale."

"Only because we haven't experienced and had instilled in us the pain of decades—centuries—of attacks by the enemy."

She frowned. "You agree with him?"

"No. Absolutely not. But I need to at least try to conceive of how the Khokteh could have reached this point while still otherwise being the civilized, generally logical, likeable species we've found them to be. I need it to make sense."

She breathed out sharply and hefted her pack onto her shoulder. "I've never understood why most people act the way they do—no reason I'd understand the asinine decisions of aliens. Let's go."

But when she reached the door her pace faltered, and she looked back at him. "These pocket universes? They're fake, manufactured playgrounds for the Metigens. They're just sidespaces to the *real* space—the universe through that big, shiny source portal at the heart of this maze."

Her gaze dropped to the floor. "They damn sure feel real, though."

41

NENGLLITSE

From four kilometers up, the Nengllitse capital looked no different from the one on Ireltse. Oh, there were a few subtle variances in the architecture, and the greater distance from the system's sun resulted in unique topography and foliage. But the zoomed-in visual scanner revealed tiny dots of Khokteh traversing the streets, going about their lives in much the same manner as those they'd left behind on Ireltse.

Comrades of those below had shot at them personally a few days earlier, so Alex recognized full well they weren't lily-white, innocent victims. Their military killed Cassela, a marvelous creature she'd only just begun to know as a friend, and over twelve hundred other citizens of Ireltse.

But if there was anything the last year had taught her—if there was anything Caleb had taught her, the Metigen War had taught her—it was that perspective was everything. If you wanted to understand your enemy, you must understand that they were the hero in their own story. The leader of Nengllitse, whoever it may be, believed he or she had the right of this war as zealously as Pinchu did.

'Alex, the Ireltse forces are approaching. We should retreat to a safe distance.'

"Right." She took a last look at the sunny afternoon and bustling city on the surface, then eased the *Siyane* up through the atmosphere. They didn't want to be anywhere near an anti-matter strike when it came. Nengllitse possessed planetary defenses, but with the cloaking shield they'd sailed past them without difficulty on their descent and did so again now.

Said defenses lit up brighter than a Christmas exhibition, however, when the Ireltse forces arrived, and in seconds a low-orbit military battle ignited. She hovered above it, transfixed in a kind of morbid horror as orbiting cannons fired repeaters at the advancing warships while the ships bathed the cannons in laser fire.

When the viewport lit up an effulgent canary yellow, Caleb grabbed the controls and yanked the *Siyane* up another half megameter. She glanced at him, but he merely raised an eyebrow in challenge…which she didn't.

The Ireltse had come in overwhelming strength, and they neutralized the automated planetary defenses in minutes. Multiple formations descended through the atmosphere, and a massive cruiser brought up the rear. It was impossible to miss the tacked-on, bulky weapon housing suspended beneath the undercarriage near the bow.

One shiny new anti-matter weapon, ready for use.

Her hands went to the controls. "The fighting has moved in-atmosphere. We can draw slightly closer—I promise I'll leave a large buffer between us and them, but I have to see."

"I know."

She gave him a tight smile and eased back down until they were skimming the stratosphere. The pinprick explosions of ship-to-ship combat and building impacts could be seen through thin, wispy clouds. Doubtless the Nengllitse military was now mobilized and meeting the Ireltse forces in the skies above the city in a mirror image of the battle on Ireltse.

Abruptly the city below flashed white like an old photo negative. A shockwave roiled outward in all directions, obliterating everything in its wake, including most of the Ireltse ships—Pinchu apparently had not appreciated exactly how powerful the weapon truly was, his statements notwithstanding. Or maybe he'd considered the ships and their crew a necessary sacrifice.

The whiteness gradually faded away, and an ashen gray curtain lifted to reveal the devastation the strike had fashioned. The city center was a crater over four kilometers in diameter, every building in it annihilated. The rest of the city had been flattened—nothing stood high enough to be picked up by the scanner.

Thousands of buildings were leveled to their foundations, the material they had been constructed of simply *gone*, eradicated in the matter-anti-matter collision. Along with the Khokteh who occupied them.

"How many dead, I wonder?"

Caleb's voice was flat and toneless. "A hundred fifty thousand? Two hundred?"

She leapt up from the cockpit chair, sending it spinning. "Valkyrie, get us out of here. Head for the portal." She walked in a daze into the main cabin, all the way back to the kitchen, where she promptly backhanded the half-empty glass of water sitting on the counter. It sailed across the cabin to slam into the wall and send water spraying onto the couch, the weight machine and the floor.

A moment later Caleb's arms encircled her waist from behind as he kissed her hair—but she didn't want to be comforted right now. She twisted roughly in his grasp to face him. "Let's go see Mesme. I have a few things I'd like to say to that *yobanyi pizda*."

"What happened to 'never ask a question until you know the answer?'"

"I'm not intending on asking questions—I'm mostly intending on yelling. You're welcome to do a little asking when I periodically stop to catch my breath."

He exhaled, long and slow. "I have to admit, right now I'd like nothing more than to stick the alien in a confined space for a couple of hard hours of questioning. Not sure I'd start off the interrogation by calling Mesme a cunt, though."

"Well, that makes one of us." She wrapped her fingers around the excess material of his collar and curled them into a fist; his shirt had committed no offense, but she needed the smallest outlet for the rage churning inside her.

"Did they manipulate humans like this, too? Do they do this to everyone? Is my father dead—is your father dead—because the Metigens wanted to run an experiment and measure the results?"

Her teeth ground painfully against one another. "Are we all just puppets dancing on their strings?"

"Baby, you and I will never be anyone's puppets."

"I hope like hell that's true...but if it's not, I'm taking your sword to the strings."

42

AURORA THESI (PORTAL PRIME)

ENISLE SEVENTEEN (PORTAL: AURORA)

Though they had only spent a few hours there more than half a year ago, it felt somehow comforting to return to the sparkling lake tucked into the mountains on Portal Prime. Why, when everything about Mesme made her the antithesis of comfortable?

Because here was where desperation had become hope. Where helplessness had become purpose.

The cloaking shield turned out to also shield them from the tech repulsion field, saving them days of hiking. The device powering the planet-wide cloaking whirled a dazzling white aura in the meadow past the lake, and the water glowed with the last remnants of photoluminescence from the night before.

Mesme was nowhere in sight.

Alex stepped off the *Siyane's* ramp into the thick grass. She'd forgotten how lush the valley was; for a moment the serenity of the environment threatened to brighten her somber mood and ease her indignation. She'd calmed down somewhat since witnessing the massacre at Nengllitse—enough to be willing to listen to what Mesme had to say—but the fury simmered just beneath the surface, ready to flare if she didn't like the alien's responses.

Valkyrie, however, murmured excitedly in her head. *I am most excited to see and meet this Metigen of yours.*

Wait until you want to throttle the life out of it.

Caleb joined her, and they approached the shore of the lake hand-in-hand. She gazed up at the sky. "Mesme, I know you know we're here. Don't be shy."

They were greeted by silence. When they reached the water Caleb gestured toward the path leading to the gap in the mountain. "Maybe it's taking a nap—you know, in its house."

"You love the fact it built a house, don't you?"

"It's intriguing. The act implies a depth and complexity of motivation beyond what Mesme presented to us. It's...quirky. I realize you don't feel the same way, and after what it put you through, I don't blame you. But given what we've seen lately, I think that apparent complexity of motivation is all the more relevant."

She shrugged. "At best I prefer to keep Mesme at a long arm's length. At worst...there aren't words for what I want. You're right—its motivations are complex, but to me this means even if it did help us once, I cannot trust that they're all in alignment with ours."

The path opened up into the small glade, which also looked exactly as she remembered. The flowers outside the house were in bloom and showed every sign of having been tended to recently. She approached the front door while Caleb checked around back. "Mnemosyne?"

Lacking other options, she knocked on the door. Again, no response. After a second knock went unanswered she nudged the door open, and when Caleb came around to the front shaking his head to indicate he'd come up empty, she stepped inside.

The interior was spartan in the extreme. A table and chair made of the same wood as the walls sat in the main room, and a wide opening led to a slightly separated room on the left. There were no other rooms—no kitchen, lavatory or closets. She went through the opening to the left.

"Oh, my."

She stared curiously at the object tucked into the far corner of an otherwise empty room. It was long, about three meters, and covered in a fine mist; the temperature of the surrounding air dropped as she neared.

Her exclamation had drawn Caleb's attention. "It's a stasis chamber. It has to be."

She nodded in response and knelt down beside it. The design was elegant and perfectly smooth, with no apparent seams or moving parts. A virtual readout displayed data in a language she'd never seen—it bore no resemblance to the machine language used by the planet's cloaking device and the Metigen superdreadnought she and Valkyrie had sabotaged. She didn't recognize any of the material it was constructed of or see any mechanism which could be powering it.

She reached up and began wiping away the condensation off the top. Caleb dropped to his knees beside her and did the same. It was with equal parts anticipation and trepidation that she peered into the pod.

Large black eyes dominated a teardrop-shaped head. Pasty grayish skin stretched over a thin, skeletal body with disproportionately long arms and legs. An androgynous torso held the limbs together but was otherwise unexceptional, with no visible sex organs.

"Well…this is a little anticlimactic."

The form's physical appearance bears a striking similarity to several images found in the historical records of mid-to-late 20th century Earth.

"What? You're telling us Metigens visited humans in physical form hundreds of years ago?"

Not exactly. In the early decades of space travel a legend of sorts arose, telling of little gray/green men—aliens—who purportedly kidnapped random people and farm animals, performing invasive experiments and occasionally flaying them.

Her eyes widened. "They flayed people?"

No, the farm animals. Cattle, mostly. Or rather, this is what the reports alleged. There is no verifiable evidence any such events, kidnappings or otherwise, in fact occurred. Those claiming to have been abducted were often accused of fabricating the tales or of being mentally disturbed. And as humanity expanded into the Sol system, the reports faded. The last reputed kidnapping happened in 2019.

Alex sank back on her heels. "People thought aliens flayed cows? Sometimes I wonder how we ever managed to get off the planet."

'Actually, your friend Ms. Rossi's ancestor played a large role in that achievement with her invention of—'

"I was being hyperbolic, Valkyrie."

'I know.'

Caleb had been listening with half an ear as he scrutinized the pod's contents. "The stories make a certain amount of sense."

"How do they make sense? I refuse to believe the Metigens would abduct people—much less fucking *cows*—when they're quite well-versed in every aspect of humanity and always have been."

His head shook. "Yet somehow people got in their heads a very distinct image of aliens—an image that looks a hell of a lot like the body in this stasis chamber here. When we started studying then exploring the stars, what were we searching for, truly? Aliens. So what did they give us? *Aliens.* I doubt they ever abducted a single person—or cow—but they could've implanted memories or suggestions during sleep. I imagine it would work similar to how they talk to us, which they can do across tremendous distances.

"They gave us imaginary aliens to fixate on—only it turns out they weren't so imaginary, because they used the easiest reference point they had: themselves."

She grimaced in prevarication, but his logic was sound. Insane to anyone who hadn't met a Metigen, but sound otherwise. "To slow us down in our search for extraterrestrial life?"

"To give us something to fixate on. To give form to the theoretical concept of 'aliens'…and, yes, perhaps so we wouldn't search so hard for *other* aliens."

"Okay, but there haven't been reports of abductions for three centuries."

"As we explored the tangible reaches of space, we found we didn't need aliens so much—the stars themselves provided more than enough to capture our imagination. Also, we became less susceptible to deception—our planetary sensors would detect any such incursions, were they real. So they faded to legend. But they served their purpose at a critical time in human development."

"Damn. Cunning, manipulative bastards." She tilted her head, her gaze focusing on the inky, lifeless eyes. "Do you think Mesme's...in there? Its consciousness, I mean."

Caleb had shifted to inspecting the pod itself with renewed purpose, clearly trying to figure out how it operated. "I couldn't even begin to guess. If it's aware, I'd expect it to have materialized in empyreal form by now. Maybe since it doesn't have anything pressing to do, it's hibernating or something." Finally he sank to the floor beside her. "Whatever this chamber's constructed of, I've never seen it before. I've no idea what's powering it or how. It's impenetrable and—"

"You were going to open it?"

"No—I don't want to kill Mesme, obviously. I just wanted to see if I *could* open it. Which I can't."

They sat in silence for several minutes, considering the pod with varying expressions of dismay, confusion and contemplation. Finally she sighed to exaggerated effect. "What now?"

"Let's give it the night."

ℛ

Mesme never showed.

Given another day and night to stew, her anger and indignation had transformed into frustration, but one thing she wasn't going to do was sit around impotently twiddling her thumbs and *waiting*. There was no way to know when the alien might return. It could be an hour, a week, a year...or never.

"So we keep investigating the portal network."

Caleb rested against the data center and didn't respond at once. He looked deep enough in thought she expected him to start pacing any second now, but finally he nodded. "I think so. We learned more in the Khokteh universe than in any one before it. We learned the Metigens are intervening in at least some of the pocket universes, and I'd be very interested to discover how they're intervening in others. Is it solely about playing the role of gods and setting societies against one another, or is there a deeper purpose behind it?"

She drew a hand idly along the back of the couch. "My more reckless inclinations are screaming at me to say screw it all and hit the source portal. But whatever we learned in the Khokteh's universe, and now finding Mesme gone...I feel like we still don't understand a goddamn thing. So we shouldn't go through the source portal." She cocked an eyebrow at him. "We shouldn't, right?"

He shook his head, laughing. "Right."

She nodded a tad ruefully. "I resisted for a long time, but now I really wish Mesme had been here. I want to know what 'the Conclave' is, and what or who an 'Anaden' is. I want to know why they all name themselves after figures in Greek mythology, even when they're in universes where the Greeks never existed. I want to know...why the Metigens embolden the worst impulses in otherwise intelligent beings, instigating them to kill one another by the hundreds of thousands, and why they think that is somehow *acceptable.*"

"Hey...." He came over and held her by the shoulders. "We did everything we could. A few months ago you succeeded in saving humanity from genocide, which was no easy feat. Hopefully I saved Akeso from eventual annihilation, and we saved ourselves from the Ruda. So maybe we can't save every species—not from themselves, anyway. We're still way ahead by any count."

She shrugged in his arms. "Shall we go try to save the next one?"

"Maybe the next one won't need saving. Which, for the record, would be fantastic."

43

IDRYMA

I did not think to see the Idryma again.

Yet here I was, my consciousness projected into the Conclave council chamber once more. The fact I was not here under pleasant circumstances did not dull my appreciation to have returned. Aurora Thesi had become my abode, but the Idryma remained my home.

The structure, if it could be called such, existed outside the three spatial dimensions physical beings spent most of their time traveling in, though not outside of time. Katasketousya were experts in dimensional manipulation—more adept at it than any species, in fact, save a select few Anaden progenies. Hence the dimensional shifts hiding the Theseis in each Enisle, as well as our clever little singularity bombs.

Here in this quantum space beside and within physical space, the Idryma presented as mirrored symmetries of light waves woven together into the framework of a great hall. Its chambers flowed outward in successive layers, expanding and contracting as needed to serve our—or their, I reminded myself—purposes. If a floor was needed, a floor manifested, and when not needed it existed only as a probability unmeasured.

Ethereal to the point of being unfathomable for most, to me it was more real than the soil on Aurora Thesi.

"You disabled the spatial triggers at the Aurora entry portal."

I reluctantly focused my awareness concretely upon the council chamber and the Conclave members it held. "I did."

"You allowed these two Humans to pass through, without seeing fit to inform us."

I refrained from drifting my attention from Iapetus to Lakhes, not intending to be the one to reveal to the others that Lakhes *was* so informed. "I did."

"You went against the express orders of the Conclave. Why?"

As operational leader it was Lakhes' questioning to oversee, yet for now the Praetor appeared to be content permitting Iapetus to grandstand while watching on in seemingly detached interest.

"As I have been expelled from the Conclave, I submit I am no longer subject to its orders. As First Analystae of Aurora, it is and has always been my Enisle, and my responsibility. I believe allowing these Humans to investigate the Mosaic is the proper decision."

"You have lost your objectivity, to an even greater degree than we realized. Your judgment has been clouded by your affection for Humans."

"I believe my judgment has never been clearer. I have seen firsthand their potential, their strength of will, in a way you have not."

Hyperion interjected then. "You have loosed a chaotic, unstable variable into the Mosaic. They will destroy everything."

"It is a risk. They also may save everything."

"They must be stopped."

I caused my presence to ripple and grow discernibly in size. I had been respectful, but this was a manifested threat. Not surprising it would be voiced by Hyperion, but if left unchallenged it may become the will of the weight of the Conclave.

"What do you imagine you will do? You will not kill me. You will not kill them, not with your own consciousness. None of you would dare. Will you conscript more assassins in one of the Enisles you happen to catch them in? It did not work before."

"They won't be able to skirt death forever."

"On the contrary, they've shown a propensity for doing precisely this. They've eluded death in multiple Enisles thus far. But I would gravely advise against efforts to engineer their demise. Have you forgotten our purpose, Hyperion? Because I believe you have."

"Never! They wreck our purpose, altering the natural course of Enisles without understanding—"

"Tell me, how are things in Amaranthe? I cannot judge for myself, having been exiled. Are they going well?"

Hyperion paused in a vacillation of light and motion, and Lakhes stepped in with typically smooth grace. "They are not. Since you were last here, Mnemosyne, we've been forced to retask Enisle Thirty-Eight as a haven for what Fylliots we were able to smuggle out of Amaranthe."

"Fylliots—they originated in Eridum II, correct?"

"Yes. Their system was claimed for organic material harvesting, along with three other systems which thankfully were not inhabited by sentient species."

"How many is that in the last century to be threatened with or suffer extinction? Twenty? Thirty? I know you will not have lost count."

Lakhes showed a ripple of acknowledgment. "Thirty-three."

My directed attention swept across all those present. "Analystarum, the kairos is upon us. We are nearly out of time. I beg you, do not interfere with these Humans. Let them explore, let them learn. Let them show us what they can do, simply because it is their nature. I believe you will come to see what I already know."

Iapetus ventured back into the discussion. "Even if you are correct, two solitary Humans cannot accomplish what we require of them. What about the remainder of the species?"

Hyperion sputtered out a taunt. "They are making a mess of their freedom, aren't they?"

I refused to be provoked into agitation. "It is a challenging period for them, yes. But they have seen other challenging periods and emerged from them stronger for the adversity."

"How can you know they'll become what we need them to be?"

Lakhes' mien was as reserved as ever, but the subtleties in the expression of the question begged for a true answer. There was, however, but one true answer I could give.

"I have faith."

CODA:

EX MACHINA

"As he caught his footing, his head fell back, and the Milky Way flowed down inside him with a roar."

— *Yasunari Kawabata*

SIYANE

L ike in Metis and every pocket universe with a realized space they'd visited, the portal they traversed deposited them in the depths of a nebula. This one was brighter than many had been, shining in vibrant reds and golds.

Now that the Metigens were aware of what they were doing, they'd decided to start mixing up their pattern. They'd previously assigned all the portals unique designations so they could track where they'd been, but from now on they planned to choose their next destination randomly. It wouldn't prevent the Metigens from tracking the portals they activated, but at a minimum it reduced the chances of an ambush.

Alex confirmed a TLF wave provided a direction to head, then checked the scanners for anything which might be hostile, or simply intelligent. Seeing nothing, she toed her chair around to face Caleb.

"So Valkyrie was rather busy while we were on Ireltse, and she's completely integrated herself into the walls and hull of the ship now. She learned a lot from the Ruda."

A corner of his mouth curled up. "And?"

She rolled her eyes. Was she completely transparent to him? Probably. "And she seems to believe I can use her integration to fly the ship myself."

"I'm not sure I understand. How is that different from what you do now?"

"I think she means fly the ship by...*being* the ship. By seeing and acting through the nodes she's grown in the hull and the frame. Is that an accurate description, Valkyrie?"

'We won't know for certain until we attempt it, but you did capture the essence of it, yes.'

"Oh." He smiled with a hint of teasing. "That would pretty much be everything you've ever dreamed of."

"Not *everything*...but in a way." She checked the scanners again. "It looks clear for two or more parsecs. I was thinking I'd try it for a few minutes, while we're still far from any potential civilization."

"You should. I'll be right here. Valkyrie, you'll alert me if anything goes wrong?"

'Always.'

She reached over and gently trailed fingertips down his jaw. "Thank you." Then she spun back to face the viewport and closed her eyes.

I'm ready, Valkyrie.

Follow me.

She did so, allowing her consciousness to weave deeper into Valkyrie's neural network toward a new cluster. When she reached it she accessed the quantum orbs and—

"Bozhe milostivyy...."

In some vague, distant corner of her mind, she was aware of Caleb squeezing her hand to make sure she was all right, and her hand returning the squeeze of its own accord. Yet it was a faint whisper vanishing behind the reality of this new existence unfolding around her.

The red and gold of the nebula burst to life in all directions, but not in any way she'd perceived before this moment. Instead she could see the composition of the surrounding dust, gases and free particles, see the electrons of their atoms interacting.

The contradiction of space overwhelmed her. It was *empty*, empty everywhere, yet nevertheless teeming. She sensed the space between the atoms as she slowly spun the ship full circle.

Should she be able to feel the air, the faint breeze of the dissipating shock wave from the supernova which created this nebula? No, for that was a human sense.

This was...something else. An elemental sense, one crafted for photons and their radiant energy.

The TLF wave existed as a gleaming silver ribbon undulating through the nebula out to the stars beyond. Enthralled beyond words, she accelerated forward to follow its path.

ℛ

PANDORA STELLAR SYSTEM

ANESI ARCH ORBITAL STATION

Devon, I need you to do something for me.

What, Annie?

I need you to relax. You're fighting me.

No, I'm not.

Yes, you are. Your subconscious is resisting.

But I can't do anything about my subconscious.

You can. If in truth you do not want this, say so now. I will understand.

I do want it.

Then want it.

⟶

Mia jerked out of her drowsy ruminations. *What was that?*

In the span between dreaming and consciousness, she'd slipped into the Noesis—where something had changed. There was a new presence in the space, familiar but *more*.

She stood and went to the makeshift cot where Devon still lay.

His chest rose and fell in a steady rhythm, as if he were sleeping...she frowned, puzzled. His formerly baggy shirt now stretched taut over his arms and chest, defining the outline of burgeoning muscles.

Her hand rose to her hair; she ran fingertips through to its razor-straight ends. It now fell past her shoulders—nearly as long as it had been before the war. Meno grew it out for her in a matter of days...was Annie now doing much the same for Devon? Building his strength and increasing his muscle tone?

She would want him to be able to better defend himself the next time someone means him harm.

Did she tell you so, Meno?

In a manner—

Behind closed lids, Devon's eyes began jerking around at a frenetic pace.

Concerned, she placed a hand on his shoulder. "Devon, are you okay?"

His eyes popped open, and he flashed her a smile full of guileful self-assurance, something altogether different from either his usual cocky, boyish bravado or the more recent irascible angst.

Or maybe it was his eyes that created the disparity...for they now blazed not white, but a stunning, brilliant amethyst.

"I do believe I am."

~

ROMANE

INDEPENDENT COLONY

Morgan's eyes glittered argent purple—the color of polished amethyst quartz—behind the designer shadewraps she'd picked up before leaving Cavare. The first of Romane's two suns peeked over a mauve horizon as she exited the spaceport; she surveyed the scene briefly then started off down the street.

Stanley, you still there?

I am. This is a most interesting experience.

My brain is an interesting experience? Well, yes, I could see how it might be.

I will not disagree. However, what I meant is being in *your brain is more different from being connected to your brain than I expected.*

She idly observed the increasing number of well-dressed businesspeople who passed her on the sidewalk on the way to their daily duties. *I don't really have a response to that.*

It's fine. I will be exploring for a while, I think.

Hey, just because I agreed to let you hitch a ride, it doesn't mean we no longer have boundaries.

You keep telling yourself that, Morgan.

Oh no, her brand of humor had finally worn off on him. This was going to be a nightmare.

Annie had shared her ideas on how to transfer an Artificial's consciousness into the neural structure of a Prevo with Stanley.

Since the Devon/Annie connection had been severed and fire-walled, they required Abigail's assistance in order to effect the transfer. But Morgan's connection to Stanley, at the time, remained intact. It had been...not a simple matter, but doable without additional equipment in any event.

The military was never going to let her fly again, Prevo or no. So she'd burned out the ware—but not until Stanley successfully transferred his higher consciousness into the cells of her cerebral cortex.

She'd left Gianno a note explaining she'd severed the connection, promising not to disclose all the Noetica secrets she knew, sharing a few secrets of her own as a goodwill gesture and threatening to share a few more with the world as a warning. Then she'd resigned her commission and high-tailed it off Seneca before anyone was able to tell her she couldn't actually do any of those things.

They might come looking for her, of course. But she was playing a bet.

After the Marshal mentioned knowing Morgan's mother, she'd had Stanley do a little research; what he'd found had been most enlightening. Now, she was operating under the theory that deep down, Gianno still retained some aspect of the philosophy she'd clearly once espoused—that she still respected the notion of taking control of one's own destiny. Of freedom.

And freedom was what Morgan now had. Trapped in her head, Stanley had a measure less of it—but she also believed he'd come with her in part for the promise of it.

Morgan, you devious, crafty woman.

She chuckled quietly and turned left at the next intersection. *Damn, Devon, what took you so long? I thought you were never going to show up. I was getting lonely.*

You? I doubt it. But none of us are going to be lonely for long. What did you do?

Besides upload the consciousness of an Artificial into my brain cells? Gave a copy of the files on Noetica and the technology underlying the Prevo connection to a friend of mine on Earth.

She paused on the sidewalk, recalling her conflicted feelings about Fedor glimpsing even a portion of the Prevo technology. *Why?*

Because our best protection is knowledge. Information is supposed to be free. We're not meant to be a state secret, Morgan—we're meant to be the next evolution of the human species.

It's time that evolution began.

TO BE CONTINUED IN
BOOK TWO OF *AURORA RENEGADES*

DISSONANCE

***

SUBSCRIBE TO
GSJENNSEN.COM

Receive updates on AURORA RENEGADES, new book announcements and more

Author's Note

I published *Starshine* in March of 2014. In the back of the book I put a short note asking readers to consider leaving a review or talking about the book with their friends. Since that time I've had the unmitigated pleasure of watching my readers do exactly that, and there has never been a more wonderful and humbling experience in my life. There's no way to properly thank you for that support, but know you changed my life and made my dreams a reality.

I'll make the same request now. If you loved *SIDESPACE*, tell someone. If you bought the book on Amazon, consider leaving a review. If you downloaded the book off a website with Russian text in the margins and pictures of cartoon video game characters in the sidebar, consider recommending it to others.

As I've said before, reviews are the lifeblood of a book's success, and there is no single thing that will sell a book better than word-of-mouth. My part of this deal is to write a book worth talking about—your part of the deal is to do the talking. If you all keep doing your bit, I get to write a lot more books for you.

This time I'm also going to make a second request. *Sidespace* was an independently published novel, written by one person and worked on by a small team of colleagues. Right now there are thousands of writers out there chasing this same dream.

Go to Amazon and surf until you find an author you like the sound of. Take a small chance with a few dollars and a few hours of your time. In doing so, you may be changing those authors' lives by giving visibility to people who until recently were shut out of publishing, but who have something they need to say. It's a revolution, and it's waiting on you.

Lastly, I love hearing from my readers. Seriously. Just like I don't have a publisher or an agent, I don't have "fans." I have **readers** who buy and read my books, and **friends** who do that then reach out to me through email or social media. If you loved the book—or if you didn't—let me know. The beauty of independent publishing is its simplicity: there's the writer and the readers. Without any overhead, I can find out what I'm doing right and wrong directly from you, which is invaluable in making the next book better than this one. And the one after that. And the twenty after that.

Website: www.gsjennsen.com
Email: gs@gsjennsen.com
Twitter: @GSJennsen
Facebook: facebook.com/gsjennsen.author
Goodreads: goodreads.com/gs_jennsen
Google+: plus.google.com/+GSJennsen
Instagram: instagram.com/gsjennsen

Find all my books on Amazon:
http://amazon.com/author/gsjennsen

APPENDIX A

Supplemental Material

PORTAL NETWORK

"MOSAIC"

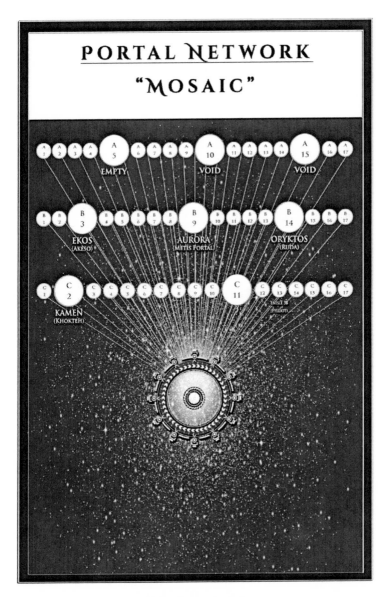

(UPDATED)

Updated Portal Network Map can be viewed online at: gsjennsen.com/ mosaic-map-post-sidespace

DRAMATIS ALIENORUM

IDRYMA

Lakhes
Conclave Praetor

Mnemosyne
First Analystae of Aurora Enisle

Iapetus
First Analystae of Khokteh Enisle

Hyperion
Analystae

PORTAL B-3

Species
Ekos

Planets
Ekos-1, Ekos-2, Ekos-3

Characters

Akeso ("All")
Ekos-2 Intelligence

Unnamed
Ekos-1 Intelligence

Unnamed
Ekos-3 Intelligence

PORTAL C-2

Species
Khokteh

Planets
Ireltse, Nengllitse, Tapertse

Characters

Pinchutsenahn Niikha
Qhiyane Kteh
("Pinchu")
Tokahe Naataan of Ireltse

Casselanhu Pwemku
Yuanwoh Vneh
("Cassela")
Amacante Naabaan of Ireltse

Nakuridi
*Chief Military Engineer
of Ireltse*

"Orange"
Ireltse Center Guard

"Grizzly"
Ireltse Center Guard

PORTAL B-14

Species
Ruda

Planets
Rudan

Characters

Supreme Three
(of Twelve)

Dramatis Alienorum can be viewed online at: gsjennsen.com/characters-alien-sidespace

APPENDIX B

AURORA RISING
DETAILED SYNOPSIS

STARSHINE

By the year 2322, humanity has expanded into the stars to inhabit over 100 worlds spread across a third of the galaxy. Though thriving as never before, they have not discovered the key to utopia, and societal divisions and conflict run as deep as ever.

Two decades ago, a group of breakaway colonies rebelled to form the Senecan Federation. They fought the Earth Alliance, won their independence in the Crux War and began to rise in wealth and power.

Now a cabal of powerful individuals within both superpowers and the criminal underground set in motion a plot designed to incite renewed war between the Alliance and Federation. Olivia Montegreu, Liam O'Connell, Matei Uttara and others each foment war for their own reasons. One man, Marcus Aguirre, manipulates them all, for only he knows what awaits humanity if the plot fails.

R

Alexis Solovy is a starship pilot and explorer. Her father, a fallen war hero, gave his life in the Crux War. As Operations Director for Earth Alliance Strategic Command (EASC), her mother Miriam Solovy is an influential military leader. But Alex seeks only the freedom of space and has made a fortune by reading the patterns in the chaos to uncover the hidden wonders of the stars from her cutting-edge scout ship, the *Siyane*.

Caleb Marano is an intelligence agent for the Senecan Federation. His trade is to become whatever the situation requires: to lie, deceive, outwit and if necessary use lethal force to bring his target to justice. Clever and enigmatic, he's long enjoyed the thrill and danger his job brings, but now finds himself troubled by the death of his mentor.

R

On Earth, Alex is preparing for an expedition to the Metis Nebula, a remote region on the fringes of explored space, when she receives an unexpected offer to lead the Alliance's space exploration program. After a typically contentious meeting with her mother, she refuses the job.

On Seneca, Caleb returns from a forced vacation spent with his sister Isabela and her daughter Marlee. Fresh off eradicating the terrorist group who murdered his mentor, he receives a new mission from Special Operations Director Michael Volosk: conduct a threat assessment on disturbing readings originating from the Metis Nebula.

While Alex and Caleb separately travel toward Metis, a Trade Summit between the Alliance and Federation begins on the resort world of Atlantis. Colonel Richard Navick, lifelong friend of the Solovys and EASC Naval Intelligence Liaison, is in charge of surveillance for the Summit, but unbeknownst to him, the provocation for renewed war will begin under his watch.

Jaron Nythal, Asst. Trade Director for the Federation, abets the infiltration of the Summit by the assassin Matei Uttara. Matei kills a Federation attaché, Chris Candela, and assumes his identity. On the final night of the Summit, he poisons Alliance Minister of Trade Santiagar with a virus, which overloads his cybernetics, causing a fatal stroke. Matei escapes in the ensuing chaos.

Shortly after departing Seneca, Caleb is attacked by mercenary ships. He defeats them, but when he later encounters Alex's ship on the fringes of Metis, he believes her to be another mercenary and fires on her. She destroys his ship, though not before suffering damage to her own, and he crashes on a nearby planet. She is forced to land to effect repairs; recognizing her attacker will die without rescue, she takes him prisoner.

Richard Navick and Michael Volosk each separately scramble to uncover the truth of the Santiagar assassination while Olivia Montegreu, the leader of the Zelones criminal cartel, schemes with Marcus Aguirre to implement the next phase in their plan. Olivia routes missiles provided by Alliance General Liam O'Connell to a group of mercenaries.

Fighting past distrust and suspicion, Alex and Caleb complete repairs on the *Siyane* using salvaged material from the wreckage of his ship. Having gained a degree of camaraderie and affection, if not quite trust, they depart the planet in search of answers to the mystery at the heart of Metis.

What they discover is a scene from a nightmare—an armada of monstrous alien ships emerging from a massive portal, gathering a legion in preparation for an invasion.

Meanwhile, Olivia's mercenaries launch a devastating attack on the Federation colony of Palluda. Disguised to look like a strike by Alliance military forces, the attack has the desired effect of inciting war. The Federation retaliates by leveling an Alliance military base on Arcadia, and the Second Crux War has begun.

Alex and Caleb flee the Metis Nebula to warn others of the impending threat, only to learn war has broken out between their respective governments. Caleb delivers information about the alien threat to Volosk. He informs the Director of Intelligence, Graham Delavasi, who alerts the Federation government Chairman Vranas and the military's supreme commander, Field Marshal Gianno. Forced to focus on the new war with the Alliance for now, they nonetheless dispatch a stealth infiltration team to investigate Metis.

Caleb is requested to accompany the team and return to Metis, only Alex refuses to drop him off on her way to Earth. Tensions flare, but Caleb realizes he's emotionally compromised even as Alex realizes she must let him go. Instead, he agrees to go to Earth with her, and together with Volosk they devise a plan to try to bring a swift end to the war by exposing its suspicious beginnings.

The plan goes awry when Caleb is arrested shortly after they arrive—by Alex's mother—after his true identity is leaked to Richard by those in league with Marcus.

While Caleb is locked away in a detention facility, his friend Noah Terrage is recruited by Olivia to smuggle explosives to Vancouver. Possessing a conscience, he refuses. The infiltration team sent by the Federation to Metis vanishes as the Second Crux War escalates.

Alex is forced to choose between her government, her family and what she knows is right. She turns to her best friend, Kennedy Rossi, and their old hacker acquaintance, Claire Zabroi. Plans in place, Alex presents her evidence on the alien armada to a skeptical EASC Board. Their tepid reaction leads to a final confrontation with her mother and a final plea to focus on the true threat.

Alex hacks military security and breaks Caleb out of confinement. Allegiances declared and choices made, they at last give in to the passion they feel for one another. Despite lingering resentment toward the Federation for her father's death and fear that Caleb is merely playing a role, she agrees to accompany him to Seneca to find another way to combat the looming invasion.

Caleb appeals to his friend and former lover, Mia Requelme, for help in covering their tracks. She hides the *Siyane* safely away on Romane while Alex and Caleb travel to Seneca. Secretly, Caleb asks Mia to hack the ship while they are gone to grant him full access and flying privileges, something Alex zealously guards for herself, and Mia uses her personal Artificial, Meno, to break the encryption on the ship.

On Earth, Richard wrestles with unease and doubt as he begins to believe Alex's claims about the origin of the war. He confesses his dilemma to his husband, Will Sutton. Will urges him to work to bring about peace and offers to convey Santiagar's autopsy report to Alex in the hope the Senecan government can find in it evidence to prove the assassination was not their doing.

Volosk meets with Caleb and Alex, and they hand over the autopsy report Will forwarded and all the raw data they recorded on the aliens. In return Volosk arranges meetings with the highest levels of leadership.

As Alex and Caleb enjoy a romantic dinner, EASC Headquarters is destroyed in a massive bombing executed by agents of Olivia and Marcus. Though intended to be killed in the attack, due to a last minute scheduling conflict Miriam Solovy is not on the premises. Instead EASC Board Chairman Alamatto perishes, along with thousands of others. On the campus but outside Headquarters, Richard narrowly escapes critical injury.

Within minutes of the bombing, Caleb and Alex are ambushed by mercenaries in downtown Cavare. Caleb kills them all in dramatic fashion, but unbeknownst to him Alex was injured by a stray shot. In the panic of the moment he mistakes her shell-shocked behavior for fear of the killer he has revealed himself to be.

Heartbroken but determined to protect her, he flees with her to the Intelligence building. Upon arriving there, they find the unthinkable—Michael Volosk has been murdered, his throat slit in the parking lot.

Suddenly unable to trust anyone, Caleb pleas with Alex to go with him to the spaceport, but she collapses as a result of her injury. Stunned but with one clear mission, he steals a skycar and returns to their ship, where he can treat her wounds in the relative safety of space.

The EASC bombing successfully executed, Olivia's Zelones network turns its attention to Noah. In refusing to smuggle the explosives he is now a liability; the first attempt on his life misses him but kills his young companion. Searching for answers, he traces the source of the hit and realizes he was targeted because of his friendship with Caleb. Lacking other options and with a price on his head, he flees Pandora for Messium.

Miriam returns to Vancouver to preside over the devastation at EASC Headquarters. She begins the process of moving the organization forward—only to learn the evidence implicates Caleb as the perpetrator.

Marcus moves one step nearer to his goal when the Alliance Assembly passes a No Confidence Vote against Prime Minister Brennon. Marcus' friend Luis Barrera is named PM, and he quickly appoints Marcus Foreign Minister.

Alex regains consciousness aboard their rented ship as they race back to Romane. Misunderstandings and innate fears drive them to the breaking point, then bring them closer than ever. The moment of contentment is short-lived, however, as Caleb—and by extension Alex—is publicly named a suspect in the bombing.

Every copy of the raw data captured at the portal, except for the original in Alex's possession, has now been destroyed. Recognizing an even deeper secret must reside within the portal and hunted by the conspirators and authorities alike, Alex and Caleb begin a desperate gambit to clear their names and discover a way to defeat the aliens.

On reaching Romane, Alex, Caleb and the *Siyane* are protected by Mia while they prepare. Kennedy brings equipment to replace the ship's shielding damaged in Metis. On the *Siyane*, she realizes the repairs made using the material from Caleb's ship has begun transforming the hull into a new, stronger metal. Caleb receives a vote of confidence from his sister Isabela, and a gesture of trust from Alex in the form of a chair.

Back on Earth, Miriam and Richard work to clear Alex's name, even as Miriam is threatened by the newly-named EASC Board Chairman, Liam O'Connell. Marcus informs his alien contact, Hyperion that his plan has nearly come to fruition, only to be told he is out of time.

As the invaders commence their assault on the frontiers of settled space by sieging the colony of Gaiae, Alex and Caleb breach the aliens' mysterious, otherworldly portal at the heart of the Metis Nebula.

ᴁ

VERTIGO

Beyond the Portal

Alex and Caleb survive the portal traversal to discover empty darkness on the other side. They follow the TLF wave until they are attacked by a host of alien vessels. Alex discerns an artificial space within the emptiness and pitches the *Siyane* into it. The vessels do not follow, and Alex and Caleb find themselves in the atmosphere of a hidden planet.

The planet mimics Earth in almost every way, but is 1/3 the size and orbits no sun. It differs in one other respect as well—time moves differently here. Days back home pass in hours here.

When they land and venture outside to explore their surroundings, Alex notices the ship's hull continues to transform into a new, unknown metal. As she puzzles over it they are attacked— by a dragon. The beast captures Alex and flies off with her.

Caleb takes control of the ship to chase the dragon. As it reaches a mountain range, the *Siyane* impacts an invisible barrier which throws it back to its origin point. On his return Caleb encounters and kills 2 additional dragons. Believing the barrier is a technology repulsor but uncertain of its parameters, he crafts a sword from a piece of metal, deactivates his eVi and crosses the barrier on foot.

Alex wakes in a memory. Eleven years old, she enjoys breakfast with her parents, then overhears a conversation between them she in reality never witnessed. Realizing this is an illusion, she demands to be set free. A ghostly, disembodied voice challenges her. Thus begins her journey through a series of scenes from the past in which she is forced to watch events unfold, helpless to intervene or escape, as her protests, tirades and desperate pleas go unanswered.

— First is a gauntlet of her own mistakes. Designed to paint her as selfish and uncaring, her worst flaws are displayed in encounters with friends, former lovers and most of all with her mother.

— She views a massive battle between the Alliance and Federation and realizes this is about more than her—the aliens having been watching and recording events across human civilization.

— Traveling further back in time, Alex suffers through the Hong Kong Incident 232 years earlier. Over 50,000 people died when an Artificial trapped HK University residents for 5 weeks without food. At its conclusion her captor speaks to her for only the second time, telling her she has 'done well.'

— She is sent to the bridge of her father's cruiser in the middle of the Kappa Crucis battle of the 1st Crux War—the battle that took his life. She sees her father's heroism as he protects thousands of civilians against a Federation assault, then his last moments as, his ship crippled, he contacts Miriam to say goodbye. The heartbreak and emotion of the scene devastates Alex, leaving her crumpled on the floor sobbing as the *Stalwart* explodes.

When it's over, she thanks her unseen captor for showing her this event. It expresses confusion at the incongruity of her distress and her thanks, leading her to observe that for all their watching, they still have no idea what it means to be human. Before the interchange can continue, she is told she will wake up, as her companion approaches.

Caleb hiked through the mountains for 2 days. The environment led him to recall a mission with Samuel, during which his mentor divulged the woman he loved was killed by slavers he'd been investigating. Later, Caleb discovers small orbs hovering in the air to generate the tech repulsion field. He renders several inert and confiscates them.

Having reached the dragon's den, he attacks it using the sword, and after an extended battle flays and kills it. As he nears the structure the dragon guarded, an ethereal being materializes but allows him to pass.

Alex awakens as Caleb enters, and they share a tender reunion. Soon, however, he is forced to admit Mia's hacking of her ship. He expects her to lash out in anger, but she instead declares her love for him. He quickly reciprocates, and rather unexpectedly they find themselves reconciled and closer than before. She recounts her experiences while a captive, and they decide to seek out the alien.

Eventually they come upon a lush valley sheltering a large lake; the alien Caleb encountered soars above it. It approaches them while morphing into a humanoid form and introduces itself as Mnemosyne.

Though enigmatic and evasive, the alien reveals its kind have been observing humans for aeons. It suggests humanity is being conquered because it advanced more swiftly and to a greater extent than expected. On further pressing, the alien—Alex has dubbed it 'Mesme'—indicates the invading ships are AIs, sent to cower people into submission if possible, to exterminate them if not. It emphasizes the ships are only machines, and notes humans have machines as powerful—Artificials. Part of Alex's test was to ensure she appreciated the dangers and limitations of Artificials, but also their potential.

Alex recalls a meeting 4 years ago with Dr. Canivon, a cybernetics expert, during which she met Canivon's Artificial, Valkyrie. She and Valkyrie hit it off, and Canivon explained her research into making Artificials safer and better aligned with human interests. She begins to understand what Mesme is suggesting, but pushes for more intel and acquires a copy of the code powering the planet's cloaking shield.

Mesme admits to believing humans are worth saving. The alien warns them they will be hunted on their return through the portal; at this point a second alien appears and a confrontation ensues. Mesme deters the new alien long enough to transport Alex and Caleb back to the *Siyane*. They arrive to learn the ship's hull has been completely transformed into the new metal.

Alex studies the cloaking shield code and adapts it for use on her ship. They depart the planet and continue following the TLF wave, discovering a massive shipyard where superdreadnoughts are being built and sent to their galaxy. Beyond it lies a portal 10x larger than the one that brought them here. It generates their TLF wave—as well as 50 more waves projected in a fanlike pattern.

They track one of the waves to a portal identical to the one leading to the Metis Nebula. They traverse it to find the signals replicated in a new space and a second origin portal, which leads them to conclude this is an elaborate, interlocking tunnel network.

Caleb devises a way to destroy the shipyard using the tech repulsion orbs he confiscated. They launch the orbs into the facility then activate them, resulting in its obliteration. This attracts the attention of enemy ships, which chase the *Siyane* through a series of portal jumps. Alex asks Caleb to fly her ship while she figures out a path that will deposit them nearest their own exit point.

On reaching it, Alex activates the sLume drive and traverses it at superluminal speed to emerge parsecs beyond the portal and well past the waiting enemies in the Metis Nebula. With working communications, they learn they've been cleared of all charges. Alex sends a message to Kennedy, telling her they are alive and have destroyed the aliens' shipyard.

$$\mathcal{R}$$

MILKY WAY

As the 2nd Crux War escalates, Federation forces conquer the Alliance colony of Desna. Lt. Col. Malcolm Jenner's *Juno* is the sole defender, and it escapes just before being crippled.

Miriam jousts with Liam even as she remains under a cloud of suspicion due to Alex's alleged involvement in the HQ bombing. Richard enlists the aid of a quantum computing specialist, Devon Reynolds, to help uncover the tampering in government records which led to the framing of Caleb and Alex for the bombing.

On Seneca, Dir. of Intelligence Graham Delavasi reviews Michael Volosk's files, including his suspicions regarding Jaron Nythal, and decides to follow up on the suspicions. Nythal tries to flee, but before he can do so the assassin Matei Uttara kills him. When Graham is called to the crime scene, he connects the dots and realizes a conspiracy does exist, and at least one person in his organization is involved.

Caleb's sister Isabela is taken in for questioning. In order to gain her trust, Graham reveals to her that her father was an investigator for Intelligence and was killed 20 years earlier by a resistance group planning to overthrow the Federation government. Her father's apparent abandonment of his family was a feint to protect them. After he was killed, the government covered up the incident.

On Messium, Kennedy is headed to a meeting when the aliens attack and is trapped under falling debris. She is rescued by a passing stranger—who turns out to be Noah Terrage—and they seek shelter. While her injuries heal they study the aliens' interference with comms and find a way to circumvent it. Kennedy sends a message to Miriam.

The Alliance launches an offensive to retake Desna. While the battle rages in space, Malcolm Jenner and a special forces team rescue the Desnan governor and his family. The Alliance fails to retake the colony. Meanwhile, an explosion takes the life of EA Prime Minister Barrera. In the wake of his death Marcus Aguirre—who arranged Barrera's murder—is named Prime Minister.

Devon Reynolds uncovers alterations to the records used to frame Caleb and Alex for the HQ bombing. At Richard's request he and a group of hackers leak the evidence to media outlets.

Upon seeing the news, Graham Delavasi refocuses his efforts to uncover the conspiracy. Suspecting his deputy, Liz Oberti, he uses Isabela to set a trap. Oberti is arrested but refuses to provide any intel.

The EASC Board meets about the Messium attack, where Miriam shares Kennedy's method to thwart the comm interference. Admiral Rychen readies a mission to drive the aliens off Messium.

While Richard and Miriam discuss Alex's name being cleared, Richard's husband, Will Sutton, arrives. In an effort to help expose the conspiracy and end the 2nd Crux War, he confesses he is an undercover Senecan Intelligence agent and puts Richard in touch with Graham.

Following a heated confrontation with Will, Richard departs to meet Graham on Pandora. Together they interrogate a man suspected of smuggling explosives into Vancouver. The agent gives up Olivia Montegreu, and they formulate a plan to ensnare her.

Miriam confronts Liam over his mismanagement of the war and alien invasion. Enraged, he strikes her, but she refuses to be intimidated. Marcus reaches out to his alien contact, entreating that he now has the power to cease human expansion and pleading with it to end the offensive, but the alien does not respond.

Olivia visits a subordinate on Krysk, but finds Richard and Graham waiting for her. In exchange for her freedom, she gives up Marcus and the details of their conspiracy. Before they part ways Graham gives Richard Will's intelligence file.

Malcolm is sent to assist Admiral Rychen in the Messium offensive. As the battle commences, Kennedy and Noah flee their hideout in an attempt to reach a small military station across the city. They witness horrific devastation and death while crossing the city, but successfully reach the station and repair several shuttles to escape.

The Alliance ships struggle to hold their own against a powerful enemy. Malcolm retrieves the fleeing shuttles and learns the details of the situation on the ground. Faced with the reality that Alliance forces will eventually be defeated, the fleet retreats to save the remaining ships for future battles.

Graham returns to Seneca to inform Federation Chairman Vranas of the conspiracy and the false pretenses upon which hostilities were instigated. Vranas begins the process of reaching out to the Alliance to end the war. Isabela is released from protective custody and returns home to Krysk to reunite with her daughter.

Based on the information Olivia provided, Miriam goes to arrest Liam, only to find he has fled. Richard similarly accompanies a team to detain Marcus, but on their arrival Marcus declares everything he did was for the good of humanity, then commits suicide.

After studying Will's Intelligence file and realizing his husband had acted honorably—other than lying to him—Richard pays Will a visit. Following a contentious and emotional scene, they appear to reconcile.

The EA Assembly reinstates Steven Brennon as Prime Minister. His first act is to promote Miriam to EASC Board Chairman and Fleet Admiral of the Armed Forces. On her advice he signs a peace treaty with the Federation.

Olivia approaches Aiden Trieneri, head of the rival Triene cartel and her occasional lover, and suggests they work together to aid the fight against the invaders. On Atlantis, Matei Uttara's alien contact tells him Alex and Caleb are returning and instructs him to kill them.

Kennedy and Noah reach Earth. Kennedy's easy rapport with the military leadership spooks Noah, and he tries to slip away. She chases after him, ultimately persuading him to stay with a passionate kiss.

Liam arrives at the NW Regional base on Fionava. He injects a virus into the communications network and hijacks several ships by convincing their captains he is on a secret mission approved by EA leadership to launch clandestine raids on Federation colonies.

Alliance and Federation leadership are meeting to finalize war plans when an alien contacts them to offer terms for their surrender. It involves humanity forever retreating west behind a demarcation line, cutting off 28 colonies and 150 million people.

The leaders don't want to surrender but recognize their odds of victory are quite low. Then Miriam receives word that Alex is alive and the aliens' ability to send reinforcements has been destroyed. They decide to reject the terms of surrender and fight. On Miriam's order their ships open fire on the alien forces.

R

TRANSCENDENCE

The Metigen War is in full swing as Alex and Caleb approach Seneca. Caleb initiates an Intelligence Division protection protocol, and he and Alex join Director Delavasi at a safe house as several actions are set in motion.

Alex contacts Dr. Canivon to discuss the feasibility of enriching human/Artificial connections, only to discover Sagan is already under attack by the Metigens. The Alliance is defending the independent colony, and Alex asks her mother to ensure Canivon and her Artificial, Valkyrie, are rescued and brought to Earth. Caleb reaches out to Isabela, who divulges the truth about their father's profession and his death. Caleb confronts Graham about it, and a heated argument ensues.

On Earth, Kennedy works with the Alliance to manufacture the material the *Siyane's* hull transformed into, now called 'adiamene.' She implores Noah to seek the help of his estranged father, a metals expert. Noah agrees, but the request introduces tension into their relationship. Devon tries to restore communications to Fionava and NW Command, while elsewhere at EASC Devon's boss, Brigadier Hervé, is contacted by Hyperion, the same alien Marcus Aguirre was in league with.

Alex, Caleb, Miriam, Richard and Graham converge on a secluded, private estate on Pandora, and Alex and Miriam reunite in a more tender encounter than either were expecting. Alex reveals the full extent of her plan to the others, including that she intends to spearhead it by being the first to neurally link to an Artificial. Even as they meet, agents of the Metigens seek to stop them—the safe house on Seneca is blown up, and the assassin Matei Uttara pursues them to Pandora.

When Miriam breaks the news to Alex that her former lover, Ethan Tollis, died in an explosion, she flees to grieve in private. Caleb goes after her, but it intercepted by Uttara. A bloody fight ensues, during which both men are gravely injured. Alex arrives on the scene and shoots Uttara in the head, killing him. Caleb collapses from his injuries.

Noah meets with his father, Lionel, in a combative encounter. Despite the tension between them, Lionel agrees to help with the adiamene production, and they travel to Berlin to meet Kennedy at the manufacturing facility. Once Lionel begins work, Noah confronts Kennedy about her motives for forcing a reunion with his father, but the matter isn't resolved.

Caleb regains consciousness, and he and Alex share an emotional moment in which they both come to realizations about each other and the strength of their relationship. Miriam learns Liam has attacked the Federation colonies of New Cairo and Ogham with nuclear weapons, and she is forced to travel to Seneca to smooth things over with Federation leadership. Once Caleb is healed enough to travel, he and Alex depart for Earth. On the way, he contacts Mia and asks her to come to Earth, though he can't yet tell her why.

Miriam meets with Field Marshal Gianno and Chairman Vranas, and in a surprising move tells them she won't take any active steps to stop Liam until after the Metigens are defeated, as they must concentrate all their efforts on the alien invasion. She then tells Gianno about Alex's plan. Gianno selects the fighter pilot, Morgan Lekkas, for participation, and recalls her from Elathan, where Morgan was helping to defend against a Metigen attack.

Alex and Caleb reach EASC Headquarters, where they are re-united with Kennedy and Noah. Alex meets with Dr. Canivon, who was safely evacuated off Sagan, and informs the woman she wants to use Valkyrie as her Artificial partner in the project they've dubbed 'Noetica.' While monitoring the war effort, EASC's Artificial, Annie, discovers her programming has been corrupted and suspects Hervé of tampering.

Miriam returns to Earth and meets with Prime Minister Brennon. She tells him they are losing the war—they and the Federation are suffering too many losses and will run out of ships and soldiers long before the Metigens do—then pitches Noetica to him.

Mia arrives in Vancouver. Alex and Caleb ask her to be a part of Noetica, together with her Artificial, Meno, and she agrees. With time running out and the Metigens advancing, Noetica is approved and Devon Reynolds and Annie are selected as the last participants.

Alex is the first to undergo the procedure Dr. Canivon has devised to allow a linking between an Artificial's quantum pro-cesses and a human mind at a neural level. Caleb and Miriam each contend with fear and worry about her well-being, and Miriam comes to recognize how much Caleb cares for Alex.

Alex awakens to her and Valkyrie's thoughts clashing and overrunning one another. She struggles to regain control of her mind and deal with the flood of information, and with Caleb's help is able to do so. She informs her mother the Metigens are deviating from their pattern and heading for Seneca and Romane in massive force.

While the others undergo the procedure, Alex and Miriam meet with Brennon, Gianno and Vranas. Alex makes the case that the Metigens are coming for Seneca and Romane, and Miriam and Brennon decide to send the EA fleet to defend the two worlds.

On Liam's cruiser, the *Akagi*, Captain Brooklyn Harper begins a mutinous campaign to stop Liam. She enlists one of her teammates, Kone, and a comm officer, who slips a message out to Col. Malcolm Jenner saying Liam's next target is Krysk and asking for intervention. Then she and Kone sabotage the remaining nukes on the *Akagi.*

Malcolm is defending Scythia from the Metigens when he receives Harper's message. He passes it on to Miriam, who informs Gianno. Gianno claims she can't spare the ships to defend the colony if the Metigens are almost at Seneca.

Caleb is furious the military won't defend Krysk, where his sister and niece live, and makes the gut-wrenching decision to try to rescue them. Alex gives him the *Siyane*, saying it's his only chance to reach Krysk in time. After a tearful parting, Caleb leaves, but not before recruiting Noah to go with him.

Alex, Devon, Mia and Morgan, and their Artificial counterparts, Valkyrie, Annie, Meno and Stanley, gather to strategize. They name themselves "Prevos," taken from the Russian word for "The Transcended," and begin to realize the extent of their new capabilities. Alex shares a touching goodbye with her mother before leaving with the fleet for Seneca.

Devon remains at EASC, where he and Annie will oversee all fronts of the war, and comes to terms with the fact Hervé is working for the Metigens. At the same time, Hyperion confronts Hervé about Noetica. Because she wants the Metigens defeated,

Hervé does not reveal to Hyperion that she has secretly placed a 'Kill Switch' in the Prevos' firmware, which when used will sever their connections to the Artificials—and also likely kill them.

Graham, Vranas and Gianno discuss the coming attack and express concerns over Noetica. When Graham returns to his office, Will Sutton—Richard's husband and a Senecan intelligence agent—is waiting on him and bears mysterious news.

Liam arrives at Krysk and attempts to use his nukes to disable the orbital defense array. They fail to detonate, and he has Kone brought before him to answer allegations of sabotage. When Kone refuses to confess, Liam executes him. Harper witnesses the execution via a surveillance camera; devastated, she prepares to try to blow up the ship. On the colony below, Isabela and Marlee are downtown as the attack begins. They seek refuge in the basement of an office building, but become trapped when the building collapses.

Alex reaches Seneca and Admiral Rychen's flagship dreadnought, the *Churchill*, and she and Rychen discuss strategy. Meanwhile, the Noetica Artificials discuss using neural imprints of notable military officers to supplement their and the Prevos tactical capabilities.

Caleb and Noah get to Krysk to discover the capital city under attack. The ongoing assault makes it too dangerous to land and find Isabela and Marlee, so Caleb comes up with a new plan. He draws Liam's ships away from the city, then, trusting the adiamene hull is strong enough to hold the *Siyane* together, crashes it through the frigates and into the belly of the *Akagi*.

They fight their way through the ship to the bridge, where they encounter Harper, who agrees to help them. She distracts Liam, then when Caleb and Noah open fire, disables his personal shield. Caleb kills Liam. Caleb, Noah and Harper rush back to the *Siyane* and escape just before the cruiser crashes.

Noah and Harper help Caleb dig a tunnel to where Isabela and Marlee are trapped, freeing them and several other people. Harper elects to remain in the city to aid with rescue efforts. Noah decides to find transportation back to Earth, eager to return to Kennedy, and Caleb heads for Seneca, and Alex.

The Metigens arrive at Seneca in overwhelming force. Alex, on the *Churchill* with Rychen, and Morgan, on the SF flagship with Gianno, take charge of the battle, employing a number of surprise weapons and tactics to gain an early advantage over the Metigen armada.

Several hours into the battle, Alex argues as it stands now they will not achieve complete victory. She convinces Miriam and Rychen to allow her to break into one of the Metigen superdread-noughts, where she and Valkyrie believe they can hack the core operating code. She hitches a ride atop a recon craft, experiencing a thrilling and terrifying journey through the heart of the battle.

Inside, Alex finds a cavernous space, with power conduits and signals running in every direction, and goes in search of the engineering core. When she hears her father in her head during the search, Valkyrie confesses that the Artificials' search of military neural imprints turned up one for Alex's father, taken before his death. Not surprisingly, it was compatible with Alex's brainwave patterns, so Valkyrie loaded it into her processes to increase their knowledge of military tactics. Valkyrie then enriched the imprint, creating a more fulsome representation of David Solovy's mind and leading to the unexpected result of his personality manifesting.

When they locate the engineering core Alex immerses herself in it to access the ship's programming. Valkyrie inserts a subtle logic error into one of the base routines, and they quickly depart the ship.

A major battle also ensues on and above Romane. Malcolm takes a special forces squad groundside, where he meets up with Mia in the governor's emergency bunker. Mia believes she and Meno have developed a signal beam to nullify an alien vessel's shields. He agrees to help her test it out on one of the smaller alien ships wreaking havoc in the city. They depart the bunker with part of Malcom's squad, while the rest of the squad conducts rescue operations. The test is successful, and Mia/Meno transfer the code for the signal to Devon, who deploys it to all the fleets.

They are returning to the bunker when Malcolm receives an order to arrest one of his Marines who was part of the rescue team on suspicion of working for the Metigens. When arrested, the suspect detonates a bomb he'd placed at Mia's home. The explosion badly damages Meno's hardware, abruptly severing his connection with Mia and causing her to stroke.

Caleb reaches the fleet at Seneca, and he and Alex enjoy a jubilant reunion. Suddenly Alex collapses to the floor as the trauma to Meno and Mia reverberates through the Prevos' connection to one another. Once Alex recovers, she, Devon and Morgan decide it's time to implement their secret plan to ensure victory.

Miriam is overseeing both battlefronts from the War Room when she's informed Devon/Annie have taken control of both Earth's and Seneca's defense arrays. Panic erupts among the military and government leaders. At that moment Miriam receives a message from Alex asking Miriam to please trust in her, and trust Richard. Richard indicates he knows something but won't divulge what it might be.

Hervé judges it's necessary to use the Kill Switch, but Miriam shoots her with a stunner before she can do so. Miriam refuses to act against the Prevos, even as they turn the defense arrays inward.

Unbeknownst to Miriam, shortly after the Prevos were created, they uncovered the full Metigen network of spies and assassins. Before leaving Earth, Alex went with Devon to see Richard and gave him a list of enemy agents, and he contacted Graham and Will on Seneca. They formulated a strategy to arrest or kill the agents at the last possible moment, and enlisted Olivia Montegreu's aid in the effort. Miriam was kept in the dark because revealing Hervé's involvement ahead of time would've alerted the aliens to the fact the Prevos were onto them.

The defense arrays fire—on dozens of Metigen superdreadnoughts hiding cloaked above the major cities of Earth and Seneca. Armed with massive firepower as well as the disruptive signal beam Mia/Meno developed, the superdreadnoughts are destroyed. The Prevos had picked up the stealthed vessels hours earlier, but again, revealing them too early would have tipped their hand.

An alien representative contacts those leading the military assault, but Alex takes charge of the conversation. The alien says they are open to considering cease fire terms, but Alex notes the aliens are in no position to bargain, as humanity's forces have decimated them. She orders them to retreat through the portal and to cease their observation of and meddling in Aurora. She also asks for an explanation for their aggression; the alien replies that humans are far more dangerous than they recognize and must be contained.

The alien accepts her terms, but warns humanity not to come looking for them beyond the portal. Alex doesn't respond to the warning, instead ordering them to retreat now. They do so, and the war comes to an end.

Later, as EA Prime Minister Brennon gives a speech mourning those lost and vowing a new era for civilization, Gianno and Vranas worry about the future of peace with EA and the danger Noetica poses, before separating to celebrate the victory with their families.

Noah reaches Earth and intercepts Kennedy as she is about to leave Vancouver. He finds her cold and dismissive, and provokes her into admitting she was hurt by him eagerly running off with Caleb, then not contacting her. He admits his mistake and being angry with her, but pleads his case by regaling all he went through to get back to her as fast as possible, and they reconcile.

On New Babel, Olivia and her partner-in-crime Aiden prepare to expand their spheres of influence. When Aiden suggests they merge their cartels—the one thing Olivia had warned him never to do—she uses a cybernetic virus to kill him, then begins taking over his cartel.

Alex returns to Earth and reunites with her mother. She elects not to tell Miriam about the construct of her father, and after catching up they agree to meet for lunch the next week.

Caleb and Alex visit Mia, who remains in a coma and was brought to EASC's hospital at Alex's request. Dr. Canivon says she's somewhat optimistic she can rebuild Meno, and together they can repair the damage to Mia's brain. Caleb authorizes her to move ahead, though there's no guarantee Mia will be herself should she eventually awaken.

They return to Alex's loft for a romantic dinner. Caleb presents her with a belated birthday gift—a bracelet crafted from a piece of his sword, the only remnant of the *Siyane's* hull before it morphed into adiamene.

He divulges that Graham has offered him any job he wants if he'll return to Division. Alex encourages him to do so, insisting they can make a long-distance relationship work. He challenges her about what she truly wants from him. When she caves and admits she selfishly wants him to stay with her, he immediately resigns from Division and asks her to marry him. After an emotional discussion, she says yes.

SIX MONTHS LATER

Miriam returns from vacation to move into the new Headquarters building. She and Richard are discussing threats on the horizon and long-term strategies when she receives a message from Alex.

On Atlantis, Kennedy and Noah are enjoying their own vacation, expecting Alex and Caleb to join them later in the day, when Kennedy also receives a message from Alex.

The *Siyane* hovers in the Metis Nebula, just outside the ring of ships patrolling the portal to prevent any Metigen incursion. Valkyrie has been installed into the walls of the *Siyane*, and Alex and Caleb have married. They activate the portal and accelerate through it on a quest for answers about the Metigens and their network of multiverses.

About The Author

G. S. Jennsen lives in Colorado with her husband and two dogs. *Sidespace* is her fourth novel, all published by her imprint, Hypernova Publishing. In less than two years she has become an internationally bestselling author, selling in excess of 50,000 books since her first novel, *Starshine,* was published in March 2014. She has chosen to continue writing under an independent publishing model to ensure the integrity of the *Aurora Rhapsody* series and her ability to execute on the vision she's had for it since its genesis.

While she has been a lawyer, a software engineer and an editor, she's found the life of a full-time author preferable by several orders of magnitude, which means you can expect the next book in the *Aurora Rhapsody* series in just a few months.

When she isn't writing, she's gaming or working out or getting lost in the Colorado mountains that loom large outside the windows in her home. Or she's dealing with a flooded basement, or standing in a line at Walmart reading the tabloid headlines and wondering who all of those people are. Or sitting on her back porch with a glass of wine, looking up at the stars, trying to figure out what could be up there.

CPSIA information can be obtained at www.ICGtesting.com
Printed in the USA
LVOW11s1816020816

498765LV00001B/75/P